## PASSIONATE ADVERSARIES

"There are several things I want from you, Victoria. I've just taken one of them."

Her hand flashed out and delivered a stinging blow to that contemptible face as she spat the damning words she thought she would never say to anyone. "You bastard!" she hissed.

Marcus grabbed her savagely and raised a hand poised to strike. Then he let her go and stepped back as he studied the pale face and wide eyes. It was just one more twist in the game he had taken so long to comprehend. "Surely, madam," he sneered, "this is no new experience for you. From all that you have implied you've felt a man's desire before. Name your price. I'll pay it." His gaze fell on her all but uncovered breasts, and the smile was insinuating. "Perhaps even so high a price as marriage."

# Constance Conant

FALLING STARS

LEISURE BOOKS  NEW YORK CITY

A LEISURE BOOK

Published by

Dorchester Publishing Co., Inc.
6 East 39th Street
New York, NY 10016

Printed in the United States of America

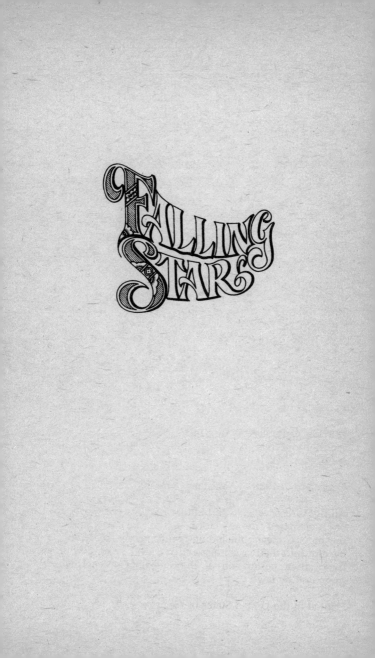

# 1

Dense fog rolled in off the Thames, dulling the highly polished boots of the slender figure muffled in a great coat. It was a raw night in early March with heavy threatening clouds blocking out any light the pale crescent moon might have offered. Soon even those clouds would be obscured by the mist that crept over the land, wrapping everything in its mantle of luminous gray.

Prudence Victoria Chisholm did not mind the fog, and despite the damp chill the opalescent vapor comforted her. She felt safe wrapped in the wisps that curled around her, hiding her from the occasional lone sailor who hurried by this desolate section of waterfront.

It had been an exhausting three months, and Victoria was weary in mind and body. The burden was heavy, and she would be grateful when these tiresome solitary voyages could be entrusted to others; for now her father insisted that she take on more and more of the responsibility of running his vast commercial empire, and that task sometimes meant traveling halfway around the world. And, all too frequently, it meant a cold, damp cabin or dangerous gale-swept seas.

It also meant vicious confrontations with men who tested her wit and her courage. It meant destroying those who stood in her way, and it meant trusting no one. It was her father's dictum, and experience had proved him right.

The last two years had been the most difficult, and they had been lonely. Always, since she had been three, she and her father had been inseparable. They had gone everywhere together, done everything together, but now they were constantly apart. The trips grew longer, the responsibilities heavier.

But soon she would be home, wrapped in all the comforts great wealth could provide. And her father would be proud of her, for he was now many thousands of pounds richer when he might very well have lost a small fortune to his enemies. She had maneuvered skillfully in a difficult situation. Her father's interests had been successfully defended.

Shuffling as the cold seeped up through the leather soles of her boots, Victoria peered into the impenetrable mist. She had sent word to Ben, her driver, that he was to pick her up here at the warehouse by nine. It wasn't like him to be late, and this part of London was not the safest place to be at night. And, always, she had to be on guard. There were treacherous and powerful men who wished her harm. Too many. Far too many.

A growing number of mercantile princes would be only too eager to see the Chisholm bastard toppled from her lofty perch. It was a dangerous place to be, a stupid place to be, but it was where her father wanted her. He had placed her there, and she would stay until he no longer needed her to safeguard everything he had spent his life building.

A wry smile tugged at Victoria's mouth, but there was no humor in it. The merchants, made clumsy by rage, could be handled easily enough, but there was a growing element of concern that occupied her thoughts more and more. Her half-brother, Edward, who hated her with a passion that bordered on madness, was making life increasingly difficult. The venom of his verbal attacks, the poisonous stories he was spreading about her were increasing in ferocity and frequency. Already she was as unwelcome as leprosy in the houses of staid old merchants who wanted none of the dirt Edward smeared on her to rub off on their wives and children.

Not that she cared about the opinions of those idiots, but there were some who could be useful to her. Indeed, alliances with a select few might even be necessary if her father's plans were to be realized. And soon Edward would no longer be satisfied with his childish war of words. He would make a move against her. It was inevitable, for he wanted what she would eventually inherit—the bulk of Andrew Chisholm's enormous wealth.

Green eyes, lightened by a subtle shading of yellow, glinted their cold light. *I'll see him in hell first!*

As she hunched deeper into her coat, Victoria was about to reenter the warehouse to instruct one of the guards to escort her home. But then she heard the sound she had been waiting for so impatiently. Ben was coming. She'd recognize the rattle and squeak of that decrepit carriage-for-hire anywhere.

As she stepped from the shadows to greet her old friend, a spark of apprehension flicked its warning. It was not Ben. The distorted, uncertain shape viewed through heavy mist was not that of Ben Ives. The man driving the carriage was too small. Ben was a big man, almost twice the size of the indistinct shape perched high on the seat above.

Every nerve in Victoria's body was taut. "Where's Ben?"

The little man turned a startled face toward the apparition that had appeared so silently from the dense fog. "Be that you, Mistress Chisholm? This 'ere fog is so bloody thick. Coo, mum, I mighta run right over ya, it's that bad, it is."

The nervousness in the coarse voice heightened Victoria's apprehension. She repeated her question as her fingers fondled the butt of the pistol she carried in her coat pocket. "Where's Ben? Why didn't he come himself?"

Finally the man remembered to doff his hat. "Ben's a bit under the weather, mum. Got the dampness in 'is chest, 'e 'as. Asked that I come fetch ya."

Uncertain and acutely aware of the number of people who would like to see her dead, Victoria hesitated. She didn't like this development. If Ben were ill, he would most certainly have sent his oldest son, Tom. He wouldn't have entrusted her safety to a stranger. "And you are . . . ?"

"Beecher, mum. Me name's Archie Beecher." Then, hopping from the high seat, the driver opened the door for his passenger. "No need to fret, mum. I'll get ya 'ome safe and sound."

Victoria felt her skin prickle with suspicion as she peered into the darkened coach. Only the outside lanterns were lit. The interior of the carriage was cast in shadow, and the shades were drawn. Something was wrong. She felt it. She could smell the fear coming from the foul unwashed body of the man Ben never would have sent.

"And Donald, Ben's son? Why didn't he come in his father's place?"

There was a brief silence before Archie Beecher replied uncertainly, "I'm not sure, miss, but I think Donald's down with the fever as well."

Cold, noncommittal eyes searched the man's sunken face. Ben Ives had no son named Donald. She had learned what she needed to know, but she also needed to know who was behind this rather clumsy attempt to abduct her, and why. Which one of her enemies had grown dangerously desperate? She would go, but not like a lamb to slaughter. She would be prepared.

"I have some papers to read. Will you light the lamps inside?"

Victoria's eyes were narrow slits as she watched Beecher's every move, and not until the twin flames flared revealing an empty carriage did she allow the man to lower the steps and assist her in. Again she fondled the pistol before extinguishing the lamps and opening the curtains as the driver began his slow, cautious journey through the almost deserted, fog-enshrouded streets.

Her mind was alert as they passed under the eerie lights cast by ineffective streetlamps. She visualized every curve, every bend along the familiar route, and then she stiffened. Beecher had turned right where he should have turned left. There was not the slightest doubt in Victoria's mind that this was more than just

an innocent error on the driver's part. He had quite
deliberately made the change in direction.

Her face was an emotionless mask as she eased
open the door and dropped lightly to the slick cobble-
stone street below. The sound of her boots striking
the uneven surface was muffled by the pervading
dampness and the rhythmic noise of the horse's
hooves as the carriage clattered slowly along.

Staying to the darkest shadows, Victoria followed
silently until the hollow echoing that bounced back to
her had ceased and the mystic aura of carriage
lanterns held steady. Beecher had quietly stopped,
and she felt no surprise as two ghostly shapes
emerged quickly from the mist and approached the
halted vehicle.

"Damn! She's not here!" exploded a voice she immediately recognized, and despite the efforts of the
second man to calm her enraged brother, Edward's
voice rose in anger and frustration as it continued to
berate the hapless driver.

"But she was there, guvner. I swear," Beecher
protested. "I picked 'er up just like ya said. Told 'er
Ben was sick, I did. She come willin' enough. Even
'ad me—" The man stopped in mid-sentence. Victoria
could feel the wave of fear wash back at her through
the mist. "The lamps! They ain't lit!" The driver's
voice was little more than a hoarse whisper as he
understood what had happened.

"What are you raving about?" Edward asked
curtly. He was irritated, but he was listening now.

"She 'ad me light them inside lamps. Now they
ain't lit. She knew! Gawd a'mighty, guvner, she
knows me name. She'll kill me. She'll 'ave me 'unted
down, she will. You know what she's like. I won't be

safe nowheres. Ya gotta 'elp me get away. Yer gonna 'ave to pay me more, so's I can get away from this 'ere town.''

"You told her your name?" Edward's voice was as slick as the filthy cobblestones beneath Victoria's feet.

"I 'ad to tell 'er somethin', I did. She asked me right out. Wanted to know 'oo I were, 'oo it were Ben 'ad sent fer 'er.''

"You fool." There was only cold contempt in Edward's voice, and then there was a gasp followed by a soft groan. Beecher had been rewarded for this night's folly.

Victoria shrugged. What happened to Beecher was of little consequence, but Edward was another matter. The man was not stupid. He would guess that she had followed and was even now watching from out of the night that had turned treacherous.

She could kill him now. She *should* kill him now. Every instinct cried out to her to finish what her half-brother had started, but she wouldn't, and she knew it. Edward was still her father's son. She would not kill him until she had no other choice.

Drawing a deep, cleansing breath, Victoria let it out slowly. Her body relaxed, and her fingers released the pistol she had been gripping tightly. There was no point in lingering. Edward would not endanger his precious neck by pursuing her any further this night. He would not probe the all-encompassing mist, for the risk of taking the shot from her gun full in his handsome face was too great. But he *knew* she was watching. And he was afraid. The faint smile that touched her lips was cold and calculating. There would be another time. A better time.

Then, melting against the darker blackness of
buildings and carefully avoiding the gin drinkers and
foot pads who would slit her throat for a guinea,
Victoria made her cautious way to the nearby home of
the man she had called uncle for as long as she could
remember.

Her pull at the bell cord was answered by the silent
opening of the small peep door. Then hinges worked
noiselessly as the heavy oak door swung wide. A
husky man in his late twenties stared at her in frank
disapproval as she stepped quickly inside and closed
the door behind her.

With a tone of familiarity in his voice, Sean Rubley
asked, "And what in the name o' the blessed saints
are ya doin' out alone at this time o' night, Miss
Victoria? And afoot at that, for sure an' there was no
carriage to be heard by these mortal ears."

She smiled into the face, which was framed by crisp
red hair that seemed to have a life of its own. "Sure
an' it's none o' your business, Sean, me boy."

But Sean would not be put off by the easy banter.
"Now, look here, missy, Mr. Byrnes would be havin'
me hide to say nothin' o' what your father would be
doin' if anything happened to ya, so let's not get quite
so uppity, if ya please!"

The smile faded from her face as Victoria pondered
the concern in the fierce reddish-brown eyes of the
man who protected Henry Byrnes with a loyalty
money could not buy. She decided to tell him the
truth. He'd learn it from his master soon enough,
anyway. "It seems that my half-brother has not yet
forgiven me for having been born and decided that
tonight would be a good time to remedy that unfortunate situation. He and some other fool got hold of

Ben's carriage and hired a rather unskilled accomplice to drive me to a deserted spot on the waterfront. You can guess what he had in mind."

Sean's face paled and the freckles stood out like flecks of dried blood. "He's gone that far, then? Sure an' we'll have to do somethin' about it now."

"Do something about what?" Henry Byrnes stood in the open doorway of his study.

At the sound of the familiar voice Victoria turned to face the tall, lean man who was in nightshirt, robe and slippers. The tassle to his nightcap hung jauntily over one ear. "Edward. He's finally made his move," she answered softly.

Henry leaned heavily on his cane. He and Victoria had discussed the possibility of an open attack and now it had come. The festering hatred Edward harbored for his half-sister had finally erupted. He had failed this time, but he would try again. "Come into my study," Henry replied in total resignation of the next move. "Give me every detail. And get out of those damp clothes," he snapped.

Silent laughter brightened Victoria's features as she shrugged out of the heavy coat and whipped the tricorn hat from her head, slapping it against her leg to remove the moisture that had collected in the turned-up brim. "I'll have some hot tea, Sean. And you'd better get Uncle Henry something stronger," she purred. "I think he needs it."

"You will take this matter seriously," Henry commanded sternly as he escorted Victoria into the book-laden room. He sat in the old chair that had accommodated itself to his bony frame through many years of use and studied the young woman who had grown from a bright, sunny child to a cold, calculating

businesswoman, a rather ruthless woman who let
nothing stand in her way. And it was all Andrew's
fault!

He listened without interrupting as Victoria
recounted the attempt on her life. "You're absolutely
sure it was Edward?"

"I heard his voice as clearly as I hear yours. Do you
think I could mistake it? But it isn't Edward who
worries me. It's the other man, the one whose voice I
*didn't* recognize. He could pass me on the street and
I'd never know him. And that, dear Uncle, does not
add to my confidence." She laughed humorlessly.

Henry's agile brain worked quickly and logically.
"Despite what he would have us believe, Edward is
an intelligent, cunning man. His accomplice would
have to be someone he trusts implicitly, which means
someone not averse to abduction or murder, someone who is as evil as he is himself."

Victoria followed her uncle's reasoning. "Edward is
a member of the Mohocks, is he not?"

"Yes," Henry drawled smugly, pleased that
Victoria's mind was working in perfect tandem with
his. "It has to be one of that band of vicious fops who
have nothing better to do than torture and even
murder some hapless victim who stumbles into their
path when they're out looking for trouble. They're a
nasty, degenerate bunch. Crueler and more diabolical
than the American Indians after whom they've
named their wretched club. Of course, nothing has
been proved against them. They're far too clever for
that, but I would wager the man with Edward was
one of that group."

It had been a long day, and Victoria stretched the
weariness from her bones. "I'll learn what I can about

them, and perhaps it's also time I kept a closer watch on my dear brother as well." But she was no longer terribly interested. Edward was just one more complication in an already complicated life.

Finishing the cup of tea Sean had placed on the table beside her, she smiled reassuringly. "Don't worry about me. I'll simply make myself a more elusive target, and that shouldn't be too difficult the way Daddy keeps me running back and forth these days."

"You could always leave Edward to me, my dear," Henry suggested mildly, but Victoria knew exactly what her uncle had in mind.

Raising her hands in mock protest, she muttered, "Don't tempt me. A convenient accident would solve *one* of my problems, at least. And I've thought about it. If it were anyone except Edward, it would be over by now, but he's still Father's son and despite all the pain he's caused, I honestly believe Daddy still loves Edward."

She shook her head in bewilderment. The terrible strain between Edward and his father was almost incomprehensible, and it was something her father simply would not discuss. She sighed in resignation. "It's beyond me, Henry. I know why my brother wants me out of the way, of course. My death would eventually mean a much larger inheritance for him; but why is he causing so much grief for Father, who has been more than generous? Daddy turned Mannering Hall over to Edward when Lady Catherine died, and he didn't have to. He could have kept it for himself. He gives Edward thousands of pounds a year, which are promptly squandered, and then bails him out again. If I acted like that, you can bet Father would have nailed my hide to the door a long time ago.''

Henry made the decision he had been pondering for months. Edward was becoming increasingly dangerous, and Victoria did not know her enemy. She knew nothing of the fierce hatred that was eating away at her half-brother, nor its cause. She had to be told, for she was carelessly placing her own life in jeopardy so that Andrew Chisholm, who was more gravely ill than even Victoria knew, might live out the rest of his days in peaceful ignorance of his son's crimes against his sister.

Edward was depending upon Victoria's love for her father, her determination to protect him from the problems that could only cause him further grief, to keep her silent. And he was right. She had told Andrew nothing, and that silence had only encouraged Edward, had made him bolder. Now it was time for both Victoria and Andrew to know the truth. But it was an unhappy truth, so he began gently.

''How much has your father told you about your mother, Jeanine?''

Only the briefest flicker of her eyes gave Henry any clue that this was a painful subject for the lovely young woman who sat across from him. ''Very little. I know she was my father's mistress and died when I was three.''

''And that's all?''

The face, which was a hardened mask, did not change expression, but the soft voice was edged with a proud defiance. ''I know that he loved her and still does.''

''Indeed he does,'' Henry replied quietly. ''He'll go

to his grave loving her. When she died he nearly lost
his mind. He cropped your hair, dressed you in boys'
clothing and ran from England. The two of you
wandered the world like nomads for almost eleven
years before he could bring himself to come home,
something he did more for your sake than for his
own.''

Henry's eyes twinkled. ''You were growing up, and
not even your masculine attire could hide the fact that
you would soon become a very beautiful young lady.
And, of course, once he made the decision to return to
England, there were certain facts you had to know.
He did not want you to learn the truth, which he had
carefully kept from you, through vicious gossip.
Unfortunately, Andrew has chosen to remain silent
about other events that are now endangering your
life.''

Victoria stared at her uncle, not understanding just
what point he was making, but she knew better than
to interrupt. She waited in patient silence while
Henry struggled to find exactly the right words.

At last Henry sighed heavily and began. ''It is not
uncommon, as you know, for a man and woman to
marry for reasons other than love. Though of the
nobility, Lady Catherine's family was in serious
financial straits. They needed a wealthy son-in-law
who would not hold too tightly to his purse strings. In
turn, your father wanted, for business reasons, the
influence and the contacts that would come with
marriage to Catherine. Little more than a year later,
Edward was born. Your father was delighted, and he
worked harder than ever to amass a greater fortune
for his son and heir. Consequently, he seldom saw the
boy. Edward's upbringing was left almost entirely to

Catherine and to servants, and he was spoiled beyond reprieve.

"When your father realized what was happening he tried to discipline the boy, but Catherine would have none of it. There were terrible arguments until finally your father had had enough. He literally tore Edward, who was screaming with fright, from Catherine's arms and dumped the boy into an unnecessarily spartan and cruel academy. For a child who had been so petted and pampered it was a living hell. With each caning, with each day on rations of bread and water, his resentment toward his father grew. Still, he refused to conform, and when Catherine learned what was happening she locked her door against Andrew. The marriage, which had been crumbling, was finished.

"Within days Andrew left Mannering Hall and never set foot in it again. For years he was content with his life and made no move to change it. Not until he met your mother. It was then that he asked Catherine for a divorce. Of course, she refused. She enjoyed the comforts and the prestige that came with being married to one of the wealthiest men in England. She was also afraid that Edward would be denied what should be his, so with the help of powerful friends she blocked the divorce action for years.

"By this time your father was desperate. He loved Jeanine, and he loved you. He was absolutely determined to free himself so he could marry your mother.

"Finally, as a last resort, he had me draw up a formal declaration stating that Catherine had denied him his conjugal rights years before he left Mannering Hall. He further expressed the doubt that Edward was the son of his flesh. Then he faced Catherine and threatened not only to make the sworn statement public but also to produce several men who would swear that they had been intimate with her.

"When faced with such insurmountable odds Catherine gave in at last, but it was too late. Jeanine died before the decree became final. And Edward, who had been raised to have a greatly exaggerated opinion of himself, who was an extremely proud and arrogant young man, never forgave Andrew, who had all but branded his son a bastard and his wife an adulteress. The long-festering resentment burst into a bitter hatred. For years he has wanted nothing more than to crush Andrew beneath his heel, to exact a terrible vengeance for the wrong he felt was done to him and to his mother."

"And he has chosen me as the instrument of his revenge," Victoria stated matter-of-factly, for she understood it now. Her death would be the cruelest blow Edward could deal his father.

"Only if you allow it," Henry stated sternly. "If you tell your father what has been going on, he can and will put a stop to it. You *must* tell him."

But she wasn't sure. She understood only too well the guilt her father had carried with him all these years. He had turned his back on his son and blamed himself for what Edward had become. The large sums of money he continued to heap on Edward, his reluctance to take a firm stand with the man—all of it in the hope of winning some morsel of forgiveness, some small portion of understanding.

"No," Victoria answered quietly. "Daddy must not know. We have no right to ask him to make such a decision, to choose one child over another. But neither do I intend to fall victim to my dear brother. I shall stay out of his way, and I shall most definitely have him watched. And now," she sighed wearily as she leaned down to kiss her uncle good night, "I'm going to bed."

Then, perfectly confident that Henry Byrnes would honor her decision, that the man who had become her dearest friend since her return to England would never betray her trust, Victoria retreated to the room that was hers whenever she was in this house.

When she had gone Henry roused himself, poked aimlessly at the fire and then settled back in his chair, mesmerized by the renewed flame. He wondered what Victoria would do when Andrew, who was the center of her life, died, as all men must.

But one thing was certain. Not another hour would pass before Andrew Chisholm was informed of the attempt that had been made on his daughter's life—and by whom. And even though Henry knew that Victoria, who was fiercely protective of her father, would be furious with him and, in fact, might never forgive him for what she would surely regard as an act of treachery, it was a risk he had to take.

He and Andrew were old men. They had lived their lives. The only thing that mattered to him now was that Jeanine's only child be protected. Nothing else was important. Not his life, not Andrew's and most certainly not Edward's.

A cunning smile spread across Henry's face. There was one way, short of killing him, that might stop Edward—the threat of total disinheritance should any harm come to Victoria. That, however, was a threat only Andrew could make.

Again Henry sighed heavily as his pen scratched over the paper. He was betraying Victoria's trust, but it had to be done. When at last he had finished the fateful letter he rang for Sean, who was to deliver it at once to Andrew Chisholm.

The following morning Henry was prepared for Victoria's anger, but not for the deep hurt that flickered in those large expressive eyes and then was gone. His voice was unsteady as he attempted to justify his actions. "I told your father everything, my dear, because I had to. There were only two choices. One was to have your brother killed, something you wish to avoid for the present, at least. The second was to inform your father so he could threaten Edward with disinheritance should any harm befall you before Andrew's death."

The twinkle reappeared in Henry's eyes, for Victoria was more interested in logic than in hurt feelings. She was following his reasoning. "Such a threat should stop Edward in his tracks, for now; it will be in his best interest to see that no harm comes to you from *any* quarter. In short, your most dangerous enemy has now become your most determined protector."

A slow, admiring smile softened Victoria's anger, and the more she understood all the ramifications of her uncle's solution to what had been a very nasty problem, the greater was her satisfaction with that solution. And by the time she and Henry, closely guarded by Sean, arrived at her father's home, the last vestige of discontent had faded.

Displeasure and determination crackled from every inch of his tall, spare frame as Henry waved Victoria from her father's room. He glowered at the bed-ridden man who had been his friend since they had been children together, a friendship that had spanned

more than sixty years, but once again Andrew anticipated him. Laughing softly, he waved Henry to a
chair.

"I've taken your suggestion," he commented
mildly. "My letter to Edward was delivered last
night. He understands that a new will is to be drawn
up immediately, that he will inherit nothing unless
Victoria is alive at the time of my death."

"And it solves nothing!" Henry retorted sharply.
"A delaying action, at best." He opened his mouth to
say more, but Andrew stopped him.

"Are you still a good friend to John Sharpe?"

Exasperation flooded Henry's face. He did not yet
see where the conversation was leading, but he knew
Andrew better than any man alive, so he waited in
silence as he nodded his head.

"And John is still very close to that simpering
courtier, Charles, the present Lord Baltimore?"

No more needed to be said. Henry understood
exactly what Andrew's plan was. "Yes. I'm sure John
can arrange advantageous terms for the purchase of
property in Maryland, and until you can have a house
built I can recommend you to some friends who live
in that colony. They'll be delighted to have you and
Victoria as houseguests until your own home is completed."

"No," Andrew stated bluntly. "That won't be
necessary. There's a planter in Annapolis who is
deeply in debt to me and as far as I can see has no
hope of ever repaying his mounting obligations. I'll be
doing him a favor by foreclosing. Victoria and I can
live there until I'm prepared to do more."

Neither man expressed the common thought
between them, for both knew that Andrew might not

live to do more. The second heart attack had been a massive one. It had occurred only days after Victoria had left on her latest voyage, and Andrew had no intention of telling her about it. The entire household had been sworn to secrecy. She was not to know. She was not to worry.

"However," Andrew continued, "such a small farm will hardly be enough for the life I intend Victoria to live. Have John purchase the largest continuous tract of land Lord Baltimore is willing to sell. But it must be close to a port and navigable water."

Andrew's smile was bittersweet as he gazed at the portrait that hung on the opposite wall. "My Jeanine would want Victoria to have every advantage money can offer, and I intend to see to it. If I can hide from the vengeful gods long enough, I shall build a mansion worthy of my daughter, but most of all, one that will be worthy of her mother. And if I do not live, if the jealous gods strike me down, then Victoria must carry on for me."

Ignoring the ramblings about a mansion that would probably never be built, Henry asked seriously, "Then you believe being an ocean away will dissuade Edward, that once Victoria is gone from England he will pursue his intentions no further?"

"I believe distance will solve the problem time has not," Andrew answered almost convincingly.

It was something Henry wanted to believe, yet the warning persisted in his brain. "Then you have no intention of going to the authorities about Edward's behavior last night? You should, Andrew. You should offer your daughter that much protection, at least."

Andrew Chisholm put his hand to his eyes as a

tremulous breath caught in his chest. "How can I, Henry? How can I? He's my son. No matter what he's done, he's still my son. And what good would it do? If I know him, nothing could ever be proved. And even worse, Victoria would have to stay in England to testify. It would be her word against his. Can you imagine the danger she'd be in every minute of every day once the charges were made? No, it's better this way."

"And Ben Ives?" Henry asked sadly. "Will his death be just another minor inconvenience for the high and mighty Andrew Chisholm?"

Andrew's eyes flicked to his old friend. His face contorted in pain as the iron weight pressed on his chest and the familiar numbness made his arm useless. He waited out the warning, then sank into the pillows. His voice was little more than a weak whisper. "Ben's dead? You didn't mention that in your letter."

"He is," Henry answered cryptically. "I wasn't sure until very early this morning when certain sources I cannot name informed me that his body was fished out of the Thames. But you needn't worry. The men I deal with are most discreet. No one will know of the inquiry. Not a breath of scandal shall touch your precious Edward. Good God!" Henry exploded in total frustration and anger, "don't you know the man is completely deranged?"

Andrew slumped deeper into the pillows. "Yes, I know. It's hopeless. One child pitted against the other. And it's my fault. If only I had handled things differently." His voice drifted away as an old man's quick tears filled his eyes. Once more he stared at the portrait of the woman he had loved so desperately, as though seeking an answer that was not to be found.

The strong sense of disapproval faded as Henry studied the face of the friend who had suddenly grown old. Andrew was right. He could not be asked to kill his own son. It *was* hopeless. "Shall I make sure Ben's family will have enough to live on? I think it should come from you."

Andrew smiled in bitter chagrin. He should have thought of it himself. "Yes. Make sure they want for nothing, either now or in the future. And Henry—take care of Victoria. Will you promise me this?"

Now was not the time for false reassurances. "As though she were my very own," Henry vowed, and wondered if Andrew had ever guessed how much he, himself, had loved Jeanine Monet.

# 2

By mid-October Victoria had returned from the extended business trip with which her father had kept her safely occupied outside the borders of England. And now Andrew was ready to move an ocean away. His numerous properties in England had been sold. Wagonloads of furniture, crates, barrels and trunks had been carted to his ships and were already on their way to Annapolis. Bullen, the only retainer who had agreed to accompany them to their new home, had also departed with the prize mares Andrew would not leave behind, for from this time on, he intended to lead the life of the landed gentry, contenting himself with raising fine horses and sipping wine.

The legal work, too, had been completed. Everything he owned now belonged to his daughter. The only thing he had held back was the enormous sum of two million pounds, which was to be divided equally between Edward and Victoria upon his death. He had stripped himself of all but the money intended as a legacy for his two children, for he dared keep nothing in his own name that he did not want Edward to get. There were to be no ugly court battles where Victoria, as the female and the younger of his two children, might lose what he intended for her. What he wanted her to have she had now, and it was a very great deal.

Andrew was content. They would spend a last pleasant week with Henry and then be on their way. By the time they arrived at their final destination their home would be ready to receive them. Everything would be in order, for Captain Crawford, who was master of his ship, the *Bayside,* had already arranged for a reliable couple from Massachusetts to run the estate for them. Several families of indentured servants who were anxious to escape the hopelessness of their lives would swell the ranks of the few slaves who had been mortgaged to him along with the house and grounds in Annapolis. Everything had been settled to the last detail.

As the carriage rolled through the streets of London, neither Andrew nor Victoria looked back. They rode in silence until they arrived at Henry's home, where they were greeted with open arms.

A formal dinner was served in the grand dining room, and the two men laughed and drank heartily to cover the sadness each felt at the imminent parting. Andrew raised his glass. "To my dear friend and good companion."

Victoria, too, raised her glass as her eyes misted. America was a long way off. It might be years before she returned again to England, for she understood exactly why her father was whisking her off to a wild and savage land. Her hatred for Edward flared brighter.

By the time the meal had ended Andrew and Henry were both a bit tipsy, and their tongues had loosened. Jeanine Monet's name had come up more frequently during the leisurely two-hour dinner than it had in the eighteen years since her death. Victoria decided it was best to leave the two old men to reminisce together. Much of what they wished to say was still not meant for her ears, so she slipped quietly from their presence and went to her room.

Hours later, at the time of darkest night, Victoria suddenly realized she was awake. It had not been a dream that had shot terror through her heart, not a dream that had left her weak with certain knowledge.

Her legs would not hold her as she strained against some unseen hand to crawl from the bed, and she sank heavily to the floor. It was as though she had been given some vile drug that separated her will from her limbs.

Desperately, she clutched at the coverlet, pulling it from the bed. Still, she could not rise. Her face was contorted in silent agony. Then a low moan, the sound of a mortally wounded animal, curled in her throat and pushed its way through clenched teeth. She felt the sharp, cutting scream rise from deep within, and she swallowed it, burying it deeper than before.

Slowly she pulled herself up and locked her knees so that her legs would not buckle under her again. Then she breathed deeply, just as the masters who had taught her in the past had insisted she practice. Her mind cleared with each cleansing breath, and the blood once more coursed through her body.

Still, her hand was trembling as she took the lighted candle and walked as though in a trance to her father's room. As she entered, the candle cast dark, fearsome shadows ahead, and the bed seemed to be lost in blackness as she approached it. She knew what she would find. Her father was dead, and part of her had died with him. Already the void had formed. The thundering silence of death assailed her ears.

She put the candle on the bedside table and sat on the edge of the high, canopied bed. Carefully, she smoothed the lines from the face that was even now growing cold, and gently, she closed the azure eyes that, when turned toward her, had always been loving. Now they were lifeless and blank. The warmth had gone from them just as it was fast fading from his body.

"Daddy. Daddy," she whispered, and in that word was all her love and all her despair, a despair too deep to be shared. She kissed her father good-bye, then made her way to her uncle's room, where she tapped lightly on the door.

Andrew Chisholm, merchant prince of London, feared and hated by many, loved and mourned by few, was entombed next to Jeanine Monet the following day. The crypt was resealed, and guards were placed to protect the body from the brazen resurrectionists.

Returning to Henry's home, Victoria was given a letter that her father had written and had entrusted to his friend's keeping. "I think he knew he would never leave England," Henry said sadly. "I was to give you this letter if he died before you set sail. Otherwise, it was to have been destroyed."

Victoria's eyes were dry as she read. The pain was too great to be assuaged by tears. Her father's words commanded her to carry on with his plans. She was to proceed immediately to America and build the Chisholm empire as she would have done had he lived. The last paragraph she read over and over again.

> Do not grieve for me, daughter, for I am confident that at last I shall rejoin your beloved mother. I have kept my promise to her. Never, in all your early years, have you been far from my side. Now, you must go on alone. My only regret is to leave you with all your problems not yet resolved. Therefore, it is my urgent command that you protect yourself. You must survive at any cost or I shall have failed.

With a throat that ached from fighting back the tears, Victoria gave the letter to Henry, who scanned it hastily then pursed his lips. "He made his choice at last. If Edward pursues you, then he is to die. But it is quite obvious that your father wants you to leave England *now.* To the very end, it was his hope that this disaster could be avoided, that you and your brother would not one day confront each other with murder in your hearts."

It was too late. Victoria hated Edward, whom she blamed for hastening her father's death, with a cold, unrelenting rage, and murder was, indeed, in her heart. "If Edward chooses to follow me to America, I will not make it difficult for him. Yet, I want him to feel that I am afraid and uncertain. I want him to be so sure of himself, so confident of success, that he will not be too careful where he steps. And you, dear uncle, are not to take the joy of killing him away from me. He is mine. This you must promise."

Henry sighed in weary resignation. If he did not promise, Victoria would not budge from England. She would deliberately seek her brother out and kill him before there was a chance for anyone to interfere. And she would not care how it was done. There would be no attempt at secrecy. It was not beyond the realm of possibility that she would simply walk up to him, put a gun to his chest and fire. Witnesses or not, at this point Victoria wouldn't care. Her father's death had devastated her, and only her hatred for Edward was sustaining her. "You have my solemn oath."

"In the meantime," Victoria continued, "I wish to draw up a will leaving everything I own to you. Edward will not profit by my death, if it comes to that."

Henry understood the cold, vengeful thinking, and he shivered. But he said nothing. Instead, he sat down to write a rough draft of the binding document. It would be finalized tomorrow and then Victoria must leave the country. He could only pray that Andrew had been right, that once Victoria was out of Edward's sight, she would also be gone from his thoughts. The money he would now inherit should keep him busy for some time.

As Henry scribbled the simple will, Victoria glanced at the paper. There was a sailing listed that interested her. The *Maryann,* a large but swift merchantman, would be sailing for Williamsburg on the early morning tide four days from now.

Quite suddenly everything fell into place. Her father's ship, the *Trident,* was riding at anchor, waiting to transport her to Annapolis, but that would be changed. Captain Hensley would leave for that small town immediately without her. Edward was undoubtedly having her watched, just as she was having his every step reported to her and from this moment on he would be lulled into a false sense of security. Everything she did would now indicate to her brother that she was afraid, that she was running.

There would be a show of secrecy. She would leave the house under cover of darkness, but in case Edward's agents were not skilled, she would sign on as Victoria Monet. She would leave a trail that could not be missed, a trail that suited her. By the time Edward had gotten as far as Williamsburg she would be aware of his presence; she would be ready for him.

Three days after Captain Hensley had quietly eased from port carrying specific instructions with him, Victoria waited out her remaining hours in England with a calm, almost detached patience. At the same time, Captain Marcus Randall, out of Richmond, Virginia, was surveying his severely damaged vessel, which now rested in a London repair yard. He had been only a short distance from his destination when he had run into a sudden, violent storm that all but sank his small ship, the *Morning Star*.

As he inspected the extensive damage, he knew he could build a new ship in America for less than the repairs would cost him here in England, but since he had already dismissed his crew to work their way home he had been in no particular hurry to make up his mind. Instead, he had enjoyed several weeks in the company of the mistress he supported in London, the mistress he had now cast aside.

Putting the ugly scene from his mind, Marcus turned his attention to what was left of his vessel. The main mast was gone, taking line and rigging with it. The hull was sprung and the keel was damaged. He had been more than lucky to make it to port, but he had been obliged to try, for the planters he served could not afford the extra charges of storage and overland transportation to London had he put into a port closer to the scene of his difficulties. As it was, it barely paid the Virginia planters to turn the soil. Not when they were forced by law to sell their tobacco only to merchants in England. And those merchants saw to it that the price was kept low.

Anger flared in his dark blue eyes, and he made his decision. He gave the order to have the ship stripped of everything that could be sold, then left the entire matter in the hands of the yard owner while he headed for the *Maryann*, which was captained by his good friend, Walter Matthews.

The two men shook hands warmly, then Marcus got to the point. "I'm in need of a berth for my return to Virginia, Walter. Do you think you could fit me on board?"

The captain laughed and put his hands on the younger man's shoulders. "Aye, you're in luck, lad. We have a small cabin that hasn't been spoken for. You won't have to sleep with the crew, and it'll do this old heart good to share your company."

With the problem settled, the two men gave their full attention to the job at hand. Captain Matthews, never known for his quiet ways, managed to get the cargo loaded in record time amid much bellowing and cursing. When satisfied that the load was well balanced and would not hinder the ship's speed by causing her to drag, the two men headed toward the captain's quarters to talk seriously and to eat a good meal.

It was Captain Matthews who broached the subject of the lost ship. "You're going to get yourself another one then?''

Marcus smiled. "You know there's no other life for me. I'll have a larger ship built, but I've decided that the time has come to give more of my attention to the farm. Ruby and Zeb have never stopped pestering me about taking a greater interest in the place.''

Walter puffed his pipe and eyed Marcus speculatively. He knew well enough the thoughts that go through a man's mind when he thinks he's about to go down to Davey Jones's locker. "So you're starting to get a little more serious about life, are you?''

Marcus shrugged his shoulders. "I think it's time for me to live a little differently.'' His smile was full of devilment. "Not *too* differently, though.''

Captain Matthews chuckled softly at his friend's implied meaning. "I don't expect you'll ever settle down completely, but you seem to have reached the point in life when you're starting to yearn for more than temporary relationships.''

Marcus sighed heavily. "No, not really. But I want children, and that's hardly possible the way I live now. So I've about decided to marry some proper young lady who won't know or care if her husband strays a little.'' Then, in an effort to divert his friend's thoughts to less troubling channels, Marcus asked about the other passengers who would be sailing with them.

Respecting Marcus's desire to change the subject, Walter told him of the young couple already on board. "They're headed for a small farm several days northwest of you, I believe. Got themselves a hundred sixty acres of wilderness.''

"I don't envy them,'' Marcus commented thoughtfully. "It won't be an easy life, and the frontier is not the safest place to be just now. There are some families in the general area, of course, but they'll have more than clearing land and starting crops to worry about."

"Frenchies gettin' the Injuns riled up again?"

Marcus turned pensive. "It's getting worse. Crops and buildings burned. Farmers left dead in the fields. Younger children carried away." His deep concern showed on his face as he continued. "The French are doing a good job of it. They're whipping the tribes to fever pitch now that some of our traders have made such inroads into the Ohio country. They don't like it, and they're determined to keep us hemmed in between the sea and the mountains no matter what they have to do to accomplish it."

A worried frown creased Walter's face. "I hope this young couple makes out all right. Maybe the husband will find a place in Richmond until their baby is born."

Marcus stared dumbfounded. "You mean the woman is going to have a child?"

"Aye, dammit," Walter scowled, more concerned than he cared to admit, for the *Maryann* was a merchantman and carried no doctor aboard. "It's going to be a race for port, lad, for if I'm any judge, the lady's past her seventh month."

Shaking his head at such stupidity, Marcus shrugged off the problem, which wasn't his. "Just the three of us then?"

Once again Captain Matthews showed his concern. "No, we have a young lady, a Miss Monet, making the trip with us. She hasn't come aboard yet, and if she doesn't get here soon, we'll be sailin' without her."

"Traveling unchaperoned?" Marcus asked hopefully.

"Aye, that she is," Walter growled, "but she's

under my protection and don't you forget it. Henry Byrnes, who's a power to be reckoned with in these parts, made the arrangements himself, and he's one man you'll not get me in trouble with. You're to keep that rovin' eye to yourself. Do I make myself clear?"

Secretly flattered by Walter's exaggerated opinion of his attractiveness to women, Marcus grinned broadly. "Don't worry, I'm sure I'll be able to resist your young lady. Probably ugly as a frog anyway. They're the only ones who travel alone, it seems."

A strong sense of disapproval flashed in Walter's eyes. Marcus had always been scornful of the ordinary. No wonder he had never found a good woman to suit him. "Too damned stubborn to look any further than some whore's bed," he thought angrily.

Sensing his friend's disapproval, Marcus ended the conversation. "It's been a long day. Think I'll go below and try to get some rest. I had better things to do last night than sleep. You know how sailors are when they're about to leave port. Want to get in all the comforts they'll be without for so long." He grinned suggestively and walked off, leaving Captain Matthews sputtering something about disrespectful young bucks.

Late that night, as Marcus lay dozing in his bunk, he heard the clatter of horse and carriage. A few minutes later he was aware of voices as several people descended the companionway. There were scraping and bumping noises as heavy objects were transferred below, then, once more, the familiar sounds of a ship at night were the only ones to be heard.

He was still sleeping when Captain Matthews's voice boomed out the order to raise sail, but he was fully awake as the rhythmic chanting of sailors bending to their task floated across the water. It was still dark, but the tide was right, and they were on their way. A few hours later Marcus was on deck.

By the time he came topside Mr. and Mrs. Ainsley, his fellow passengers, were already struggling to walk on the gently sloping deck. The woman's cape blew in the breeze, and Marcus saw that Walter was right. It would not be much longer before she'd be giving birth. He shook his head in bewilderment at any man who would be foolish enough to bring a woman that far along on what could be a rough sea voyage in the North Atlantic.

Grasping the rail, Ellen Ainsley turned and saw Marcus staring at them. Her smile was warm and friendly, and Marcus returned it as he approached the young couple. Introducing himself, he chatted amiably, pointing out various landmarks as the *Maryann* made her way rapidly toward the open sea.

It was night again before Victoria decided to venture on deck. She stood at the rail and felt the slightly increased angle of the ship as it began to labor almost imperceptibly through the waves. A deceptive swell was rolling in. The conditions were deteriorating.

The wind picked up and soon the cold, stinging spray was soaking the heavy, hooded cape she wore. She grasped the rail firmly and planted her feet as the ship bounced and plunged into a trough that had not been visible only seconds before.

A storm was brewing, and the open deck was not the place to be. Not without a lifeline, at any rate. As she turned to go below, the ship plunged, and Marcus, who had come topside to offer Walter any help he could, lost his balance and collided violently with Victoria.

She cursed as she was slammed against the rail with a force that knocked the breath out of her. Her eyes blazed as she drew a slim, razor-sharp stiletto, a weapon made for only one use.

Marcus saw the glint of steel and tried to grab Victoria's wrist, for he did not trust any woman who held a weapon, and this one looked as though she meant to use it. But Victoria spun from his grasp at the same time the blade slashed a neat path through the arm of the heavy seaman's jacket Marcus was wearing.

"Lord God," he hissed, and began to take the situation seriously. His foot shot out and knocked Victoria's legs from under her. As he attempted to pin her to the deck, she scuttled sideways, and Marcus landed heavily, grasping nothing but air.

At that moment the ship smacked into a wall of water, and both of them were washed roughly across the deck. Grabbing Victoria with one hand and the iron ring of a hatch cover with the other, Marcus hung on against the raging rush of water, but he lost his grip on Victoria when the *Maryann* nosed up like a blowing whale.

With nails digging and scratching for any hold she could find, Victoria raised the knife to plunge it deep into her attacker's throat. But Marcus rolled, and the blade burrowed harmlessly into the plank where his head had been.

Stunned by the murderous assault, he knew that if the silent struggle continued much longer, they would both be swept overboard. The woman who had come damned close to killing him was struggling against both an acutely angled deck and a heavy, sodden cape that was weighing her down, making movement almost impossible. When the *Maryann* plunged downward again, she would be swept away, and there would be no hope of rescue.

Wincing in distaste, he delivered a sharp, hard slap to Victoria's face. Her head snapped to one side and, before she recovered, Marcus managed to grab her wrist and apply a paralyzing pressure. "Drop it, dammit!" he shouted angrily above the thunder of spray and pounding waves as Victoria continued to clutch the weapon tightly.

In a final desperate effort to save them both, Marcus avoided the nails that were trying to scratch his eyes out and the flailing legs that made holding on to her almost impossible and delivered a backhanded blow to Victoria's cheek that would have stunned a man twice her size.

In the instant her world went black Marcus grabbed the knife and threw it overboard. Then he hoisted her to his shoulder and headed below.

As he struggled down the narrow stairs, Victoria regained her senses and realized that the man she had almost killed was not one of Edward's hired assassins. And when Marcus stood her on her feet in front of her door she managed a maddening smile. "I must apologize, Mr.—" There was a pause as she waited for him to fill in his name.

"Randall! Captain Marcus Randall," he snapped in irritation. "And you would do everyone aboard this ship a great favor, Mistress Monet, if you would confine yourself to quarters during rough weather. It would please us all if you would show at least some small degree of intelligence in this regard." He was still breathing hard from his efforts and was in no mood to deal with a woman too stupid to know when someone was trying to save her life.

Victoria pursed her lips and gave a thoroughly nasty look to the oaf whose clumsiness had almost knocked her head over heels into the briny deep. "And you, sir, are a menace. Surely you know better than to sneak up on a person in a rough sea. I really thought you were trying to knock me overboard since I hardly needed saving—until you came along," she added sweetly. "Really, Captain, you amaze me. Do you actually believe I would put myself into a situation I couldn't handle?"

Marcus almost blushed. What she was implying was true. He was the one who had caused the problem, but he wasn't about to admit it.

While he stood glaring, not able to find a suitable answer, Victoria's smile became friendlier. She knew he felt like an idiot. And regardless of how it had turned out, he had been trying to help her. "I seem to have caused you a great deal of trouble. May I make amends by offering you a drop of brandy? And I promise to leave the door open so as not to compromise your reputation."

Her rather caustic sense of humor did not escape Marcus. He laughed softly and gave her a look she did not misunderstand. Suddenly deciding that this rather violent, arrogant young woman might add some spice to an otherwise dull voyage, he accepted the invitation and followed her into the small cabin.

Victoria motioned him to a chair and threw him a thick, luxuriant towel. While he removed his drenched jacket and dried his hair and face he watched as she made herself more comfortable. The first thing she got rid of was the sodden cape, which fell like lead to the floor. Then, quite unself-consciously, she removed her wet shoes and hose. Marcus smiled. He liked what he saw.

Slowly and deliberately, his eyes perused her from the damp golden mane of hair that tumbled about her shoulders to the smooth golden glow of her skin. Then his open gaze wandered down to the high firm breasts and the narrow waist. The prospects of this voyage had definitely improved.

With no embarrassment and some obvious amusement, Victoria purred, "I hope, Captain, that my assets outweigh my liabilities on your balance sheet."

Marcus flashed her a wicked grin. She had caught him assessing her like some prize mare, but if she didn't mind, neither did he. "They do, indeed, ma'am. Though you have a few assets I'd just as soon forget about. Your ability to stick cold steel into a man, for one. Do you know how close we both came to being washed away?"

What had turned out to be an unwarranted attack on this man was something Victoria did not wish to discuss, so she lifted a brow in a show of total unconcern. "Let's not worry about something that didn't happen." Then she turned toward the stand whose closed doors protected the mugs and promised brandy, and as she crossed the cabin, Marcus noted the unconscious grace with which she moved, even as the ship plowed through the rough sea.

Closing the space between them, Victoria handed Marcus his cup and seated herself across from him. As he sipped the strong, warming drink, he was impressed by the large emerald and diamond ring on her hand. Then he frowned as his gaze wandered to the cheek that still showed the mark of the vicious slap he had inflicted.

"I'm terribly sorry," he apologized, reaching over to touch the reddened skin with gentle fingers. "I didn't want to hurt you."

This time Victoria's expression of surprise was genuine, surprise that such a little thing should concern him. "Forget it, Captain. I've suffered from worse. Shall we talk about something more pleasant? You, for instance?"

The dazzling, half-teasing smile that accompanied her words fascinated Marcus, and he felt the first faint stirrings of something more than casual interest. He stared into the unusual eyes that did not waver under his own, then smiled self-consciously. He had forgotten all about the questions he had intended to ask. "I fear there's little of interest to tell."

Nevertheless, within minutes he found himself opening up as the brandy and Victoria's soft murmurs of admiration loosened his tongue, for she had recognized almost at once that Captain Randall was a man who could be very useful to her. She encouraged confidences that Marcus began to realize could be extremely dangerous in the wrong hands.

But Victoria played skillfully upon his vanity. She laughed with him over his small triumphs and frowned in disappointment at his defeats. Several times she touched his hand in sympathetic understanding even as she refilled his cup.

It was not long before she knew of several ports where underpaid deputies could be bribed to ignore the more onerous laws of navigation that weighed so heavily on the colonials. It had been a stroke of great good fortune meeting Marcus Randall. He would tell her more of what she needed to know in order to compete with American shippers whose vessels slipped quietly into forbidden ports carrying forbidden cargo.

The man was a fool, but a most useful one, and she would encourage the growing interest that gleamed in those dark blue eyes. She had manipulated men like Marcus Randall before, and they had not recognized her tactics until it had been too late. Neither, she hoped, would he.

Victoria pouted prettily. "Yes, Captain, I can understand your resentment. It seems that the obtuse German who sits on the throne is being poorly advised."

"Indeed he is, ma'am, if he expects us to suffer forever under laws that give all the advantage to English merchants and none to the American—laws that force honest men to become criminals just to survive." His expression was bitter as he pondered the injustice. "But I fear it's the grasping English merchant who's more to blame than the king. They're a powerful lot, and they seem to get their way no matter how strongly we protest the laws that line their pockets and empty ours."

Victoria knew of the inequities to which Captain Randall referred, the laws that had served her father and other English merchants so well, laws that had been flouted with such impunity by the colonials and enforced with such incompetence by the Crown. But Captain Randall had told her enough for now. If she carried the subtle inquisition any further, even he would understand her purpose. She was amazed that his suspicions had not yet been aroused.

She smiled as she refilled Marcus's cup. It had not been necessary for her to introduce herself. He had already known her name. The good captain was eager to step into the snare, and she would take advantage of that eagerness. Then she grew weary of a contest that was no contest at all, of a game that now bored her because it had been won with such ease.

Still, she would cultivate the overly eager provincial until she was certain he could be of no further use to her. And as Victoria surveyed the man's darkly handsome face, the weather-roughened, bronzed skin and the thick black hair whose deep waves defied the ribbon at the nape of his neck, she thought that she just might enjoy this particular encounter no matter how one-sided. He would be a welcome change from the bewigged, pasty-faced posturers she so frequently dealt with.

Then her attention was diverted as the ship hovered almost motionless on the crest of a wave. Knowing from long experience what was to come in the next instant, Victoria grabbed for the bottle of brandy just before Marcus gripped her forearms in work-hardened hands. He half stood, leaning heavily against the table, which was bolted to the floor, and tightened his hold on the woman who might easily be thrown backward from a chair that was not secured.

The *Maryann* nosed down and skidded to the bottom of the trough before shuddering under the impact of the next wave. When the vessel plowed upward and righted itself Victoria saw the question in Marcus's eyes. She had reacted to the danger a split second before he had. She had aroused his curiosity, and that could lead to questions she did not intend to answer. Not truthfully, at any rate.

"You've been to sea in rough weather before," he stated simply, but it was a question.

"I once ran into a storm on a miserable Channel

crossing," Victoria lied smoothly, "but certainly nothing like this." Then she cursed silently at the unskilled lie. He was an experienced seaman. He would put it all together. Perhaps not right away—but eventually.

Marcus was puzzled and somewhat disappointed by the answer, but there was no time to pursue the matter. "Will you be all right by yourself?"

"I hope so," Victoria replied uncertainly. She had to be more careful. The man wasn't *that* gullible.

Marcus looked at her as though waiting for her to say more, and when she remained silent he nodded in resignation. "In that case, I'd better go topside. Captain Matthews will need every able-bodied seaman aboard if this storm worsens."

Raising her hand to his lips, he smiled. "Next time we must talk more about you."

"Anytime, Captain." She laughed, but her eyes narrowed as Marcus left the small cabin. He knew she had lied, but he didn't understand why. And she had no intention of telling him. He was a man who said too much when in his cups, and she had no doubt that Edward could persuade him to talk as easily as she.

# 3

Rough water continued to buffet the ship during the night, but by morning the pounding had subsided noticeably. Still, the sea was less than calm, the footing less than sure as Victoria made her way along the deck and noticed Captain Randall busily helping with the complicated procedure of getting a sailing vessel safely from one point to another. She watched him for a few minutes, admiring his obvious skill. The expression on his face showed the exhilaration he felt fighting the elements with his two hands.

Marcus glanced up and threw her a rakish grin. Victoria smiled warmly and waved to acknowledge the greeting, then turned her back to study the horizon ahead. The signs were good as the distant sky showed blue. She squinted against the glare of far-off sun reflecting from the sea. Another few hours and they would have clear sailing.

As she stood holding to the lines, the noise of a banging door caught her attention. Turning casually toward the source of the disturbance, Victoria saw two passengers, a man and a heavily cloaked woman, struggling to come on deck. The door to the companionway had been whipped from the man's careless hand and was now causing a problem. It was being swung back toward him by the motion of the ship, and he was striving valiantly but ineffectually with the door as well as the woman by his side.

At that moment the *Maryann* pitched upward, and the woman lurched, losing her balance. She tried desperately to save herself by grabbing at the door-frame, and by this time Victoria saw that the still choppy water was only part of the problem. The woman's swollen body would have kept her off balance on firm ground.

As soon as the ship steadied, Victoria rapidly closed the distance between herself and the couple. Balancing herself against the ship's motion, she put her arm around the woman's enlarged waist. Planting her feet firmly, she grabbed the threatening door and gently applied a leaning pressure that forced the young woman back onto the stair. Then she guided her burden down the steps to her own cabin.

After seating the stranger Victoria turned to shut the door and saw Captain Randall looking at her quizzically while holding onto the pale-faced youth. She clenched her teeth in frustration. Once more Marcus had witnessed her competence at sea. If he hadn't been sure last night that she had lied, he was absolutely certain of it now. But it couldn't be helped. She'd explain it away somehow, for she could hardly allow a pregnant woman to go tumbling across the deck like some tar barrel that had broken loose.

Blowing out an exasperated breath, Victoria motioned for Marcus to seat the man and turned to get the bottle of brandy, which she put in front of the obviously seasick passengers.

William looked up wanly and shook his head. "Please, ma'am, if you'd just get my wife to our cabin."

Captain Randall put his large hand none too gently on William Ainsley's shoulder. "We'll take care of you *and* your wife, if you'll be good enough to give me the key to your door."

The tone in Marcus's voice was belittling, and William was embarrassed by his own helplessness as he rummaged around in his pockets before finding the elusive key. "Thank you, Captain. Ellie was feeling so sickly this morning, I thought a walk in the fresh air would do her good. And I wasn't feeling much better myself," he added guiltily.

Brushing aside the man's dejected apology for being so useless, Marcus looked over at Victoria. There was a trace of sarcasm in his voice. "I assume you'll be able to care for Mrs. Ainsley while I get her husband to their cabin."

"Of course," Victoria assured him cooly, ignoring the impolite tone that had been meant to intimidate, for she had already decided on an explanation should Marcus question her further. She would admit a little more—just enough to cover the stupid lie she had blundered into.

When Marcus returned he put a powerful arm around Ellen's shoulders and all but carried the woman from the room. He got back just as Victoria was putting the brandy away.

"Don't hide it yet," he muttered. "I could use a nip or two myself."

Victoria showed her teeth in silent laughter and

poured a double portion. Marcus sat down, emptied the mug and let out a sigh of profound relief.

Sympathizing with Marcus's unwanted role of dealing with seasick passengers, Victoria smiled in understanding. "I don't imagine rescuing pregnant women is exactly your line of work, Captain."

Marcus was in no mood for frivolous banter. In fact, he was irritated by what was now obvious. Victoria had lied to him, and he was deeply disappointed in her less than honest behavior. Nor did he understand the purpose of such deviousness unless she were playing some coy feminine game. But why? It certainly wasn't very becoming to a woman so capable of looking after herself. He directed a disgruntled look her way. "Young ladies of breeding are usually too delicate of speech to use that term, madam."

For an instant Victoria didn't understand, and when she did her temper flared. Marcus Randall was taking it upon himself to reprimand her for using the word *pregnant*, a word obviously considered to be less than genteel in the simpering, hypocritical society in which he apparently moved.

Her smile was nasty as she decided to give this terribly dull, opinionated provincial something to chew on. "Would another term change the cause, Captain? Or are you too delicate of mind, too pure of thought to conjure up such images? Forgive me if I have corrupted your innocence."

Marcus winced under the vicious attack and the undisguised contempt in the syrupy voice. The fact that Victoria might be justified in defending herself didn't improve his mood. "No, madam," he drawled, controlling the anger, "no matter what word you use to describe the condition, the cause remains the same, and I hope it doesn't change."

"You and every other man I've ever met," she purred. "And if you will not think me too forward, I might even confess that I have known one or two women who have also thoroughly enjoyed the cause if not consequence. Or is that, too, something ladies of breeding would not say?"

"I believe it would be most proper under very specific circumstances," Marcus answered stiffly, but he had been taken by surprise. Sweet, charming, sympathetic Mistress Monet had been transformed. She was tough, and despite the softness of that well-modulated, educated voice, she was crude, as crude as any sailor in any alehouse.

And that business with the knife. It had been more than just fright, more than just protecting herself. He had seen enraged whores slash at each other before they could be separated. It had not been a pretty sight. Victoria's reaction last night on deck had been the same. Cooler, perhaps. With less passion, but the same. A slow, calculating smile spread across his face as he thought that he just might have hit on the truth.

"Tell me, my dear, how is it you're crossing the Atlantic alone? Have you no one who could look after you? No husband or father or—anyone else to accompany you?"

Victoria did not miss the meaningful hesitation in his voice. She knew exactly what he was asking, and she decided to give him yet another morsel to digest.

"I feel quite certain that one or two gentlemen of my acquaintance would have been most eager to accompany me on this tiresome journey, but then I hardly think that my darling Aunt Prudence would understand such conduct. After dear papa died Aunt

Pru insisted that I make my home with her and would give me no rest until I agreed," Victoria lied smoothly.

"You're not married then?" It was a stupid question to which he already knew the answer. What he really wanted to know was whether or not she had a lover, a provider, but he could hardly come straight out with it.

Victoria was satisfied. She had diverted his suspicions to a path he could understand, a path that would explain her secretiveness and would cover the unforgivable blunder. "Ah, no, Captain," she sighed forlornly. "Alas, that happy state has passed me by."

Almost as one, they laughed silently. Victoria's eyes sparkled with humor, and Marcus realized that she was laughing at him. But he didn't mind. In fact, he was beginning to enjoy her less than orthodox behavior.

"Come now," he coaxed, "are you really joining relatives?"

"But of course," she assured him, flirting with her eyes, "and looking for some way to escape them as quickly as possible."

Marcus frowned in annoyance. He didn't like the implications, but if what he suspected were true, it certainly explained her lack of honesty—even to the point of lying. "That, my dear, should be no problem."

Victoria lowered her lashes demurely. "I think perhaps you are right, Captain. The only problem will be finding someone who can pay my price." She smiled brightly and added almost as an afterthought, "But one can always compromise."

The game had turned sour, and Marcus found himself itching to shake some sense into her. She had far too much to offer a man to live the life of a whore. He barely restrained the hand that seemed to have a will of its own. "You've had your little joke, madam," he growled. "Enough is enough!"

"But of course, if you say so, Captain. More brandy, sir? You seem to have come up dry." The dripping sarcasm of the last sentence eluded him. He was too preoccupied with his own thoughts. He nodded and pushed his cup toward her.

"Yes," he sighed in defeat. "I think I could use another drink."

The barest quiver touched Victoria's lips as she poured the amber liquid. He believed exactly what she wanted him to believe, that she was a woman looking for a man, and that man didn't necessarily have to marry her. Then she leaned back in her chair and watched him try to sort through his confusion, but she could not play too rough a game with this little mouse. There was more he could teach her. Once again she changed her tactics.

"It was good of you to help with Mrs. Ainsley, and it's very kind of you to take the time to keep me company. I'm really grateful to have someone to talk to and joke with a little."

Not sure just what kind of woman he was dealing with, Marcus was wary. He had no intention of being ensnared by a whore, no matter how beautiful or how interesting. He would be the laughing stock of Richmond. "Well, my dear, there's always Ellen. I imagine the poor child would be happy to have female companionship at a time like this."

"Yes, you're right. I'll do what I can for her. It must be dreadful being *enceinte* as well as seasick."

Marcus noted the effortless substitution of the
French word that somehow sounded so much more
genteel coming from her lips than its English
equivalent. At the same time the word *hypocrite*
flashed through Victoria's mind as she read the look
of smug approval on his face at her toned-down
language. Pregnant was pregnant, no matter the word
used to describe it.

Deciding that he had no good excuse for prolonging
the visit, Marcus drained his cup and stood to leave,
but he was extremely curious about Mistress Monet.
She might very well be the kind of woman who could
add measurably to his enjoyment of this trip, but he
had to be sure. If he made a mistake, Walter would
have his scalp. It was time he found out.

"Perhaps you would do me the honor of dining with
me this evening. I'm sure Captain Matthews can
come up with something special for the two of us."

Victoria managed to show the most delicate of
frowns with exactly the right hint of a disappointed
pout on her face. She had no intention of joining
Marcus Randall in an intimate dinner for two.
"Thank you for your thoughtfulness, Captain, but
tonight I think I should invite the Ainsleys to dine
with me. You are quite right when you suggest that
Mrs. Ainsley needs a woman's company and that I
have been remiss in my duty toward her. But of
course you would be most welcome to join us," she
added brightly.

Disappointed by the answer, Marcus knew he had
no one to blame but himself. It had been he who had
suggested Victoria pay more attention to Ellen. She
was, after all, merely accepting that suggestion. He
gave an exasperated sigh. "I'll escort the lady to your

cabin myself."

"And who," Victoria teased, "will escort Mr. Ainsley?"

His eyes answered the twinkle in her own. "That, dear lady, will be his problem. Until this evening then?"

He bowed over her hand and left with the distinct impression that he had just been outmaneuvered. His lips twitched in wry humor. Miss Monet was a most intriguing bit of baggage.

Victoria waited several hours before approaching the Ainsley cabin. She tapped lightly so she would not disturb them if they were resting.

Now that the sea had calmed, a healthier looking William opened the door. He beamed his welcome. "Please, come in. How kind of you to visit."

"Thank you," Victoria replied and stepped inside. "I must say, you and your wife look much better than you did on deck this morning."

Both young people laughed in good humor. "We're feeling ever so much better, but we're terribly sorry to have put you and Captain Randall to so much bother," Ellen apologized.

"No bother," Victoria assured them. "It was only too obvious that neither of you has ever been to sea. I had almost forgotten how upsetting it can be. Perhaps you're feeling well enough to join me for dinner in my cabin. I believe Captain Randall will also attend."

The Ainsleys were flattered and delighted. They accepted immediately and insisted that Victoria stay to chat with them awhile. Their open friendliness relaxed her completely. She had almost forgotten how pleasant it could be just to talk with someone who demanded nothing, who expected nothing—someone who offered friendship with no ulterior motive to spoil the gesture. The pleasant interlude passed all too quickly.

Regretfully, she excused herself and returned to her quarters, where she gave much thought of projecting exactly the right image. She would wear a gown that flattered but gave little hint of the great wealth that was hers. She was not ready for that complication. It would take far too much explaining and would arouse entirely too much curiosity. No. Marcus had accepted her unsubtle hints. He must continue to accept them. The trail Edward would follow must not be too clearly marked.

At the appointed hour Marcus Randall escorted Ellen Ainsley through the door without bothering to knock. William trailed behind. The cook, whom Victoria had bribed shamelessly, had produced from some mysterious cache food that had almost certainly been intended for the captain and his officers.

Each dish brought in by Tommy, the cabin boy, was well prepared and beautifully presented. The four of them did justice to the Madeira, the fish chowder and the thinly sliced ham swimming in raisin sauce. Herbed potatoes, hot crusty rolls and roasted onions testified to the cook's skill. Ellen and William were duly impressed.

As they sat munching the after-dinner cheeses and fruit, Marcus questioned William about his plans once they dropped anchor in Virginia waters. The man's answers were an affront to Victoria's meticulous nature, for William had planned no further ahead than getting to the land he had purchased.

With concern showing plainly in his voice, Marcus pursued the subject. "What supplies *have* you brought with you?"

"After purchasing the land and paying our passage, we had very little left to buy the recommended goods. Ellie brought some linens and other household items to our marriage, and we have warm clothing for the winter. That and what I can build with my own two hands ought to get us started."

"What about seed and food to last till your first harvest? Do you have the tools you need to work the soil, and you cannot go into the back country without a musket and shot. What about stock?" Marcus questioned relentlessly.

William was obviously upset by this line of interrogation, but it was Ellen who spoke up. "We have over twenty pounds sterling with us and thought that would surely purchase enough to see us through. We understood that things were so much cheaper in the colonies."

A bitter laugh escaped his lips as Marcus commented, "Not for goods that come from England. Such things will cost you three times more in the colonies. And even at that price you're likely to get inferior products."

For the first time in many days, Victoria felt an honest emotion as she saw Ellen's unsuccessful effort to hide the fear as her hand moved unconsciously to the unborn baby within her. "Enough, Captain." She laughed. "I'm afraid that any more of this conversation will cause these two to turn around and go back to England."

Marcus was outraged at her cavalier disregard for the safety of the two young people whose lives would depend on being prepared. His question was curt. "And what, madam, do *you* know about rough living?"

"Very little," came the deliberate lie, "but surely it cannot be as bad as you paint it."

The contempt that flooded Marcus's face did not disturb Victoria. She had already made up her mind to talk to the Ainsleys in private, for she did not intend to stand idly by while William, through inexperience, pulled his wife down with him. The girl deserved better. Besides, she had the beginning of an idea that they might prove useful to her later on.

Ellen filled the strained silence by asking Captain Randall about his own situation, and Victoria listened as he repeated some of what she already knew. The almost impoverished young couple listened as wide-eyed as children as Marcus described Serenity, his eight-hundred-acre estate near Richmond, and the rich timberlands he owned to the northwest of the James River. He concluded his answer to Ellen's question.

"My interest lies not so much in raising tobacco, which is a pesky crop at best, but in shipping. The life of the sea suits me far better, I fear, than farming."

"Does your wife not mind your long absences, Captain?" Ellen asked with an innocence that caused Marcus to smile wistfully.

"I'm afraid no woman would have me, madam. As yet, I still lead the gay bachelor's life."

He had meant the remark to be flippant, but something in his voice prompted Ellen to murmur, "Oh—I'm so very sorry, Captain, but surely there must be some good woman who would be willing to care for you."

Victoria almost strangled on her tea. Little Ellen had
managed to cut Marcus Randall off at the knees, and
he just sat there with a stunned expression on his
face.

To hide his embarrassed discomfort, Marcus
reached for the wine bottle and shared the last of the
Madeira with William. As the men sipped the
soothing liquid, the two women talked softly, and
Victoria learned a great deal about the two children
who had all the bravery of ignorance as they faced the
formidable task before them. Finally William stood,
expressed his thanks and then helped his wife back to
their own quarters.

Marcus lingered over his drink while Tommy
cleared the table, and after the boy had gone he spoke
bluntly. "Can you really be so ignorant that you
actually meant that nonsense when you implied I
painted too stark a picture of frontier life?"

"I generally say what I mean," Victoria answered
calmly.

Marcus compressed his lips in disgust. "You're a
damned fool, and you should keep your mouth shut
when you don't know what you're talking about. The
Ainsleys *must* realize what they're facing. They *must*
be prepared if they are to survive. False hope won't
help them."

Victoria eyed him coldly. "Neither will useless fear.
Or do you make it a habit to frighten children? And I
might add, Captain Randall, that your great concern
for their safety seems to stop just short of any *real*
help. Or did I miss your offer?"

Marcus flinched under her censure. She was right,
but he wasn't about to apologize or become further
involved with the Ainsleys. He bowed stiffly to his

hostess and returned to his cabin, which suddenly seemed an emptier, drearier place.

He was edgy. His close brush with death on a raging sea almost a month ago had forced him to look at himself honestly, and he hadn't liked what he had seen.

Sleep came with great difficulty as Marcus lay wondering about the woman who seemed to understand him better than he did himself. Certainly she understood him better than he understood her.

# 4

Victoria remained in her cabin the next day, poring over charts and maps of the colonies that she had gone over dozens of times before. But at this moment her purpose for studying them was a little different. She would ask William exactly where his property was located. His answer would determine the extent of her involvement with him.

Opening her trunk, Victoria took out one of several large pouches of hard coin and emptied it on the table. She separated a number of gold discs from the silver ones and put the rest back. Then she tied the coins in a handkerchief, satisfied that the amount of money she intended to lend William would make his first year in the wilderness as secure as possible.

Then, if he succeeded in raising a crop, any surplus would come to her at deflated harvest-time prices as partial payment on the loan. The loan would also alert other settlers in Virginia to a possible source of scarce cash, and if they forfeited on their payments, she would own vast stretches of land for a paltry sum.

The thought pleased Victoria, for she intended to expand into every aspect of American business, and felt that this would be one of the few constructive things she had accomplished since her father's death.

When she asked William and Ellen to join her in her cabin William pointed to the general area where his homestead was located, and Victoria was satisfied. He could be of use to her.

Carefully, she explained her proposition, edging cautiously toward the topic that was her real interest in the Ainsleys. She told them something that was very near the truth—that her father had been dealing in the fur trade for several years and had a minor interest in the Ohio Company. "It would be very convenient to have a small way station for men and animals making the journey to and from the Ohio. It would also be a means for you to earn a little cash."

The Ainsleys were willing victims. They agreed immediately to the arrangement. "You can count on me, ma'am," William boasted.

Victoria wasn't willing to concede William's dependability just yet, but she thought there was a chance that he and Ellen might survive to give her what she needed—a trading post on the edge of the frontier. And now that the deal had been struck it was to Victoria's advantage to see that these two young people *did* succeed where so many others had failed. There was only one more step to be taken to complete her plans, but that step was a long way off and would have to be handled with great skill.

As they were about to leave, Ellen asked the obvious question. "But how will we reach you, Miss Victoria?"

"You will not need to contact me, Ellen. I will

contact you." She pondered for a minute before continuing. "However, there is one more thing I hardly feel it necessary to mention, but since you are probably unaware of the need for secrecy in many business matters, I must ask for your solemn oath that you will discuss our arrangements with no one."

"Not even Captain Randall?" William asked innocently.

Victoria's smile was enigmatic. "Not even Captain Randall." And as she closed the door after them, Victoria's spirits lifted. She would make another fortune with very little risk, for with William's help the fur trade would come to her. And because of Marcus Randall she knew exactly how to get those furs to foreign ports where the prices were high. Chisholm would be a name to be reckoned with in the colonies as well as in the rest of the world. Her father would have been pleased. And Edward. She would deal with him when the time came. No matter what the cost.

Completely satisfied that she would soon have a trading post on the very edge of the frontier, Victoria slept soundly while Marcus tossed restlessly in his bed. Alien thoughts and feelings tortured him. He had been outrageous in his behavior toward Victoria and had badly shaken the confidence of William, who already had more than enough to worry about.

Finally Marcus gave up the struggle for sleep. Staring at his haggard reflection in the shaving mirror, he shook his head. He didn't understand what was happening to him. For almost a year now he had grown increasingly restless and dissatisfied. Maybe Walter was right. Maybe it was time to settle down.

When the first uncertain light of morning crept into his cabin Marcus roused himself from his despondent lethargy and went topside. He was disappointed that Victoria was not there. She had stayed in her cabin all day yesterday, and though he had lingered on deck well into the night, she had not appeared. She was avoiding him, and he didn't blame her. He had managed to get on everybody's nerves, including his own.

Then his spirits lifted as Victoria emerged from the companionway door. Even the cold look she directed toward him as she turned to walk in the opposite direction didn't dampen those spirits. He felt much better as he approached her.

"Fine day for sailing," he commented inanely.

Victoria gave him a disgusted look. "That, Captain Randall, is something any child would know. Am I to congratulate you on your keen insight?"

The bronzed skin turned ruddy. Marcus was not skilled at making amends, and Victoria had the tongue of a serpent. It wouldn't be easy to reestablish a congenial relationship, but he intended to try. Somehow, it seemed important.

"No. Hardly. Actually, I only intruded to apologize. I said some rather nasty things, and I'm sorry."

The expression on Victoria's face all but withered his hopes. Then she changed her mind. There were other ways to cut Marcus Randall down to size. A great many people called her a great many things, but none had been stupid enough to think her a fool. Before she was done, this boorish oaf would learn who was the fool.

Once more she slipped behind a charming facade. "We have a long voyage ahead, Captain, and since we can hardly avoid one another altogether, it might be wise to call a truce. Your apology is accepted."

Greatly pleased by her capitulation, Marcus

blundered on. "Thank you, my dear. I fear I've all but forgotten how to behave in polite company. Your forgiveness makes me feel much better, particularly since you are no longer confining yourself to your quarters sulking over a remark I really didn't mean."

Victoria almost laughed out loud. He actually believed she had spent the day pouting over his insults. She didn't know whether to despise him or pity him. "No, Captain, I was not sulking in my cabin, and to be very honest I gave your remarks very little thought."

Somewhat deflated, Marcus continued lamely, "I'm relieved to hear that. I'm afraid I'm unaccustomed to dealing with women on a serious basis and could only think that I had hurt your feelings."

Victoria's brows arched slightly. "Oh, and on what basis do you deal with women?" She was having a marvelous time baiting him. He was unbelievable. His arrogance. His *conceit*.

"Come now," he chided, "you know very well what I'm saying. Women prattle on for hours, and when they're all done they haven't said a damned thing. You must admit that your sex is hardly equipped to deal with serious matters, something you, yourself, proved only two days ago."

This time the laughter would not be suppressed. Victoria thought Marcus Randall one of the most ridiculous men she had ever met, and he was so serious! So earnest! "And just what are women equipped to deal with, Captain—in your considered opinion?"

She was laughing at him, and he knew it. "They would be very wise to confine themselves to womanly duties. Something they have the capacity of

understanding," he responded sharply, thoroughly
irritated by her badgering. He had meant this to be a
pleasant conversation, and it was going all wrong.

But Victoria wouldn't let the matter drop. "Pray,
enlighten me, sir. What are these womanly duties to
which you refer?"

Dark blue eyes blazed in anger. "Being *where*
you're wanted *when* you're wanted. But then you
should know that, madam, if what you imply of your
own background is true."

Victoria glanced down at the tip of her shoe, which
moved in a brief semi-circular pattern across the
planking. Then she raised eyes that had lost all traces
of amusement and responded in weary resignation.
"I've heard those words or words very much like
them before, Captain Randall. Many times and in
many languages. I suppose you, too, like others
before you, will now offer to do me the supreme kindness of instructing me in those duties you feel I have
yet to master."

Abruptly, Victoria stopped speaking. She had
revealed too much. "No matter, Captain. Forgive me.
I fear we shall once more be at each other's throats if
we continue this conversation." Pulling her cape
closer, she shivered with an inward chill. "If you'll
excuse me, I think I'll go below. I've had quite
enough fresh air for one morning."

Itching with curiosity, Marcus had no intention of
letting Victoria escape so easily. He wanted very
much to learn about the other men in her life, the men
she so openly admitted had also offered to teach her
the art of pleasing them. "Yes, it is turning raw," he
agreed. "Would you mind if I join you? I'm sure we
can find more pleasant subjects to discuss."

Victoria's hesitation was barely perceptible. "I'm sure we can, Captain. Perhaps you would even be good enough to continue our last conversation on the intricacies of trade from the colonies. There's so much I still don't understand."

Exasperation flicked over Marcus's face. "Only if you insist, madam. And to be very honest, I can't imagine why you should be interested in such a dull topic."

Certain that the request would arouse his curiosity, Victoria was ready with her own explanation. "But, Captain, even a mere woman who is unskilled in her duties would like to understand a little of the conversation that so seems to engross our menfolk. I should hate to appear totally ignorant when dear Aunt Pru's husband and friends discuss their affairs."

A hint of sadness darkened Marcus's eyes. Once again Victoria had plunged the verbal blade deep. But it was more than that which disturbed him. Never in the few days he had known her had she relaxed her guard, and he suspected that not once had she spoken the truth. "My dear, you already know enough to have me hanged if you choose to repeat what I've told you."

Victoria stared thoughtfully at the man who understood that she could, indeed, make life difficult for him. He knew only too well the possible consequences of his impulsive confidences, and he had said nothing until now. Neither had he been taken in by her simpering posturing, but he had answered her questions anyway. And those answers had been truthful.

It wasn't fair to burden her with this trust. He wasn't playing according to any of the rules that governed her own life. She sighed heavily. "I have no intention of repeating anything you have told me, Captain. That much, at least, you can believe."

"I do," he stated simply. "Now, shall we go below? There's no need for us to freeze while satisfying your curiosity."

The questions Victoria asked were carefully worded. She approached everything from an oblique angle. Frequently she changed direction only to cut back to the same path. She laughed with Marcus, making some joking comment that elicited a deeper truth, and he was totally fascinated by the *tour de force*. Never in his life had he been questioned by a more skillful interrogator. And the questions were not those of some ignorant little mistress whose only interest was catching a rich man to support her. Yet that was precisely what she had said. She would stay with her aunt and uncle who lived somewhere along the Susquehanna River only long enough to find a man who could afford her price.

Doubt and disbelief cast perplexing shadows over everything Victoria had so skillfully led him to believe. And for the first time Marcus noticed that those hands did not belong to a pampered rich man's toy. But the thing that troubled him most was what he now recognized as a deliberate insincerity in her relationship with him from the very beginning. And why had she thought he wanted to push her overboard when all he had done was try to save her from a fatal dunking in the cold waters of the North Atlantic?

He did not understand the game she was playing. Certainly the charade could not be for his benefit, for she had practically confessed to having been some man's mistress. There was no need to continue the half-truths and outright lies.

He stared into eyes that revealed nothing. "And you, Victoria? What about you?" he asked at last.

She shrugged. "There's very little to tell, Captain. I'm alone, and I'll make my way as best I can."

The next question was difficult, for Marcus remembered with embarrassment his recent parting from the woman who had served him for more than four years whenever he found himself in London. "And your lover? Did he not provide you with enough money for a fresh start? It's the least he could have done."

"I'm not destitute, Captain, and the life I prefer to live is really none of your business, is it?"

No matter how softly spoken, the words cut deep, and Marcus did not understand why. Neither did he understand why he should care, but he did.

Thoroughly confused, he left the cabin and returned topside to lose himself in the hard labor demanded of every common seaman, but it didn't help. Then, just before dusk, he retreated to his own quarters, where he paced restlessly in the confinement of the small room.

He was jumpy and on edge. Every nerve seemed to twitch. "Damn women aboard ship!" he cursed, and slammed the door behind him as he sought escape on the open deck. And there the dark mood lifted. An unconscious smile brightened his face. Victoria was at the rail. He approached her with an unreasonable happiness coursing through him.

"Lovely night," he began, gazing up at the brilliant starlit sky.

"Mmmm," she murmured absently, her attention riveted on a falling star. "Did you make a wish?" she asked as the fiery bit of celestial ash disappeared below the horizon.

"Yes." Marcus smiled as he turned her to face him. "I wished that there might be truth between us. And you?"

Her face was soft and unguarded, her eyes moist with sudden tears. She nodded. "I wished that someone I love most dearly has found happiness."

"A friend?"

Her smile was wistful. "Yes," she replied softly and said no more, but the longing in her voice reached out and touched him. Without thinking, Marcus took her in his arms to comfort her.

"Someone you miss very much."

Tears that had been too long constrained threatened to spill down her face. "Yes—very much," she whispered as the glistening drops finally broke free.

With an unconscious tenderness, Marcus wiped each tear away with his finger. "Would it help to talk about it?"

The eyes focused and became aware. "No," she answered softly and turned to look skyward once again as though searching for some solution to a problem he knew nothing of.

Turning seaward, Marcus commented quietly as he gazed across the vast expanse of ocean, "Barely a ripple as far as the eye can see."

"Yes. It's a lonely sea we sail, Captain. A very lonely sea."

Once again he heard the sadness and the longing in that soft voice, and he knew that she was referring to much more than the calm waters that stretched as empty as her life apparently was to the far horizon. How well he knew the feeling, and when he turned her to him again he held her more tightly as his lips brushed hers.

Victoria did not pull away. She leaned against the

hard body and was comforted by the warmth of his closeness. Her arms encircled his waist as she pressed closer, desperately seeking to hide from the desolation that threatened to overwhelm her.

In all this world there was no one to love her, no one but Henry, and even he was passing from her life. She shivered and stepped back. "Thank you, Captain. Thank you for your kindness."

Dark blue eyes searched the now unreadable face. "I think it's more than kindness," he said at last, sheltering her protectively within his arms, drawn to her by some force he didn't try to understand. His touch was gentle, but now he was seeking something from her in return.

Victoria had felt herself drowning in the empty devastation of her life, and she clung to the man who held her as she would to a drifting spar in a stormy sea. Her defenses had given way; her resolve was shaken, and she returned the softness of his kiss even as her hand caressed his cheek.

Marcus felt the hesitant, almost shy response. Her reaction was that of some little schoolgirl instead of the experienced mistress she was. He smiled as he recognized the coy whore's game and slipped his hands under the cumbersome cape, molding her body to his.

His lips teased and cajoled; his arms tightened, and Marcus felt the all too familiar need course through him and through Victoria as well as she slipped her arms around his neck and answered his urging.

The soft breath of Victoria's tremulous sigh touched his lips, and Marcus pressed deeper. His lovemaking became more insistent, and Victoria stiffened as the low pulsing of awakening desire sounded its warning.

She shuddered and stepped back. Her eyes sought the face that was lost in shadow. Then she turned to escape the danger to which she was vulnerable, a yearning and a need that were new and frightening to her.

"No," Marcus whispered, and pulled her close again. "Not yet. Love me," he pleaded, and was startled by the words. A whore wasn't for loving; she was for taking.

When Victoria pushed away he did not try to stop her. Instead he clenched his fists in frustration and unfulfilled need and admitted the truth. He wanted more than just her compliant body. He wanted her to love him.

There was bitterness in his soft laughter. She was extremely skilled at her particular little game. She played it well, but he was no longer certain of his ground or of his purpose. Troubled, brooding eyes watched as Victoria made her escape below, where her thoughts returned once more to the blazing path of the falling star. It had been to her an omen, a portent. It marked the end of her life to this point. What the future held she did not know. She was stepping onto uncharted territory. She must use all her wiles and all the skills her father had imparted to her to survive.

# 5

Captain Matthews was pleased with the perfect weather he had encountered this past week. They were almost halfway to their destination and, if the wind held, he would make it to port with time to spare before Mrs. Ainsley was due to have her child.

Feeling extraordinarily relieved and therefore expansive, he decided that he had not been particularly gracious toward his passengers. He knew that Marcus had, more or less, taken the odd assortment under his wing, even the strange and aloof Mistress Monet, who had never bothered to seek him out for any reason but had mingled with the others on rare occasions.

A twinge of guilt tugged at him, and he decided that perhaps it wouldn't be too much trouble to invite his passengers to his private quarters for an evening meal. He might even get out his guitar, an instrument he played not so much with skill as with enthusiasm.

"The very thing," he thought happily. "I've neglected the ladies shamefully."

When Marcus joined him as he usually did for several hours each day Walter asked if he thought the Ainsleys and Mistress Monet might like to join them for an evening.

"I'm sure William and Ellen will be delighted. As for Miss Monet," he continued uncertainly, "I'm never sure what she will or won't do. The lady hasn't been out of her cabin for a week. Shall I extend the invitations or will you?"

"You seem to know them better than I. Why don't you do the honors? This evening sound all right to you?"

After agreeing that this evening should be fine Marcus felt a good deal happier now that he had the perfect excuse for stopping by Victoria's cabin. She had been avoiding him since that night on deck, the night she had stirred more than just his desire. "Damn," he muttered as he tapped on her door.

When Victoria answered the knock Marcus stepped through uninvited, forcing her to give ground, for she wanted no further physical contact with Captain Randall. It had taken days to beat down the longing and the need he had aroused, and her mind still refused to let go of the memory. The softness of his lips, the soap-clean smell of his skin lingered still.

Marcus noticed the quick backward step and laughed softly. "I would almost think you're afraid of me," he teased, but his past experience with women caused him to guess rather accurately that Victoria Monet was not too comfortable at this moment, and he took pleasure in that knowledge. Why should he be the only one to suffer?

"I imagine your visit has some purpose, Captain." Her voice was cool and impersonal, and Marcus studied the calm, composed woman who was so different from the one who had responded to his touch. He had felt her warmth and the need that had been strong in her as well. But it had only lasted a moment—not nearly long enough.

He sighed in resignation and extended Walter's invitation. Pleasantly surprised by her acceptance, he stood waiting for her to say more, to give some indication that he was welcome, but Victoria was silent. Disappointed and embarrassed for having made a fool of himself by begging a whore to love him, he gave a slight, mocking bow and left.

As soon as Marcus had gone, Victoria let out the breath she had been holding. Her behavior was ridiculous. There was no room in her life for any man, much less this overbearing, conceited planter from Virginia. Still she gave a great deal of thought to what she would wear and then laughed at herself as she realized that she wanted to impress the man she should be guarding against. But surely it could do no harm. When this trip was over she would never see Marcus Randall again.

So she proceeded to dress with unusual care in a scandalous off-white woolen gown. She brushed her hair until it glistened and coiled it in a great golden bun that covered the crown of her head. When the knock came she was ready.

Throwing her cape around her shoulders and pulling the hood over her meticulously arranged hair, Victoria unbolted the door and admitted Captain Randall, the man who had almost persuaded her to forget why she was aboard the *Maryann*. Almost but not quite.

With courteous reserve Marcus escorted Victoria to

Walter's quarters and helped her off with the heavy, concealing cape. As he removed it from her shoulders, he and Walter stood speechless. The dress was far from modest and revealed the soft enticing glow of bare arms, the graceful curve of neck that flowed to lovely shoulders. Marcus took a deep breath as his gaze slid to the rounded gleaming breasts that worked their magic against the delicate shade of the gown.

He felt an uneasy stirring and turned his back to hang the cape from a peg on the opposite wall, wondering bitterly which of her paramours had bought her that too revealing gown. It was the sort of thing one bought for a mistress—not a wife. A man did not expose the body of the woman he loved to the world.

Captain Matthews recovered first. Complimenting her on her remarkable appearance, he led Victoria to a chair. She accepted the glass of wine and sipped it slowly, enjoying Captain Randall's obvious struggle with his emotions and will. He had caused her a few uncomfortable hours; now it was his turn. But far back in her mind Victoria knew she had started this whole nasty business, and she was less than happy with herself. Her mood darkened further as she squirmed uncomfortably under the memory of the time she had suffered because of a man she didn't even like.

William and Ellen interrupted her gloomy thoughts as they arrived attired in their very best. The animated Ellen seemed prepared to have a good time, but the numerous bows attached to the dangerously strained bodice only accentuated the swollen breasts and the too thick waist. "Not quite appropriate for a

married woman heavy with child," Victoria thought
snidely, and then bitterly chastised herself for the
uncharitable turn of her mind. It wasn't Ellen she was
furious with. It was herself.

Knowing that this young couple would have little
enough gaiety in their future, Victoria decided to put
a good face on it and make it a happy evening for their
sakes. Just because she was miserable was no reason
everyone else should be.

Captain Matthews was a good host. He drew out the
usually shy William. The young couple chattered like
the two happy children they were, and their faces
beamed with pleasure at being the center of attention.

Marcus and Victoria listened politely, inserting a
quiet comment or question from time to time. They
knew that this occasion belonged to the Ainsleys, and
they were content to share in their pleasure.

It was not until Tommy had cleared away the last of
the dishes that the mood changed from one of
energetic cheer to one of more subdued relaxation.
The food had been excellent and the wine worthy of
the best tables. Now they were satisfied to sit back
and bask in the warm afterglow.

Walter got out his somewhat battered guitar and
began to strum an old ballad. Victoria hummed softly
to the familiar chords and Captain Matthews, thus
encouraged, began to sing the words. As he prepared
to put the instrument down, Victoria asked if she
might try it out, and when he gave it to her she
strummed a few bars before falling into a haunting,
melancholy tune that somehow suited her mood.

Originally it had been a Spanish love song but had
been translated into English and was now very
popular in that country. Walter recognized it and

began to sing in his clear, rich tenor while Victoria joined him in a soft harmony that was barely audible but seemed to blend with and complement the man's voice perfectly.

When the lovers in the song had died and the final note still trembled in the air Ellen wiped her eyes. "Oh, that was lovely," she sobbed. "Such a sad song. Do lovers always have to die?" she questioned with a wistfulness that brought a look of tenderness to Walter's eyes.

"The lovers or the love," Victoria answered cynically.

Marcus had not taken his eyes off her since the song had begun, but now the bittersweet expression that had touched his face hardened at the unnecessarily cruel answer. Ellen was barely seventeen, and William wasn't much older. The hope of unworldly innocence still shone in their warm brown eyes, eyes that were now cast down in confusion, a confusion caused by a hardness, a brittleness they could never comprehend.

And quite suddenly everything seemed to fall in place. All of it made sense. Victoria was no more than a wanton tease who took perverse pleasure in destroying a man. She was alone because her last lover had probably thrown her out. And no wonder, for beneath that lovely face and body was a cruelty he, himself, had suffered under.

He had met such women before, women who used every conceivable trick of mind and body to lure a man only to make him feel small and somehow degraded when he sought to fulfill the ultimate promise. It had been many years since he had been caught in that snare, not since he had been an untried youth. Now it was happening again. Only this time it was going to end differently. He was no longer a raw, love-smitten child of fifteen.

His eyes glittered. He was furious. It was long past time Miss Monet was taught the lesson she so richly deserved. Now that he understood her game it was time she learned his.

Victoria's fingers coming down on the strings startled them all as she thumped out a rousing, rather bawdy song known to every sailor. Walter, who had had too much wine, whooped lustily and joined her in lyrics that caused Ellen, a farm girl all her life, to blush, while Marcus glowered his displeasure. His fingers twitched to slap the smiling face that mouthed the bold, suggestive words.

The singing lasted for another half hour until Victoria, who could no longer ignore the speculative, half-mocking gleam in Marcus's eyes, stood to take her leave. Instantly he was at her side to escort her back to her cabin.

When they reached her door Marcus bent his head and pressed a hard, lingering kiss on her mouth that announced his intentions, but Victoria backed away and forced an uneasy smile.

"Good night, Captain. It was a lovely evening. One I'm sure the Ainsleys will remember for a long time."

"Not just the Ainsleys," he drawled, fully intending that this would be one night *she* would not forget, either.

Then he closed in, but Victoria slipped sideways, determined to keep her distance. "Good night, Captain," she repeated emphatically as anger edged her words, but as she stepped inside her cabin and attempted to close the door in his face, Marcus braced his hand against it and walked in. He bolted it behind him.

Victoria stood her ground and faced him. "I thought I made it quite clear that I do not wish to prolong the evening."

The breath of his quiet laughter brushed her face. "That, my dear, is unfortunate. You've had your way for some time. Now it's my turn."

Wasting no energy in futile protest, Victoria made one swift move toward the door, but Marcus reached out and spun her back roughly, crushing her to him. His grin was infuriating as he bent his head to reach her mouth. Victoria strained to turn her face away, but his fingers curled tightly in her hair as he demonstrated the futility of resistance.

"Not this time, pet," he murmured against her cheek. "I've had quite enough of your little game. Now we play mine." His eyes glinted maliciously as he slowly and painfully forced her face to his.

The suggestive sound of his soft laughter tugged at the corner of Victoria's fear and sent it flowing through her limbs. Her heart raced under the alien emotion, and she fought against it with an even greater ferocity than she fought Marcus. She had felt his passion before and had been tempted by it. Her body, if not her mind, had responded to the urgency that had caught her so totally by surprise. Now she wanted no more of that treacherous weakness, and she renewed her desperate struggle.

She tried to sink her teeth into lips that teased, but Marcus tugged at her hair, forcing her head back a fraction. He was amused. "My dear, you'll find I know every whore's trick that has ever been invented. You'll have to do better than that. Much better."

His taunting infuriated her, but she drew in a quick, sharp breath as his mouth moved to the hollow in her throat and then to her breasts. One muscular arm tightened around her, effectively pinning hers to her sides as experienced fingers unfastened the low-cut gown. Then his hand slid inside her garment to stroke the smooth bare skin, working its way to her waist and then her buttocks.

Victoria squirmed helplessly and moaned her distress as his teasing sent sparks of fire shooting through her. A sharp cry of protest was wrung from her lips. "No!" she sobbed as Marcus took her to the floor with him. She struggled to be free, yet her resistance was less than convincing.

Marcus was torturing her with a touch as light as a butterfly's wing. It was an exquisite torture, one she was reluctant to end before its purpose was fulfilled. And when Marcus once again brought his lips to hers Victoria's arms encircled him. Her body pressed closer. There was an urgency now to her movements; a silent plea flashed from her eyes to his.

In that trembling instant Marcus pushed her roughly from him and sat up. Victoria stared at him in confusion. Her eyes were shadowed by longing. She drew a deep breath to still the uncertain pulse that raced and would not be quiet. It was then that she saw the narrowed eyes glint with satisfaction as the mouth curved downward in a cruel, insulting smile.

Finally the truth crashed in on her. "No," she whispered, trying desperately not to believe what was happening. But it was true, and she closed her eyes to blot out the mocking light of contempt in his. She understood it all.

He had planned this final humiliation from the beginning. His every move had been carefully calculated. And she had come to heel like some obedient bitch on a short leash. The icy rage consumed Victoria.

Scrambling to her feet, she stumbled to the stand. Almost tearing the door from its hinges, she reached in and pulled out the gun that was never far from her. But before she could pull the hammer to full cock, before she could squeeze her trembling finger against the trigger, Marcus grabbed her wrist and applied a pressure that sent her to her knees as he wrested the pistol from her hand. Then he stood her on her feet and forced her to look at him. His eyes were cold, without warmth of any kind, and there was an ominous warning in his voice. "There are several things I want from you, Victoria. I've just taken one of them."

Her hand flashed out and delivered a stinging blow to that contemptible face as she spat the damning words she thought she would never say to anyone. "You bastard!" she hissed.

Marcus grabbed her savagely and raised a hand poised to strike. Then he let her go and stepped back as he studied the pale face and wide eyes. It was just one more twist in the game he had taken so long to comprehend. "Surely, madam," he sneered, "this is no new experience for you. From all that you have implied you've felt a man's desire before. Name your price. I'll pay it." His gaze fell to her all but uncovered breasts, and the smile was insinuating. "Perhaps even so high a price as marriage."

Victoria strangled on her rage. Her eyes blazed with fury, and she lunged for him. Her nails raked his face,

and Marcus threw up his arm to protect his eyes.
"Damn!" he hissed in shocked surprise as he felt the
blood ooze from the wounds and run down his face.
But he, too, was racked by a torment no less than
Victoria's, and this final assault ripped through the
last vestige of restraint. "By God, this will stop!" he
snarled. "You *will* learn. If I have to kill you, you will
learn."

His fingers dug into her shoulders, and he crushed
her face against his chest so she could not breathe.
One arm encircled hers, pinning them uselessly to her
sides. Victoria squirmed and kicked, using up
precious air, but Marcus held her tight until the
struggling stopped and her body slumped. Then he
loosened his hold a little, just enough to let her turn
her head and gulp in cold, damp air. His voice was
husky with emotion out of control. "You've amused
yourself at my expense for some time, love, but that's
over," and before she could react a mouth that had
turned cruel closed over hers.

Then Marcus cradled her cheek against his chest.
He was trembling with emotions he did not want to
recognize or admit, and his voice was heavy with
regret. "The next time you begin to play your nasty
game, my dear, be sure you haven't taken on an
expert."

Releasing her, he unbolted the door and returned to
his cabin, but it had been a costly victory. He wanted
her. He wanted that vicious, half-wild little tart more
than he had ever wanted any woman.

Victoria stood on legs that would barely support
her. Her face was drained of color, and she swallowed
hard to bring some semblance of calm to a brain that
refused to function logically. Pain darkened her

luminous eyes. He was going to pay. "Damn his soul to hell," she raged. "He will pay!"

Even as she stalked the length of the small cabin, damning and cursing Marcus Randall in several languages, Victoria knew that she would get even—more than even. She would crush the arrogant colonial under her foot like the loathsome scorpion he was. He would be made to suffer the same burning defeat he had just heaped on her.

Victoria's eyes narrowed. Already she savored the sweetness of her revenge. Marcus Randall would suffer much more at her hands than she ever could at his. But it was neither rage nor the desire for vengeance that consumed her as she slumped to a chair, fighting uselessly against the torrent of need that would not be stilled.

# 6

Almost before the pale, cheerless sun broke the horizon Victoria was on deck. She would not admit the devastating defeat to herself, much less to Marcus Randall. He would not be given the satisfaction of seeing her cower in her cabin, afraid to show her face.

She gritted her teeth as she prepared herself to confront the man who was going to regret the day they met. She had already devised her plan. Whether or not it succeeded depended upon Marcus Randall and the depth of his vanity.

For more than an hour she paced like some caged animal, smiling mechanically at the sailors who greeted her, but Marcus did not come topside. Victoria compressed her lips grimly as she recognized the tactics. He thought to let her burn herself out in useless, directionless anger. But he was mistaken; her anger was no longer directionless.

Wasting no more time waiting for him to appear, Victoria climbed the steep stairs to the forbidden quarter-deck where Captain Matthews was chatting to the sailor at the wheel. "Good morning," she said brightly. "I hope my presence does not disturb you."

Walter doffed his cap. "Not at all, Mistress Monet. It's my pleasure to see you looking so fresh this morning." Then Walter turned worried eyes back to the distant sky and shook his head. "Weather doesn't look too promising up ahead," he muttered more to himself than to Victoria.

Still smarting under the harsh humiliation Marcus had inflicted, Victoria wasn't the least interested in the weather, but she obediently took the cue and turned her attention to the subject that was so obviously disturbing Captain Matthews. Then she, too, became concerned. "Maybe we'll miss it," she replied hopefully, and then dismissed the possible danger from her mind. "But I really came to thank you for a lovely evening. I think William and Ellen were extremely pleased with your kindness, and so was I."

As Walter looked into that beguiling face, he wondered why he had ever thought her cold and aloof. She had shown last night that she was a pleasant, charming woman. Not a prude, either. "My pleasure, ma'am, and may I wish you well in my country."

She smiled her thanks. "How much longer do you think it will be before we reach port?"

"At the rate we're going, I would say another two weeks at most."

Thanking him again for an enjoyable evening, Victoria returned to her cabin. She was quite satisfied with herself; she had revealed her true destination to no one, and that fact was going to be put to good use.

Marcus Randall had beaten her, but only temporarily.

Hours after Victoria had gone below, Marcus joined Walter for lunch in his quarters, where he learned that Mistress Monet had been strolling the deck earlier. "I must say," Walter commented expansively, "she was extremely pleasant. Showed every sign of good breeding in her courtesy toward me."

Marcus stared at his friend in bewilderment. He had been certain Victoria would have gone running to Walter to complain. In fact, he had waited half the night for the knock to come at his door, and it had been one of the reasons he had not taken her completely there on the floor of her cabin. If he had, Walter would have strung him from the nearest yardarm, friend or no friend. Still he had almost risked it. He had wanted her that badly.

Thoroughly confused and more than a little uneasy, Marcus stood to leave when Walter offered an unasked for bit of advice. "From the looks of your face, lad, I'd say you'd tangled with a wildcat. But whatever caused those slashes, I wouldn't let it happen again. If the lady comes to me with a complaint, I'll settle it just as I would if you were a stranger."

"That will hardly be necessary," Marcus replied coldly. "The lady has already made her point." But he was deeply embarrassed. He had made an ass of himself in the eyes of one of the few men whose opinion he respected, whose friendship he valued. Still uncertain, he asked bluntly, "Miss Monet told you nothing at all?"

Pursing his lips to hide the smile, Walter answered in laconic tones. "Not a word. Never mentioned your name. Guess she thought she could handle it by herself.'' His eyes sparkled with laughter as he continued. ''And from the looks of you and the looks of her, I'd say you got the worst of it.''

''Yes,'' Marcus agreed sourly and walked from the room. As he passed Victoria's door he thought briefly of apologizing, then decided against it. He had swallowed enough of his pride for one day. And why should she forgive him? He hadn't yet forgiven himself.

However, he was unable to resist the temptation of pressing his ear against her door, straining to hear any sound. But there was absolute silence from within. ''Probably resting,'' he thought guiltily, for he knew he had been brutal in his treatment of her. It had gone further than he had intended. He sighed heavily as he continued on to his cabin. It wasn't like him to treat a woman that way, and the victory he had won at such great cost to himself turned to bitter defeat.

Victoria was not resting. She was laboring her way through a terribly dull book her father had bought concerning the latest scientific principles of farming, but she couldn't concentrate. Her thoughts kept returning to the man who had taught her a lesson she would never forget, and when the day became suddenly dark, she was glad for an excuse to stop.

Stepping to the window, she saw the distinct line of the squall that was now almost on top of them. She lit the lamp and watched as it swung in a wider arc than it should. At the same time the ship's movements became more pronounced. Victoria threw her cape around her shoulders and headed for the main deck to see exactly what they were in for, and when she did her heart sank. Not only were they in the fierce crosswinds of the squall, but ahead were the

ominous black clouds that had worried Captain
Matthews only hours ago.

As she stood there assessing the danger, it began to
rain. At first there were large gentle drops, but almost
immediately a sheet of water hit her as the wind came
with a roar, bringing fear with it. She had seen it all
before. A gale this time of year in the North Atlantic
was a serious matter.

Hastily, she returned below, where she drowned
the coals in the small charcoal heater, lashed her
trunk to the foot of her bed and put anything that
might be hurled across the room under cover. Just
before extinguishing the oil lamp she tied a rope
across her bed. It would give her something to hold on
to, something to keep her from being tossed from the
bunk. Then she wedged her pillows in the corner,
braced her feet against the frame of the bed and
prepared to ride out the storm.

She could imagine the struggle that was only beginning topside. Every seaman aboard knew what
was coming, and even now the cook would be extinguishing the fire, for one wrong move, one careless
miscalculation could condemn them all to a watery
grave.

At that moment, the *Maryann* shuddered and
trembled as though she were breaking apart. The full
force of the gale was on them. Victoria's smile was
bitter. The pleasure Edward would derive from her
death was not to be endured. Then she stiffened. If
the ship went down, Marcus would die too.

"Holy mother, Isis," she moaned, totally disgusted
with herself. Yet she felt cheated. It wasn't his death
she wanted but, rather, her own particular brand of
revenge. He had taken her pride and now she was

determined to destroy his. She knew that he was up on that gale-swept deck doing what he could to save them all, but it didn't matter. She only wanted him to live long enough to feel the lash of her fury.

Victoria spent what seemed an eternity fighting the rope, burning her hands as she was tossed and bruised by the raging sea. She braced herself more fiercely until her strength threatened to desert her. The rhythmic thumping of manned pumps dulled her mind.

Exhausting hours passed. The gale shrieked like some demon from hell, sucking at the planking, curling through the smallest space, invading her cabin with the damp chill of certain death.

"Damn Edward!" she hissed. If it hadn't been for him, she would still be in England, safe and warm in her own bed. The rage that flooded through her diverted her thoughts so completely that it was some minutes before she realized something had changed. The pitching and rolling of the ship had subsided. The terrible groaning of timbers under stress was less ominous. She no longer had to brace herself so fiercely, but could relax with little danger of being dumped to the floor.

When she felt it was safe Victoria sat on the edge of the bunk massaging her cramped legs and blowing on rope-burned hands. She was totally exhausted from the physical and mental strain. Removing only her shoes, she stretched out under the blanket, drained of all feeling. In minutes she was asleep.

From the depths of great weariness, Victoria was dimly aware of a persistent noise that she could not place in her sleep-drugged state. Irritably, she turned and pulled the blanket over her head, but still the

noise continued. As she forced open heavy lids, she
realized at last that someone was pounding on her
door.

Finally she threw back the blanket with arms that
barely responded to her will and struggled to a sitting
position, waiting for her mind to clear. As she sat with
head in hands, feeling half sick, the cabin door
opened and Marcus was striding toward her. She
stared at him, trying to understand what was happening.

Then she felt harsh hands at her shoulders as he
shook her roughly. The cold voice cut through the fog
in her tired brain. "Victoria! *Listen* to me, damn it!
Ellen needs you!"

She struggled to clear her head as the meaning of
the words began to make an impression. Her eyes
were more alert. "What's the matter?"

"Breech birth," he answered grimly. "She's been
struggling for hours, and she's worn out. We've done
all we can, and now we can only pray to God that you
can help, or is making a eunuch of a man your only
talent?"

Victoria flinched as she recognized the burning
contempt in his voice. Then her eyes blazed. She had
had enough of Marcus Randall. Rising from the bunk,
she aimed a vicious kick at her tormentor's shin, a
kick that hurt her shoeless foot more than it did the
object of her wrath. Then she limped to the Ainsley
cabin, and as she entered her senses were assaulted
by the stench and reek of the struggle to give birth
gone wrong. Fighting against the odor that hit her like
a physical blow, Victoria bent to examine the young
woman.

Ellen was moving feebly, sobbing softly for her

mother. There was no more strength to scream out against the pain. Gently, Victoria turned her on her side and pushed the girl's knees toward her stomach. She stared in horror as she saw the problem. Protruding from the mother's racked and tortured body was a tiny foot, and Victoria wondered how long Ellen had been trying to force her child into the life-giving air.

Removing her ring, she cupped one hand into as small an object as she could and gently followed the tiny leg into the mother's body. The trouble was obvious to her probing fingers. The baby's other leg was bent and could not pass through. The child was in an unnatural, broken position.

Gritting her teeth and summoning every ounce of courage she possessed, Victoria took the baby's foot in her free hand and eased it carefully back into the mother's body just far enough to allow her to straighten the other leg and bring it down so the child could pass from the canal.

She was desperate. The maneuver had to work. If it didn't, her only other choice would be turning the baby, and that was something she didn't want to attempt.

Despite the chill in the cabin, Victoria felt the trickle of perspiration run down her face. "When you feel the next pain, Ellie, push! Push as hard as you can," she pleaded. "I'll help."

As the next wave of pain swept over her, Ellen bore down as hard as she could. Released from the prison of his mother's body, the baby came into Victoria's hands. Instantly another pair of strong, suntanned hands cut the cord and removed the child from her slippery grasp. From the corner of her eye Victoria saw Marcus trying to clear the infant's nose and mouth of blood. Then she gave her full attention to the mother, wondering why he was attempting to save an infant who was already dead.

After tending to Ellen and making sure there was no hemorrhaging Victoria stripped the quilt from the bed, dumped it on the floor, then removed the fouled and bloody sheet from under the incoherent woman. Finally she pulled Ellen's gown down around her legs and stood wearily. Staring numbly at her bloody arms and hands and at her blood-spattered dress, Victoria stumbled to the water basin and washed herself perfunctorily, too tired to do more than rinse off in the cold water.

Then she returned to her own cabin only long enough to strip her bed and bring the bedding back to Ellen. She dumped the blanket and sheets into William's arms just as Marcus wrapped the tiny body in a cloth and walked with it from the cabin.

Suddenly Victoria was weary unto death. The strength she had summoned to battle for Ellen's life deserted her. "The hell with them," she thought bitterly, feeling totally defeated. "Let William explain to his wife about the death of their son. I'm through."

All the strain of the past hours weighed down her body and spirit as she groped her way to her own cabin. Through sheer force of habit she raised her arms to unfasten the many small buttons that went down the back of her dress.

Almost weeping in frustration and despair, she felt a pair of warm, comforting hands put her own at her side. She stood numb and unprotesting as Marcus unfastened her dress and removed the bloody souvenir from her body.

Neither did she protest when he picked her up and

carried her to a chair. She was only vaguely aware that he had left the cabin, but she was more alert when he returned, bringing fresh linens. She watched with little interest as he made up her bed, then lifted her in his arms once more and put her down on the bunk.

Leaning over, he kissed her on the forehead and stroked the damp tendrils of hair from her face. "Sleep now, my love. God knows you've earned it."

He sat on the edge of the bed for the few minutes it took her to fall asleep. When he was sure she would be all right Marcus stood and stretched muscles that ached from his long struggle, first with the storm on deck and then with the stunning tragedy in the Ainsley cabin.

It wasn't until he was about to leave that he remembered Victoria's ring, which he had rescued from the washstand in the Ainsleys' cabin. Easing the blanket down, he placed the large, shimmering jewel on her finger and smiled as he saw what an incomplete job she had done of washing off. Nothing would have pleased him more than to obliterate all traces of her ordeal from those small, competent hands, but he would not disturb her now. She needed sleep much more than she needed a bath. So he contented himself with tucking her in before walking from the room, closing the door quietly behind him.

Weary to the bone, he trudged to Walter's quarters, where he accepted a mug of strong rum. Captain Matthews had been waiting anxiously for some news, and Marcus filled him in on the whole terrible event that had begun during the height of the storm.

"You say Miss Monet seemed to know what she was doing?" Walter asked, almost too tired to care, for he, too, had been severely tested these past hours.

"Yes." Marcus sighed. The rum was hitting him hard, and his words were slurred. "The baby's body has been wrapped. William might want you to read a few words over his son later."

"It was a boy, then," Walter said quietly as his eyes glistened and his voice broke.

"Aye," Marcus confirmed heavily. "It was a son." He rose before he made a complete fool of himself. Tears were close to the surface. For a man to lose his son was too much to bear.

When he reached his cabin he collapsed on the bunk, too weary to undress. His last conscious thought was of Victoria. She was everything he disliked in a woman, but she was the woman he was going to marry. He laughed tipsily. "Whether she likes it or not," he declared to no one in particular.

It was well past noon when Marcus finally roused himself. His body was stiff and sore, but it was nothing that wouldn't work out quickly. His next thought was of the woman he now considered his, and he wondered if Victoria were awake.

As he remembered the quiet courage she had displayed in the early morning hours, he decided to forgive her for the unladylike conduct she had exhibited once again, but it must be impressed upon her that he would stand for no more of that quick temper or her nasty little game. There was just so much he would tolerate, even from her. A lopsided grin spread across his face as he rubbed the spot where she had landed the kick that had hurt her more than it had him.

Less than half an hour later he invaded Victoria's cabin, balancing a large tray of food in one hand and gripping a pitcher of hot water in the other. Unburdening himself, he walked to the bunk and stood for several minutes, content just to watch her sleep. Then he bent over and kissed her on the lips. She opened her eyes instantly.

"Good afternoon, my dear. I've invited myself for a late breakfast," he informed her confidently.

Stretching herself awake, Victoria threw her legs over the side and blew out a deep breath. She felt better. Without questioning the source of hot water, she scrubbed her skin until it glowed. Then she took her robe from a peg, slipped it over her under-garments and sat down at the table. It had been a long time since she had put any food in her stomach and she was famished.

As Marcus heaped her bowl with porridge and buttered their biscuits, he was pleasantly surprised to hear her apologize for her earlier actions. "I hope you will forgive me; it was uncalled for. I regret having lost my temper."

Marcus stared at her as he realized that she was not really apologizing for the blows she had so roundly heaped on him, but, rather, for losing her temper, which she seemed to consider a much more serious matter.

He answered in sardonic tones. "I certainly forgive you, my dear, but it's only fair to warn you that any further conduct of that sort will have serious con-sequences. I believe that was the third time you've seen fit to show your temper."

"The first two were justified," she replied evenly, but her eyes challenged him to contradict.

Marcus laughed. "Eat your breakfast and let me eat mine in peace, madam. We can discuss the merits of the case later. More to the point, I wanted to thank you for your help with Ellen. You seem to have had some training."

Victoria shrugged away the question. There would
be no confidences between her and the man she
intended to hurt as deeply as he had hurt her. "Anyone who has ever helped a mare foal would have
known what to do."

"And you have?" Marcus asked, totally intrigued
by this small, apparently honest glimpse into her life,
a life that seemed to be a series of contradictions.

"Once or twice." Then, seeming to notice her ring
for the first time, she changed the subject. "Thank
you for returning my ring. I would hate to lose it."

Sullen eyes focused on the large emerald surrounded by diamonds. "A gift from some paramour, I
suppose," Marcus muttered.

Smiling sweetly, Victoria led him exactly where she
wanted him to go. "The man who gave it to me loved
me very much." Her voice was smug, and Marcus
clenched his fists in frustration. The food turned to
dust in his mouth and he sighed heavily.

"Captain Matthews will be reading a brief service
for the Ainsley baby at three o'clock. We'll carry
Ellen on deck in a chair if she's up to it. It might give
her some comfort in years to come to know that her
son was given proper burial at sea. She would appreciate it if you could be there with her."

A few weeks ago Victoria would have refused, but
as she remembered the terrible pain of her own grief,
she decided that she would attend the pitiful service
she had seen many times before. She closed her eyes
against the memories. "I'll be there."

Exactly at three Victoria proceeded topside. Everyone else had already gathered, and she stood quietly
to the side of the group while Captain Matthews read
the service. When the tiny bundle splashed into the

water Ellen sobbed uncontrollably. William knelt at her side, put his arm around her waist and wept with her.

All the pain of her father's death came rushing back, and Victoria could bear no more. As she turned to go below, she saw the tears in Marcus Randall's eyes even as she felt the sting of salt in her own. Her shoulders slumped. She should have known that Ellen would need help. But, no! Instead of going to the girl's cabin she had thought of no one but herself. She had been concerned only for her own comfort and her own safety, and now Ellen's son was dead. At the height of the storm the girl had struggled against fear and against pain. "I should have been there," Victoria sobbed softly.

Wiping unfamiliar tears from her eyes, she entered the small cheerless cabin and sank into the nearest chair. No one was blaming her, but she blamed herself. She could have saved Ellen's baby.

Suddenly she became very angry. Angry with herself and angry with William and angry with Marcus. She hardened her mind against what was yet to come. There would be more suffering—not only for her but for anyone who got in her way. And Marcus Randall had definitely gotten in her way. He had challenged her, and she would meet the challenge. Just as her father had taught her to do.

# 7

The remaining days passed swiftly as the *Mary-ann* made near record time under every scrap of canvas that could be raised, and Marcus spent much of that time with Victoria. He wooed her skillfully, taking only the smallest of liberties, being careful not to press, not to frighten her into throwing up the defenses that were slowly coming down.

Captain Matthews watched the courtship with an approving eye, and he was fully prepared to marry them at sea if they should ask. But neither of them did. The lady, it appeared, wasn't quite ready even though Marcus was obviously chaffing under the un-accustomed restraint.

Walter laughed out loud. He had thought that he would never see the day Marcus Randall fell hope-lessly in love, but he had, and he was overjoyed for his friend. Miss Monet was a fine, striking woman, and they made a most handsome couple. Marcus was a very fortunate man, indeed.

After a week of confinement Ellen, too, began to

take an interest in this shipboard romance. Seeing two
people so much in love helped ease her own loss a
little. And William loved her every bit as much as
Captain Randall loved Miss Victoria. She sighed and
let go of the baby she had never seen. There would be
other children.

Only two days out of port Victoria stood on a towel
squeezing water from a sponge down her body when
she heard her door open. Turning toward the source
of intrusion, she saw Marcus standing in the doorway. His body stiffened as his eyes traveled over
every inch of her.

"Lord God," he whispered, then realized that the
door to Victoria's cabin was still wide open.
Slamming it shut, he asked irritably, "Won't you ever
learn to bolt your door?"

Victoria laughed softly, totally unconcerned as she
reached for her robe. "And will you ever learn to
knock? Even Tommy has better manners."

Marcus didn't answer. Instead he walked to the
nearest chair and sank heavily into it. He could not
take his eyes off her, and he wanted nothing more
than to touch that wet, glistening skin, to caress those
small, rounded breasts. He drew a deep breath to
calm the sudden, unwanted reaction of his body as his
gaze drifted to the long sleek legs.

Victoria did not hurry. Calmly, she adjusted her
robe over her damp body and tied the sash. "What's
on your mind?" she asked. Her low, throaty laugh
sent chills through Marcus, for Victoria knew only too
well what was on his mind. "Perhaps I'd better
reword that question. What brings you here so unexpectedly?"

She stood in front of him in a beautiful silk wrapper that did very little to hide her enchanting, hard, slender body. The dampness of her skin caused the flimsy material to cling and become almost transparent where it caressed the curves and hollows, but she seemed unaware of her own appearance or of the effect it was having on Marcus Randall.

Patiently, Victoria stood waiting for Marcus to answer her question. The woman who had been raised for so many years as a boy in the company of men was not the least embarrassed, and Marcus wondered bitterly how many others had seen her like this. For how many others had she strutted and posed? And had they been privileged to run their hands over that soft, golden skin—touch the satin of those thighs?

He could not believe that any woman could be so unaware of her effect on a man or be so totally innocent as Victoria looked standing there, taunting him with her unconcern. He pulled his mind away from the agonizing scenes, the jealous fantasies he had created, and looked at her with a longing and a desire he was barely able to control.

Only a few seconds had gone by, but to Marcus it seemed an eternity before he was able to collect his thoughts, to speak rationally. "I came to tell you we're nearing our destination. Another few days and we'll be putting into port. Have you made arrangements for transportation to your uncle's home? If not, I would be happy to take care of the matter for you."

"I'm quite sure my uncle has made the necessary arrangements," Victoria replied easily, knowing that a ship would, indeed, be waiting for her if Captain Hensley had brought the *Trident* safely to port in Annapolis. "At the very least, there should be some sort of message giving me further instructions. I wrote to Aunt Pru several days before I sailed telling her that I would be arriving in Williamsburg aboard the *Maryann*."

A slow-breaking smile of pure delight spread across Marcus's face. "My dear, you will find that in this country a few days is not nearly enough time for a letter to precede you. I doubt that your aunt and uncle will claim it or even know of its existence for weeks after we disembark. You might have a very long wait ahead of you."

Victoria frowned, but Marcus was extraordinarily pleased. "I hardly dared hope that you might be detained for any length of time, but almost certainly you will be. And perhaps we can put that time to good use. While you're waiting to hear from your aunt, I can show you the town; you can meet part of my family, and you might even honor me with a brief visit to my home in Richmond."

Victoria flashed him a charming smile. "Perhaps. We'll just have to wait and see, but it's very kind of you to be concerned about me."

Marcus hated these games she insisted on playing. Victoria knew full well how he felt about her, and she certainly had at least some suspicion that he wanted to marry her. "It's quite a bit more than concern, my dear," he drawled. "Certainly you know that I am very much in love with you, and despite a rather unsavory reputation, which I've warned you about, you've given me every reason to believe those feelings are returned in full measure." Suspicion gleamed from the narrowed eyes. "Or are you still parrying, waiting to find an opening to a vital spot?"

The first twinge of guilt skipped across Victoria's

heart. Marcus was right, of course. She *was* waiting
for the opportune moment to plunge the blade deep,
to bring down his arrogance and pride, to humiliate
him as he had humiliated her. "Perhaps I am being
overly cautious," she admitted at last. "And you're
right. My feelings for you run deep. I'd be lying if I
said anything else. You're an extremely handsome
man. It wouldn't be difficult to listen to the heart
instead of the mind. I imagine a great many women
have already made that mistake."

An uneasy premonition pricked at Marcus. The
conversation had taken a turn he didn't like. Victoria
had put her finger on a very sensitive spot.

He nodded in confirmation. "There have been
others, but none I've ever considered marrying. And
there are no claims on me. I've been very careful to
avoid the usual entanglements." His lips twitched in a
rueful smile. "I assure you there will be no breach-of-
promise suits, nor are there any illegitimate offspring,
for I've never wanted any bastards cluttering up my
life."

The momentary lowering of Victoria's eyes and the
brief flicker of bitterness that crossed her face caused
him some alarm. He had admitted too much.

With every muscle taut, he leaned forward in the
chair as though trying to touch her physically with the
words. "I love you, Vickie. God only knows how
much. And I want you. Not as a mistress, not as I've
wanted other women, but as my wife. And I need to
know that you love me, that you will marry me."

The light of triumph glinted in Victoria's eyes as she
seated herself opposite the man she was going to
bring to his knees. "If you're sure—" she began uncertainly, then laughed away all doubt. "Of course I

love you, you idiot. Why else would I have put up with you all these weeks?''

It was enough for Marcus. He pulled her from the chair and hugged her close. She was going to marry him. Once again Serenity would become a home, a happy place resounding with the sound of children's laughter. "I love you," he murmured before stepping back to stare into those luminous eyes. "I wonder if you know how much."

"Yes," she answered in a voice that was suddenly unsteady. "I believe I do."

The *Maryann* had passed the capes and now navigated the James River. Victoria stood on deck eagerly awaiting her first view of the port that represented the start of a new life and the end of her association with Marcus Randall.

Even as she thought of him, he approached and put a possessive arm around her waist. "There she is!" he exclaimed exultantly as the ship veered and sailors scrambled to make ready to drop anchor.

Victoria looked at the unimposing little port and tried to sound enthuiastic. "It'll be good to get on firm ground again," was as much as she could manage.

Marcus laughed. For a woman who was used to the elegance and grandeur of London, Williamsburg wasn't much. Still, it had a charm of its own, one Victoria would come to appreciate in time.

It was a cold blustery day, and Victoria's cape whipped around her, but Marcus seemed unmindful of the weather. His thoughts were racing to make suitable plans for the woman who was going to become his wife. He hugged her closer and smiled confidently. "I think I've finally decided to settle down and pay more attention to my farm as befits a married man. Or would you rather I limit the size of our family by staying at sea?" he teased.

"I think the sea suits you best," Victoria answered softly.

They were not the words Marcus had expected to hear, and his face showed his disappointment. "But not for too long, my dear. I want a house full of children, and I want to be very sure they're all mine."

Ignoring the less than subtle insult, Victoria flirted with her eyes. "Then by all means, Marcus, you must spend your time at home."

Accepting the false smile as real and accepting her words as ones of invitation, Marcus heaved a sigh of relief. "Thank God you're not one of those women who would refuse her husband because she didn't want to spoil her figure by giving him sons."

Victoria laughed in genuine amusement. "And would you love a woman who had grown fat? I think not."

Pensive eyes stared unseeing into the rough, white-capped water below. "I will love you no matter what changes overtake us both. And I will love our children. As much as my father loved me—and my older brother."

Suddenly Marcus was not with her. He was somewhere in the past, a past that held memories that drained the color from his face and created the illusion of dark shadows beneath the blue eyes. Victoria was fascinated by the sudden change in the man she thought she knew. It was the first time he had made any mention of his family, and she was curious. But at that moment the anchor splashed down, effectively closing their conversation, and Victoria felt a twinge of regret at the lost opportunity to begin peeling back the layers of lacquer that covered and protected Marcus Randall.

The next few moments were busy ones. From the instant he swung Victoria into the long boat that would carry them to the landing, Marcus took complete charge of her life. Several of Victoria's trunks, which had been stored in the hold, were transported to a nearby warehouse where they would remain until she was ready to sail north. Only the single trunk that had been in her cabin was lashed to the carriage that took them to the large, white inn Marcus had chosen for her.

After seeing her settled in one of the finest rooms he ordered a light lunch and a tub. "I think that takes care of everything. If I've forgotten anything, just ask the maid, but be ready by seven-thirty. Will you miss me?" he asked, confident of her response.

And Victoria did not disappoint him. "Very much." She smiled.

Kissing her lightly, Marcus departed with a lively step, whistling as he descended the stairs. The clerk looked up and smiled, recognizing a man unmistakably in love.

Minutes after he had gone a parade of servants brought the tub and several pails of pleasantly warm water. A young maid no more than fourteen bobbed politely. "Me name's Peggy, miss. The cap'n says for me to see to your comfort. He thought maybe you'd like to be havin' your bath before you ate. That suit ya, miss?"

"Fine, Peggy," Victoria answered absently. Her mind was not on the creature comforts but on the message that should have come by now. Her agent in Annapolis knew she would be arriving in Williamsburg aboard the *Maryann*, and someone should have been there to contact her immediately.

Dismissing everyone except Peggy, Victoria stripped and slipped into the water, enjoying the unaccustomed luxury of having someone else scrub her back. She relaxed and listened indulgently as the maid chattered away.

"I saw ya comin' in with Cap'n Randall, miss. Ain't he a handsome devil? Though some would say he's got a soul black as Satan."

"You know him?" Victoria asked, surprised by the easy familiarity of the girl, who had a great deal to learn about the proper way to conduct herself in her job.

"Oh, yes, miss." Peggy giggled. "He's well known about these parts, but then I expect you'd be knowin' all about that. Still, there's many a lady who'd like to trade places with ya."

"Whatever for?" Victoria asked sarcastically, almost snarling at the maid who stood with sponge poised in midair.

Young though she was, Peggy suddenly realized that she was talking too much, but Mistress Monet was staring right at her, waiting for an answer. There was no escape, and Peggy's eyes fell as she answered. "There's them that says he has quite a way with the ladies, mum, and he ain't above openin' his purse for them what pleases him," the girl finished miserably, blushing furiously.

Marcus had told her of what he had called his unenviable reputation, but still it came as a shock to hear this young girl discuss him so openly. He apparently did exactly what he pleased and didn't care who knew about it. And Peggy, that simpleton, had automatically assumed that she was just one more of Captain Randall's whores.

At any other time Victoria would have been amused, but she was not amused now. She was embarrassed and angry. The first pangs of jealousy tugged at her, and she did not recognize them.

Her eyes glittered. If Marcus wanted to be the talk of Williamsburg, she would help him. Stepping out of the tub and into the towel Peggy held waiting, Victoria pointed to her trunk. "There's a gold dress in there that I'll wear tonight. Please lay it out for me. And get my robe. I can't stand around in this towel all day," she snapped.

"Yes, miss," Peggy answered fearfully and scurried to do what she had been told, but when she lifted the only gold dress in the trunk, she gasped in shock.

"I'll have lunch now," Victoria said as she slipped into her robe. "And this dress will be our little secret. At least until tonight. Agreed?" She smiled at the girl and pressed a silver coin into her hand.

Peggy heaved a sigh of relief. The lady wasn't going to report her. She wasn't going to lose her job. Then she looked down at the coin and smiled happily. "Oh, yes, miss. Not a word. I promise."

Victoria had not yet finished her meal when a knock came at the door. A porter bowed politely and gave her a note. "There's a sailor gentleman downstairs who asked me to deliver this, miss. He asked that I wait for a reply if you have one."

Breaking the seal, Victoria read the contents and crossed to a small writing desk. She scrawled a lengthy message and gave it to the waiting porter along with a gold piece. "There will be two seamen calling to pick up my luggage early tomorrow morning. You are to show them directly to my room, and you are to mention these arrangements to no one.

Is that understood?''

Her eyes were hard, and the man bowed, impressed by the amount of money she had given him as well as by her commanding tone. "Yes, miss. I'll follow your instructions to the letter. No one will know about this from me. Thank you, miss," he said as he bowed himself out of the room.

Then Victoria turned to study the dress, which had been part of a costume she had worn to one of the more scandalous parties indulged in by the upper-class snobs who populated London, people she had cultivated because of their usefulness to her father. There, in that licentious company, the dress had been only one of many unusual and daring creations, but here in this provincial town it would cause quite a stir. Marcus Randall would most definitely be noticed tonight. So would she.

At precisely seven-thirty Marcus knocked at her door, and Victoria was ready. Placing herself where the candlelight would include her in its soft caress, she called for him to enter, and when he did he stood rigid and motionless, his hand gripping the doorknob so tightly his knuckles showed white.

Every muscle tensed as he felt the blood rush to his groin and the restraining pressure of his tight-fitting breeches. Longing fringed by pain shadowed the eyes that took in the slim garment of shimmering gold that followed and molded every curve of her body.

The bodice, which was little more than two cleverly cut bits of cloth, was split almost to her waist. And only thin straps of braided gold, the barest whispers of shadows against her skin, stood between her and total disaster as they curved their sensuous way to a clasp at the back of her neck.

Victoria turned slowly, allowing him to admire the back, which was totally bare to a point just below the waist, and as she moved, the sleek, smooth skin of her leg showed briefly where the narrow skirt was slit on one side. It was obvious that she wore nothing underneath, and she was one beautiful, fluid line from the tips of her golden wedge-heeled sandals to the shimmering upswept hair that was adorned by emerald- and diamond-encrusted combs of gold. But as shameless a garment as it was, it somehow suited her.

Spellbound, and totally unable to resist the siren's call of this golden Lorelei, Marcus started toward Victoria but was shocked out of his intent by the nervous giggle of Peggy, who had followed him to see for herself the newest woman to claim Captain Randall's attention, the woman who was so shamefully attired in the precious cloth-of-gold.

With eyes flashing their anger, Marcus turned menacingly toward the source of this unforgivable intrusion, and the frightened maid paled as she took a step backward. Then he laughed humorlessly. "Ah, my pretty young miss. You see before you a man totally undone by a beauty that rivals even one so fair as you."

Peggy's hands flew to her cheeks. She blushed visibly, then turned to run down the stairs where she could not wait to tell the other servants of the shameless doxy who dressed like a naked heathen goddess and of Captain Randall who had caused her to blush with his bold and daring compliment.

Victoria purred in amusement. "I see that your reputation for charming the ladies is well deserved.

I'm sure young Peggy is totally enamored of you and will have great difficulty sleeping tonight."

A slow, crooked smile spread across his face. "Then I fear that the child will die of a broken heart. I have eyes for no one but you, and you have captured me completely."

Then he studied the gown more dispassionately, and a frown hardened his face. Victoria smiled as she read his doubts and misgivings. She was going to be quite an embarrassment to the man whose outrageous reputation had caused her a good measure of humiliation only hours ago.

"Are you sure this is the gown you want to wear?" Marcus asked in reasonable tones that contained no hint of his belated displeasure.

Extracting her full measure of revenge, Victoria answered in innocent surprise. "But surely my appearance does not distress you. That's hardly possible for one about whom I have already heard so many fascinating stories. In fact, I was led to believe you preferred your women undressed. However, if you do not wish to escort me as I am, I am quite willing to forgo this evening with you."

Marcus raised a brow in understanding, and a small muscle in his jaw moved as he clenched his teeth. The gossip had reached her already, and she was quite capable of making him pay for past sins. "My dear, I would not think of denying you the pleasure of your spiteful revenge, but I did warn you that my reputation will not bear close scrutiny. And I will gladly escort you to hell and back if that is your wish, but I don't think you will enjoy the journey quite so much as you might imagine."

Picking up her cape and fastening it at her throat,

Marcus thought that this woman had a great deal of explaining to do after he had her safely wed. If that priceless dress and those emerald combs that were worth a king's ransom had come from her previous lover, they would be returned. And she would tell him the man's name if he had to beat the truth out of her.

After helping Victoria into the closed carriage, Marcus took the seat next to her, an unfashionable move that would have crushed the style so in vogue, but with what she had on it hardly mattered. Then, taking her hand in his, he leaned back against the cushions, closed his eyes and remained quiet for a moment before turning toward her.

"I thought we had agreed that our past is behind us. Yours *and* mine. Is this your way of telling me that my indiscretions cannot be forgotten or forgiven?"

Victoria heard the pain in his voice and lowered her eyes as she drew in a deep breath to ease the tightness in her chest. The stupid little chambermaid's gossip had found its mark. She hated the thought of Marcus making love to other women, and probably in the very room he had chosen for her. It shouldn't matter, but it did. It mattered very much, and it hurt more than she wanted to admit.

And he was right. Her outrageous attire had been meant to hold him up to public ridicule, to humiliate him in front of people he knew, to punish him for the thoughts that tortured her.

Now that it was almost done there was no satisfaction in her revenge or in the deeper wound she was yet to inflict, for the game had gone too far and for the first time she would grieve over one of her victims.

"You're right," she answered at last. "Our past is

behind us, and most especially mine." Then she
smiled brightly. "Shall we turn back? There's always
the white wool."

"As I remember, that particular gown would not be
much of an improvement," Marcus murmured as his
mind turned back to that night aboard the *Maryann*.
He sighed in regret and then focused his thoughts on
the present. "No, we're late as it is. Both of us will
just have to suffer through it."

Victoria heard the peevish note in his voice
and compressed her lips in disgust. She certainly had
not the least intention of suffering through anything
and wondered why Marcus should care what she
looked like. She had seen worse in the kind of
establishment to which he was undoubtedly taking
her.

They rode in prickly silence a short while longer.
When the carriage halted in front of an imposing
house situated on what was obviously a fashionable
side street, Victoria accepted Marcus's hand and
stepped to the ground, allowing herself to be led into
the spacious entrance of his uncle's Williamsburg
home. She smiled spitefully as he removed the cape
from her shoulders with a defiant flourish and gave it
to the stylishly wigged and handsomely liveried black
servant. Then her spine stiffened as she realized her
mistake.

Her gaze flicked first to the brass chandelier, which
was ablaze with expensive, bright-burning spermaceti
candles and then to the wall sconces, which helped il-
luminate the paintings gracing the walls. And they
were not the type of paintings to be found in pleasure
palaces—East or West. They were unmistakably
family portraits.

Victoria drew her breath in sharply and whirled to face her tormentor. "Why didn't you tell me we were coming to a respectable home?"

A maddening grin spread slowly over Marcus's face as he drawled innocently, "But, my dear, a respectable home is the *only* place I would ever take you." The smile ended in soft laughter when he noticed the sparks of anger dancing ever so briefly in her eyes, for he understood exactly what she had expected this evening—a whore's night out in some bawdy establishment and a quick tumble in her bed as repayment. "Lord God," he thought, almost panicking, "how much *did* Peggy tell her?"

But neither of them had time to pursue the subject. Their attention was diverted by a tall, blond man, younger than Marcus, who approached them with an infectious smile lighting his handsome features. Victoria returned the smile, but she did not miss the strength in the faultlessly attired, deceptively languid frame. And the grunt Marcus let out as he was embraced by a crushing hug confirmed her assessment of the young Virginian.

Stepping back, Marcus clasped his cousin's shoulder, his face reflecting both love and pleasure. "Good to see you, Clay. Missed you earlier when I stopped by to invite myself to supper."

Claiborne Lee's light blue eyes sparkled with devilment. "Sorry I wasn't here. Got trapped by a good friend of yours when I was picking up a shipment for Mother at the docks. The lady was asking about you. Seems she's missed you and was about to settle for me!"

At that point in the one-sided conversation Clay laughed out loud, fully expecting his cousin to share the humor of the situation, but Marcus was grim. He was not amused. And to make matters worse Victoria's expression made it very clear that she understood *exactly* what Clay was saying.

A little confused by his cousin's reaction, Clay shrugged and turned his attention to Victoria. His eyes missed nothing. Not the indecent attire, not the natural golden beauty almost hidden beneath the skillfully painted face, nor the slanted, kohl-darkened eyes that smoldered with an inner fire.

His smile broadened as he assumed more than he should. His cousin's latest strumpet was seething with jealousy. "Why, cousin," he drawled suggestively, "you should have told us you would be bringing a new lady love, and such a beauty at that. But then you always were the lucky one." He laughed only to sober immediately as Marcus flashed him a warning glance.

Only then did Clay realize his mistake. Never had Marcus brought any of his whores to this house. But the woman's appearance! What else could she be? No decent woman would enter his mother's home dressed like that. He frowned and looked full into his cousin's eyes and blushed a hot pink.

Almost stammering, Clay bowed and smoothed the situation over as best he could. "I'm truly delighted to meet you, ma'am," he murmured sincerely and then turned repentant eyes to Marcus. "I'd appreciate a proper introduction to the lady."

The damage had been done and Marcus could only hope the evening might yet be salvaged, but the worst was still ahead of them. If Clay had assumed that Victoria was no more than a companion of the evening, then God only knew what his aunt and uncle were going to think.

Breathing deeply and holding tightly to Victoria's hand, Marcus made the announcement. "Clay, I have the honor of presenting Miss Victoria Monet. We plan to be married sometime in the very near future. Victoria, my sometimes obtuse cousin, Claiborne Lee."

Clay was stunned. The shock he felt registered in his eyes. He stared at Marcus and blinked back the disbelief. Then a dazzling smile of pleasure spread over his face. "Marcus!" He laughed and hugged his cousin to him in another fierce embrace. "*Damn*, but I'd just about given up on you," he crowed, and then brought himself up short. "Beg pardon, ma'am," he apologized hastily to Victoria. "An unfortunate slip of the tongue. Hope the rough language didn't offend you."

Victoria smiled wistfully at the genuine concern and the gentleness in Clay's voice. The charming young man had already displayed a fierce loyalty to his cousin, and when she made an enemy of Marcus Randall she would also make an enemy of Claiborne Lee. It was to be regretted, but it could not be avoided.

"My dear Mr. Lee," she responded softly, "I very much doubt that you could ever offend anyone." Then her eyes sparkled in mischief. "And that, sir, makes you very unlike your cousin!"

Clay laughed in pure pleasure. She had forgiven him! She was not going to pout and sulk and make him apologize a hundred times over for his unforgivable blunder. Tucking Victoria's arm under his, he squeezed her hand affectionately. "And now you must allow me the pleasure of presenting you to my parents."

Outwardly, Clay was calm, but his mind was

scrambling for some way to avert disaster. "Damn!" he cursed to himself. Marcus should never have brought his intended into this house dressed as she was. He could only pray that his father would not turn purple with rage or his mother have an attack of the vapors when they saw Victoria. There was no way around it. He was just going to have to blurt out the fact that Marcus and Victoria were going to be married before there was any discourtesy toward his cousin's bride-to-be.

An audible gasp greeted Victoria's entrance into the resplendent drawing room as other guests turned shocked eyes in her direction. Unconsciously, Clay took her left hand in his and slipped his right arm around her waist, pressing her closer to him, trying instinctively to shield her as Marcus closed in protectively from the other side.

But Victoria remained totally unconcerned and seemed not to notice Mr. Lee's cold, disapproving eyes as they flicked for the briefest of moments over her less than acceptable attire. However, a small, satisfied smile touched her lips as Clay hurried through an introduction that was more a warning.

"Mama, Papa, I have the honor of presenting Miss Victoria Monet, who is soon to be Mrs. Marcus Randall," he announced in a firm, confident voice that was heard to the far corners of the suddenly stilled room.

Before her son could say any more, Josephine Lee jerked her head toward Marcus, who nodded in silent confirmation, and she was overjoyed. It was the news she had been waiting to hear for years, and she didn't care what the scantily dressed woman did or did not wear, for it was going to take more than some simpering little belle to tame her impossible nephew.

With an accuracy gained through long experience, Josephine Lee assessed Victoria shrewdly. Then, with her usual facility for ignoring whatever did not please her, she embraced the woman whose face still wore the smug look of some unknown victory.

"Oh, my dear," Josephine cooed. "What a delightful surprise! And what a perfectly marvelous gown! Why, it must have cost a fortune. Is it the latest thing? We're so dreadfully behind the times when it comes to fashion."

Victoria recognized the opening Mrs. Lee was giving her and moved in, for it did not suit her plans to be rejected by Marcus's family. No—that would make future explanations far too easy for him. He would not suffer nearly enough.

A warm, engaging smile softened her features. "It was *quite* expensive, madame, but it would be more appropriate in the harems of the East where the style originated, I believe. Or so my dressmaker assured me. But please. Forgive me. I understood this to be a costume ball," she lied smoothly.

David Lee read the guilty expression on his nephew's face accurately and realized that a scandalous blunder had just been covered quickly and skillfully but certainly not truthfully. Yet it hardly mattered, for this was the first woman Marcus had ever brought to this house and that very fact indicated that his nephew was absolutely serious in his intentions. He pursed his lips in satisfaction. Marcus would see to it that this young woman's mode of attire changed drastically.

Inclining his head in gracious acceptance, Mr. Lee fell in with the lie. "I'm sure you will notice one or

two other guests who also suffered under the same mis-
apprehension,'' he replied cordially. ''Especially the
widow Benson, who arrived in enough plumes and
feathers to stuff a mattress.''

Victoria flashed him a noncommittal smile and
inclined her head in the politest of dismissals as she
slipped her hand under Marcus's arm in a silent
signal that she wished to move on. There was more to
be done, and her eyes glinted in triumph as every
gaze in the room fixed upon her and a low murmur
rippled through the gathering as a sudden breeze
rustles the leaves of a tree.

Primly, she perched on the edge of a straight-
backed chair and struggled to subdue the laughter
that was bubbling toward the surface. Large apple-
green eyes that were devoid of all guile watched as
Clay grinned sheepishly at Marcus.

''Looks as though you'll have to endure a little more
gossip, cousin.''

''For the last time, I hope!'' Marcus replied with
feeling.

''You reap what you sow,'' Clay muttered sourly,
for like his parents he, too, had grown exasperated
with his older cousin's lack of discretion and
numerous affairs of the heart.

Lightly running his fingers down Victoria's bare
back, Marcus smiled into Clay's stormy eyes. ''Not
too quickly, I hope, but when the harvest does come
ripe, perhaps I'll name one of my sons after you, dear
cousin.''

Clay winced visibly at his cousin's insensitivity and
looked at Victoria through eyes that were awash with
unspoken sympathy. He saw that his concern was unnecessary, for Victoria's expression had changed.

There was a subtle hardness to her face, and he recognized the combative glitter in those slanted eyes.

Briefly he was tempted to remove himself from the line of fire, but a hopeful curiosity kept him close by Victoria's side. For once he would like to see his domineering cousin set back on his heels. Maybe, just maybe, Victoria would be the one to do it. And if she could, he didn't want to miss it.

Blithely ignoring Marcus, Clay tucked Victoria's arm under his and escorted her to the table when dinner was announced. After seating her he slipped quickly into the chair beside her, thus forcing Marcus to sit across from them at the only other available place.

"Shall we make him suffer? Just a little?" Victoria pouted as she stared adoringly into her dinner partner's eyes.

Clay smiled in agreement. She was ready to extract her measure of revenge for Marcus's overly possessive behavior, and she intended to establish quite clearly that she belonged to no one.

It was something he had sensed instantly. One look at the proud, straight back, a glimpse into those pale, defiant eyes had been enough. The very worst thing Marcus could have done was to brand her in public as belonging to him.

Now she was about to assert her independence, and Clay was only too willing to help. It was time Marcus was brought down a peg or two. He fell laughingly into the trap.

As Victoria flirted coyly, Clay responded gallantly. The more Marcus glowered, the more Clay enjoyed the whole exercise. And when Victoria openly rested her hand on his knee as she half turned in her chair to flutter her lashes at him Clay roared with laughter.

Smiling appreciatively as every head turned in their direction to share in whatever had amused the usually restrained Clay, Victoria decided her little conspiracy had gone far enough. She had made her point.

But for Marcus it had gone too far. He was angry and jealous and more than annoyed with both Victoria and Clay. Before speaking, he placed his napkin on the table with extraordinary care.

"My dear cousin," he said slowly and distinctly, "I will not tolerate your encroachment, no matter how innocent. And, if necessary, I shall be only too happy to take you outside in order to teach you proper respect for property rights. Do I make myself clear?"

Clay's usually cheerful countenance darkened with outrage, but before he could respond, Victoria plunged the knife deeper. "Property rights, Marcus?" she asked sweetly. "But you have no rights, my angel. At least not yet.

"I thought I had made that quite clear aboard the *Maryann*. Have you forgotten so soon the grief you brought upon yourself by attempting to treat me like some vassal, like some witless creature who had no choice but to submit to your vilest behavior?"

Controlling her mounting rage, Victoria frowned as though considering the problem and then nodded at having found a solution. "Yes, perhaps you should visit the friend Clay mentioned earlier. The one who lives along the docks. The lady's services might improve your disposition and your manners."

The words found their mark. Even Clay was stunned at the vicious turn the harmless game had taken, for Victoria had made it appear that Marcus had tried to force himself upon her, and his cousin had never forced any woman. And to make it worse she had scorned him. She had dismissed him with an unforgivable coldness, suggesting that he satisfy the animal needs she found so disgusting in the bed of some whore.

Not certain of how Marcus would react, Clay braced himself. But Marcus's anger was contained. Though his eyes glittered, he merely inclined his head in Victoria's direction, acknowledging the accuracy and the venom of her barb. A mocking smile twisted his lips, but he was mocking himself, and suddenly Clay understood it all.

His cousin was hopelessly in love with a woman who would not hesitate to slash him to the bone then leave him dying in his own blood. And Marcus knew it. He *knew* the cruel nature lying just beneath that lovely surface.

Clay breathed deeply to ease the heaviness in his chest, and he struggled to shake off the frightening premonition. There was just so much Marcus would tolerate, even from Victoria. She must not push him too far. If she did, the consequences would be more than she could pay, for Marcus had the devil's own pride and would demand a terrible price from her for destroying it.

But as he studied Victoria's serene, unconcerned profile, a slow-breaking smile brought the sparkle back to Clay's eyes. Marcus was not going to have an easy time of it, for he had chosen a woman who had the courage of a gladiator and the arrogant pride of a French chevalier. It was not a happy combination for any woman, least of all for one who was going to marry his cousin, but it was an even more unhappy combination for the man she chose to marry.

"Poor Marcus," Clay clucked as he raised Victoria's

hand to his lips. "But pray, madam, do not be too
hard on him, for under that prideful exterior is quite a
remarkable man."

Victoria returned Clay's smile, but she was restless.
Now that her victory was almost complete she was
anxious to be done with all of it. And when dinner
was over, when everyone had returned to the more
comfortable drawing room, the ladies clustered
around Victoria while the men formed a companionable circle around Marcus. Everyone wanted to know
more about the shipboard romance. Both victims
were faultless in their behavior and both tolerated a
battery of personal questions with all the courteous
evasiveness that only a lifetime of good breeding
could impart.

Finally, and to her great relief, the men ambled
toward them, still chuckling over some story that had
just been told. From the rueful smile and helpless
shrug of his shoulders, Victoria knew that Marcus,
too, had undergone quite an interrogation. She
laughed openly, nodding her head to let him know
that her ordeal had been no less trying than his, and
their eyes met in agreement. It was time to escape.

Minutes later, with Victoria clinging to his arm,
Marcus inched his way past family and friends,
accepting their good wishes as well as their
invitations. Victoria bit her lip in unexpected chagrin
as he extended invitations of his own in both their
names. She still wanted him to suffer; she still insisted
on revenge, but this was more than she had counted
on. Perhaps even more than she wanted. He was
going to look like a fool.

Hunching inside her cape, Victoria shivered as she
was assisted into the carriage, which was only a little

warmer than the blustery night. Gratefully, she
accepted the ministrations of a slave, who put a small
iron box filled with hot coals under her feet. And
Marcus had thought to bring a blanket, for he knew
how bitterly cold the nights could become, how
quickly the temperature could plunge as winter
approached.

Drawing her closer, Marcus cradled Victoria
against him as he tucked the blanket around her.
Gradually her body relaxed, and she snuggled deeper
into the warmth. She detested being cold. So much of
her early life had been spent in lands that sweltered
under a blazing sun that now the ice and snow of
more northern climes worked a hardship on her. But
it was something she would have to endure. She
didn't know how long she was going to be stuck in
this miserable land nor how long she would have to
wait for Edward to make his move. Her eyes glittered
in anticipation.

Interpreting her silence as unhappiness, Marcus
tilted Victoria's face up to his. "Something troubling
you?"

"No," she lied. "I was just wondering if your
family really approves of me. They were very kind, of
course, especially Clay and Aunt Jo, but I made a
terrible mistake dressing the way I did."

It was as close to an apology as she would come,
and Marcus accepted it. "I'm sure everyone loved
you. I know the men did, especially Clay." He
laughed. "Had one devil of a time, though, explaining
that damned dress. Or rather the lack of a dress. And
my uncle had a few sharp comments of his own concerning your combs and ring. Told him they were
family heirlooms from your mother's side of the

family.''

Soft, purring laughter escaped Victoria's lips. Already Marcus was twisting and squirming. Already he was lying for her. At least he thought he was. Actually, he was very near the truth, but he didn't know that, and Victoria almost gloated in the discomfort he was already beginning to feel. ''Then, by all means, I shall tell him the very same thing if he ever asks,'' she agreed smugly.

The cold, calculating working of her brain brought a sharp reaction from Marcus. ''It doesn't matter to you that I'm lying to my family to protect your reputation, does it? You don't feel the slightest twinge of remorse over your past behavior!''

A sly, satisfied smile slipped across Victoria's face. ''Should I?'' she asked innocently. Then the question turned sharp. ''And you? Is there some remorse in your heart?''

''My dear,'' Marcus sighed unhappily, ''don't you know? Don't you know that I would gladly undo the past if I could. Yours and mine.''

Victoria heard the sorrow and the regret in his voice. She watched as the flame from the lantern danced in his dark blue eyes. Before the deed had been accomplished she wished it had never begun. ''Shall we begin anew?'' she asked softly, putting her hand to his cheek. ''Shall we each make a fresh start?''

Unaware of the true meaning of her words, Marcus smiled down into the face he loved. His lips were gentle and lingered longingly on hers. ''Shall we begin now? This instant?'' he whispered, slipping his hands under the cape to caress the flawless skin.

Knowing that this would be the last time she would

ever hold Marcus Randall close, the last time she would ever feel the beat of his heart against hers, Victoria embraced him tightly. For her it was farewell. It was the ending of something that should never have begun.

For Marcus the clinging arms promised a future. They promised love and happiness, not just for now, but for as long as they both lived. "Marry me now," he pleaded. "I love you and need you, and I'm struggling desperately to wait for you. And it's just as difficult for you. I know it is. Tell me!" he urged, burying his face in her hair. "Tell me you need me too!"

"Yes," Victoria admitted to herself as much as to Marcus, "I want you, and I've wanted you in the past."

"Then there's no need to wait. I'll stay with you tonight. We can be married tomorrow. There'll be no problem obtaining a special license."

Victoria put her hands to his face and smiled in genuine amusement. "So! You'll stay with me tonight. And will you be found in my bed tomorrow morning when Peggy comes bursting through the door?" Her laughter taunted. "And what lie will you tell your uncle to protect my reputation from that bit of gossip? Besides, my dear, it was you who said you wanted no bastards cluttering your life. And a child conceived before his parents are married would still qualify, I believe."

There was suddenly something very hard and very cruel in Victoria's voice. Marcus cringed visibly. But she was right. "Yes," he replied unsteadily. "In the backwoods it wouldn't matter, but here in Williamsburg my bedding you before we were married *would* matter. You would suffer and so would my child. No, I'll wait. But you will marry me tomorrow?''

"Of course, my dearest," Victoria promised as she allowed herself to be kissed once again.

As Marcus released her from this final embrace, the carriage stopped. Marcus stepped down and swung Victoria to the ground, holding her closer than he should, not wanting to let her go. Finally he escorted her through the door of the inn.

It was late, and the lower floor was almost, but not quite, deserted. However, Marcus was not interested in the two seamen finishing the last of the ale in their mugs. Instead, he turned his full attention to Victoria. His arm encircled her waist, his head lowered as he spoke softly while they ascended the stairs. And when they reached her room he took the key from her hand, unlocked the door and swung it open. But he made no move to go in. Raising her hand to his chest, he pressed it hard against his heart.

"God willing, my love, this will be the last night ever to see a locked door between us. I'll come for you tomorrow at one-thirty. Will that give you time enough for all the primping and powdering you'll want to do?" He laughed indulgently.

"Yes, Marcus. One-thirty will give me more than enough time," she replied, slipping her hand from his grasp. "Good night, my dear," Victoria said softly as she closed the door.

Enormously happy, Marcus headed for the stairs, whistled a cheery tune as he descended and winked broadly to the two seamen, who had obviously finished their ale and were now heading for the front door.

Preparing for bed, Victoria removed the precious garment she had worn and slipped into a warm robe, for despite the dying fire the room was damp and cold. Meticulously, she folded the scanty cloth-of-gold gown with layers of protective rice paper and put it carefully in the trunk. Only those things she would need in the morning were left out, and after an almost sleepless night she gave up and dressed earlier than necessary. She was pacing the floor restlessly when the soft knock came at her door a little before six. In these latitudes the sun had not yet broken the horizon, and it was still dark.

Answering the quiet summons, Victoria admitted the two seamen, who waited patiently for her instructions, but there was something more urgent on her mind. "Have you seen to Mr. and Mrs. Ainsley as you were told in my note yesterday?"

"Aye, ma'am," Robb answered. "They'll be on board a small vessel headed for Richmond on the morning tide. They've got most of what they'll need to give them a good start. We told them you'd be getting in touch with them in a few months."

Satisfied that her plans were in place and working, Victoria instructed the two men to remove her luggage to the waiting carriage, and while they were carrying her trunk down the stairs, she looked around to make sure she was leaving no trace of herself in this room. Then she picked up her jewel box, walked to the main floor and asked the clerk for an accounting.

The man looked at her oddly. "Captain Randall took care of that as usual, miss. In fact, the fee is paid for tonight as well."

"Yes, how stupid of me," Victoria answered sarcastically as she reached into the pocket of the man's coat she was wearing and retrieved a gold coin. "See that Captain Randall receives this when he calls later today. Tell him it is for services rendered. If I ever have need of his particular skills again, I shall send for him, but for now I consider our account closed.''

The stunned expression on the clerk's face gave Victoria an immense feeling of satisfaction. She watched as the man looked down at the Dutch joe in his hand, then back to her. He believed it! Soon all of Williamsburg would be buzzing with the speculation that Marcus Randall had degenerated into nothing more than a male whore! Her soft laughter insinuated what had been left unsaid, and the clerk's gaze followed the slender figure of the woman garbed in men's clothing. He let out a soft whistle as he watched Mistress Monet climb into a waiting carriage accompanied by two burly seamen. He would be sure to give Captain Randall the lady's message. Word for word.

As she rode toward the harbor, Victoria strained to make out the shapes and forms of the buildings just becoming visible in the gray of pre-dawn. Then, no longer interested in the passing scene, she slumped into the corner of the seat and hunched deeper into the caped greatcoat. Her sigh of regret was audible to the two men riding with her.

''Anything wrong, miss?'' Robb asked with concern.

''No, Robb,'' she answered as though from a great distance. ''I was just thinking how impossible it is to know where the wheels we set in motion will take us.''

''That's something, miss, that only time gives the answer to.''

Victoria smiled at the sailor's practical wisdom and then lapsed into silence. Robb knew better than to intrude upon any female who was in the kind of mood

Miss Victoria was in, so he, too, remained silent until the dockside warehouses loomed before them in the first true light of dawn.

Almost at once Robb spotted Captain Crawford pacing impatiently. The orders had stressed utmost secrecy, and the captain had hoped to be on his way before full light.

With little ceremony, Captain Robert Crawford hustled his employer from the carriage, giving her only the curtest of greetings. With the receipt Victoria had given them, Robb and Tim claimed the trunks from the warehouse, and the small group made its way to the landing. The luggage was safely stored in the bow of the longboat and Victoria was rowed to her vessel, which had dropped anchor just outside the harbor.

# 8

Marcus arrived at the inn a few minutes before one-thirty and asked the clerk to send a servant to announce his presence to Mistress Monet. He was determined to do things properly, to start his marriage off on the right foot.

The clerk stared in apprehension and decided that perhaps it might not be wise to relay the lady's message exactly since it was well known that when roused the captain had a murderous temper. "I'm sorry, sir, but Mistress Monet is no longer staying with us."

The confusion Marcus felt was reflected in his face. "Not staying at the inn? What happened? Where did she go?"

"I don't know where the lady went, sir. She was met here this morning by two seamen and headed for the docks in a carriage the men had brought with them. As a matter of fact, I didn't even recognize her until she spoke. She was dressed head to foot in a man's clothes, but she did ask me to give you this, sir.

Said to tell you that she considers the account closed. She'll let you know if she needs your services again. Whatever that means, cap'n," the clerk stammered nervously as he placed the gold coin in Marcus's hand.

Stunned by the implied meaning of payment, payment publicly made, Marcus fought against the crippling pain that flooded his brain. The shock of what Victoria had done choked the breath from his body. Slowly his fingers closed like bands of steel over the coin, which seemed to sear his flesh. He understood it now. She had paid him in gold, but he had paid the ultimate price, his pride, for she had crushed him under her heel. But before it was done it would also cost him his life, for he would find her. He would kill her for this. "Damn her!" his mind exploded, as the pain that had flooded his eyes was replaced by anger, a much easier emotion to bear. "If she thinks she can get away with this, she's a fool. I'll kill the little bitch," his brain thundered as the blood pounded in his ears.

The rage that burned in him guided his footsteps to the door of one Mr. Leroy Jones. This gentleman of slight stature and unremarkable features was sitting behind his desk when Marcus entered his office. Through years of experience he managed to hide his surprise and curiosity upon seeing Marcus Randall standing before him. The last person he would ever have expected to pay him a business call was this brash gentleman who had always been so very capable of handling any matter that might arise in his rather callous life.

Mr. Jones stood. "Good afternoon, Captain. From the look on your face I judge that you have some urgent business to discuss. Please follow me into the back room where we are not likely to be disturbed.''

The smoothness of the man did not escape Marcus's notice, for now the burning rage had cooled to a deadly anger and a determination for revenge. He accepted the proffered chair and sat, silently collecting his thoughts.

As usual when Leroy Jones wished to observe a client more closely he made a studied practice of filling his pipe, lighting and drawing on it several times, all the while seeming to give his visitor only casual attention. And at this moment Mr. Jones felt the greatest sympathy for the person who had caused this arrogant sea captain and planter to seek out a man who traded in digging out very private and personal facts about others.

Quietly, he inquired, "What is it that has brought you here to me, Captain?"

Marcus stared at the man through eyes that were cold and bleak. His voice was calm, but there was a flatness of tone that Mr. Jones knew meant trouble for someone. "I wish you to use your specific talents and connections to track down a young woman who presumably sailed this morning for parts unknown."

Mr. Jones pursed his lips and pondered silently. Then he asked, "Does this lady have a name?"

"Her name is Victoria Monet, and she left the inn early this morning with two sailors. Apparently they were headed for the docks."

"And you have no idea where she might be bound?"

Marcus frowned slightly and hesitated to tell the story Victoria had related to him. He was going to look like an ass, for he doubted that anything she had said was true. The entire episode had been carefully planned, and he had been completely taken in.

An almost imperceptible sneer distorted his lips. "The lady *said* she has relatives who live somewhere along the Susquehanna River, so she might be headed for Maryland or points north."

Mr. Jones puffed on his pipe several times, trying to put first things first, then his calm, contemplative voice continued. "And where did you first meet the lady in question? Sometimes that is of more use than an uncertain destination."

"Mistress Monet boarded the *Maryann* in London. I understand from the captain that all arrangements for her passage were made by Mr. Henry Byrnes. He brought her aboard late at night, so I personally did not see the gentleman."

Mr. Jones's eyes opened wider at the mention of Henry Byrnes. "Do you mean the barrister and merchant, Captain?"

Annoyed by the sudden note of respect and caution that had crept into Mr. Jones's voice, Marcus answered tersely, "Yes. I understand he's quite well known in London and seems to wield some influence."

Despite himself, Leroy Jones smiled. "That is an understatement, sir. Along with his partner, the late Andrew Chisholm, Mr. Byrnes is one of the wealthiest and most powerful figures in England, not just London. Your lady travels in exalted circles."

"I know nothng of her background. All I know is that she is to be found!"

"Patience, Captain, patience. I know it's difficult for you to go through this questioning, but I think you will be amazed at just how much you *can* tell me of the lady's background. Just a few more questions if you want my help," Mr. Jones added pointedly.

So Marcus endured the pain and the humiliation as he answered each question that was put to him. He produced the special license that was now just a hateful scrap of paper, and he slapped the Dutch joe on the desk.

"No, Mr. Jones, it will take a great deal more than a gold coin to settle this account," Marcus stated bitterly.

Ignoring the implied threat, Mr. Jones continued. "You say she left the inn this morning accompanied by two sailors. That certainly suggests that wherever she is going it is by ship. It should be no difficult matter to find someone along the docks who saw her. Can you give me a description of the young lady?"

Marcus slumped deeper into his chair and was silent for a long moment before describing the image he conjured in his mind. "Miss Monet is above average in height, and she is extremely slender."

A bittersweet smile touched his lips. "Her hair is soft to the touch and resembles liquid sunshine. Her skin has a golden cast to it and is as smooth as satin. It's absolutely flawless. Not a mark or scar anywhere on her."

His smile broadened, and there was a happier look to his face as he remembered the feel of her, the scent of the sweet-smelling oil she used on her skin and the bright, pealing laughter when she was amused.

Leroy Jones hid his smile. Marcus Randall was a man very much in love. It was an unfortunate affair of the heart, a proud man humbled. "Go on," he urged as Marcus stopped speaking, lost in his own reverie.

Straightening in the chair, Marcus continued in a

more matter-of-fact voice. "Her eyes are the one characteristic that will tell you if you have found the right person. I can't describe them exactly, but they're a unique yellowish-green. And they glow with the joy of life. At least that's the way it seemed to me," Marcus finished lamely. "But one thing you probably should know. The clerk at the inn said that she was dressed in men's clothing."

Mr. Jones raised an eyebrow. "Most unusual," he mused. "Is there anything else about her clothing that is noteworthy?"

"Yes," Marcus admitted reluctantly. "Her gowns are expensive, and she's never without a rather spectacular diamond and emerald ring."

There was an uneasiness stirring in the back of Leroy Jones's mind, but he could not define it so he continued with the practicalities. "Did Mistress Monet have any type of cargo or luggage that might need to be transferred to another ship?"

Remembering the trunks that had been taken from the *Maryann*, Marcus answered with some hope. "Yes. Some of her things were stored in a warehouse. The workers there could probably tell you the name of the ship to which they were transferred."

"In that case, Captain, there might be no need for my services. Surely your contacts on the docks are as good as mine. Perhaps you would prefer to pursue this matter yourself."

Mr. Jones had felt obligated to point out this simple fact to Captain Randall, but his curiosity was aroused, and he hoped the man would not withdraw the commission. He was extremely pleased when Marcus declined the opportunity to carry on alone.

"No, I think it best to leave this entirely in your

hands until something definite has been turned up. Frankly, I do not trust myself to act with any discretion in the matter. Besides, I have a business to run and a plantation to care for."

After a slight hesitation Marcus added, "Finding her is only part of your job, Mr. Jones. I shall want every scrap of information about the lady you can dig up. I will want to know not only her whereabouts but her habits and associates as well. This will take more time than I can give right now."

A nasty smile marred his features as Marcus finished his reasoning. "It is most important that the lady not know she is being pursued until it suits my purpose."

Leroy Jones studied the man in front of him. He saw the determination in every line of face and body. He would not wish to be the object of the captain's wrath, for Marcus Randall had a temper that was well known along the waterfront. It was also well known that he was quite the roué, but there had never been the slightest hint of any violence where his women were concerned. This apparent desire to cause Mistress Monet physical harm was totally out of character. But then, so was the indisputable fact that he had proposed marriage to the lady.

It seemed the good captain had run into someone he couldn't handle with his usual methods. He had been slapped down and not gently. But not for long. Not if he took the case.

These and a great many other thoughts passed swiftly through Mr. Jones's agile brain. He felt sure that Captain Randall was in for quite a struggle, and despite himself the little man smiled faintly into that tense and stormy face.

Marcus's eyes flashed dangerously. "Something amuses you, sir?"

"I could not help but think that you just might have met someone who has a great deal of pride and arrogance herself. To be very honest with you, I believe that even if I find Mistress Monet, you are still in for quite a battle; but more important than my idle thought is any further information you can give me, no matter how trivial it may seem. Sometimes it is the small, seemingly inconsequential detail that proves to be our most valuable ally in work of this sort."

"I can think of nothing else except that the lady seems to be well educated and has a great curiosity about the intricacies of business."

Uncertain that he should say what was uppermost in his mind, Marcus hesitated before adding in a voice that was not quite steady, "The lady also led me to believe that she was once mistress to a man of substantial means. But that is something I would rather forget," he added stiffly.

Mr. Jones was cynically amused by the last words and wondered why it was that the corrupters always searched for the incorruptible and were so surprised when they didn't find it. Captain Randall was turning out to be somewhat puritanical despite his many *affaires d'amour*, which were so frequently the topic of local gossip.

"So, Captain, because it pleases you to think the lady virtuous, she becomes so in your eyes," Mr. Jones commented unctuously. "That type of wishful thinking will lead me far astray, sir, for to find a certain type of person one must look in a certain type of place, if you follow my meaning. To misread the lady's character will certainly assure failure."

For the first time since he had entered this musty back room Marcus relaxed. He looked steadily at the rather small man seated behind the desk and gave a grudging sound of approval. "There seems to be more to you than first meets the eye," he commented dryly. "You have rather deliberately forced me to look at myself, and I'm not sure I like what I see."

"Your quarry apparently knows you, sir, and if I am to think as she does, I, too, must be able to see you as she does."

"It's a rather unflattering view, I fear," Marcus drawled sarcastically. "Let us say that she sees me in such a light as to cause her to run after I had obtained a license for our marriage, after I had introduced her to my family. She literally dumped me in such a manner that I'm afraid I must look quite the fool to a number of people at this point."

"Then your motive is revenge, Captain? Revenge for injured feelings, for being made to feel the fool, as you put it?"

Marcus looked into those shrewd eye and said icily, "At this point, Mr. Jones, I think if I could get my hands on her, I would gladly strangle her, but not too quickly—not too quickly," he muttered, and his voice trailed off into uneasy silence.

Puffing contentedly on his pipe, Mr. Jones studied the sullen face before him. He was more than a little surprised that such a practical, seafaring man refused to face the truth. Mistress Monet had wounded the captain deeply, so deeply that his pride would not allow him to seek her out for any other reason *but* revenge.

Mr. Jones smiled in understanding. Marcus Randall had to find the woman who jilted him, but it was not

for revenge. Aloud, he asked several brisk questions
that might be of use in ferreting out the young lady for
whom he was beginning to feel a perverse admiration.

Closing the painful inquisition at last, Marcus
concluded, "I've told you all I know. Now I want her
found. At any price!"

He was extremely agitated at having to tell so much
that made him look like a schoolboy, and again he
slouched in the chair as he covered his eyes with his
hand. His body showed the great weariness that had
descended upon him. Recalling every detail, every
emotion was too much. Struggling against overwhelming despair, Marcus straightened and looked
full into Mr. Jones's sympathetic face, and when that
intelligent, discerning man saw the naked pain that
Marcus could not hide he was satisfied. He would
help. And not just for Captain Randall's sake. The
possible outcome of this case fascinated him.

"We will find Mistress Monet, Captain. From what
you have told me it might take some doing, but I have
never failed and don't intend to do so now. Besides,"
he added cheerfully, "I am anxious to meet this rather
remarkable woman myself!"

Mr. Jones was a master at his craft because he was a
discerning student of human nature. He knew that
there was much more to Mistress Monet's actions
than either he or Captain Randall understood at the
moment. And several of the pieces did not fit. There
were glaring inconsistencies.

"Well!" he exclaimed at last, bringing himself back
to the business at hand. "We have enough for a good
beginning, Captain Randall. Where will I be able to
reach you if need be?"

Marcus shook his head wearily. "I must return to my estate briefly. Then I'll be sailing for Philadelphia to commission a new ship to be built by the Penrose yard. I'll stop here before I sail and again when I return. I hope there'll be some news before then."

"I'll do my best, but do not become impatient. The lady seems to know what she's about."

Marcus's numbed mind was still working clearly enough to realize that Mr. Jones had just paid the compliment of respect to Victoria, and for some reason that fact provided a small degree of comfort and hope. At least the man was not underestimating Victoria as he had done to his everlasting regret.

When the distraught planter had gone Mr. Jones sat for a long time scribbling on a sheet of paper. All the bits and pieces of information were placed in order down the page. The uneasiness he had felt earlier increased. The name Monet kept pulling at his memory. He had heard it many years ago, and if he were not growing old and senile, it had been in connection with Andrew Chisholm, the powerful merchant whose death had been reported only today in the local paper.

Rousing himself, he retrieved the latest issue of the *Virginia Gazette,* which contained the article concerning Mr. Chisholm. This time he read more carefully. It was all there, including the name of Mr. Henry Byrnes, who was listed as a minor partner in the mercantile empire ruled by Andrew Chisholm and his daughter.

Leroy Jones stared at the one sentence reporting that Mistress Prudence Victoria Chisholm, only daughter of the deceased, had gone into seclusion and was not available for comment. Once more, the intuition he trusted more than the facts, the intuition that was seldom wrong flashed the possible answer through his mind. Might not Miss Chisholm's seclusion have been sought aboard the *Maryann?*

It fit. More so than the story Marcus Randall told. This was not some outcast mistress running to relatives. No. Impossible. Not with a costume fashioned from the prohibitive cloth-of-gold. Not with emeralds, and most especially not with diamonds. Diamonds were for royalty, not for some little trollop who had failed to please her benefactor.

But there was more. Her facility aboard ship, her arrogant confidence, and the ease with which she had manipulated an experienced man like Captain Randall. Victoria Chisholm was known for her cunning and her cruelty. Mistress Monet would seem to be no less cruel, no less cunning.

He shook his head, not daring to believe what every instinct told him was true. Marcus Randall had tangled with the Chisholm bastard and had come off second best.

The word *bastard* struck a responsive chord. That was it! Monet! The name of Andrew Chisholm's mistress. Years ago, there had been a terrible scandal and then it had simply faded away and no more was heard. But the woman's name had been Monet. And now there was Victoria Monet. Was it coincidence or was the elusive Mistress Monet in reality that marauding shark of commerce, the infamous Victoria Chisholm?

Apprehension so strong that it bordered on fear closed in on Leroy Jones. He was in deep water. He must move with great care. If what he suspected were true, it was entirely possible he might not live to see the resolution of this case.

There was an operative in London, a man of great skill, a man who had worked wonders for him before. Yes. He would contact him, emphasizing the need for utmost caution and secrecy.

Many minutes later Leroy Jones applied the distinctive red wax to the lengthy correspondence he had just completed and headed for the docks. This was going to be a most expensive undertaking for Marcus Randall.

The master of the packet assured Mr. Jones that his ship would keep to the scheduled departure date and that the urgent message would be delivered in London within four to six weeks, depending upon wind and weather.

Confident that he was on the right track, Mr. Jones next made his way to the warehouse, where he questioned the workers. One of them recalled the early morning loading of the trunks in question. And yes, he had seen the name on the transom of the ship as the sun broke through. It was the *Bayside.*

After several more minutes of questioning Mr. Jones was satisfied that he had learned all he could and he proceeded to the inn, where he knew several servants who could be induced to answer discreet inquiries for pay. The first person he would seek out was young Peggy, who seemed to know everything that went on at the inn and could be relied upon to embellish whatever she might know of Mistress Monet.

# 9

Captain Crawford snapped concise orders to his crew and before many minutes had passed the *Bayside* was made snug against the private dock. Howard Coster, Andrew Chisholm's agent, paced nervously. He had been apprehensive about his future since Richard Hensley had limped into port with the news of the owner's death. From what he could understand a woman was now in charge. Victoria Chisholm would take command of her father's vast interests.

Howard spat into the cold, filthy waters of the harbor in disgust. It was bad enough that a female was running things, but this one was too young. Nobody would take her seriously, least of all the men she was going to have to deal with.

"Hell," he muttered sourly and squinted against the sun as four men disembarked, but he didn't see the woman he was looking for.

It came as a shock, then, when Robert's words finally registered in his brain, and he gaped impolitely at the bundled-up youth whose hand was extended in greeting. Hastily, he grasped the slim, gloved hand in his. It seemed to be what she expected.

Then, doffing his hat, he gave a slight bow. "We were all saddened to learn of your father's death, miss. It came as a shock, and we've all been treadin' water since, not sure just what you'd want done. Didn't know if your father's orders still stood or if you had a mind to do things your own way."

Howard Coster shrugged awkwardly, almost apologetically, under the cold, narrow-eyed smile that hardened on his employer's face. "A new broom sweeps clean, eh, Mr. Coster?" Victoria purred, and then chilled the man's blood with the soft, sibilant laughter that was not laughter at all. "But for now everything will remain the same, just as my father planned. You have nothing to fear but incompetence."

Howard winced under the clear and unmistakable warning. His job was safe only so long as he pleased her. Unconsciously, he assumed a servile stance, and Victoria was satisfied. Howard Coster might not like being ordered about by a woman, but he would obey.

Following him into the large brick warehouse, she froze in her tracks. The majority of her father's possessions and furnishings were still stored in this damp, ruinous barn.

None of the chagrin showed on her face or in her voice. "I suppose, Howard, there's some reasonable explanation as to why my orders have not been followed. There were several barrels and crates that were to be kept under close guard, but the rest was to have been sent to the Sherman farm."

The man looked at her and hesitated. She could be a

mean one, and he didn't want to get Bess in trouble. But a man had to look after his own skin first. "Mrs. Hubbard, your housekeeper, refused to allow another stick of furniture to be moved in. I had little choice but to keep it here."

"Why?" Victoria asked, thinking her meaning perfectly clear.

"I couldn't just let valuable pieces sit out in the weather, miss. I had to keep your things here."

Victoria expelled a long, slow breath. "No, Howard. Why did Mrs. Hubbard refuse to obey my father's orders? Did she not understand what was required of her?"

Something in the soft, patient voice irritated Howard Coster. It was as though she were talking to some idiot who needed pictures drawn in the dust before he could understand. "The Sherman house is bulging to the rafters with furniture now, Miss Chisholm. Apparently your home in London was at least three times larger than your new quarters. There simply isn't any more room." He finished with a snap to his eyes that defied her to find fault where none was due.

The smile on Victoria's face was genuine. It was most comforting to know that even though Mr. Coster was fearful of losing his job he would not be trampled on. When he was right he would stick to his guns. "Mrs. Hubbard's decision seems to be a sensible one," she drawled, not giving ground, but not taking any, either. The matter was settled, and they both knew it.

"Now," she continued matter-of-factly, "if you will have the special items loaded on a wagon, Tim and Robb will see them safely to the farm. And meanwhile I trust you can procure some form of conveyance for me and Captain Crawford."

It was Howard's turn to smile. "I've had a carriage waiting at the front since we sighted the *Bayside* from the hill," he answered as he looked up toward the mounting land that dominated the small port town. "I've also taken the liberty of having your luggage put aboard. So, if you'll follow me, Miss Chisholm, I'll start you safely on your way."

Victoria had missed the silent signal with which Howard had conveyed his wishes to his men. Apparently everything had been worked out beforehand and the operations of this warehouse moved as quietly and as efficiently as a well-greased wheel. She nodded her approval, and Howard Coster suddenly felt a lot more secure in his job.

The ride to the house was slow and wearisome. The roads were extremely primitive and once outside the small town they became little more than deeply rutted paths.

Victoria hunched deeper into her coat as she lifted the curtain to look out upon a bleak countryside whose drab colors and barren features proclaimed the nearness of winter. Her mood was sullen as she wondered what she would find at the impoverished farm. She had no great expectations, for the Shermans had proved themselves to be poor managers and worse farmers. The lowliest peasant along the Nile understood what they apparently did not. The land must be replenished. You could not continue, year after year, to take, for if you did, nature would exact her full penalty.

She sighed and smiled ruefully at Robert. "It becomes increasingly obvious with each jolting mile that I will need a house in town. A place much nearer the harbor. This is no easy ride and wastes valuable time.''

Robert arched a brow and replied almost apologetically, ''The roads are about as good as they get, I'm afraid. Right now the ground is solid, but after the snows and spring thaws I'm not sure you'll even make it to town unless you cut cross-country on horseback. I'll have Mr. Coster find something for you. He knows most everything that's going on in Annapolis.''

Lapsing once more into silence, Victoria studied Captain Crawford from behind lowered lids. He was a fine seaman from a seafaring family. And he was a quiet man. Like many sailors who had faced the spectre of death, Robert saw no need to waste precious time on matters of little consequence. She knew the feeling, and she also knew that except for Walter Matthews she might very well be drifting in a murky grave.

As her mind wandered, she thought of another captain, one whose eyes were darkest blue, one who had for so brief a time captivated her, and one she could not easily put from her mind. A wistful smile touched her lips.

Robert's voice prodded gently. ''What are you smiling about?''

She looked into the pleasant face and left her reverie behind. ''I was wondering what a certain gentleman in Williamsburg might be thinking at this moment, and I'm afraid there is enough vanity in my soul to hope that his thoughts are not too restful.''

''Captain Randall, you mean,'' Robert stated bluntly.

Victoria's pale eyes locked with the young man's, a

man who was not yet twenty-six. He had overreached himself. "You seem to have had your spies in place," she stated just as bluntly. "May I ask why you took such a presumptuous liberty?"

Robert's face was stern; he wore his disapproval like a badge of honor. "I felt it was necessary. From the moment you set foot in Williamsburg you were my responsibility, though I hardly think Tim and Robb would qualify as spies. However, they are trustworthy and resourceful, so I sent them ashore to keep an eye out for your safety. When they learned who your companion was they were rightfully concerned and managed to stick like burrs. They were never far from your side."

The skin that covered Victoria's high cheekbones seemed to tighten. The eyes were devoid of expression, but Robert was a valuable employee so she chose her words carefully. "It is most comforting to know that you take your responsibilities so seriously, even those no one has asked you to assume. But there is one thing that must be made very clear—where my personal life begins your responsibility ends."

Captain Crawford did not waver under the reprimand. His gaze held steady. "Had you chosen anyone other than Randall for your affair," he commented testily, "then perhaps I would not have *presumed*, as you put it. Unfortunately, the man can be as dangerous as a viper when crossed, even though he would sometimes appear to be no more than a degenerate fop."

Victoria was on the verge of discharging this brash young man, then thought better of it. "If Marcus Randall is as dangerous as you say, I must, indeed, thank you for your loyal dedication to my service.

However, since I am quite sure he is well on his way to forgetting all about me, you need concern yourself no further."

"I do not believe he will forget Victoria Monet so quickly. And if you had run out on me the way you ran out on him, you'd have reason to be concerned," Robert warned. "A man can be driven just so far."

"You seem to be very well informed."

"Tim and Robb are experts at gathering information, and, of course, it was not difficult to understand the situation when Randall went immediately from your embrace to the home of some unfortunate government clerk where he pounded on the door, though it was after midnight, until the poor man stuck his head out of the upstairs window to enquire what was the trouble. The entire neighborhood must have heard the captain bribe the clerk shamelessly until the man promised to have a special license approved and ready to be picked up the following morning. A license for the marriage of Marcus Randall to one Victoria Monet. A marriage that was to take place the following day."

"I take it you don't approve, Robert. Of me or of my actions."

"Does it really matter?" he asked sadly.

"No, it really doesn't," she answered smoothly. Her decision had been made. Robert would be promoted to a larger ship. His home port would be Philadelphia, not Annapolis as it was now. The charming young man who had reported to her father on several happy occasions was no longer quite so charming. She would not tolerate anyone meddling in her affairs. The sooner he was gone, the better.

At that moment the driver announced their arrival, and an instant later the carriage swerved as it entered the lane to the Sherman farm. Victoria stepped to the ground and stood looking at the almost graceless brick structure in front of her. She twitched her nose in distaste. The place was unfinished. Only the central portion of the house had been built. The wings, which would have added balance and beauty, had never been started.

As she stood staring glumly at the front door, it swung wide and a motherly, graying lady in cap and apron bustled across the small portico, hurried down the few steps and took both of Victoria's hands in hers. Bright, birdlike eyes that reminded Victoria of some saucy English sparrow smiled up at her with genuine pleasure and warmth. "Welcome home, Mistress Chisholm. We've been waiting on pins and needles for you to arrive."

Before Victoria had a chance to reply, a tall, lanky man whose friendly eyes belied his sober face joined them. "Welcome, miss. I'm right glad you've arrived. Poor Bess was about to collapse with curiosity."

Then, realizing that Victoria didn't know either of them, he added, "I'm Josiah Hubbard and this, in case you haven't guessed, is my wife, Bess. Welcome to Chisholm House."

Victoria felt a sudden burning moisture in her eyes and for some reason the graceless, unfinished state of this home no longer seemed to be important. "Chisholm House. Of course, Josiah, you have christened it. If only my father—" She broke off, unable to continue with any dignity.

Bess, who had suffered the grievous loss of her children, understood Victoria's difficulty and hastened to fill in. Sweeping her young mistress up the stairs, she kept up a constant stream of conversation, stopping only long enough to direct the men to take the luggage to the south bedroom.

Not until the men had finished their task did Bess escort her mistress up the surprisingly graceful staircase to a cheerful bedroom where a bright fire was burning. "Mr. Coster sent a rider as soon as you were sighted to let us know you were coming," Bess explained. "I'll fetch the hot water now so you can clean up a bit and get out of those clothes."

Victoria smiled at her housekeeper's disapproving frown but said nothing. Sitting in the nearest chair, she struggled with the riding boots, then removed the breeches, jacket and shirt. Clad only in the warm woolen hose and a skimpy shift, she rooted in her trunk for the blue wool. By the time she had slipped it over her head, Bess was back with water so hot, steam rose from the pitcher.

"Now you get yourself washed off as fast as you can, then come down to the kitchen. I've had a stew simmering for hours." And with that Bess was out of the room and halfway down the stairs.

Victoria's eyes widened in disbelief. The kitchen was for servants! And neither had Bess offered to help her unpack! "Really!" she muttered under her breath and made a few choice comments about help in the colonies.

Nevertheless, her growling stomach propelled her unerringly in the direction of a delicious aroma, and she decided she'd take up these minor annoyances with her housekeeper tomorrow. Even the fact that Bess had set a place for all of them somehow did not surprise Victoria, and since the kitchen was warm and cozy while the rest of the house was damp and chill, Victoria allowed Robert to hold her chair for her while she held her tongue. She had hunched over campfires to share a bit of goat's meat with bandits and murderers. She could endure this enforced cordiality. But only for tonight.

Josiah popped a bit of gravy-soaked bread into his mouth, washed it down with coffee, then turned a serious face toward his employer. "Seems to me, miss, you have a great many valuables in this house. More than's safe, I think. There've been far too many robberies hereabouts lately, and I'd feel a lot better if some provision was made for the protection of your property."

Casting a sidelong glance at Robert, Victoria agreed. "I'll see if Tim and Robb are willing to take the job. Captain Crawford assures me they are both rather remarkable men as well as being shrewd judges of character."

Robert chuckled. He had wondered how long it would take her to rub his nose in the dirt. "You'll need to provide them with weapons. The few guns I have aboard ship can't be safely spared."

"It's settled, then. Will you be staying the night, Robert?"

With brown eyes sparkling, Robert jerked his head in silent laughter. "No, ma'am, I think I've about worn out my welcome." Then his face became serious. "We wanted your arrival to be a happy occasion. We wanted you to feel at home in a strange land, and we wanted you to know that there are people here who are prepared to care for you, to help you, if you'll let us."

A momentary flickering of the eyes was the only indication Victoria gave of her discomfort. They meant to be kind, all of them, but all she wanted was to be left alone, to travel her own path in her own way, to be about her father's business.

"Thank you, Robert," she answered coldly. "If I need your help, I'll ask for it. And now," she continued, turning to Josiah, "shall we inspect what little we can before it gets dark?"

For an instant no one moved. Her chilling dismissal of Robert's kindness had stunned them all. Bess and Josiah stared at their employer as though they couldn't believe such rudeness to one who was only trying to help. Robert's eyes lingered on Victoria's face for a moment, and then he stood. "If you have no objection, Miss Chisholm, I'll wait here until Tim and Robb arrive. Then I'll be taking my leave, ma'am."

"Thank you, Robert, and I'll expect to see you about ten tomorrow morning." Without a backward look or thought, Victoria retrieved her coat and accompanied her farm manager on a tour of inspection.

Since it was growing near the time when the sun would dip below the horizon, Victoria decided to inspect the slave quarters first. Bullen would come next, since she wanted to spend some time with the old retainer who had become more than a servant to her father over the past few years.

The few slave cabins were about what she had expected. There were no windows, the floors were of dirt and the makeshift chimneys spewed almost as much smoke back into the one-room shacks as they carried to the outside. Most of the buildings were shabby and showed signs of long neglect, but the small hovels that housed the black slaves were undoubtedly the worst.

However, even they showed signs of recent

improvements. Tough leather hinges and stout wooden bars held new doors tight against the wind. Each cabin contained a few odd pieces of rough furniture, kitchen utensils, a small crock of cornmeal, a generous firkin of lard and a pitcher of molasses. Most of the food, as Josiah had already explained, was portioned out daily from the cellar and pantry of the main house. Whether or not that practice would continue was in doubt. Victoria would wait to see how it worked before making any changes.

Josiah knocked on the door of the final slave cabin to be inspected. A tall, thin black man of indeterminate age opened it cautiously. "Afternoon, Mr. Hubbard. Somethin' I can do for you?"

"Afternoon, Elias. This is Mistress Chisholm, the new owner of the farm. She's come to inspect your quarters."

The dark man's eyes turned suspiciously to Victoria. "Afternoon, ma'am. Please come in," Elias responded politely, but fear and mistrust showed in his face.

Ignoring the man's apprehension, Victoria brushed past the slave, took a few steps forward and then stopped. A furtive movement in a dark corner had caught her attention. As her eyes adjusted to the dim interior, Victoria's gaze flicked over the woman who shielded two small children behind her. It was a protective gesture Victoria understood, for as they had trudged from one cabin to another, Josiah had brought her up to date on conditions at the farm.

The slave, Elias, was the father of five sons. Only the two youngest ones remained on this estate. The three older boys had been sold off when the farm had changed hands. It was obvious that Elias and his woman feared for their two remaining children.

Josiah, too, understood the fear. "Sally, this is Mistress Chisholm, the new owner of the farm," he repeated by way of introduction.

The woman responded by bobbing politely, but her eyes pleaded with Victoria as two small children peeked shyly from behind their mother's skirt. "My two boys, David and Saul," she admitted softly, the fear of losing her children etched deeply in her face.

Victoria smiled at the names. "Do you have any training, Sally?"

"Miz Sherman, she thought my sewin' and broiderin' was mighty fair," Sally responded hopefully.

"In that case," Victoria continued, "I'll see to it that you receive enough material to make a shirt for each of your boys. When you've finished bring them to me so that I might judge whether your skills are fine enough for my needs."

Again Sally gave a quick curtsy. "Yes'm. I'll do the best I can, ma'am."

Victoria looked the black woman squarely in the eye. "That's exactly what I shall demand from you—at all times. If you and your family do what is expected of you, there will be nothing to fear from me. Not for yourself nor for your children."

The message was clear and Sally understood it. She felt faint from the wave of relief that washed through her. Elias put a supporting arm around his woman and met Victoria's steady gaze. "We'll do our very best, ma'am, same as we did for the Shermans."

Victoria's sardonic smile indicated that she appreciated the underlying bitterness of Elias's words. "And they rewarded you by selling three of your children."

The man's shoulders slumped. White masters

wouldn't tolerate complaining slaves, and the woman with the golden hair and green eyes had understood him only too well. Had understood his hatred.

"I think you will find," Victoria continued in a quiet voice that, nevertheless, gave fair warning, "that your own efforts will determine your fate. However, if conditions here are not to your liking, I'm sure we can make other arrangements for you elsewhere."

"Yes'm," the black replied contritely and then sought refuge in silence.

"And now," Victoria persisted, knowing that the black had understood the warning clearly, "what special tasks did you perform for the Shermans?"

"Mostly, I work in the fields, ma'am. But when I gits the time I do a fair piece of work with wood. Made that bench yonder by the fireplace. Did a few things for the main house. Helped build the barn. Lotsa things I done, ma'am. All over this here farm."

"And there's a great deal more yet to be done," Victoria admitted, sighing as she thought of all the work ahead. Then, indicating to Josiah that she was finished here, she walked into the chilling air and made her decision.

"How old are Sally's three sons?"

"Seven, eight and nine," Josiah answered with a strong sound of disapproval in his voice.

"If you know where they are, buy them back."

"Yes, ma'am!" Josiah exclaimed with great joy and admiration. "I know just exactly where they are, and I'll take care of it first thing in the morning."

By this time Victoria decided that she had seen enough of the farm for one day, and she headed for the large brick stable that housed Bullen's quarters. Before she reached the well-maintained building,

Bullen came out. He had been waiting for her since he first heard she had arrived.

"Miss Victoria," he cried. "Thank God you've finally come. I learned of the death of Mr. Chisholm just days ago. I don't know what to say, miss."

It was the conversation she had dreaded most, but Victoria breathed deeply and kept her emotions under control. "There's nothing to say, Bullen. We are all going to miss him very much. And I shall certainly miss his advice, which means I'll be depending upon you even more now that he is not here to build the herd himself."

"He knew his horses, that he did, miss," was all the aging man could think of in the way of conversation at this moment, for Bullen had respected Andrew Chisholm's knowledge of the prime interest in his own life.

Brightening a little, he added, "But don't you fret, miss. I'll take good care of his horses just like always."

Both sadness and gratitude tinged the small smile Victoria managed to direct toward Bullen. She nodded in silent agreement. Then, after making sure that this faithful servant was well cared for, she returned reluctantly to the house even as Tim and Robb pulled up in the slow-moving farm wagon. She was not yet finished for the day. This place needed money to put it in shape, a great deal of money. The sad crop of tobacco curing in the sheds would never bring enough to buy food for the winter, much less pay for all the other needs of the place.

Pressing her lips together, she stared at the cask that had been unloaded from the cart. "Open that one," she directed, and Tim pried it open, standing back afterward to await further instructions.

"Dump it," Victoria commanded, and as Tim followed orders, pouches of coins and billowing sawdust spilled out onto the floor.

Hefting one of the numerous pouches in her hand, Victoria explained, "Each purse contains exactly one hundred pounds sterling. You are to use what you need. You're not to bother me with details. Do what must be done to secure this place for winter. We'll discuss the rest later. And now, if you'll excuse me, I still have a great deal of unpacking to do."

Not once doubting that her orders would be followed exactly, Victoria retreated to her bedroom, leaving five astounded people behind. Bess was the first to recover. Stooping, she began separating pouches of coins from the sawdust. Josiah and the others bent to help her, but no one could think of a safe place to hide such great wealth. Finally Robert suggested suspending large canvas bags, each containing an equal number of smaller pouches, down the privy that was located under the cellar stairs. "Of course," he laughed, "you'll have to make sure no one uses it."

The tension was broken and laughter filled the room. Upstairs, busy at her forlorn task, Victoria heard the gaiety and smiled to herself. It would work out. She needed time to deal with Edward, but after that her father's wishes would be carried out to the last detail.

Gradually Victoria began to relax in her new surroundings. She no longer saw danger behind every shadow. Once more she found pleasure in human companionship.

Before the first silent snowflake drifted downward one still December night the farm was ready for the fierce storms that would come raging inland from the bay, bringing deep drifts that would make travel difficult if not impossible, but Victoria had not the slightest intention of being stranded on this desolate farm.

It was time to leave this place of sanctuary. Edward would not brave the winter gales at sea to follow her. He would wait. How long, she didn't know. But he would not come now.

Robert, too, was anxious to get started before the rivers and even the bays began to freeze as they sometimes did in severe weather. Philadelphia was not that far away, but in winter it could be a dangerous voyage. He'd feel much better once they were safe in port. They sailed the next day.

While Captain Crawford spent time at the Penrose shipyards making clear Victoria's specifications for the two additional ships she had ordered, his employer was free to enjoy the fine shops as well as the smaller ones, where the crafts of the countryside were to be found. Victoria spent hours browsing and buying, piling the arms of Tim and Robb high with her purchases.

They stayed at the fanciest inn, ate the finest food, and Tim and Robb drank their fill of the best wines and ales. Still, they obviously preferred their potent grog to even the most expensive of the imported wines.

For the two sailors the highlight of the trip was the visit to a highly recommended gunsmith. They spent hours examining various weapons, hefting one pistol after another and generally making a nuisance of themselves before deciding on two pistols and two Swiss rifles, the finest and most accurate guns money could buy.

To these purchases Victoria added two quality fowling pieces for Bullen and Josiah, as well as a uniquely crafted small pistol for her personal use. The German gunsmith, who spoke very little English, was delighted to learn that the wealthy lady was fluent in his language, and he went into great detail as he explained the intricacies of each weapon. Satisfied at last that the products he had so lovingly crafted would be properly cared for, he accepted the handful of gold coins that more than compensated him for his efforts.

While Robert Crawford was kept busy approving or disapproving every detail of the plans that would eventually come to life as two sleek sister ships, Tim and Robb accompanied their mistress everywhere, and they found her to be as good a companion as any lad who ever sailed the seas.

Victoria clutched these brief, happy days to her. Not even the traitorous pounding of her heart when she heard that Captain Randall had also visited the Penrose shipyard could spoil the joy of this too brief respite from the burdens and cares that must be resumed before long. And with each day the affection between Victoria, who had everything, and Tim and Robb, who had no home but the sea and no family but each other, grew stronger.

# 10

January had ended before Victoria returned to Annapolis. The homecoming was noisy and joyous. There was the following piece for Josiah and yards of fine cloth for Bess. Gaily decorated tinware was given to each household—slave and indentured servant alike. Inside the smaller tins were nutmegs, cinnamon bark and vanilla beans. Dozens of prized dressmaker pins as well as needles and thread filled others. Long lengths of homespun were added to each family's hoard of treasures.

For the first time Victoria confided in Bess and Josiah concerning the plans she had made to expand the house. As soon as the ground warmed up, work would begin. She had hired two of the finest hydro-engineers to be found in Pennsylvania to help with the modernization and completion of Chisholm House.

Less than a week after her return Victoria hired the local surveyor and his two assistants to travel north to Baltimore, where her father's two thousand acres of land were located. They would clearly establish and mark metes and bounds so there would be no question of ownership.

Victoria and her two constant companions became a familiar sight on the streets of Annapolis. The three of them frequently rode through town in a garishly expensive carriage done in pale green, decorated and embellished with numerous raised, curved ornamentations expertly finished in gilt. Even the leather seats matched the exterior color, and the inside was paneled in fine velvet of darkest green. Gold shades covered the windows when privacy was desired. Brass trim and sparkling lanterns dazzled the eye. All in all, it was a most luxurious and sumptuous vehicle much admired by the natives, who felt themselves to be hopelessly behind the fashion when they saw the latest import from Philadelphia.

Clothing Victoria had seldom worn, velvets and satins, fur-lined capes and the most expensive Egyptian cottons, became her everyday attire. Only the most exclusive shops were patronized by her personally, and the precious English coin that was so scarce in this bartering colony, this colony which used tobacco as money, began to flow from Victoria's purse.

Within days, the town knew her name and her habits. They could only guess, however, as to the extent of her wealth. And those estimates were revised upward daily as each purchase was duly noted.

Dozens of terribly expensive oranges were sent to the farm. The best of the hams, the choicest cuts of pork preserved in brine, the largest cones of sugar, as well as exotic spices, were transported to Chisholm

House. Even now the miller was loading hundred-pound barrels of wheat flour aboard the wagon that would be heading directly for the old Sherman place in a matter of minutes.

Very soon invitations from the best families began to arrive both at Victoria's small home in Annapolis and at Chisholm House itself, which was an inconvenient distance from the capital. One invitation was from Government House and had been signed by Governor Ogle, himself. It was at this extravagant reception that Victoria had been overwhelmingly accepted by the cream of Annapolis society.

As was expected, Victoria reciprocated. However, everyone understood that the poor little house she occupied in town, the only one that had been available, for lease, simply would not be suitable for entertaining, and they were most delighted when she rented the largest hall in Annapolis and hired the most expensive caterer to run her grand affair. Her gown of pale golden satin, the empress-style necklace of emeralds and diamonds along with the matching ring, combs and earrings were the envy of every woman who saw them. Their cost was incalculable.

Neither did it harm her reputation when she hired a man who was greatly admired and respected by the townspeople as her lawyer, Mr. Stephen Bordley. This same well-mannered, well-educated Mr. Bordley soon became Victoria's steady escort to the numerous theater parties and balls. She was putting on quite a show. She had come out of hiding. Victoria was now ready for Edward.

It was at this point that she remembered Marcus Randall and the warning Robert had voiced when he had told her in plain language that Captain Randall's reputation was known in ports both here and in England. He was a dangerous man, a man of black moods and evil temper. It was unlikely that he would allow an insult such as the one she had inflicted on him to go unavenged.

At first Victoria had dismissed the warning, but the more she considered it, the more she thought she had better take it seriously. Still, she did not wish to reveal her private life to others, so she chose a more devious method of calling attention to the good captain should he succeed in getting to her despite the constant protection provided by Tim and Robb.

Stephen raised his eyebrows as Victoria presented him with inventories and enumerated each and every item of her almost uncountable wealth. He recorded each and every bequest that was to be included in her new will.

Bess and Josiah were generously provided for. Bullen was also remembered. Neither Tim nor Robb was forgotten, but the bulk of her possessions and money were to go to one Marcus Randall, presently of Richmond, Virginia, owner of the plantation known as Serenity. Stephen was curious, but he asked no questions, and Victoria offered no further information.

When she signed the various copies of the will that Stephen's clerk had laboriously made, Victoria decided that the time had come to tell those most closely associated with her the truth about Edward. Mr. Coster, Tim and Robb were the first to learn of her brother's attempt on her life and of the danger he represented. When next she returned to the farm Bess and Josiah, as well as Bullen, were also informed of the murderous intent of her brother.

Suddenly each of her employees understood the need for the rifles, the pistols and the tight security that was always maintained at the farm. No peddler, no tinker or, for that matter, no guest was allowed to set foot on the place without specific clearance. But this was a farm, not a fortress, a fact that presented a constant problem to those determined to protect Victoria from harm.

But it was a problem Bess could solve. The woman, who had spent many years on an isolated farm in the northern reaches of the Massachusetts colony, knew the absolute necessity of early warning if a family hoped to survive.

Many times Bess had gathered her children, herding them to the root cellar when marauding Indians had threatened. They had been given time to prepare against an attack because the geese she kept about the farm raised a racket that could be heard all the way to the neighbor's house whenever a stranger approached.

"Yes, miss," Bess concluded with an emphatic nod of her head, "those big Norwegian geese are the kind to have. Better than watch dogs, they are."

So it was agreed. In addition to armed men, the farm would be guarded by the noisy geese whose raucous honking could be heard half a mile away.

As Victoria studied each face that was turned toward her, she was aware of the genuine concern and the love she saw there. These people cared about her and, almost against her will, she admitted that she cared for them as well. And because she cared, she allowed them to edge a little further into her life. She would include them in her plans. She would tell them of her determination to travel to the Ohio country with the man who was her father's agent in the dangerous business of sneaking furs out of hostile territory, for they would worry if she suddenly disappeared for weeks with no word of explanation.

However, there was no need to confide her intentions of using the Ainsleys as an important cog in the closed circle of her father's venture into the fur trade. It might not work out and until it did she would say nothing.

When she had made clear her intention of venturing into country the French were guarding jealously to those who sat around the kitchen table with her the expressions on their faces elicited a smile of amusement from Victoria. They were so cautious, so timid. Such people would never build great wealth or construct financial empires as her father had done. Risks must be taken, sometimes great personal risks, but there was no other way. The bold inherited the earth—not the meek. That was another lesson her father had seared into her brain. She would not forget it.

Robb was the first to recover. "You can't be serious!" he sputtered. "Why, it ain't safe for an Englishman west of the Alleghenies. Trappers and traders gettin' themselves scalped every day. And worse," he muttered sourly.

"I hardly think Monsieur Pelletier will kill the goose that lays the golden egg," Victoria offered reasonably, defending the Frenchman who arranged for the furs to be collected on the other side of the mountain. "After all, he stands to gain a percentage from every pelt I purchase through him. No," she added, quite certain of her ground, "the French might be a prideful breed, and they might be quick to anger, but where money is concerned they are not fools."

"Frenchies don't always have the say as to what them Injuns do," Robb mumbled, and then decided where his duty lay. "Well, miss, go you might, but not without Tim and me. And that's that!"

For the first time since her father's death a hearty laugh of genuine pleasure rolled from deep within Victoria's being. And with that laughter real healing began. Clasping Robb's hand in both of hers, she agreed. "And that's the way it will be."

Later that week, the news arrived from Annapolis. James Bryce had arrived to pick up the horses and trade goods that he was to take into the wilderness. Victoria, dressed once more in the more practical men's attire, and her two constant companions hurried into town ready to accompany Mr. Bryce and his men on their journey.

James was not pleased at the prospect of having a woman tag along. He had enough to worry about without being burdened by the presence of some fool female.

However, since he had already made arrangements to rendezvous with the Frenchman, Philippe Pelletier, this side of the shifting boundary, he thought just maybe Victoria's presence might not be too great a hindrance. He was paid well for his services in hard cash and he hated to give up the money because of some female's whim.

Reluctantly he laid out his plan for Victoria, and she agreed that it was a good one. They would stay just this side of the Ohio valley and let the Frenchman come to them. The change in procedure fit in very well with her own hopes and plans. If the Frenchman had already agreed to cross out of his own territory, perhaps he would come even a little further—to the

Ainsley cabin. And that was the reason she had chosen to risk her neck. To persuade Philippe Pelletier to come to her.

She turned her full attention to James Bryce and his men. He had a good reputation and had always succeeded in his mission, but Victoria would be placing her life in his hands and she wanted to be very sure that they were competent ones. Tim and Robb were also uneasy as they studied the backwoodsmen with great suspicion and absolute mistrust.

These shaggy, half-wild creatures were a breed apart, and neither sailor liked the idea of Miss Victoria traveling in their company. Their buckskins were filthy and grease-smeared. It was hard to tell where the coonskin caps ended and the dirty, unkempt hair began. Most of them looked as though they hadn't seen a razor all winter, and the odor that emanated from the four mountain men was enough to kill a mule. Apparently they hadn't seen a tub all winter, either.

But Victoria was satisfied. Each of the strangers carried a flintlock rifle and a hand gun. Each wore a hatchet and knife hanging from his belt. Their eyes glinted coldly as they, in turn, studied her.

They were all searching for the answer to the same question. How reliable would each be in a tight spot? Would any prove to be excess baggage or, worse yet, would any break and run under life-threatening conditions where every gun was needed?

James was the first of the men to nod his acceptance. The young woman in front of him was dressed like some fool dandy from the tidewater, but her eyes were clear and steady, her frame lean and trim with not an ounce of fat to slow her down. But, more important, she carried a fine pistol and her two men were armed with handguns and the modern Pennsylvania rifles.

While Tim and Robb were still trying to make up their minds about the evil-smelling strangers, James twanged out the conditions under which he would allow Victoria to accompany the packtrain. She would be expected to sit the saddle for long hours without complaint, and she would have to follow orders without question or he would send her back regardless of where they were at the time.

Having traveled under similar conditions through more merciless terrain than that which confronted her now, Victoria assured James that his rules were acceptable. While on the trail he would be undisputed leader, and she would obey without question.

"Hope so, ma'am," he drawled and spat the evil tobacco juice on the warehouse floor. "Cause it'll be your funeral if'n you don't."

Within days they were ready to leave the safety of Annapolis, and the tone of the journey was set immediately. Neither Mr. Bryce nor Luke, who rode with him, engaged in any unnecessary conversation. Clint and Aaron, who brought up the rear of the train, were also miserly with words, so Victoria and her two friends remained silent as well, though it worked a severe hardship on the gregarious Robb.

That night, when the first camp was set up, Victoria, Tim and Robb pitched their tents. They ignored the looks of amused superiority on the faces of Mr. Bryce's men, who only cut a few pine boughs to nestle in some protected spot. The three lowlanders just looked at each other, compressed their lips and endured the unspoken contempt in silence.

As the small party climbed the mounting land, detours were often necessary to ford swollen creeks and fast-running rivers, for the weather had turned warm, and the snow in the mountains was melting fast. But regardless of how the pack train twisted and turned, they always came back to a straight line of approach. Then, two days out of Annapolis, Mr. Bryce and his men started leaving hay and small bags of oats along the trail for the journey back. Forage was scarce in the heavily wooded mountains that were just awakening from winter.

The distance between farms became greater, and James gave orders for cold camps. No fires meant no cooking, and they began to subsist on the daily ration of ground corn mixed with coarse sugar as well as a small portion of the tough, dried meat that was next to impossible to chew.

Just short of a week of steady travel, James conferred with Victoria. It was a singular honor, one he would not have bestowed upon many women, but he had come to admire the toughness of her character as well as her hide.

They were almost at their destination now. Another day would put them in position to light the signal fire, and if they were lucky, that fire would be answered by friendlies.

That evening there was absolute silence. Sound traveled a long way at night, and they were on dangerous ground. Tension settled over the camp like a prickly rash, but despite the danger, despite the discomfort, Victoria felt a kind of contentment come over her as she watched the last of the twilight give way to the sudden, star-laden velvet of night. For the first time in months she slept undisturbed by the nightmares that had plagued her since the death of Andrew Chisholm.

There was no hurry to get started in the morning. Their final destination was just hours away, so most of that day was passed in cautious silence, and Victoria spent that quiet time observing every detail of her surroundings. They were wild and starkly beautiful. It was much to her liking. Birds were everywhere, nestled in every protective pine, leaving their tracks in the snow, struggling for every seed, every bit of food. She sat very still. Some of the tiny creatures ventured so close that she could see the swift and steady beating of thir hearts under the warm down of their breasts. And once a rare woods buffalo crashed his way across the trail.

Underneath the blanket of snow, water was running off to the streams and creeks that found their way to the river. The pleasant, trickling sound was everywhere, and the ground was like a fragrant sponge. Spring was touching the high country.

After another cold meal that was eaten before the winter sun had started to descend, they broke camp and traveled to their point of rendezvous. It was night again before James and two of his men inched their way to the rim of the high, windswept pass. Small twigs caught and flared, then the bright flames outlined the retreating figures clearly as the men stationed themselves at a spot where they might see a return signal. In a few minutes they extinguished the fire and walked noiselessly to the dark camp.

"Answerin' fire to the northwest. We'll have company tomorrow, and I hope it's the company we're expectin'. But I'd advise all of you to stay alert just in case," James stated.

Victoria fingered her pistol and saw that Tim and
Robb had drawn the long rifles across their laps.
Sleepless, they waited through the long, cold night
until, just after dawn, the weary watchers saw three
men appear from out of the rising ground fog and
cautiously approach the cold ashes of the signal fire.
All of them were dressed much like James and his
men, except that the shortest man wore a bright
blanket jacket while the two Indians had bearskins
draped over their deerskin leggings and shirts.

The short, white man spoke softly, but his voice
carried to them in the absolute and eerie stillness of
the mist-shrouded dawn. "Monsieur Bryce?"

James motioned for Victoria to follow him. Tim and
Robb, though uninvited, were less than a step behind,
rifles resting loosely in the crook of their arms.

The tallest of the three strangers was facing them,
and he watched in silence as they approached. He
showed no emotion, but his gaze never wavered from
Victoria's face. The dark, piercing eyes locked with
her pale ones.

James raised his hand in greeting. "Mr. Pelletier.
Good to see ya again. The man I worked for died. This
here's his daughter, Victoria Chisholm. She's in
charge now."

A wide smile spread slowly over the Frenchman's
face. His friendly, dark eyes missed nothing as they
barely flicked over Tim and Robb, who were
fingering their rifles nervously, before returning to
study this bare-headed, golden-haired creature in
front of him, a woman whose pistol was on half-cock
and was being held by a very steady hand.

Philippe clucked and shook his head. "Ah,
mademoiselle, it is my great pleasure to meet one so

charming." A trace of sarcasm edged his words. "But you have no need of that little toy. And would you know how to use it?"

Victoria made her point. "*Oui*, monsieur, I could have put a shot through your back some time ago, but we came to trade, not to fight."

Philippe bowed. She was right. Giving a typical Gallic shrug, he continued, "So, mademoiselle, we try each other and now we know, *n'est ce-pas?*"

"*Oui*, monsieur." She smiled. "We both prefer making money to fighting, so let us get on with it." Then Victoria slipped with ease into French, the language that had been her mother's native tongue.

Running Dear, the younger of the two Indians, had been watching in fascination. He studied the subtle shadings of her golden coloring, the cold, pale eyes that reflected the light, allowing no man to see into them, and the small even teeth that flashed white when her mouth smiled even while her eyes did not.

"*Le cougar*," he whispered uneasily to the older man, who nodded his head and grunted in agreement.

James heard the comment and understood it. He shifted uneasily as he introduced Victoria to Spotted Wolf and his son, Running Deer. There was no telling what these fool Indians would take into their heads to do, and he stood ready to spring. The Frenchie was probably a little more civilized than the Indians, but he would have little control over them once they made up their minds to act.

The mountain cat to which Running Deer had compared Victoria was the totem of this tribe. It was not beyond the realm of reason that they would consider her a lucky charm, an omen. In that case it would take more than his small group to get Victoria back should the Indians decide they wanted her.

Philippe broke the tension. He spoke rapidly in French to his two companions, and they drifted away in the direction from which they had come as Philippe explained, ''They will signal the others to come with the furs. When you have inspected them we will do business.''

Immediately James gave the sign for his men to bring up the string of pack horses, and while they followed his silent instructions, Victoria leaned against a tree. Robb backed off a few steps and also remained standing. He was not at ease. He had heard too many tales of Indian massacres and torture. He kept his finger and thumb poised on the musket.

Robb's apprehension and mistrust were obvious to Philippe, who knew that one wrong move could cause a great deal of trouble, and it was possible that he could lose his pay for a winter's work. His tone was harsh with anger. ''Please assure your man, mademoiselle, that he is safe with us. This meeting is to be mutually profitable after all, is it not?''

''Robb knows he's safe, monsieur. It is simply that he has the admirable trait of never being foolhardy or too trusting,'' Victoria replied in English so Robb would understand.

Philippe laughed softly in appreciation. ''And you, mademoiselle, you do not trust too easily either, I think.''

Victoria chose not to answer. Instead she watched as the heavily laden pack animals were brought forward only to be surrounded by a larger contingency of Indian ponies carrying the wealth of an entire people on their backs. Bundles of furs were dumped and spread for inspection. Victoria waited quietly for James to comment.

''These are prime pelts,'' he said at last. ''Mr.

Pelletier has brought you the best." Then he signaled for his men to spread the blankets and the trade goods. This powwow could take a while.

Solemnly, the Indians gathered around the wealth of items the backwoodsmen displayed. They were all business as they picked out the kegs of rum that were so necessary in trading with the tribes further west. Next to go were the shorter French muskets, which were preferred to the longer, more awkward English weapon. Powder, lead for shot and the superior English flints were set aside along with kettles, knives, hatchets and salt.

Once the necessities had been obtained, the Indians turned to the brightly colored cloth for their women. Some of the younger braves took the glass beads, mirrors, combs and gaudy shawls. Blankets and dyes were added to the mounting pile and when at last they indicated that they had chosen all they wanted Victoria turned to James.

"Is it an acceptable trade on both sides, Mr. Bryce?"

After handing Philippe his commission in silver James calculated the worth of the entire amount and answered, "I'd say at the goin' price they were gettin' short-changed a mite. The furs are worth another three, four pounds, mebbe. Yessir," he mused, "even countin' a right smart price for the muskets, it's still a bit short."

Victoria made no comment but produced a leather pouch from her pocket and counted out four coins onto the blanket. No one moved to pick them up and Victoria understood. When one more coin was added Spotted Wolf grunted in approval and scooped them up. They were of little use to him, but the French would trade more guns and powder for these heavy metal discs. They gave little for furs, whose price was strictly controlled, but for the white man's money they would give much.

Philippe bowed over Victoria's hand. "Not only are you beautiful, mademoiselle, but you are honest. A sadly rare combination, I think."

"Ah, but I wish to deal with you again, *monsieur*. It would be unwise to be less than honest, do you not agree? Besides," she added wryly, "you outnumber us."

The Frenchman's laughter echoed through the hills. "Ah, *cherie*, you do your devious race proud. It is my pleasure to deal with you as long as it suits us both."

Now was the time. Once this opportunity was lost it might never come again. "I should like to make a proposal, monsieur. One which might save us both some problems with the French authorities. A friend of mine, a most discreet friend, has built a cabin nearby. I should like to persuade you and your companions to deliver your furs there in the future. War between our two nations is very close, I think. Before long this part of the country could be running red with blood. I prefer that mine not be among the others. You, too, I imagine, would rather do business in the privacy of a home where prying eyes would not spot you as quickly. Especially if you come and go at night."

Philippe pursed his lips and stared for a long moment at Victoria. She was right. The fur trade was strictly controlled by the authorities. His smuggling was every bit as dangerous for him as capture by the French could be for Victoria's men. An inconspicuous cabin entered at night, a barn in which to hide the horses, these would be good.

He nodded in agreement. Then he turned to Spotted

Wolf to discuss the matter, but the Indian spoke directly to Victoria in her own language. "We will have to meet this friend before we can answer. And if it comes to war, my people's blood will not be shed for the white man."

The warmth of Victoria's smile glowed in her eyes. She had dealt with wily elders before, men who pretended not to understand a word you said until it suited their purpose. "I will show you the place. We can leave whenever you're ready."

The Indian's features softened, and his dark eyes returned the smile. He read the respect in the countenance of the young white woman whom his son had likened to the golden mountain cat revered by his people. She had been raised well.

He turned to his men and spoke a few words. All but Running Deer gathered their possessions and turned back in the direction from which they had come. Then Spotted Wolf surprised Victoria and terrified James. Reaching under his cape, he removed a necklace of beads and bear claws. From it hung a finely carved head of a mountain lion.

"I believe you were sent to us as a good omen. We will fast and pray to the Great Spirit as we think upon its meaning. Wear this when you come this way again. It will be recognized, and you will be safe."

Victoria accepted the gift with gratitude and humility, emotions she did not often experience. The Indian was giving her something that was very valuable to him. More importantly, he was offering her friendship and protection just so long as she proved worthy of them. She would do her best not to disappoint him.

At this point Philippe, who was also growing wary, broke in, asking where the cabin of her friend was located. Victoria went to her horse and removed a map from the saddlebag. She pointed to the spot she had stared at for so long aboard the *Maryann*.

Estimating the Ainsley cabin to be less than a day's journey distant, Philippe started the group to the south. They did not stop until the sun had disappeared from view, leaving their trail in darkness. Another cold meal was quickly consumed before the group settled down to wait for morning.

They reached the Ainsley cabin early the next day, being careful to avoid the few lonely farms in the area. As a precautionary measure, Tim, Robb and Victoria approached the cabin alone, calling out when within hailing distance.

The first sign of life they saw was the barrel of a musket easing around the corner of the cabin. Next, William's head followed. Victoria tried not to laugh. "It's Victoria Monet, William," she reassured him and swept the hat from her head.

"I couldn't believe my ears. I thought that was your voice, but I couldn't be sure," William rattled on in happy relief before calling to Ellen that it was safe.

Ellen rushed out of the cabin, tears of relief still swimming in her eyes. "Miss Victoria," she sobbed. "Thank God it's you. We've been so afraid," she began, then choked back the words that only fed her terror.

With great courage, Ellen gathered herself together. "But I'm forgetting my manners. Please, come in. You must be tired and hungry."

"No," Victoria answered, making every effort to speak casually, "the last few days have been easy ones. However, we're not alone. There are ten of us in all. A Frenchman, two Indians and four of my men are waiting to be called in."

Ellen tripped over the high step into the cabin. "Indians? And the French?" Her face was white, her eyes haunted.

Victoria smiled into that fear. "Nothing to worry about," she replied easily. "We outnumber them."

The large brown eyes, made more prominent by sleepless nights and terror-stricken days, gazed full into Victoria's. "I trust you," Ellen stated simply. "You saved my life once, and I believe you're doing it again."

Tim and Robb stared at Ellen. This was the first they had heard about Ellen's life being in danger. Where and how had Miss Victoria come to her rescue? But they were questions that would have to wait, for their employer was even now calling to the rest of their group.

Hastily, Ellen stepped back outside the cabin. She would have none of those heathens in her home. Why, she and William could be murdered in their bed!

Philippe and his companions read the fear in Ellen's face and the tension in every line of William's body. They understood it, for this was an outlying farm. It was easy pickings for any wandering raiding party looking for trouble.

By mutual and silent agreement, they settled themselves on their blankets in the clearing, where the sun had melted the snow and had warmed the earth. No one made any move to approach the Ainsleys until Victoria introduced them all around.

Only then did Spotted Wolf, Running Deer and Philippe turn their eyes to the white strangers. Solemnly, the two Indians acknowledged the existence of the young couple while Philippe smiled his charming smile and got right to the point.

"Monsieur, madame, Miss Chisholm has told me so much about you, including the fact that you are most trustworthy and most discreet. I hope this is so, for then we shall be good partners, *non?*"

Instantly Ellen's curiosity pushed aside the fear. She frowned her uncertainty. "Miss Chisholm? Are you talking about Miss Victoria? But her name is not Chisholm. It's Monet. I don't understand."

Every eye turned toward Victoria. Only two of her companions knew that she had, indeed, sailed under false colors. Now they all understood that something was wrong, something that might affect their dealings with her.

The narrowed, mistrusting eyes of Philippe and the two Indians, as well as the speculative gaze of the backwoodsmen made it quite clear to Victoria that an explanation was necessary. An explanation that was at least close to the truth, for if she lied only Ellen and William would not know it. Still she wished to keep as much to herself as possible.

Briefly, she related part of the story. She told them of Edward's attempt on her life and of her decision to put an ocean between them. "So you see," she continued, "I changed my name only briefly and only for the purpose of throwing my half-brother off the track. Sometimes it is wiser to run from trouble than it is to meet it head on. This, I thought, was one of those times. Of course, once I had reached my final destination, there was no more need for deception."

Philippe shrugged and accepted the explanation, but Spotted Wolf was not so sure, so he listened closely as Ellen pursued the matter.

"But Captain Randall," Ellen began. "Why, what must he think of all this?"

Victoria barely controlled her anger. Ellen could not

possibly be that stupid! She was blurting out things Victoria very definitely wanted kept private.

In condescending tones Victoria answered cooly, "Captain Randall knows nothing of my reasons for leaving England, nor does he know anything about my brother. So you need not concern yourself any further, Ellen."

Refusing to be put off by the coldness of Victoria's voice, Ellen persisted. "But if you're to be married, he must be told!" she said firmly, paying not the least attention to William's frantic signals for her to be quiet.

"Captain Randall and I are not going to be married," Victoria answered somewhat more patiently. "And since I am quite sure that he has forgotten all about me by now, there is certainly no need to burden him with my problems."

"No," Ellen said sadly and shook her head in denial. "He has not forgotten you. How could he? He adored you, Miss Victoria. I never saw a man more in love. What happened?"

Victoria shrugged and sought to end this unpleasant inquisition. "Let us say that the game had been played to the end. There was no need to prolong it. What is done is done. It's over," Victoria replied with finality.

"You never intended to marry him," Ellen said softly, finally understanding what had happened but not why. "You must have hurt him very deeply." There was no accusation in her voice, only great sadness and pity, and all of it was not for Marcus Randall.

Victoria heard and did not like it. She turned to walk away, but Spotted Wolf encircled her wrist with strong fingers. He had understood everything Ellen had said and everything she had only implied. He frowned his concern and questioned Victoria in French.

"This man loved you?"

The answer came slowly as Victoria faced both herself and the truth. "In his own way. Yes, I think he did."

"And you loved him. You led him to believe you would share his blanket?" It was an extremely blunt question, and Victoria answered just as bluntly.

"Yes."

"And then you ran."

She shrugged. "Why not? He had served his purpose."

Spotted Wolf's face grew even darker. Le Cougar was well named. She had all the cat's cruel, vicious nature. "You have done a dangerous thing," the Indian said thoughtfully as he released Victoria's wrist. "You have caused this man Randall to pant and howl like a lone wolf at the moon, then you turned the heel of scorn to him. I think it is not yet settled. It would not be had you done this thing to me. Does he have no pride that he should meekly suffer this shame at your hands?"

Victoria bristled at the implication. "He is a very proud man. In fact, too much so. That was one of the problems. He has enough vanity for ten men. I performed a slight surgery on that vanity. Nothing more."

A long sigh escaped Spotted Wolf's lips. "He will come," the Indian stated with certainty. "You must guard your back, for what harms you could one day harm my people. You can be of no use to us dead. Only alive."

Her smile was warm and friendly. Even her eyes danced with appreciation for the older man's practical wisdom and his wry humor. "I will certainly do my best," Victoria laughed, "but he knows me only by the name of Monet. By the time he learns my true identity, if he cares enough to make the effort, I will know about it. There are those who watch for me."

The Indian nodded his approval, then turned his mind to other, more pressing matters. He would worry about Le Cougar some other time. Once more he switched to English so that all present would understand him. "Enough talk. My stomach grows empty. It is time to silence its complaining."

Without being asked, Running Deer and James Bryce melted into the surrounding forest. Within minutes the fatal shot rang out, and the two men came back carrying a young buck who still had the winter covering on his small, budding antlers. He would need little roasting and would be tender and juicy to the bite. Spotted Wolf's tongue played with a bothersome tooth and he grunted in satisfaction. A hot meal of tender meat was what he needed.

Ellen added what she could spare. There were biscuits with which to sop up the hot, red juices, and she warmed up a pot of leftover beans that had been cooked with meaty chunks of bacon. There was the honey William had found only days ago. However, the greatest treat was the pot of sliced dried apples that had been simmered over the fire and were now plump, sweet and juicy. Even Victoria devoured her share of this unexpected bounty. She had endured the meager trail rations as well as the cold camps. Now it was time to enjoy this rare hot and delicious meal.

When everyone had stuffed himself full each person sought a more comfortable position, leaning against the cabin or against a sturdy tree, eyes closed, face turned to the warmth of the sun.

Finally William tore himself away, entered the cabin and returned with a pail of Spruce Beer and several good dippers. He offered the makeshift brew around and the men's mood mellowed even more as they drank the fermented liquid and got to know one another better.

Victoria turned her attention to Ellen. The two women chatted amiably and said no more about Captain Randall. Neither did Victoria push Spotted Wolf for a decision. To do so would be a mistake.

Finally the Indian made up his mind. Next season, the furs would be brought to this cabin. They would come by night and they would leave before morning light. But for now Spotted Wolf was anxious to sit by his own fire. He was growing old and these long journeys tired him. It was time for the council to decide on a new chief.

But not just yet. Not until a few more winters had passed. Not until the white man settled the war that was coming. He must stay long enough to control the hotheads, long enough to keep his people out of the conflict. They must no longer spill their blood for the French. The time would come soon enough when the red man's blood would be spilled in his own cause.

And when that day came, when his people must face the endless tide of the white man, when they could no longer find refuge in the lands to the west, they would need the friendship and the guns such as Le Cougar could provide. She would be the means of saving his people from disappearing forever from the forests and meadows of this land that had welcomed them when they had fled from the shores of the great waters to the east.

Because of the waking dream that had troubled his mind for so many sleepless hours last night, Spotted Wolf was convinced he knew the reason the golden-haired woman had been sent to him and his people from out of the lands he once knew. And because William and Ellen Ainsley would be his link to her he piled an odd configuration of stones at every approach to the cabin and hung feathers from nearby trees. This farm was now under the protection of his people.

He explained the meaning of these symbols to the Ainsleys, whose eyes spoke eloquently of their gratitude. Neither did Ellen forget to thank the woman who had made all of this possible. Victoria Chisholm or Victoria Monet, it did not matter. This beautiful woman of strange moods had saved her life once before and now she was doing it again. For Ellen understood that it was because of Victoria that she and her husband were under the protection of Spotted Wolf. Any Indian who came this way would read the signs and would leave them unmolested. What they could do for their benefactress was very small in comparison.

But it was not small to Victoria. The final phase of her plan for the Ainsleys was now completed. She had her trading post on the very edge of the wilderness. It was only the beginning.

# 11

Accompanied by Tim and Robb, Victoria left the warehouse where the furs had been stored temporarily and walked to the ordinary that served the best food in Annapolis. She paid little more than cursory attention to the small, inconspicuous man seated at a table in the corner, enjoying his pipe and sipping his drink, apparently engrossed in the local newspaper.

Mr. Jones could hardly believe his good fortune. He had heard the talk about the woman who had arrived from England months ago, but this was the first time he had gotten a glimpse of the elusive Miss Chisholm. Now there was not the slightest doubt that what he had suspected when Captain Randall had first visited his office was true.

He should have come here immediately when he had discovered that the *Bayside* operated out of this small town. But no, he had gone off on a wild-goose chase up and down the Susquehanna. He sighed. It had been quite a hunt, but now it was over.

Allowing his gaze to drift in her direction, Mr. Jones took in the coloring, the emerald and diamond ring as it sparkled when she lifted her cup, as well as those unique eyes. This was, indeed, Mistress Monet. There was no mistake about it. And her name was Chisholm!

A few days more of discreet inquiries and he would be ready to go back to Williamsburg. By that time an answer to the letter he had sent to London should be awaiting him.

Mr. Jones did quite a bit of walking that afternoon as Mistress Chisholm and the two men who stuck like burrs stopped in one shop after another. By the time they finally headed toward the fringe of town they were juggling a considerable number of bundles, but Leroy Jones was not prepared for what he considered to be great good fortune when the trio entered a small home in a desolate area. There were no other houses nearby, and the two men, after depositing the day's purchases, had headed back to the more populous area, leaving Mistress Chisholm in the house, apparently alone. That small bit of information should prove interesting to Captain Randall.

Leroy Jones waited into the night and allowed himself the luxury of a smile as he watched the first floor of the house go dark. Shortly afterward there was a faint light in the front bedroom and a window was opened. Then the light dimmed and disappeared, but not suddenly, as though a candle had been snuffed. The person carrying the candle had gone into another room, and that small action told him that Miss Chisholm very probably slept in the back of the house. Another interesting point to note.

Satisfied at last that the two men were not coming

back at this hour, Mr. Jones got up and walked stiffly toward Mr. Inch's tavern. There were still a great many questions to be answered, but his work must be done quickly. Captain Randall was growing impatient.

Marcus was returning from a profitable trip to the West Indies. The small craft he had bought from a planter in financial difficulties sped him homeward. When the new *Morning Star* was slipped into the waves he would own two ships. *One and a half*, he thought, smiling ruefully.

Then the dark frown that so frequently marred his handsome face these days once again creased his brow as he thought that Leroy Jones was taking an extraordinarily long time tracking down one slip of a woman.

As he had done so often these past months, Marcus dredged up every detail of the cruel treatment he had suffered at Victoria's hands. His aunt and uncle had been the souls of discretion when he had been forced to offer some lame excuse for her abrupt departure, but Clay had not spared him the embarrassment of a few barbed comments. Marcus had come danger-ously close to soundly thrashing his younger cousin several times during the brief stops he had made in Williamsburg to check with Mr. Jones. But the elusive gentleman had never been there. Only a message of "no progress" had been handed to him by a clerk. Marcus's smile was evil as he thought of what he would do when he finally caught up to Victoria.

His bowed head was filled with malevolently pleasing visions when he was abruptly shaken from his imagined vengeance by Lyle Saunders, his second in command. "Will you be dropping anchor at Williamsburg or going on to Richmond, Cap'n?"

"We'll drop anchor at the capital," Marcus answered in the short-tempered tones Lyle had heard all too frequently since December past.

"Aye, sir," the mate answered, and was as perplexed as ever at the captain's foul mood, but he dismissed the problem and concerned himself with the more pressing one of bringing the ship into the crowded harbor.

As soon as the anchor splashed down, Marcus was rowed to the landing. From there he hurried the short distance to Mr. Jones's office. He had no desire to run into Clay, who would surely engage him in conversation about Victoria.

When Marcus walked through the door Mr. Jones stood to shake his hand. "Well, Captain, it's good to see you at last, sir. When I received no answer to the message I sent upriver several weeks ago I wondered if you had lost interest in my commission."

"Hardly," Marcus growled. "I've not been home yet. More reports of no progress, Mr. Jones?" he asked wearily with little hope.

Leroy Jones could not help smiling broadly as he escorted his client to the back room. "Not this time, Captain! I can now give you a full report of complete success. Mission accomplished, sir!" the little man crowed in great satisfaction and self-esteem.

"You've found her!" Marcus was almost afraid to say it.

"That I have, Captain Randall. That I have!" Leroy beamed. "In Annapolis!"

With a grand gesture, he continued. "Be seated, sir, and you shall learn quite a bit about your mysterious

Mistress Monet."

Reaching into his desk, Leroy removed a packet of papers. Before giving them to his client he said, "First, Captain, you should know that Mistress Monet is in reality Mistress Prudence Victoria Chisholm, daughter of the late Andrew Chisholm. This fact will help you better understand what you are about to read."

Giving the totally stunned man several sheets of paper covered with the fine, small script of the London agent who had done such a remarkable job, Mr. Jones leaned back in his chair and watched the incredulous sea captain turn his attention to the papers he held like a lifeline in unsteady hands.

The first fact leaped out at Marcus. Victoria had been born in 1729 to a Mademoiselle Jeanine Monet and her lover, Mr. Andrew Chisholm who, at the time of Victoria's birth, had been inconveniently married to someone else and already had a grown son.

Marcus felt his face burn as the significance of this first bit of information struck him. He recalled all too clearly the remark he had made to her about not wanting any bastards cluttering up his life. He groaned and wished to God he could recall that pompous, self-righteous, unintentional hurt, but it was too late for that. He could not recall the spoken word and what was worse, he was not at all sure Victoria would ever forgive him for having uttered it. Now he understood. Now that it was too late he understood the veil that had descended, blocking all expression from that lovely face.

Struggling to regain his composure and to clear his blurred vision, Marcus continued to read an infinitely detailed report on Mistress Chisholm, and his respect

for the ability of Mr. Jones and men like him grew
with each succeeding sentence. He began to see a
small girl deprived of the softening effects only a
woman's touch could provide when her mother died
young. He visualized the distraught father trying desperately to hold what was left to him, taking the child
with him wherever he went, trying to raise her as a
boy until even he had to face the fact that she was a
young woman.

There had been lengthy stays in various countries of
the East, where they had been guests of wealthy and
influential men, and Marcus smiled at the wording of
the report. "Undoubtedly the young Miss Chisholm,
being of tender years, was unduly influenced by
customs and beliefs that we in England might not
wish her to emulate." A most diplomatic man, this
agent.

Further on he read of the death of Andrew
Chisholm and of the steadfast friendship between
Victoria and Henry Byrnes, a partner in some of her
father's ventures, but the next paragraph burned into
his brain. It was as clear a warning as the perceptive
investigator would give.

> One of my most skilled operatives had
> occasion to follow a lead in London. Edward
> Chisholm, half-brother to the lady in question,
> along with another gentleman of obvious
> station had settled themselves in a local
> tavern. Mr. Chisholm was deep in his cups
> and was overheard in drunken conversation.
> The little my man could make out is repeated
> here, "—missed her the last time but will
> kill—next time—vixen-eyed bastard." These
> words seem to give some credence to the
> vague rumor that an attempt had been made

upon Miss Chisholm's life some time before
she sailed for America. However, we are
unable to confirm this without making our
inquiries obvious. As you requested, our investigation thus far has remained most discreet and will continue in that vein until we
have further instructions from you. It was
deemed most prudent, however, in the light of
the conversation just mentioned, that we
make a cursory investigation into the actions
of Mr. Chisholm.

Marcus breathed deeply to steady himself from the
shock he had just been given. Then he continued
reading, hoping that he would not find what he
already knew he would.

It seems that he is a known homosexual with
tendencies toward violence. He belongs to a
vicious group that calls itself the Mohocks. I
believe the name alludes to one of your
American Indian tribes.
The men who are members of this organ-
ization are rumored to have perpetrated
several crimes of brutal, senseless violence.
However, nothing can be proved. But it is a
poorly kept secret that Mr. Chisholm despises
the lady in question and seems to be the
object of some derision for having failed to
carry out his mission against her.
Further, Edward Chisholm was left a considerable fortune by his late father but from
what we can learn, the two men had little in
common and scrupulously avoided each other.

As he read on about Victoria's brother, Marcus felt
fear prick at his skin. The man was a dangerous
lunatic and belonged chained in an asylum, not
running loose on the streets.

The lengthy report concluded with a single sentence that was almost an afterthought. "Mistress Chisholm is known to some as *la gata dorada*, the golden cat, and it is our understanding that the afore-mentioned appellation has been earned."

Marcus looked up at Leroy Jones, who was sitting back puffing his pipe, missing none of the emotions that had played across Captain Randall's face. He had almost been able to tell which line and which para-graph Marcus was reading by his expression. This was not a remote, cold man bent on vengeance. It was just as he had suspected. Captain Randall was still very much in love but had yet to face that fact.

"What do you think of this business about Victoria's half-brother?"

Mr. Jones smiled at the question. Of all the information in the report, Marcus Randall asked first about the one possible source of danger. "I think, Captain, that my colleague reads the situation correctly. I have reason to trust his intuition implicitly, and I believe that Edward Chisholm most certainly did make an attempt on his sister's life.

"That might account for her traveling under an assumed name and being cautious about who knew her true identity and destination. The lies were not solely for your benefit, Captain. There were com-pelling reasons, I believe, for many of her actions. Reasons we might not yet fully understand, for if you remember, she used the name Monet, her mother's name. It would appear that she was attempting to hide, to slip unnoticed from England, but, surely, in that case she would have assumed a name that had no connection with her past. No, she wants her trail to be followed, but only so far as Williamsburg. For once her pursuers trace her that far, they must then begin to make inquiries, beating the bushes in hopes of flushing her out, but, of course, she will not be here. Yet she will not be so far away that she will not hear them thrashing about in their frustration, for I have no doubt Miss Chisholm has men everywhere, but most especially in our small town.''

The thought was new to Marcus. His eyes widened and his expression was troubled. Then he smiled. She could very well be having him watched just as he was having her every movement chronicled. ''You're right,'' he admitted, ''but forewarned is forearmed, I believe.''

''I thought you might wish to exercise some caution,'' Mr. Jones agreed, then continued with his own line of reasoning.

''From everything I can learn it would seem that Miss Chisholm fled from certain danger after her father's death, but only to make sure of her ground before she took on a fight for her life. Now,'' he said slowly and distinctly, ''I think she's ready.

''There was no trace of her for about a month after her arrival in Annapolis. Then, quite suddenly, she came out into the open, purchasing a small isolated house in town, attending social functions, visiting several of the more important residents and generally doing an extremely poor job of remaining in hiding.

''Yes,'' Mr. Jones reiterated, ''I think the lady is ready to be found.''

The fear showed in his eyes as Marcus put into words what they both knew. ''She's going to kill her brother.''

Mr. Jones pursed his lips, but his eyes twinkled. ''She is most certainly going to try, Captain. However, her brother seems to be every bit as devious as she.

It's just possible he might get to her first."

The face that had been bronzed and roughened by sun and sea went deathly pale as Marcus realized the terrible danger Victoria was in. Then he relaxed. Very soon now she would be where no one would find her, not even her brother. He stood to settle accounts, but Mr. Jones waved him back down to his chair.

"There is more, Captain. The report you have just read covers Miss Chisholm's life only to a certain point. There are a few facts that duty compels me to impress upon you."

With great care Mr. Jones made sure Marcus understood Victoria's immense power before telling him that he had learned from one of her warehouse employees, who had happily downed the rum he bought him, that one of Victoria's ships would be taking on cargo in England sometime in June. He had hinted broadly that it was very special cargo and would require immediate attention when the ship put into Annapolis. Her agent would have his hands full.

Quickly Marcus put together the bits of information that might serve him well. "So, sometime in July or August Mr. Coster will be at a crucial point in Miss Chisholm's plans. And if that gentleman met with some unfortunate accident and could not carry out those urgent duties, who would take over?"

There was absolute understanding in the look Leroy Jones directed toward Marcus. "From what I have seen of the lady in question I am fairly certain that she would look after her interests in Annapolis personally."

"And she would most likely stay at her home in town, which you said is in a rather isolated location."

"Probably, Captain, but don't say any more. If I am

ever questioned by the authorities, I wish to be able to tell them in all honesty that you did not confide in me, that I have no idea what you planned to do with the information I obtained for you."

Marcus smiled with a flash of his old arrogance. "Have no fear, Mr. Jones. I have no intention of telling you or anyone else what my plans are. But what makes you think anyone would point to me if some harm should befall Miss Chisholm? Surely she has a great many enemies if half of what I've read is true."

Mr. Jones shifted uneasily. This handsome, self-centered seaman who refused to admit the truth even to himself still underestimated the young woman he pursued. It was time to play the last card and hope this planter and captain who had the power of life and death over slave and sailor alike had enough sense to change course.

"But none, I fear, with so compelling a motive," Leroy said smoothly, and began to play a little game on his own.

"It is amazing what can be learned from low-ranking subordinates when they are flattered a little. A minor clerk who penned several copies of a legal document for Miss Chisholm's lawyer was only too happy to impress me with his importance by sharing a little of the contents. The document was the lady's last will and testament."

He let that sink in before continuing. "There were numerous bequests to employees and to Mr. Byrnes, but the largest share of her considerable fortune was left to you."

Marcus sat as though turned to stone. This thunderbolt Mr. Jones had so quietly and casually unleashed left him speechless. His mind worked swiftly, then he laughed out loud and slapped his hand on the desk in front of him. "By God, the little witch has just as much named me should any sudden accident befall her, for the authorities are quick to suspect the one who has the most to gain. And certainly her friends will understand the finger of accusation she has pointed in my direction. Yes," he hissed between clenched teeth, "it's something she would do, something only her treacherous mind would consider."

Then he fell silent and lowered long, black lashes to shade the pain in his eyes. Victoria was watching for two enemies: her brother and him. She was ready to do battle with either of them or both. And that battle would be to the death. He must be very careful, for that consequence must be avoided at all costs.

"No," he murmured softly, more to himself than to Mr. Jones, "Victoria might end up wishing to die, but she will not. Not by my hand. And not by her brother's, either, if I can help it, for that would defeat my purpose entirely."

This time Leroy Jones made not the least effort to hide the broad smile. He had been right from the very beginning about this man who imagined a revenge he did not want. So, with a clear conscience he completed his report, something he would not have done had he not been absolutely sure that Marcus Randall constituted no real danger to Andrew Chisholm's daughter.

"There's only a little more, Captain," he remarked absently while rummaging in his desk. "This," he continued as he found what he had been seeking, "is a drawing of the exact location of Miss Chisholm's house in Annapolis. On the back is a diagram of the interior. And this," he crowed as he put a key into Marcus's hand, "fits the back door."

A slow-breaking smile of pure joy spread across Marcus's face. It was done, and he was almost ready to make his move. He was almost ready to show a certain young lady what suffering was all about.

There were a great many lessons she had yet to learn, and he intended to teach them well. But only his most trusted men would accompany him, for what he had in mind was a hanging offense. Therefore he must move with great stealth and lay down a false trail so neither the authorities nor the men who, even now, might be watching would suspect anything.

# 12

Victoria watched approvingly as a small army of workmen proceeded at a rapid pace to complete Chisholm House. Governor Ogle had recommended an architect who now worked enthusiastically with the two engineers she had hired when she had visited Philadelphia.

There would be a hot water system that would heat the yet-to-be-completed orangerie, and a complete system would be incorporated into the new portions of her home. As far as the manor house was concerned, malodorous privies and the tedious task of heating buckets of water would be things of the past.

Continuing past the busy construction sites, Victoria strolled toward a newly plowed field and breathed deeply as the unmistakable odor of newly turned earth drifted toward her on the soft summer breeze. Josiah had been right when he decided that there would be no more tobacco grown on the farm, for it drained the soil and barely repaid the cost of growing it. Instead there would be undulating waves of grain gracing her land. And soon the air would be fragrant from blossoms in the small orchard her manager had planted. Already the pungent odor of the new herb garden filled the air, and on this beautiful day, Victoria felt only great admiration for the man who was meeting the needs of the farm with experience and skill.

Even the needs of the children had not been forgotten, and with Victoria's consent Josiah had written to a nephew still in Massachusetts. The young man, who was one of fifteen children, would be arriving next month to assist his uncle in running the farm, and would also take on the thankless chore of teaching the children to read and write, for Bess was steadfast in her belief that an educated worker was a much more valuable employee than one who could only make his mark. And only after the small house for this newest employee was finished would the work on the slave quarters begin.

Victoria's smile was smug as her thoughts jumped from one small triumph to another. She was very pleased with herself, for she had finally convinced Bess that allowing Mrs. Thompson, a highly capable indentured servant, and her daughter, Suellen, to help with the household chores would in no way diminish her own authority.

And Howard Coster was justifying her growing confidence in him. Not only was he running the operation here in Annapolis with great cunning and skill, he had also found the perfect agent to take charge of the new office in Baltimore town. Buck Arnold was an ambitious, enterprising young man whose vision was outpaced only by his enthusiasm. Already he had bought up modest bits of land spurned by the larger speculators and was in the process of selling those parcels to farmers who could afford nothing larger. Soon their crops and their animals would be transported to the pickling plant and the slaughterhouse that were even now being constructed on the west bank of the shallow basin that served the small vessels bringing tobacco to the Crown's warehouse, where it would be officially graded and reshipped to England.

Victoria laughed aloud with the sheer joy of accomplishment and ran for the stable. It had been a long time since she had felt so certain, so sure of success.

Not waiting for help from Ned, one of the stable-boys Bullen was training to take his place, Victoria threw a saddle on Lady Fair, the aging mare who nickered impatiently and was as anxious as Victoria to be off. The instant Victoria's weight hit the stirrup the horse took the bit between her teeth and bolted for freedom. Clutching the saddle, Victoria managed to throw her right leg across the mare's back just as Lady Fair reached the fence and soared over.

Shouting her exhilaration and giving voice to the ancient desert call of triumph, Victoria pressed her boots down against the stirrups and settled herself more firmly in the saddle. She gave Lady Fair her head, and, intoxicated by the sounds and smells of the day, neither horse nor rider cared in which direction they raced.

Anyone watching the wild, reckless ride through field and wood might have thought some demon chased both woman and beast alike. Finally, unaccustomed to such strenuous effort, Lady Fair pulled up snorting and blowing, but her spirits were still high.

She reared and pranced as the spray from the waterfall hit her sensitive nose. Victoria laughed, hugged the mare's neck, then steadied her, for she was not yet ready to continue the ride.

They had come to the place where the two hydro-engineers would oversee the construction of the building that was to house pumps and boilers and other mechanical marvels about which Victoria understood only the barest essentials. She was not in the least concerned, for she had chosen the men carefully, men who had mastered the ancient knowledge as well as the new.

Further on, where the water still swirled and raced, there would be a mill, first for lumber as the land was cleared and then for grain. The skills needed to run those mills would be provided by several men her father had chosen to work for him as indentured servants. Now they would work for her for a period of seven years before they earned the right to work for themselves.

Coaxing Lady Fair into motion, Victoria began a slower inspection of the farm. She smiled her happiness for Elias as he straightened from his task of enlarging the ice house and swept the hat from his head in greeting. Gratitude for the return of his three children brightened his eyes. His oldest son, now ten, returned her smile as Victoria waved and rode on.

The sound of shingles being sliced and thumped from a roughly squared length of wood caught her attention, and she watched for several minutes as workers repaired the roof of the spring house. Further on, Tim and Robb used their skills caulking and tightening the smokehouse, which would see little rest during the butchering season.

Things were going well. There had been no illness, no accidents, and the families from England worked

side by side with the blackamoors, something many
white laborers born and raised in this country refused
to do.

Victoria's gaze, which was becoming ever more discerning, rested on the sturdy cabins Josiah had had
built for the indentured servants. They were well constructed and were tight against the wind. Each cabin
had two windows that let in light and air. The field-
stone chimneys had been expertly crafted and
worked well. There was little danger of fire, a disaster
that must be constantly guarded against. Donald
Hubbard, Josiah's nephew, would live in just such a
house.

Once more Victoria's mind returned to several
questions she had been pondering. After watching the
operation of the farm and the work performed by
each laborer she was now ready to implement her
decisions. Bess would continue to dole out to each
family only the highly perishable foods, which were
kept under lock and key in various locations, but
those supplies that could be conveniently kept in each
house would be disbursed in quantity to each family.

Second, the ovens of the main house would no
longer be kept going from morning to night to provide
the bread for everyone on this farm. A large, separate
bakehouse would be built just as soon as work was
done on the slave cabins. The women who were most
skilled in the art of coaxing dough into light, crusty
loaves would take over the chore of producing bread
for everyone except those who lived in the manor
house. Bess would never forgive her if she allowed
bread and rolls baked by some other woman to be
served at her table.

And third, Josiah would be given the authority to
pay each laborer a few pennies a week. If any worker

did not perform to Josiah's expectations, his pay would be diminished or withheld. It was the most powerful incentive Victoria knew of.

She gazed over the fields, pasture and wood in satisfaction. This was her home and, except for Henry, she yearned for nothing left behind in England.

As she walked toward the house after leaving Lady Fair in Ned's capable hands, Victoria came to grips with a task she had been avoiding since she first set foot on this farm. Her father's personal belongings, as well as several cherished items, were still packed in numerous trunks and crates, some in the cellar and some in the bedroom that was to have been his.

Unshed tears stung Victoria's eyes, and she stumbled over the doorstep as she entered the house, remembering what a fuss her father always made on her birthday. No matter where they had found themselves, no matter how primitive the surroundings, he always found some special gift for her. She still had every one, and she treasured them all.

She sighed heavily and got on with the painful task. She began with the crates and trunks stored in the cellar, then tackled the things that had been taken to her father's bedroom before this household had known that Victoria would be coming alone.

The portrait of her mother, painted by an expert hand almost a quarter century ago, was hung in her father's room where it had always been. The family portrait, a happy picture of the three of them, was given a place of honor in the drawing room. It hung above the fireplace, and Victoria stared at it a long time, strangely comforted by its presence.

Finally all manner of clothing was pulled from

trunks and heaped in various piles. Much of it would be given away, but those things that had been her father's favorites would remain in his room, a room that would not be left barren and desolate. Victoria was not yet ready for such finality.

The rest didn't matter. The men of her household, including Bullen, could take what they wanted. Anything that was left would then be given to the male workers on the farm, who would welcome any addition to their meager wardrobes.

Her father's jewelry, which included a marvelous watch that had fascinated her as a child, would be put in safekeeping in the unlikely event she might one day marry and have a son of her own. A bittersweet smile touched her lips as her thoughts drifted back to the *Maryann* and Marcus Randall.

When at last it was done Victoria took refuge in her father's room and stared into her mother's emerald eyes. If only she could remember her.


Days crowded by work and accomplishment flew by. The gentle heat of early summer had given way to the hot, moisture-laden air of mid-July, which weighed heavily on body and spirit. It was on such a sultry night that Victoria, tossing restlessly in her bed, unable to sleep, heard the frantic sounds of a rider coming too fast in the dark, shouting at the top of his lungs.

Hastily she pulled on a robe and raced for the stairs, nearly tripping over Josiah, who was also hurrying toward the disturbance. Together, they listened to the story in growing dismay. Howard Coster had been set upon by thieves earlier in the night. His scalp had been split open, his face was bruised and swollen and his leg had been broken.

"Do you know who did it?" Victoria asked the messenger.

"No, ma'am. All we know is that Mr. Coster was found unconscious along the side of the road about eleven."

The man paused for breath and then continued. "Mrs. Coster had the doctor in. Stitched up Howard's head and set the leg. But he's going to be flat on his back for weeks. Just keeps mumbling about a special shipment coming in, and he's got to get back to the warehouse."

Victoria knew exactly which shipment Howard was talking about, and someone had to be at the warehouse to receive the message and give orders for the immediate disbursement of the contraband. "Go back to town and tell Howard not to worry. I'll take care of things myself until he's well enough to resume his duties. And assure him," she added as an after-thought, "that his salary will continue during his confinement."

There was no sleep for anyone in the house for the rest of the night. Victoria was suspicious of Howard's accident and said so. She knew only too well that this whole incident could be a trap. It had the smell of her brother about it, but he was still in England; Henry's last letter confirmed that fact. And the men she had stationed in Williamsburg and Richmond had reported nothing unusual. Still she was uneasy.

Before the sun broke through the steamy haze, Victoria, accompanied by Tim and Robb, arrived in Annapolis. Beatrice, Howard's wife, was almost inconsolable, but Victoria did the best she could while Tim and Robb entertained the younger children in this large family.

They stayed long enough for Victoria to assure herself that Mr. Coster would make a complete recovery, and long enough for her to be filled in on all the details of this latest operation, which would pass unnoticed almost under the noses of the customs agents. Once Victoria was satisfied that every precaution had been taken, she left for the warehouse for what might prove to be a very long wait. It might be days or weeks before Captain Rutherford, master of her ship *Eye of Osiris*, splashed anchor just outside the harbor.

All that day and even into the night Victoria kept busy while waiting for a message that did not come. It was well past dark when she at last gave up and left the warehouse in the capable hands of the nightwatchmen. She would return again tomorrow and as many tomorrows as it took until word of her ship arrived.

Tim and Robb saw her safely to her Annapolis home and waited while Victoria made sure that both doors as well as all the windows on the lower level were well secured. Only then did the two men drive the carriage to the tavern by the battery, where they would quench their thirst before retiring to whatever accommodations were available for the rest of the night.

After seeing to the safety of the carriage and to the comfort of the horses Tim and Robb entered the taproom and gazed around in search of some congenial seaman with whom they might strike up a pleasant conversation. Tonight they were in luck. There were two lonely sailors off by themselves in a corner who were more than happy to swap drinks and stories.

Neither Tim nor Robb noticed that while their two

newly found friends plied them with cup after cup of grog, they, themselves, barely touched the ale in their mugs.

It was not long before Victoria's bodyguards were deep in their cups, and they laughed and sang as their jovial companions helped them up the stairs to their beds.

The two strangers waited impatiently until both Tim and Robb were deep in a drunken sleep. Then they walked from the inn to the water's edge. They retrieved a lantern from its hiding place and slowly swung it back and forth. Then, extinguishing the light, they waited until the soft sound of muffled oars dipping into water broke the silence. An instant later a small boat nudged the pilings of the dock.

Marcus Randall climbed the ladder and stepped ashore. He handed a large wicker trunk to Terrence while he tucked an empty seabag under his arm. Quietly the three men made their way through the deserted streets and waited, well hidden, in a small grove of trees located just behind Victoria's Annapolis home.

Marcus fingered the key in his pocket and looked up at the sky for the tenth time. Heavy storm clouds obliterated the feeble light of the moon. It was very dark, and that suited his purpose. His luck could have been no better. The threatening storm would keep even the late stragglers indoors.

As he watched patiently, the faint glow at the back window held steady. There seemed to be no movement of any kind except for curtains blowing at the open upstairs window.

Motioning for Terrence and Lyle to follow, Marcus advanced stealthily across the yard to the back door of the house. He inserted the key Mr. Jones had given him into the lock and met with resistance.

The key with which Victoria had locked the door was still in the lock, but that should prove to be only a small problem. Slowly and carefully Marcus used his key to jiggle and push the one inside free of the lock. He breathed a sigh of relief when there was no sound as it fell to the floor. Apparently there was some sort of mat or rug, which had muffled any noise that might have been made. Everything was working for him, and he was sure of himself. The knob turned and they were inside.

Turning to Lyle and Terrence, he whispered, "Wait for me here, and for God's sake don't move. I'll call when I want you to bring the trunk."

Feeling his way cautiously through the dark kitchen and into the front room, Marcus pictured every detail of the diagram Mr. Jones had made of the interior. Keeping close to the wall, he worked his way noiselessly to the second floor. The faint glow from the back room still concerned him, and he stepped in warily.

A small brass Bhatinda lamp rested on a table in the corner of the room. The delicate cutwork in the brass sleeve that covered the candle allowed only a faint glow to escape and lessen the dark shadows at that end of the bedchamber.

Marcus did not bother to extinguish the light, for he would be between it and his victim. Besides, he didn't care if Victoria recognized him. In fact, he rather hoped she would. It would make this abduction so much sweeter if she called his name, if she begged for mercy. But no! There must be no noise, no screams, no pleading. He must get her away from here as quickly and as silently as possible. Satisfaction must wait, for Victoria had powerful friends, friends who would see him hang for what he planned to do this night.

Just as Marcus was about to reach for Victoria, he saw the dull glint of metal on the bedside stand. He almost laughed out loud. Had he extinguished the light, he would have missed it. He picked up the small pistol and put it in his belt.

With a movement that was both swift and sure, Marcus grasped Victoria's face in his hand and applied the downward pressure that opened her mouth so he could stuff the wad of cloth in. In that same instant Victoria came to snarling, biting, clawing consciousness.

Marcus jerked his hand away from the teeth that drew blood, but the gag held. In almost the same split second Victoria's nails raked the unknown intruder's face, then her hand groped across her nightstand as she felt for the gun that was no longer there. Her curse of rage, though muffled, was unmistakable as she turned on her attacker with renewed fury. Her fingers found the vulnerable eyes, but before she could gouge them out Marcus jerked his head back sharply. He had suffered under one of her vicious attacks before. He knew how she fought, and he was prepared to minimize the damage, though he thought he wasn't doing too well at the moment.

Holding onto her was like trying to hold a slippery, wriggling eel. Again Victoria squirmed from his grasp. Her fingers fumbled for the knife under her pillow, and she slashed at the dark form that hovered over her. A grunt of pain escaped Marcus's lips as the blade seared his flesh and began the backward arc for a second, more accurate thrust.

The move was so swift, Marcus barely had time to grab Victoria's wrist and apply the twisting pressure to paralyze fingers that refused to let go of the weapon. In desperation, Victoria clawed with her free hand, and once again her nails found his face.

Breathing hard and dripping sweat and blood, Marcus managed to contain both her wrists in his left hand. As Victoria fought against his grip Marcus whipped a length of rope around her wrists, then tied a handkerchief over her mouth so she could not work the first gag out with her tongue.

It was over. With two quick motions Marcus tied the rope which held her wrists. Then he tied her ankles and wrapped her in the tangled sheet that had fallen to the floor very early in the struggle. Finally he dared leave her long enough to walk to the door and call softly for his men.

Lyle and Terrence brought the wicker trunk into the room, and Marcus stuffed Victoria in. He grabbed whatever clothes that were in drawers and wardrobe and crammed them into the trunk around and over her, securing the lid. At a more leisurely pace he put the remaining personal articles from the two upstairs rooms into his seabag. It must look as though she had packed her things herself. Her own trunk would be hidden in the small shed at the rear of the house.

Bending close to the bed, he checked for blood. The bottom sheet was stained, and he removed it, stuffing it in his bag as well. Everything else looked normal. Most of his blood had been soaked up by the linen shirt and the light jacket he was wearing. Some had dripped on Victoria, but that didn't matter. What was important was the fact that he could leave no signs of struggle in this room.

Then he lowered the small lamp close to the bed. The mattress was not stained, nor was the rug by the side of the bed. It would be all right.

Satisfied, he signaled his men to carry Victoria downstairs while he lugged the seabag and her trunk, which was to be hidden out back. Then, once out of the house, he locked the door, got rid of Victoria's trunk and led his men back to the dock. They met no one.

Victoria struggled against the sheet that covered her like a winding cloth. She managed to loosen it enough to get her hands to her mouth and get rid of the gag, which was all but strangling her. Then she set to work on the rope that bound her wrists, but the knot was on the opposite side and she could not get a good hold on it with her teeth. Neither could she slide the rope around her wrists so the knot would come to her. The narrow confines of her prison prevented her from maneuvering enough to help herself.

Finally she screamed, but the sound was muffled and useless. Her captors dumped her unceremoniously onto an uncertain surface. Then she understood as the sound of oars striking water reached her ears. Were they rowing her to deep water to throw her overboard? Drowning was not a pretty death, and there was no escape from this cramped prison. But who? Who was it? She resumed her struggle to save herself, and as she did so her senses were overwhelmed with delayed recognition. The strength of his hands. The smell of his skin. Marcus! But how?

Victoria slumped and stopped her struggle. It wasn't possible, yet she couldn't deny the truth. Marcus was about to dump her into the murky waters of the port. Hers would be just one more body found bumping against the seawall as the tide rolled in. No. He could have killed her already.

But time passed, and once more there was

movement. Once again she was being carried somewhere. Then she heard the sound of a door opening and
she was bumped roughly to the floor.

"That'll be all," Marcus said, dismissing the men
who had helped him, and he locked the door to his
cabin after them as they left.

He pocketed the key and, as an added precaution, threw the bolt. Lighting extra candles, he
approached the trunk. There was a smile of
satisfaction on his scarred face. For a long, rewarding
moment he just stood looking down at Victoria's
prison. He was savoring his moment of triumph.

But before he freed her he washed the worst of the
blood from his face and removed the stained and
slashed jacket and shirt. He looked in his mirror and
clenched his teeth in anger. Some of the marks she
had inflicted would go with him to his grave. Miss
Chisholm had a great deal to make up for. Much more
than a Dutch joe could ever repay.

Not willing to delay his revenge any longer, Marcus
unfastened the lid of the trunk and pushed it back.
Scattering the clothing about, he lifted Victoria out
and stripped the sheet from her body. There was none
of the usual pristine neatness about Victoria now. Her
hair was wild and disheveled. The low-cut sleeveless
gown was smeared with blood. So were her face and
arms. And she was wobbling dangerously on bound
feet, trying desperately to maintain her balance.

Grasping her face in his hand, Marcus turned it
sharply to one side. There would be a wicked bruise,
but the skin was not broken. The blood that was
smeared on her was his, and Marcus was surprised
when he realized he was actually relieved not to have
done too much damage to the object of his wrath.

Until this moment neither of them had spoken. Then
Marcus made the mistake of laughing softly into the
eyes that glittered with fury.

"You fool!" Victoria hissed in anger. But it was her
turn to smile, for the damage she had inflicted gave
her a modicum of satisfaction. And he hadn't killed
her. Not yet. There was still hope. She tossed her head
in rebellious defiance.

Marcus laughed out loud, for despite the stinging
and burning of his various wounds, none of which
was serious, he was immensely pleased. All the
arrogance and all the pride he remembered so well
were still there. Breaking her was going to be the most
pleasurable experience of his life. He was going to
enjoy every moment of his vengeance.

"My love, that fire in your eyes does not intimidate
me. On the contrary, I find it exciting, and believe
me, I do not need any more stimulation, as you will
soon discover."

His voice was as smooth and as oily as the castor
bean, and just as dangerous. No one needed to spell
out the meaning of his words to Victoria. She understood them well enough. She had to think. There had
to be some way out of this.

Only Victoria's eyes betrayed her frustration as she
struggled to control her rising anger. Neither did she
resist when Marcus held her tight against him while
the fingers of his free hand closed around her face,
bending her head back, forcing her to look up at him.

His eyes narrowed in satisfaction. "It is most
gratifying to see that you are trying to control that vile
temper of yours, and you are quite right to save a little
of that fire for other more pleasurable passions."

Victoria's eyes glinted coldly. If Marcus Randall

thought she would give him the pleasure of crying and pleading like some schoolgirl, he could not be more mistaken. She was not accustomed to begging anyone for anything. Not even her life. And she had no intention of starting now.

Instead she waited calmly as he untied the knot that still held the handkerchief he had used to hold the gag in her mouth around her neck. As he drew his knife to slit the ropes that had burned her wrists as she had tried to work free, her position was still one of docile acceptance. It was not until Marcus dropped to one knee to free her ankles that Victoria, without warning, brought her knee up sharply under his chin. Marcus dropped heavily, but as he did he threw his arms around Victoria's legs and brought her down with him.

As she struggled to free her legs from the dead weight of his body, Marcus fought to clear his head. Pulling loose at last, Victoria lunged for the door and shot the bolt free. But there was another lock, and the key was gone. She looked for another avenue of escape but found none.

She turned to face Marcus, not sure of his reaction to her latest attack, but there was no urgency to Marcus's movements. She was trapped and he knew it. Neither had she made any attempt to use the knife he had dropped under the force of her knee meeting his chin. The minute the rope had been cut she had charged, but the knife still lay there between them. He stooped to pick it up.

He suspected he was very lucky. For a moment he had lain stunned and unable to defend himself. Victoria could very easily have buried the blade deep in his back, but she had not done so. His smile was smug as he stood dangling the key in front of him. "Looking for this?" he asked with maddening innocence.

Victoria stood stiff and silent. Her eyes flicked briefly to the knife that Marcus was locking away in his sea chest. She should have used it. She should not have hesitated. Whatever happened now was her own doing.

Turning back to face his captive, Marcus raised an eyebrow in mock surprise. "What, madam, nothing to say? Where's all your spirit, girl? Have you given up so soon, then?" But she would not answer, not even when his laughter taunted and infuriated her.

"I suggest you relax, my dear," he said reasonably. "I much prefer not to hurt you, something you have made all but impossible." He shook his head sorrowfully, but his eyes gleamed with perverse pleasure. "I fear you have all the instincts of an alley cat, in which case I humbly suggest that a gentler demeanor will most definitely be rewarded by kinder treatment. But if you insist on trying to tear me to shreds, I will meet force with force, and you will not like it."

Victoria's eyes flicked in exasperation. She needed time to think, time to turn this nasty situation to her advantage. Yet she wasn't sorry she had not plunged the knife into his defenseless back.

Cautiously, she began to ease away from him, but Marcus put out a hand and stopped her. She did not resist. Then, with movements as ritualized and graceful as any temple dancer, he slid the sleeveless garment she wore from her shoulders, down to her waist and past her hips, allowing the soft, almost transparent cloth to fall softly to the floor.

His fingers brushed the smooth, bare skin. His eyes moved slowly and took in every hollow and every gentle curve. Marcus was in no hurry. He remembered a night long ago, and Victoria remembered also. She had wanted him then, and he had scorned her.

"Are we not yet even?" she questioned softly, then once more lapsed into silence as Marcus's eyes lifted to meet hers. He did not have to speak. She read the answer on his face. He had not yet exacted the last drop of vengeance. And she would not grovel at his feet. She stood tall and proud. Her eyes challenged him, and Marcus responded.

"Turn around, my dear." When she refused to budge his tone became more demanding. "Turn, I said."

But she would not. Her pride was as fierce as his. She had no intention of making this easy for him. "You, sir," she responded icily, "can go to hell."

Marcus flashed a dazzling smile. "If I do, madam, you may rest assured that I'll take you with me."

Putting his hands on his hips, he proceeded to walk slowly around her. She was stubborn, but not for long. He remembered the fire that smoldered deep beneath that beautiful, golden surface. She had wanted him once. She would again. This time he would oblige her.

Sighing audibly, he backed away a step. "You'll find a robe on the peg. You can put it on if you choose."

He smiled at the surprised look on Victoria's face and continued the game he had waited so long to play. "Or, if you'd rather, you may be seated exactly as you are. In fact, I would like that. I prefer my women with a little more meat on their bones, but, still, you're pleasing enough. Besides, when a man is hungry, any meal will do."

Totally incensed by his crude, insulting words, Victoria glared at him and spun defiantly on her heel. Marching haughtily to the other side of the small cabin, she snatched the robe from the peg and threw it to the floor. "I won't wear another woman's clothes," Victoria stated flatly. "You brought my things with you; I'll wear them."

"You'll wear what I tell you to or wear nothing at all, my dear; it makes no difference to me. Besides," he added, enjoying her show of temper, "I went to great pains to have the robe made especially for you."

Victoria stared at him blankly. She had made a fool of herself. Picking the robe up, she felt the sleek softness of it in her hands. The ruby satin glowed warmly in the candlelight. Paler velvet adorned the rolled collar and wide-cuffed sleeves. Tiny velvet-covered buttons transformed the tight bodice into a corselet. It was quite lovely and quite expensive. And Marcus had had it made for her. The ground began to shift beneath her feet.

Marcus laughed at her obvious uncertainty. "When a gentleman goes courting he usually takes a gift," he drawled sarcastically.

Victoria stared at him as though he had lost his mind. Her lips parted as if she were about to speak and then closed as quickly. She kept her own counsel as she shrugged into the robe. Once again the sand shifted. There was something here she did not understand.

But there was no time to ponder the situation. Marcus walked to the washstand, splashed more water into the basin and threw Victoria a towel.

"You're a mess. Get yourself cleaned up. And do something with that hair!"

Stung by this additional slur to her physical appearance, Victoria snapped back. "You did it!"

The petulant scowl on Victoria's face was too much for Marcus. He threw his head back and laughed until the tears rolled from his eyes. "I hope you will pardon me, my dear. I had no idea you were so sensitive to my opinion. I did not mean to hurt your feelings. But no matter, I find you entirely enchanting, dirty or clean, full-curved or flat-chested."

Compressing her lips to hold back the curse, Victoria wet the towel and scrubbed at her face. Marcus was right. She was a mess.

When she had finished washing her arms she opened the robe and looked in the mirror at her body. There were still some bloodstains on her breast, and she rubbed gently until Marcus took the towel from her and lingered over the task he enjoyed performing.

Unable to wait as he had planned, Marcus pushed the robe from Victoria's shoulders and pressed her against his bare chest. The sound that came from him was very much like a sob, and Victoria shivered.

Marcus picked her up and placed her in the narrow captain's bed. "Stay there," he warned, "or I shall be forced to tie you down."

Victoria did as she was told. Marcus was in no mood to be disobeyed. She had witnessed this kind of barely controlled desire in men before. It was a wild need that was more brutal than loving, and Victoria did not want to be its victim.

As she was trying to think of some way out of her predicament, she stared absently at Marcus, who had his back to her and was removing the rest of his

clothing. She had seen enough male bodies to
appreciate his. The shoulders were broad and heavily
muscled, the waist and hips narrow, and the legs
strong. She stared in frank and open admiration. It
wasn't often the gods put together all the right
elements in one form, but they had apparently done
so with Marcus.

Her idle wanderings were short-lived, for when
Marcus turned to face her she saw that any plan she
might contrive for avoiding or delaying his passion
was futile. Every muscle in her body tightened and
prepared for battle, but that was not the way to
handle him. As she forced her body to relax, her mind
raced to find some escape, but Marcus was already
easing in beside her.

The swift, painful assault she had feared did not
come. Instead, Marcus struggled against the raw
animal need that refused to subside. He slipped one
arm around Victoria and the open robe she still wore.

The heady fragrance of the scented oil she used on
her skin filled his senses as he turned her on her side
to face him. His fingers teased. His lips caressed, and
slowly but surely Marcus coaxed a small flame from
the reluctant ashes.

Before the flame could be nurtured Marcus lost his
battle to the raging urgency within. He could wait no
longer. Moving and positioning Victoria to his will,
Marcus sought release from the flooding tide, the
release only Victoria could give him.

He was out of control and groaned with the effort to
rein in the lust that could ruin everything. But there
was no resisting the relentless force that surged
through him.

After nine months of celibacy his body refused to
obey his will. Emotion, which had been too long pent

up, broke free in a wild, raging storm he was helpless to fight.

When it was over Victoria turned her head away from him so he would not see the anguish and the need in her face. He had played a very cruel game just as she had so many months ago. She took a deep breath as her body stiffened against unfulfilled desire.

Marcus was spent. He lay there for long minutes before turning to Victoria, who lay quiet and still, her arm across her eyes. She wanted no more of him.

"Please put out the candles." Her voice was barely audible, but Marcus heard the desolation and it angered him, for he did not like being reminded of his inadequate performance.

"No, my dear, it gives me great pleasure just to look at you. You will just have to suffer it. Besides," he smiled tenderly and brushed her lips with his, "you will not be one of those wives who only make love at night in the dark."

The shifting sand collapsed under Victoria's feet. She stared in disbelief at the man who had learned nothing. "Wife?"

"Of course, my darling," Marcus replied. "I can hardly send you packing after tonight." He laughed softly. "I'm afraid I'll just have to make an honest woman out of you. You goose," he teased, "did you really think I wouldn't marry you?"

It was Victoria's turn to inflict pain. "And you, Captain Randall, as I told you earlier tonight are a fool! No, I won't marry you. I'd rather spend eternity in hell."

Marcus clenched his teeth against the fury that almost blinded him. His eyes glittered with cold fire. "We'll see what you prefer after a few months of my tender ministrations. Perhaps hell will lose its appeal, my dear. It's possible."

Victoria changed her tactics and swallowed her pride. "Haven't you had your revenge? Haven't I paid a high enough price? Please, let me go."

His face was hard and unyielding. "No, Victoria, the price is much higher than the one you have paid so far. You owe me a great deal more, and I intend to collect. Besides, how can I let you go? Surely you would run to the authorities, and I would find myself dangling from the end of a short rope."

"I won't," Victoria promised. "I won't tell anyone. Please, Marcus, I can't marry a man who wants me only as a convenience and a brood mare. You could get better and more willing service from any of your whores. I could not live with a husband who jumps into any bed that happens to be handy."

Marcus flushed in embarrassment. Then his eyes narrowed in anger. His words dripped with malice. "It's delightful to know what you expect of me, pet. I shall try not to disappoint you."

"You are not going to disappoint me," Victoria flared, "because I am not going to marry you. Really! I think you've lost your wits altogether!"

Then she added the final blow. "Actually, Marcus, I expect absolutely nothing from you. Not even honor."

He propped his head on his hand. His face was very close to hers. "That is really very considerate of you, my precious. It makes what I have in mind so much easier to do. Now get out of bed and get washed. I want you clean when I make love to you again."

Victoria's skin tightened over the high cheekbones. She would like to scratch his eyes out, but she had already tried that and it hadn't worked. "*Damn*," she muttered to herself. She should have used the knife when she had the chance, if only to wound him, to slow him down.

She sighed in defeat and walked toward the discolored water in the wash basin. Opening the bottom of the cabinet, Victoria removed the chamber pot and poured the dirty water into it. Then she refilled the shallow basin with clean water from the pitcher and proceeded to scrub every inch of her body. She didn't care if Marcus watched or not. Nothing mattered but escape. She had to get away from him before he made her pregnant.

Her mouth twisted in a wry grimace as she recalled how Marcus hated that word, and she risked a surreptitious glance in his direction. He had put on a robe and was setting out paper and pen on the table.

Marcus turned toward her and smiled. "Be seated, my dear. You are to write a letter to your friends. I would not wish them to become suspicious of what might turn out to be a very long absence on your part."

Victoria held her breath. For the first time Marcus saw fear in those pale eyes. "How long?" she asked, and Marcus understood.

He shrugged. "For as long as it pleases me. But no more questions. I want your letter to arrive before morning."

Victoria shook her head. "No, I won't write it," she stated flatly.

"I think you will, my dear," he assured her in level tones. "The pain you have already suffered would be child's play compared to what I *can* inflict. Then, too, there is another point to consider. Unless you write the letter it will be a simple matter for my men to slip back into town and quietly bury a knife deep between the ribs of your two friends who are, even now, in a drunken sleep. They would feel nothing. There would be no noise, and you would have accomplished nothing by your stubbornness. By cooperating you will at least save their lives."

Victoria's spine stiffened, and she was tempted to call his bluff, but if she were wrong, if Marcus carried out his threat, it would be too late to change her mind. No, she must do as she was told, but she would find a way to give some clue as to what had happened to her, or where to start looking. What could she say that would help her friends find her? Marcus surely had already concocted some story she would be expected to commit to paper. "What am I supposed to write?"

"Anything will do, I think. Just so it's something written in your hand that will keep your friends from beating the bushes for you until I can get you safely away."

He paused a moment. "Let us say that some dear friend in England is very ill. Shall we make it Henry Byrnes? At any rate, you will say that you received such a message and decided to leave for England immediately. There was no time to notify them. You might also add that you will write later."

Victoria let her breath out slowly. There was still hope. No one would believe such a fantastic story, least of all Tim and Robb. They would check. They would turn Annapolis upside-down, but all that would take precious time. "And will there be other letters?" she asked, stalling for time to think.

Marcus smiled at the foolish question. "No, my dear," he answered smoothly.

Victoria's mind worked frantically, and she found her answer. She wrote in general what Marcus had told her to, but she did a little embellishing of her own. She asked that Tim and Robb express her regrets to Monsieur Pelletier and his good friend, Mr. Wolf, when they arrived at her farm later in the week. She hoped to see them upon her return from England but had no wish to continue the painful conversation she and Mr. Wolf had engaged in during her last visit to his home.

It was the best she could do. Tim and Robb *must* understand that she was telling them to go to Spotted Wolf. But would he remember the conversation when he warned her about Marcus? He had to. It was her only hope.

She watched fearfully as Marcus read the letter, and she caught her breath when he frowned and looked at her questioningly. "This conversation you refer to," he asked, "what does it concern?"

Giving the first answer that popped into her head, Victoria replied, "He has asked me to marry him. I refused. He finds my decision difficult to accept."

Marcus nodded. That was something he had great difficulty accepting himself. There wasn't a woman in the Tidewater who wouldn't jump at the chance. Then, with no further questions, he let the letter stand as written, and Victoria signed it, not as she usually did, not the plain, bold P.V. Chisholm, but rather, she signed her full name.

Satisfied that this letter would give him a day or two head start, Marcus unlocked the door and let out a piercing whistle. Seconds later Terrence took the letter from his hand and disappeared. Marcus closed and relocked the door, putting the key in his robe pocket. Then he picked up Victoria's ruined gown from the floor where it still lay. Absently, he drew the fine cloth through his half-closed hand. There was hardly any thickness to it, and it was probably the finest, most delicate length of cotton he had ever held.

"India?" he questioned.

"Egypt!" Victoria replied testily. She really didn't feel like holding a casual conversation with him at this point.

"I thought the style unusual," he said absently, his mind more on Terrence's mission than on the spoiled nightgown.

Victoria snapped her defiance. "Not everyone covers himself from chin to toe!"

Marcus most definitely did not like the tone of her voice. "Nor will you," he assured her as he walked closer. But before he had reached her side, Victoria was on her feet, edging away from him. She was in no mood for any more of his boorish attentions. The sooner she could get on deck and slip quietly over the side, the better.

But Marcus was in no mood for any nonsense. He put his hands to Victoria's shoulders and forced her back down in her chair. "How many men have you loved?"

The question caught her off balance. She thought of her father and Henry. And she thought of two very special teachers, men of great wisdom and learning. And she even remembered Ramon, the man who had been the object of her first girlish sighs.

"Very well," Marcus sighed, hoping she would tell him the truth, but certainly not expecting it. "Whether you loved them or not, how many men have you gone to bed with?"

Angry because she could not control the flaming of her cheeks, Victoria lashed out cruelly. "I lost count!"

This time when Marcus put his hands on her, she winced in pain. "How many?" he repeated softly. "And I want the truth. If you continue to lie to me, I will not hesitate to make you wish you hadn't."

Sorely tempted to tell him she had had many lovers, that she had hopped from bed to bed like a flea changing dogs, Victoria glared up at him. Then she changed her mind. If he didn't already know the answer, he wouldn't have asked. He knew entirely too much about her. He had known where to find her. And he had known about Tim and Robb. But he had not known about her dealings with Philippe and Spotted Wolf. She decided to tell the truth. "Just you," she admitted reluctantly.

The heaviness of regret was in his voice as Marcus replied quietly, "Yes, I thought as much. Your strenuous way of life left little sign of your virginity, but it left enough so that it could not be misread."

Victoria glared at him and was about to suggest a vulgar, physical impossibility when she was forestalled by a discreet knock at the door. Marcus opened the door and stood with his back to Victoria, who strained to hear the low, guarded conversation. The letter had been delivered to the inn. Tim and Robb would get it in the morning.

Marcus nodded his satisfaction. "Tell Lyle to weigh anchor. And, Terrence, I'm not to be disturbed unless there's an emergency." Then, carefully locking the door, Marcus turned back to Victoria. The insipid smile on his face caused her to put the table between them. She stood gripping the back of the chair, looking in vain for a place to run.

"There's no need to be afraid, Victoria. This time it will be better for you, I promise."

"No!" she flared. "I will not be your latest whore!"

He smiled indulgently. "But of course you will, my dear. Marry me or not, as you choose. But married or not, you will submit. Willingly or not, you will submit."

"Let me go, damn you! I've paid more than you had any right to demand!"

"But not nearly enough," Marcus said grimly as he locked Victoria in his arms and carried her struggling to the bed. Removing his own robe, Marcus turned Victoria to him and held her in an embrace she was helpless to break.

"You little fool," he whispered, his breath touching her eyes as his lips grazed her face in the softest of caresses. "If you fight me, I will not be able to keep my promise, and I want to keep it," he finished softly. "Let me show you the joy you have not yet experienced. Let me make love to you, Victoria. Let me satisfy you as I have not yet been able to do. Come to me. Come to me," he pleaded as his hands began their exploration of her tense, resisting body.

She shivered under the fingers whose touch was as light as a gossamer thread. A quick intake of breath and a tensing of her thighs betrayed the sparking of physical feelings she did not want Marcus to see. But when one finger traced its way from her navel to a point between her thighs, Victoria groaned as the insistent pulsing low in her body began its primitive rhythm.

Marcus smiled into her eyes as his lips brushed hers before moving down her body, seeking out and forcing the growth of each nipple. His teeth closed lightly over the softness of her breast as his hand moved slowly up her inner thigh toward another softness he was seeking.

Victoria's body jerked in a spasm of desire, and she made a desperate attempt to resist this betrayal of her body over her will. "No," she pleaded, her eyes filled with the pain of sure defeat. "Don't. Don't make me want you as you did once before. Leave me that much, at least."

"Do you want me?" Marcus asked unnecessarily. He could feel the responding, demanding need in every inch of her. Her body was hot against his. She was fighting herself now more than she was fighting him. Her breathing was quick and shallow with the effort to resist.

"Do you want me?" he asked again as he touched and teased the most sensitive area of her body.

Victoria let out a painful breath. She writhed under the tantalizing touch. Then she gave up fighting the desire, the need. Lifting Marcus's face to her own, she pressed a series of slow, light, tender yet demanding kisses on his lips. Her hands found his buttocks, and she tried to force the weight of him higher on her body so that he would penetrate her, so that he would fill her and turn the relentless craving, the insistent pulsing into a cascade of flowing, rushing waters, waters that would bring the unknown blessed release she instinctively knew would come.

"Yes," she whispered in answer to the question that now seemed so natural and so loving.

Victoria drew her breath in and held it as Marcus took her slowly, easing his way gently until she felt him in the innermost part of her, until the terrible torment she had only heard talked about over- whelmed her until she could endure no more.

Victoria strained against her lover, who was prolonging the ordeal beyond her strength. Marcus understood and built her passion to the heights, where it hung for an instant and then crashed down the other side with sharp climaxing peaks and valleys of split-second relief until the next sparking of passion sent the electricity of need and desire through her once again. And so Victoria twisted and clawed and writhed her way down from the summit to the calmer waters below. And when it was done she was worn out. Perspiration covered her body and her lungs ached in her chest from the exertion Marcus had demanded of her. Her breathing was tortured as she blew out the cleansing breaths that at last allowed her to draw air into her body.

She lay quiet at last, great tears of shame and defeat easing their way from the corners of her eyes. She turned on her side, her back to Marcus only to feel his hands rest on her breasts. ''I love you,'' he whispered.

Victoria drew in a deep tremulous breath as he pressed his body against hers, announcing that he was not yet through with her, that an already long night was to be made even longer, that her defeat would be reinforced one more time before the light of a new day lightened the darkness of the cabin.

# 13

Something had awakened him, and Marcus lay still trying to clear his head. He had been deep in sleep when some small noise had sounded its warning. He raised up on one elbow and realized that Victoria no longer lay next to him.

His heart pounded fiercely as his eyes strained to see the door. The bolt was still in place, but where was she? The light was dim. Only one candle was burning. Quickly he lit a second.

The flame flared, and Victoria stiffened as the light encompassed her. Then Marcus understood. "You're looking for something?" he asked pleasantly.

Victoria was tempted to lie, but stubborn pride changed her mind. "The key."

"Oh? Which key, my dear? There are several. One to my sea chest. One to the arms locker, and one to the door."

She directed a scathing glance his way. "I was looking for the key to the door, but any one of them will do."

Marcus laughed out loud. "In that case, my dear, I'm greatly relieved you didn't find any of them, for I have no doubt you would finish what you almost accomplished earlier."

"For what you put me through last night," she replied, "yes, I would."

Marcus smiled in satisfaction. He had made love to her twice more before they had fallen into an exhausted, contented sleep, and she had responded. His smile broadened. She had, indeed, responded.

She had fought him at first, but he had subdued all resistance and had gone to great pains to arouse the fires he knew were there. Then it had come—the passion that was as strong as his own, and he had taken her fully even as she had found the wild, sobbing release that would bind her to him forever.

A short time later breakfast was brought to their cabin, and Victoria fumed silently when Marcus fished for his keys in the base of an unused oil lamp. It was the one place she hadn't looked.

She watched intently as Marcus opened the door to accept the tray of food, but he did not let down his guard. Once more the door was locked, and the keys were deposited safely in the pocket of his robe. The smug, self-satisfied look on his face grated on Victoria's nerves, but since there was nothing she could do for the moment, she would be patient. She would wait. Sooner or later Marcus Randall would make a mistake.

Victoria satisfied herself with only a few spoonfuls of the steaming porridge. She glared at Marcus, who continued to stare. "Do you find my manners so atrocious that you must sit there ogling every move I make?"

He smiled away her rising temper. "No, my love, I find that my joy in seeing you across the table from me once again dulls my appetite for food."

Victoria flashed a nasty look his way. "Then that's your only appetite that has been dulled!"

He laughed and attacked his own bowl. Suddenly he felt much better. The old humor was back, and the spirit of rebellion was still strong. After an experience that had subdued her and had made her uncertain of her own strength, she was bouncing back, and she was learning.

When he had asked her about her lovers she had eventually told the truth. And when he had asked her what she was searching for she told the truth. Reluctantly, perhaps, but still the truth.

Because he was pleased Marcus decided to loosen the shackles just a bit. Besides, he wanted a bit of privacy himself. "I'll be on deck for about half an hour. That should give you enough time to take care of your needs."

Victoria's eyes flickered angrily in his direction. She hated this imprisonment and all the humiliation that went with it. "I'm sure it will," she replied coldly. "And what about your needs? Or don't you experience such problems? But then I always suspected you were something less than human," she concluded sweetly.

His laughter aggravated her, but she liked his answer even less. "I hope to prove to you again just how very human I am, but even the best of men must rest once in awhile," he replied with a rakish smile as he gathered up his clothes.

Muttering a few unkind words about his conceit, Victoria threw the bolt in place as she slammed the

door after him. She waited hopefully, but the sound
of the key being turned in the lock was as loud as a
pistol shot to her.

Victoria cursed in chagrin. Once on deck she was
free, for she was a strong swimmer and could make it
to shore. But for now she would heed Marcus's advice
and get herself ready to face the uncertain day.

When Marcus returned Victoria thought briefly of
keeping the bolt secured, but he would only break the
door down and then there would be no privacy at all.
Sullenly, she slid the bolt, but she would not turn the
knob. That he could do for himself.

The dismal day passed slowly. It was one of the
most wretched days of her life. Marcus spent hours
on deck, locking the door behind him, leaving her
with nothing to do. But it was worse when he
returned.

"Did you miss me?" he smirked as he entered the
cabin.

"No," Victoria replied as she casually turned to sort
out those items Marcus had crammed into his seabag.

This was not the sort of thing Marcus had in mind.
Taking the rope that pulled the opening of the seabag
closed from Victoria's hands, he smiled into the
evasive eyes. "We'll occupy ourselves more
pleasurably for the next hour or so. Or were you
saving some small chore to do as a means of avoiding
me?"

There was no point in lying. Marcus had seen
through the plan she had hoped might spare her any
further intimacy until she had a chance to escape. "I
had hoped you would leave me alone. I don't like
what you're doing."

"On the contrary, my dear, you seem to have an absolute passion for lovemaking. And quite a talent for it as well, I might add."

But Victoria was in no mood for lighthearted bantering or teasing. "I am not doing it willingly," she answered bitterly. "I'm doing all I can to resist responding to you. Surely you know that. Have you no pride? Must you continue to arouse the most primitive of passions in a woman who doesn't want you?"

There was no sign of the depth of the wound Victoria had inflicted. "Let us see just how unwilling you really are," Marcus said coldly as he picked Victoria up and carried her to the bed.

He knew exactly where to touch her, and he knew exactly where to brush his lips over her skin, and he knew when she could deny him no longer.

Against her will Victoria responded to the terrible urgency of her need. She strained to be done with it, to end this betrayal of the flesh. Then the sobbing began as she struggled to reach the pinnacle that must be scaled. When she was there Victoria stiffened and was motionless as Marcus once more gave her the greatest physical gratification she had ever known. The sharp cry of release came as she clung to the man who had become as addictive to her as morphia. She wanted him. She needed him.

When it was over Marcus held her close to him. He kissed away her tears of shame. "Don't you know how much I love you?" he asked quietly.

"This is not love," Victoria answered in a voice that was heavy with sadness. "This is an exercise in mean, spiteful power. If you loved me, you would let me go. You would allow me to make my own decisions. You know I don't want to share your bed, yet you continue to rouse those passions in me which make it impossible for me to resist."

There was a long silence before Marcus asked gently, "And did your father allow you to make your own decisions?"

"No, but he was my father, not my lover!" Victoria protested.

"But he did love you, did he not?"

"Yes, with all his heart," she answered softly, remembering so many things.

Marcus sighed. "Then perhaps we are not so different, he and I, for I love you with all *my* heart, but I will not let you go."

A great and painful despair filled Victoria's heart. It was no use. He was not going to let her go. She turned her face to the wall so Marcus would not see the tears she could not stop.

But Marcus knew the pain she endured. He moved closer to her and put his arms around her as if to ease the aching in her heart. But he was satisfied. He had done his best. Each time he had taken her he had planted his seed deep. Soon she would be with child. *Then* she would marry him. She must!

A few days later, just after dawn, they dropped anchor. Lyle and Terrence rowed ashore to fetch the horse and carriage, which had been put up at a nearby stable. They did not notice the two figures on the opposite bank making ready to cast their lines into the water.

James Bryce and his nephew had gotten up early to travel the short distance from the farm to the river. They would spend these few hours together before

James headed for the backwoods, where he had his cabin. Each year he spent much of the summer helping his sister and her husband with the farm chores, but it was almost time for him to leave, to return to the life he preferred.

When the carriage stopped near the bank on the opposite side of the river James watched with idle curiosity. This was a very early hour for travelers to be about. Then he saw a man emerge on deck carrying someone. As the sun cast its brightening rays of light, James was able to see that the person in the man's arms was a woman. The hood that covered her head fell back, and the golden hair tumbled free.

James sat up in surprise. He couldn't see the face; he was too far away, but he had seen that color hair or something very close to it every day for almost two weeks.

Turning to his nephew, he asked, "Whose ship is that, Billy? Do you recognize it?"

The boy squinted as he looked across the water, which was reflecting the sun. "That's the ship Cap'n Randall bought from Mr. Johnson."

James thought it over. "But Randall lives on this side of the river. What do you think he's up to over there?"

"I don't know, Uncle Jim, but Pa says the captain has some land a good day's journey from here."

The carriage pulled away, leaving James Bryce with a very uneasy feeling. He hadn't been close enough to see clearly, and the sun reflecting off the water hadn't helped much. But he had a feeling he had best be getting back to Annapolis to see if Miss Chisholm was there. He'd lose a week or so, but he was a woodsman who had survived for some years by playing his

hunches and he wasn't going to ignore this one.
Hastily he gathered his gear, thinking he was playing
the part of a fool, but if something was wrong, the
quicker he knew the better.

As the carriage jostled along at the best safe speed,
several hours passed before Victoria awoke from the
drug-induced sleep. Her head ached and her stomach
could not be trusted. Each jolt threatened to make her
ill. She moaned and buried her face against the chest
of the man who was supporting her.

Marcus ordered the carriage to pull to the side of
the narrow road and helped Victoria out, allowing her
to rest in the shade of the trees for almost half an hour
until she got over the worst of the wrenching sickness
induced by the drugged tea.

Wetting a handkerchief with water from his
canteen, Marcus bathed her face and hands. "Are you
able to continue?"

Victoria tried to nod, but her head only bobbed and
slumped. They traveled until the road became a trail,
and the carriage could go no further. Vaguely aware
that Marcus was carrying her, Victoria struggled to
clear her head, but it was a useless effort. She saw the
cabin only through a gauzy haze, and then there was
nothing. She was not aware of the seaman bringing in
the luggage, nor was she aware of Marcus putting her
to bed.

Slowly Victoria became aware of the fact that she
was awake. The sun streamed into the room from a
high, small window. Throwing her arm across her
eyes to block out the light that shot bolts of pain
through her head, Victoria moaned and rolled onto
her side. She had a splitting headache and could only
dimly remember that she was no longer aboard ship.

"A cabin," she thought disjointedly, and could not remember how she had gotten here.

With a supreme effort Victoria was able to slide her legs out of bed and sit up. Again she moaned and put her head in her hands. Marcus had drugged her! How long had she been here?

Victoria shivered and only then realized that she had been put to bed without a nightdress. She squinted her eyes against the light and saw her robe where it had fallen to the floor. As she bent to pick it up, she groaned in pain and went to her knees. "Damn him," she sobbed weakly, even as she felt strong arms supporting her and lifting her to her feet.

"My robe," she whimpered, and Marcus slipped it over her shoulders.

"A little fresh air will help. Can you walk to the necessary or would you like me to carry you?"

The question registered, and Victoria realized that she most certainly did need to visit the outdoor privy. "I'll walk if it kills me," she muttered through clenched teeth, and Marcus tried to hide his smile, for she would be in no condition to give him any trouble for many hours.

When Victoria emerged from the small, outdoor privy her robe was on properly and buttoned. She felt better, and she refused any help as she stepped gingerly in bare feet over the stones and stubble that formed a path of sorts back to the cabin. But this time Victoria saw her new house clearly.

It was built like a fort. Rough logs formed the stout walls. The few windows were high and narrow. The door was made of thick, impenetrable oak, and there was nothing to be seen outside the cabin but trees. They were in a wilderness, but where? Was it somewhere near the Ainsley cabin or was it close to the place she had met the Frenchman and the Indians? When she escaped which way should she run?

There were only questions without answers, but as Victoria's mind began to clear, she remembered the property Marcus had described to the Ainsleys aboard the *Maryann*. A day's journey northwest of Richmond, he had said. "Yes, of course," she thought triumphantly. She would head for Richmond. The sun and the stars would be her guides.

Her dark mood lifted now that she knew where she was and in which direction she would run. She needed no encouragement to help Marcus throw together a hearty breakfast of bacon and fried potatoes seasoned with bits of onion. There was even salt in the cupboard.

Marcus sat back contentedly. The coffee was hot; the cookies Ruby had baked were still edible, and later he would help Victoria make biscuits.

His smile broadened. She had eaten like a deckhand, and well she might. She had had no food in her stomach since Tuesday night and it was well past Thursday noon. Victoria had been under the effect of the drug he had put in her tea for almost two days.

"If you're feeling up to it, you might want to unpack a few of your things and settle into your new home," Marcus suggested amiably.

A defiant answer was on the tip of Victoria's tongue, but she decided against it. She had no intention of being here long enough to *settle in*. That, however, was something she would keep to herself. It would be very stupid, indeed, to put Marcus on his guard. In fact, she would try to do the very opposite.

If she were a good enough actress, she might even convince him that she was quite content in this miserable cabin in the middle of this miserable wilderness.

For the most part Victoria curbed the rebellious anger that simmered under the surface. She did what she could to make life bearable. While Marcus fetched wood, she heated water. He washed and rinsed the sheets; she took care of the smaller items. But always, Victoria looked for an opportunity to escape. An opportunity that never came, for Marcus watched her every move. She was never given an opportunity to run.

Even the few moments of privacy he allowed her were of little comfort, for Victoria lived in a state of constant apprehension. At any time of the day Marcus would come up behind her, put his arms around her and begin to rouse the passion she could not hold from him. And never did he miss a single night of lovemaking. She was left exhausted while he seemed to grow stronger. Her nerves were strained to breaking.

The fear that was always with her grew to monstrous proportions. She became short-tempered and irritable. It came to a head one day when she wandered to the small woodland pool to swim and bathe in the cool water and to seek the solitude she needed.

On some days Marcus would join her in the swimming hole. The coldness of the water would stimulate his desire and he would take her there. On other days, such as today, he would sit contentedly under a large willow, watching in fascination as his little water nymph swam and splashed until her skin crinkled. Either way he was quite content with his life.

When she had had enough Victoria climbed onto the bank and rubbed off briskly. Spreading the wet towel under her, she lay on her stomach, occasionally reaching up to fluff her hair so the sun could penetrate every layer, and Marcus drank in the beauty of her bronzed, naked body, which seemed to absorb the very glow of the sun she loved.

He breathed to ease the constriction in his chest, and he wondered if the heart could actually swell with the fullness of love. He smiled at the atypical romantic sentiment. But he *was* in love. Hopelessly so. Victoria was his heart and soul. Never, so long as he drew breath on this earth, would that love diminish.

And she loved him. From time to time he had caught her looking at him with an expression of wistful tenderness on her face. A hundred times, after the passion had been spent and she lay exhausted and content in his arms, she had whispered the words that put his heart at ease.

He smiled at his own foolishness. He had once called her scrawny. Nothing could be further from the truth. Slender, yes. But she was not skinny. The flesh was smooth and sensuous, and it covered that delicate frame with fluid grace. Her bones could not be much larger than those of a small bird, but they carried her feathery weight with a strength and an endurance that had surprised him. She was swift of foot, a fact he had discovered to his chagrin, and her movements were as light as the wind—and just as elusive.

He frowned. The uneasy stirrings had returned as

they always did when his mind dwelled too long on his golden Lorelei. And she was growing restless. The tension between them was building, but still she had not agreed to marry him, and still she was not with child.

A baby would settle her down. It had to. It was the only hope he had left. His need and passion grew stronger, and he went to her.

Kneeling at her side, his fingers traced the gentle curve of her back. His arms straddled her and he bent his head to kiss the smoothness of her shoulder. Then his hands slipped under her and he turned her to him. His lips touched the coolness of her breasts, then moved downward. His body throbbed with desire, and he began to remove his clothing, but Victoria's eyes flashed in anger and her face hardened with resolve.

"This is hardly the time or place," she muttered from between clenched teeth, unable to hide her irritation.

For an instant Marcus froze. For weeks she had loved him. She had come willingly to his bed. It was something she enjoyed as much as he. Never had she been passive. And now this shattering rejection of the strongest bond between them.

Fear gripped him, for he knew how easy it was to grow weary of one's bedpartner. He had done it himself. Many times. Now he reacted badly.

"Any time or place I choose to make love to you is right, my dear. Never forget that." His tone was flat to cover the turmoil of his mind, and his hands were rough as he attempted to enforce his will.

"No!" And to emphasize her absolute refusal, Victoria pushed away.

Unbridled anger replaced fear. Marcus curled his
fingers in the damp hair and forced Victoria's face up.
His eyes were cold. There was no room for com-
passion. *"Never* say no to me, Victoria. I will not
tolerate your refusing me. I should have thought you
would have already learned that painful lesson. I
prefer you come to me willingly, but if I must use
force, I will."

"You have no right!" she panted, stung by a fury as
great as his. "You have no right to keep me here and I
won't stay. I've had enough. I've suffered enough."

"Stop it!" Marcus commanded harshly. A stinging
slap from the flat of his hand emphasized his words.

Quick tears sprang into Victoria's eyes, but they
were tears of anger and chagrin. She slapped him
back, and the crack of her hand across his face stilled
the birds. For a long minute the whole world was
silent as Marcus stared at her in disbelief. Then it
came.

Three, then four quick, stinging blows were struck
in rapid succession. Victoria barely had time to get
her hands up, but it didn't matter. Marcus jerked
them back down and landed one last sharp, painful
slap. Then he pulled her to her feet, scooped her
under his arm and carried her like a sack of rice back
to the house.

Throwing her on the bed, he stormed out and
locked the door behind him. Victoria buried her face
in the sweet-smelling pillow, then turned on her back
and looked up at the high, small window. She sighed
in defeat. She would never get through. She had
thought of it many times before and had rejected it.

She beat her fists into the mattress, and hot, salty
tears of anguish ran from the outer corners of her eyes

into her ears and hair. Her nose was stuffed up; her head ached, and she didn't feel well.

Victoria lay still, breathing deeply, practicing the discipline she had learned as a child. Gradually her nerves calmed and she finally admitted to herself that she was never going to get away from this place without help. They would come. They had to come.

As the room darkened, Victoria roused herself. She couldn't hide here forever, and she decided to face Marcus now. She didn't know what to expect. His moods could swing as widely as her own, but she didn't care. No matter what he did to her, she didn't care.

But Marcus, too, had had time to think, time to calm his anger and fears. He watched as Victoria prepared the coffee for the evening meal and then ladled out the thick porridge that would hold them until breakfast. They were running low on supplies. Soon he would have to take her to Serenity whether he wanted to or not.

He sighed heavily. She had not changed. She was still as arrogant and just as willful and spoiled as she had been the night they first met. And just as dangerous.

Her refusal still rankled him. She had gotten away with it this time, but there would be no next time. Once more she was becoming difficult, and Marcus did not like it.

His brooding was interrupted as Victoria's words registered. He leaned back in his chair and studied the earnest, pleading face. "How long?" he repeated. "I thought I made that clear. Until I tire of you." He smiled. "And that day might be very close, indeed. You're not the most docile of creatures."

Victoria knew he was teasing her, trying to lighten her mood, but she was in deadly earnest. "I wasn't raised to be docile," she replied wearily. "Nor subservient. You must allow me to live my own life. Something you seem entirely unwilling to even consider. Please, Marcus, set me free."

"But, my dear, how can I? For surely you would have the law on my heels before I had a chance to turn around. I would not like to be forced to flee across the mountains to New France. Perhaps the West Indies would be more to my liking. When I've made a decision I'll let you know."

Victoria's eyes were solemn. Her voice pleaded. "Let me go. This is no good for either of us. We cannot spend the rest of our lives like this. I will swear to go my way and cause you no trouble. I will absolve you in writing if that's what you want. I give you my word."

There was an edge to Marcus's voice that Victoria recognized. "We'll have no more conversations on this topic. Do not ask again. Do you understand?"

She fought the frustration. "Yes, I understand." It was useless.

She had looked for every opportunity to get away from this place but had found none. She was watched constantly and was beginning to feel like an insect under the scientist's glass. Neither did she know how Marcus was able to tolerate the life they led here.

To make matters worse, she was past due, and she was afraid. What would happen when he finally realized that she was most probably pregnant, that he had, in all likelihood, fathered a bastard child? They were constantly together. He would know soon enough.

Victoria hoped desperately that Philippe and Spotted Wolf would understand the message, that they would be able to find her and soon, for unless she left him unattended, unconscious and bleeding, there was no escape from Marcus Randall. Victoria was not yet willing to risk his life for her freedom.

Her nerves were stretched tight. It took great effort to keep a calm facade, and the decisions that had to be made weighed heavily on Victoria's mind.

She needed to get away, to go somewhere where she could think without bumping into Marcus with every other step. And she had to go before it was too late. Already she had changed. She was not the same woman who had sailed from England. And she must not change. She must hold to her resolve. She must carry out her father's wishes. Marcus Randall could not be allowed to interfere or change the path that had been set out for her long before she knew he existed.

She shook her head in glum silence. It was impossible. She was right back where she had started. It was an endless maze with no way out. She enjoyed his body just as he enjoyed hers, and, in her own way, she loved him, but she doubted seriously if theirs was a love poets would immortalize. Still she would miss him.

And he was still trying to make her into something she was not. That had always been the greatest problem. She must go her own way. She had better things to do than allow a man to control her through her body, and he had done a beautiful job of that. She gave him credit even as she acknowledged it.

When the table had been cleared and the last plate dried Marcus sat in his chair and pulled Victoria onto his lap. As he rested his cheek against her head, he asked, "Are you really so unhappy, Vickie?"

"Yes," she answered truthfully, knowing it wasn't the answer he wanted. "This is not my world, and I am not willing to live in it. I cannot be what you want me to be, and I cannot change."

Then she tried to soften the pain. "We both know that I have no great love for sweeping and dusting and wouldn't do any of it if you didn't hound me. I think you would make a better housewife than I ever will."

She knew that she had succeeded in taking some of the sting out of her words and out of the actions she already regretted when he looked at her with that suggestive leer on his face and replied, "Tell me that in bed, my dear."

She laughed. "You don't leave me breath enough to talk."

As he picked her up to carry her to the bedroom, there was a knock at the door. Cursing softly, Marcus put her down and went for the pistol he kept locked away. He opened the door cautiously.

"Ah, monsieur, a thousand pardons," the stranger said in his heavily accented English. "It seems that I have lost my way and by some merciful providence, I stumbled onto your cabin. I wonder if you would be so kind as to point out the road to Richmond?"

Marcus looked at the man whose smile was open and whose dark eyes sparkled with friendliness. "Come in. I can sketch a rough map and put you on the right trail. There are several that bear away from Richmond and none of them are marked."

Victoria betrayed no emotion as she watched Philippe stand at the table while Marcus sketched the map. When it was done Marcus explained it carefully, then led the man to the door to show him the way. As he did, he was struck a vicious blow from behind with the butt of the Frenchman's pistol.

Victoria winced when she heard the sickening sound, but it had to be done. The blood would congeal and the bleeding would stop. It sounded worse than it actually was. Philippe had handled the whole matter with precise timing and great skill.

Then she heard the sound that sent her flying from the cabin. Tim and Robb were calling her name. The minute they saw her the two seamen rushed forward and embraced her in a hug she thought she might never escape. James and Spotted Wolf were more dignified in their greeting.

She put her arms through those of her bodyguards and the three of them walked side by side back to the cabin. Spotted Wolf trussed Marcus securely as Victoria watched through eyes that were troubled. She was deserting him again. He had good reason not to trust her, but he had brought this misfortune on himself. He was most fortunate to be escaping with his life. Any other man would have died weeks ago.

"Are you all right, mademoiselle?" Philippe asked as his eyes took in what was obviously a comfortable and rather charming little house and wondered if the title madame might not be more appropriate.

Victoria's eyes were bleak. "Physically, I'm in good shape if you discount the fact that I think I'm pregnant," she answered, remembering how Marcus hated that word. "My suffering has been in my thoughts and indecision. I need time to think. I need to go where Marcus can't find me unless I want to be found."

Spotted Wolf stepped forward. "You will come

with us back to my people. There you will be able to work out what troubles you."

She looked at him gratefully. "Yes, I'll come."

Turning to Tim and Robb, she gave explicit orders. "He is not to be hurt, do you understand?"

The two men glanced down at the unconscious man on the floor. They gave a disgusted grunt but nodded in compliance as she continued. "Give us until morning, then release him. By the time he gets to his estate we will have an insurmountable lead. Then you and James follow as quickly as possible. And please," she added, "make sure he's all right. He was hit quite a blow."

Then, pausing for a moment before committing herself, Victoria made the only decision she could. "Tell Captain Randall to go home. I will send a message to him as soon as I know what I'm going to do. You are not to mention the fact that I am probably carrying his child. I haven't made up my mind about that, either."

Tim and Robb looked at their mistress in shocked surprise. They understood her meaning. She was thinking of getting rid of the babe she might be carrying. They knew that some women who attempted this dangerous thing died for their efforts. To think that Miss Victoria would even consider it was madness.

Hastily Victoria rolled some of her clothing in a blanket and said to Philippe, "There's still some food left. Take whatever we'll need."

The Frenchman chose a few items to fill out their dwindling rations. "We will not do much eating, mademoiselle. Mostly we eat a bit from the saddle. We must get through the mountains as quickly as possible."

Picking up her light bundle, Victoria stopped and stared for a long moment at Marcus. "Good-bye, my love," she whispered.

Philippe let out a soft whistle. "So, it is like that?"

"Yes," Victoria answered unhappily. "It's a mess."

The confusion in the Frenchman's eyes said that he didn't understand. His unasked question was ignored as Victoria walked out of the door. Those left behind pulled up chairs and perched like birds of prey, watching until Marcus tried to move his hand to rub away the pain that throbbed in his head and found that he could not. He opened his eyes and groaned as he tried to focus on the blurred images above him. As his vision cleared, he looked into the faces of angry men.

"So, you're awake are ya, Cap'n? If we had our way, we'd cut you up in little pieces and feed ya to the sharks, but Miss Victoria said ya wasn't to be harmed, so we'll just let ya lay there where we can keep a close eye on ya," Tim snarled.

Terror showed in Marcus's eyes. "Victoria? Is she all right? If any harm comes to her . . ."

"Easy now, mate," Robb interrupted. "Miss Victoria's all right. We came to rescue her from you! Got things kinda mixed up, don't ya? We're her friends."

"Friends?" he repeated, not understanding. "But how did you know where to look?"

"Well, Cap'n," Tim volunteered, not able to disguise his malice, "the note we got from Miss Victoria kinda had some instructions in it. Somethin' you wouldn't know about. But it was clear enough to us. Then James here caught up to us. He saw ya take Miss Victoria off your boat though he wasn't sure at the time it was her. When everything was put together proper like we knew where to look, right enough."

The picture was terribly clear as Marcus realized Victoria had been waiting for these friends since she had written the letter. She had not shown the slightest sign of recognition when that man had come to the door and into the house. She had stood there like the docile, well-trained wife he wanted her to be. She had not given one word of warning but had waited and had seen the blow come.

He strained his body so he could see into the other room. "She's gone?"

Tim stared at the man in disbelief. "You don't think she'd be here. Not when . . ."

Robb stopped him. "Watch your mouth, mate. You heard the orders, same as me."

Marcus turned his head to one side, but not before Robb saw the moisture-filled eyes. He took a kinder tack and with gruff sympathy said, "What you done coulda got you killed, Cap'n. She's gone now, but she said that we was to release ya tomorrow, that you was to go home. She'll send word to ya there when she's made up her mind."

Marcus didn't understand the message. What was there to decide? He had lost her again, and this time there was not even anger to help ease the terrible grief. He could only cling to the hope that she would contact him, that somehow he would be able to find her. He would go to Annapolis. He would beg her to marry him, but she had said to wait at Serenity.

"Will she return to her farm?"

"No, Cap'n, she's gone where you'll never find her," Robb answered.

Marcus closed his eyes against the tears he could not contain. He would go home and wait. He would trust her to keep her promise. He had to.

James had been watching and listening and thought he understood the situation. He chewed his tobacco, then spat into the dying embers of the fire. He listened to the familiar hissing, then said, "You're either a fool, Cap'n, or you're love-struck. Both about the same, I reckon."

"Yes," Marcus answered quietly. "I love her."

The next morning Robb cut the thongs from wrists and ankles. The three men mounted their horses and Tim looked at Marcus, trying to decide whether or not to obey orders. This man, if Victoria was right, was the father of the child she was carrying. It seemed to him that the cap'n had a right to know. He decided against it and said instead, "You're a lucky man, Cap'n. Had Miss Victoria said the word, you'd be dead now. And if she said she'd send a message, then she'll do just that. Never known her to break her word. We'll leave your pistol further down the trail. You can come after it if you've a mind ta."

He turned and trotted off behind the others and was lost to sight. Marcus walked to the swimming hole and sat leaning against the accommodating tree. He buried his head in his arms while silent sobs racked his body.

# 14

Victoria was silent as she journeyed toward Spotted Wolf's village. Her thoughts were diffused. She made little effort to pull them together. There was a decision that must be reached, but for now she simply refused to make any conscious effort to solve the problem that had engulfed her. Instead she deliberately allowed her mind to take in the sensual perceptions that flooded upon her and filled her brain with color, sound and smell.

Riding with Philippe and Spotted Wolf, she barely looked up when the three who had guarded Marcus rejoined the small party, so unknowing had her conscious state become. It was more than the meditation she had learned and practiced in years gone by. This was a blurring of vision, and she saw as in some dark dream.

At Spotted Wolf's insistence no one disturbed Victoria as her pony obediently followed, keeping pace with the short, brisk trot of the wiry, seemingly tireless animals ahead of him.

On the second day all awareness left her mind. She was oblivious to her surroundings, responding to no one, seeing and hearing nothing of the external world. She sat unmoving on her pony for some time after the group had halted for the night. Not until the quiet, intense gaze of Spotted Wolf pierced the barrier to reality did her mind begin its descent from the mountain. She turned her head to answer the dark, penetrating eyes that reached out to her in silent communion.

"When you seek the Great Spirit and see your visions you must not forget to come back," the Indian reminded her gently.

Putting his arms up to receive her, he supported Victoria's weight as she swung a leg over the saddle and came to him in one fluid, boneless move. Tim and Robb hastened to unroll and spread her blanket. Then the two of them watched uneasily as the Indian put their mistress down and folded the protective covering around her.

"*Le Cougar* has been on a distant journey. Her spirit is tired and she must rest," he stated simply as he held Victoria's hand in his and spoke in a guttural, soothing tone until she fell into a normal sleep.

The two seamen looked at each other uneasily. Spotted Wolf had decided upon the name by which Victoria would be known to his people. It was almost as though he had laid claim to her. They didn't like it, and they shuffled over to join James Bryce.

"What's wrong with her?" Tim asked. "It's like she's dying."

James stared into the flames of the campfire. His words were slow and uncertain. "I've seen something like it in Indian ceremonies. What they call purifying themselves and communing with the spirits or ghosts. Don't know if I can explain it, but it's almost like they can forget their bodies and send their minds where they want."

Noticing that Spotted Wolf's eyes were on him, he asked, "Can you explain it a little better?"

"I can, but I will not," the Indian replied not unkindly, and then rolled himself in his own blanket, leaving the men to eat their small meal in silence.

But Spotted Wolf did not find rest for some time after he had withdrawn from the others. His mind pondered the feeling of kinship he had felt for this young woman the very first time he had seen her emerge from the swirling ground mist on a cold March morning. His son had put his own thoughts into words when he had called her *le cougar,* and this ability she possessed to send her spirit to the mountaintop as the shaman of his people did had shaken him to the deepest, most primitive part of his being.

Without the purifying smoke, the fasting or the chanting, she had put herself into the hands of the Great Spirit, and the great god of all creation had returned her safely. She had been touched gently by his hand. She had come back to him and his people.

The first rays of the sun awakened him, and he felt the pang of fear in his heart when he saw *Le Cougar's* blanket was empty. Then a faint sound caught his attention, and he turned toward it.

Spotted Wolf relaxed and smiled. *Le Cougar* had not disappeared in a puff of smoke. She was returning to camp from the woods. Her face was relaxed and peaceful. Whatever evil demon she had struggled against had been banished.

But he was not prepared for her next move. Engrossed in her own thoughts, Victoria stood on the high bluff and faced the rising sun. She raised her arms toward it and intoned a chant that was barely audible to his straining ears, but he understood.

Never had he seen the white man give thanks in the old way. Never had he seen them acknowledge the power that had created all things and that determined all things. For even though her words were strange, the cadence and purpose were unmistakable.

He waited until she turned back toward him before speaking. "Your path is clear?"

"The more urgent of my questions was answered. The second I must decide for myself."

Spotted Wolf showed his teeth in silent laughter but decided against saying anything more as Tim stomped over to see how his employer was feeling. He and Robb had been extremely concerned but had not interfered in something they did not understand for fear of doing the wrong thing.

Victoria heard the uncertainty in his voice. "I'm fine, Tim. I've made my decision," she said in a firm, steady voice, then rose to accompany her friend to the fire that would soon be extinguished.

Camp broke a few minutes later when Philippe signaled that it was time to move on. The wiry Frenchman took the lead as the small group continued its rapid pace into the mountainous terrain that stood between them and safety from the pursuers he hoped would not come. He would be very disappointed if Captain Randall did not do as he was told. The man must not follow them even if he possessed the skill to track them through this difficult terrain, something Philippe doubted.

The final climb brought them to a pass from which unfolded a view that defied description. The valley below resembled nothing so much as a haven from all care with its sparkling waters and wide expanse of forest and meadow. From where she sat her horse Victoria could see a cluster of odd, elongated huts with curved roofs among the more familiar structures. A thin wisp of smoke was coming from some of these lodges. Their pace quickened as they drew closer to this sanctuary.

Several Indians rode out to meet Spotted Wolf. All were well armed with muskets and lances, and each Indian wore a knife and hatchet. But their warlike appearance melted under the warmth of Running Deer's smile.

He greeted his father with great dignity but also with the deep love of a son for his father, and Spotted Wolf answered in the same bumpy, guttural language Victoria had yet to understand. But when he turned to her and spoke in French she realized that they had briefly discussed what was to be done with her and had come to a satisfactory solution.

The older Indian turned to Philippe. "You have room for her?"

Philippe smiled. Even if he had not one inch of space to spare, he would have said yes. Miss Chisholm would be good company for his wife, Raven's Wing. And so it was settled. Victoria was taken under the care of the motherly Raven's Wing, daughter of the Micmacs, one of the many belonging to the powerful Algonquin confederation.

And with great pride Raven's Wing escorted her guest into the spacious, three-room cabin and introduced her to the usually boisterous but suddenly shy children. Thereafter Victoria was one of the family. No one made any special effort to pamper her nor in any way make her feel an outsider. She was assigned chores and whatever her shortcomings, no one seemed to notice.

Tim and Robb were given a long list of written instructions, for Victoria had decided to stay. She would allow the child within her to live. That had been the uncertainty that had plagued her, the decision she had needed to make quickly, and she had made it.

But she would stay here. If necessary, it would not be too difficult for others to reach her, but she would be away from all the well-intentioned, not-to-be-endured, outraged sympathies of Bess and the nagging of Josiah to seek vengeance. She did not know what she was going to do about Marcus. That was the decision that was yet to be made.

However, she had accepted the fact that her child might very well be the second bastard in her father's family. Not even for the sake of this child would she subject herself to the absolute authority Marcus would have under the law if she married him. He could make life very difficult for her.

Yet she winced as she remembered the cruelty of the young ladies into whose company she had been thrown upon her return to England. They had not hesitated to inform her of her undesirability in correct society. Nor had she missed the snide glances of their elders. The pain had been dreadful, but she had survived. Badly scarred. Bitter. But she had made it.

Now those who had pointed the finger of scorn at her were in her debt. It hadn't been difficult. Some she had ruined already. Others waited in fear for their turn. And it was coming.

Victoria bowed her head. She had suffered as only a fourteen-year-old can. She did not wish that terrible agony for her child.

Robb's voice jerked her back to the present. She had thought all the old bitterness had been left behind. "James will escort you and Tim back to the farm, where he will pick up the trade goods for next season and transport them to the Ainsley cabin. Be sure Mr. Coster gets my instructions, and he'll take care of the rest."

Neither sailor wanted to leave her among these heathens with no one to protect her, and they argued fiercely. But their protests got them nowhere. Reluctantly they agreed to accompany James back across the mountains, but they clearly were not happy.

Victoria smiled and put her hands to Robb's rough face. "Thank you, my friend. This is the way you can be of best service to me. I shall wait here until you return." Then she slipped the necklace Spotted Wolf had given her around the sailor's neck. "Wear this. It will protect you, but just in case," she smiled mischievously, "be careful. And above all, listen to James. At least until you're out of the woods."

Robb smiled back, but the troubled frown was not totally erased from his face.

September was blessed with warm days and cool nights. These pleasant days passed quickly, for Victoria was kept busy helping Raven's Wing put by the stores of food her family would need to carry them through the winter. And when that was done there was still no rest, for Victoria must learn the art of readying furs that would be needed to make the parka that would keep her warm during the time of bitter cold. So she scraped, rubbed, chewed and stitched. Perspiration ran down her face from the sheer force of her concentration. Raven's Wing glanced her way and smiled frequently.

At last the parka was finished, and Victoria frequently fled the noisy confines of Philippe's cabin to visit Old Bird, a Delaware who had fled the sickness and the evil of the white man with a pitiful remnant of his tribe. He could have fled to his brothers in the north or to the Miamis a little further west, but he had chosen this neutral ground for his people, the land of the ancient mounds, the land that had been revealed to him in his vision.

And now Spotted Wolf, a practical man not given to imaginings, had brought this woman to them and had revealed his own dream. The final decision would rest with Old Bird. For this reason, and also because he had outlived his hatred, the venerable shaman instructed Victoria in the ancient knowledge.

For hours they sat by the fire while Old Bird fingered the talking sticks, the sticks that told the story of how his people, who called themselves the Lenni Lenape, had traveled from a country that now lay beyond the western sea to the lands of plenty at the edge of the eastern sea. Eyes grown dim with age stared into the fire as he recited the legend of his people.

Although Old Bird's English was very poor, Victoria was beginning to pick up the shadowy, poetic language that was his own. Together, and in both languages, they communicated and grew in respect for each other. But there were times when her heart was full of sorrow, for these people still clung to a life that was dying. If they wished to survive, they must change.

James and men like him were only the spearhead of what was to come, for the white man would sweep across this land, driving the Indian before him until there was no place left to run. Her eyes narrowed in determination. Old Bird must learn to use the white man's law for the good of his people. It could be done. And Victoria began to explain a few of the possibilities to the shaman, who listened intently. He would consider all that she had said.

Then, to amuse the children at those rare times the cabin had grown quiet during the cold winter evenings, Victoria would retell all she had heard of the story told by Old Bird and the talking sticks. Raven's Wing, who was not of the Delaware, nevertheless did not wander too far from the intimate group while keeping her hands busy making a dress for the woman who was outgrowing her own clothing and could let the waists of her few dresses out no further.

Time came to have little meaning for them as the days passed routinely. The nights were gratefully accepted as release from the small tasks that kept them all busy. And as Victoria's time came nearer, her mood darkened. She must decide soon.

But she was not sorry she had chosen to let her baby live. Each move, each stirring of the restless child within seemed to bring a contentment that was certainly unreasonable under the circumstances. Often she laughed at herself, but the laughter lost its cutting edge when she put her hand to the spot where she had felt the life that was becoming more important than her own.

Then, on a dreary day in February, one of the men who had been trapping far from the settlement returned with as many furs as he could transport. This action was repeated again and again as the men struggled home. The Great Spirit had heard their cries. The animals that had grown so scarce returned in great numbers. Never had pelts been so thick. Never had there been so many.

Spotted Wolf was silent as he listened and watched. Then he talked with Old Bird. The decision was made. She was to be one of them. They would adopt her into the tribe and the unborn child she carried as well. Both men were now convinced that *Le Cougar* had been sent to them by the force known as Manitou, and whether for good or for evil, they must accept her into their midst.

Moving more awkwardly now, Victoria stood, put her hands to the small of her back and tried to stretch out the pain. She smiled at Raven's Wing. "What do the women say my child will be?"

The squaw's eyes sparkled with her teasing. "My Philippe tells me what has happened and how you would allow no harm to come to the good *capitain*. I think you wish for a boy like his father."

Victoria frowned. "If it is a boy, and if he is anything like his father, I should drown him at birth."

The Indian smiled serenely. She knew the longing that was in this golden one's heart. She had heard the restless stirrings at night when everything was still and thoughts came to the mind. "You have decided?"

Victoria heard the question and knew the meaning. "Yes, I decided weeks ago. I will send for Marcus. If he comes, I will explain what I have in mind. If he accepts, the child will at least have a father in name if not in fact. If he doesn't come, then that will be the end of it.''

Raven's Wing and Philippe had discussed the situation as best they could piece it together. Neither could understand Victoria's reluctance to settle down and be happy with a husband and family. Finally, they had shrugged and had stopped thinking about it. It was her life, after all, and they were happy to have her here with them. It was good company for Raven's Wing, who had raised a large brood of children herself and found great joy in them.

The seasons had once again turned full circle. It was time for Spotted Wolf to lead his men to the cabin of William and Ellen Ainsley, where they would meet James Bryce. Philippe was then to send James to Serenity. He was to tell Marcus only that she wished to see him. If he agreed to come, he was to be escorted back to William's cabin. From there Philippe and Spotted Wolf would bring him to this village.

If he did not wish to come, he was to be told nothing more and no further action was to be taken. But to be sure Marcus believed the message came from her Victoria removed her ring and handed it to the Frenchman.

Philippe nodded his approval. ''One of you must show some sense. Soon there will be more than your own selfish whims to consider. I think Captain Randall will come and when he sees your condition will agree to any terms you lay down.''

Victoria smiled at her friend. ''You have more confidence than I. What I ask will not be easy for him to agree to. He has very definite ideas about what he does and does not want."

"We shall see, *ma petite,* but with such an important mission I think we must be on our way very soon. We would not want the little one to be born without his father, eh?"

His smile was kind, but Victoria's eyes were pensive. "You and Raven's Wing have been very good to me, and I shall never truly be able to repay you. One day, perhaps, the opportunity will come so that I may pay some small portion of my debt."

Philippe's dark eyes sparkled with gaiety. "Enough, mademoiselle, or my tears shall water down the soup!"

Then he turned his attention to his wife and kissed her on the cheek. "*Ma cherie,* do you think you could feed your husband, or must I take another wife to care for my needs?"

Raven's Wing rapped him smartly on the knuckles with the wooden spoon. "You do and I kill you both!" she hissed.

Philippe and Victoria laughed together, but the two women hurried to put the meal on the table. Victoria ate the same food she had only picked at for months and thought that it tasted much better than usual, but the observant Frenchman who sat quietly across from her was worried.

Although her belly had enlarged nicely to accommodate the growing child, the rest of her body had grown even thinner. Her face and neck, which were exposed by the collarless deerskin dress, looked scrawny. The shoulders of the garment that had been made to allow for the usual plumping of a soon-to-be mother hung desolately over the angles of barely

fleshed bone. And despite the outward calm, Philippe
knew of the inner torment that had been caused by
this Randall fellow and by her own foolishness.

"*Mon capitain* will come whether he wishes or no,"
he thought sourly.

The caravan transporting the furs was made ready
the next day, and Victoria watched silently as the
group of men and horses made their way into the
rising hills. There was no joy in her heart as they were
lost to sight, only doubt and uncertainty.

But Philippe, who urged his horse through the
rock- and snow-covered terrain, had no doubts. Not
for months. Not since Tim and Robb had told him of
the agony in the eyes of this Randall fellow when he
learned that Victoria had escaped him. No. The
Frenchman was surer of Captain Randall's reaction
than he was of his obstinate guest's, a woman old
enough to know that things could not always be just
exactly as one wished.

A short time after their arrival at William Ainsley's
cabin Philippe and the others had concluded their
dealings. James then agreed to travel to Serenity
while the rest of the party waited here. And William,
who had remained safe behind the feathers and
stones, showed his gratitude to Spotted Wolf and his
men. Everything he had, he shared, and Ellen used
the last of her precious spices and raisins in a bread
pudding rich with cinnamon sauce. But most
satisfying of all was the fact that they were learning to
survive in a hard country that forgave few mistakes.
And they stood all the taller for it.

At this moment of William's content James faced a
disheveled, distracted Marcus Randall at the

plantation called Serenity. Marcus stared blankly at
the ring James had put into his hand. Victoria was
asking him to come to her in the wilderness territory.
He might be going to his death, but there was not the
slightest hesitation. Of course he would go. Nothing
could stop him.

Victoria's men had told him that their mistress
would send a message. They had told him she did not
break her word. He hadn't dared believe them, but he
had hoped. Despite himself, he had hoped.

But he had almost succumbed to total despair. For
months he had not dared set foot off his property for
fear he would miss the messenger he waited for.
Then, after months of agonized waiting, after months
of drowning in a haze of drunkenness and ill temper
that caused everyone to keep out of his way, the
message had come.

The house slaves, Zeb and Ruby, jumped to carry
out the bellowing orders from their suddenly
exuberant master. They hastened to throw together
the provisions he ordered as he tore to his room to
collect several changes of clothing and his shaving
gear. They didn't know what had happened, but they
didn't care. It was enough for them that the terrible
dull pain that had been in this man's eyes since his
return from his hunting lodge had now disappeared.

As Marcus bounded down the stairs with full saddle
bags flung over his shoulder, James Bryce, having
pondered the planter's reaction to the message from
Miss Chisholm, decided to go one step further than he
had been authorized, for he had learned from
Philippe pretty much how the situation now stood.
And knowing the customs of some Indians, he
thought it only prudent that Captain Randall be

prepared for any eventuality.

Holding up his hand, the usually taciturn woodsman who was beginning to enjoy his role, said,
"Whoa there, Cap'n. Seein' as how you're goin' to be
a guest in Spotted Wolf's village for a spell, it might be
right smart to take a little present."

For if things turned out the way Philippe thought
they might, it was customary for the groom to offer a
token gift to his bride's family, and as far as James
was concerned Spotted Wolf wasn't about to be
insulted by not receiving something in return for his
adopted sister. That was no way for a man to keep his
scalp.

"Injuns," he thought wryly, "got their own way of
collectin' a dowry."

Marcus was uncertain. "What kind of gift? In God's
name, man, spell it out. I'm in no condition to think
about fancy geegaws that might appeal to the
savages."

Doing his best not to give the game away, James
rubbed the stubble of whiskers at his chin and
drawled, "Well, now, Cap'n, it's up to you a'course,
but as I rode in I saw some mighty fine horses roamin'
behind your fences. One of them would sure please a
chief like Spotted Wolf."

James smiled as he heard the worried question.
"Will one be enough?"

"Oh, I think one'll do, Cap'n. You're gonna have to
pack an extra horse with some spare oats anyway, so
you might as well make a good impression and give
the animal to the head man. Sort of a gesture of
friendship."

"I know very little about Indians, Mr. Bryce, and I'm
thankful for it, but if one horse is good, two might be

better.''

Ignoring James's broad grin, Marcus gave orders for three of his finest horses to be brought to the house. And as he waited, he was barely able to contain his impatience. He fumed silently until he and James started, at last, in the direction of the Ainsley cabin, where he would be at the tender mercies of a French *coureur de bois* and his Indian companions. Not the happiest of fates if Victoria meant to seek revenge. And he wouldn't put it past her.

The two men traveled almost without stopping, eating cold food and drinking tepid water from wooden canteens while still moving, dismounting only to rest their aching bones by walking alongside their animals. It was late the next day before they arrived at their destination.

Spotted Wolf heard the hallo of the returning frontiersman a few seconds before he heard horses' hooves crossing the clearing around the cabin. William welcomed Captain Randall profusely, and Ellen, in her innocence, told Marcus how good it was to see him and how good it had been to see Mistress Monet about this time last year.

Something in the way Ellen pronounced Monet, some guilty hesitation, caused Marcus to direct a withering look toward her. ''Did Victoria really not tell you her name is Chisholm?''

Ellen blushed furiously and William looked down at the rough floor as his wife confessed. ''She said it was a secret, Captain. Miss Victoria would not have told us her real name except she had to say something when we addressed her as Mistress Monet in front of her friends.''

''I'm sorry,'' Marcus apologized. ''You owe me no

explanation. It seems that Victoria is blessed with good and loyal friends and you are to be counted among them.''

Ellen looked up at Marcus through questioning eyes. "But how did you learn of Miss Victoria's real name, Captain?"

An evasive, somewhat guilty smile touched his lips as he replied, "Let's just say that Miss Chisholm and I met again under rather unusual circumstances and managed to learn a little more about each other. Now, if you will excuse, me, Ellen, I will join Mr. Bryce's friends, who are expecting me, I believe."

To forestall further questioning by his curious hosts, James spoke up. "We'll probably be gone by the time you folks are up in the mornin'," and leaving it at that he led the way to the storage room where Marcus was immediately aware of cold, noncommittal eyes staring at him.

"Ah, Monsieur Capitain, we meet again," Philippe purred with the same bright smile and sparkling eyes Marcus remembered from their last encounter.

"I hope to fare a little better this time, monsieur," he answered sardonically, bowing to the laughing Frenchman.

Spotted Wolf was very pleased to see the haggard appearance that told of the relentless ride this man had made to get here in response to *Le Cougar*'s message and he said, "Sit, Randall, it is good that you have come willingly."

Marcus understood the implied threat. "Nothing could have kept me back."

Fully satisfied that Captain Randall would be safe with the others, James went outside to help William, who had already started to care for the horses and was leading them toward the barn. James rescued the food Marcus had brought for human consumption and carried it back to the addition, which had become an efficient, well-run trading post.

Before the sun was up the horses had been packed and each man moved quietly in order not to disturb the couple who were still in their beds asleep. The trade had been heavy. Many furs would work their way to Richmond and then by boat to Annapolis. From there it was none of his business where they went. James didn't want to know. He was satisfied the way things were, and with very little conversation he turned his packtrain in one direction while Philippe led his group in another.

The journey through the mountains took a great deal from men and animals alike, but in his eagerness to reach Victoria, Marcus pushed the party to their limits until Philippe turned in his saddle and stopped him. "Monsieur, we will not get there at all if you do not exercise more care, and then who would explain to the mademoiselle, eh? I think you will be of little use to her lying at the bottom of some cliff. So if you please, do not ride your horse up the back of mine. Mademoiselle Chisholm will be there when we arrive. She is waiting for you."

Marcus reined his horse in and slowed the animal's pace a little so the large stallion no longer crowded the smaller pony directly in front of him. He wanted to ask a thousand questions, but the few attempts he had made while still at the Ainsleys' had proved fruitless. No one would say any more beyond the simple fact that Victoria wanted to see him. He sighed heavily. He would find out soon enough why she had sent for him and why she was in Indian territory, of all the God-forsaken places.

As his horse followed the others, Marcus was deeply immersed in his own thoughts. Victoria had said she would send a message, but this was beyond him. He did not know what to expect; he could only hope. Her men had already told him that they would just as soon cut him up for shark bait. Well, there weren't any sharks where he was going, but there were scalping knives and roasting stakes that were probably less to be feared than the torture he had undergone these past months, waiting and hoping.

For the first time in years he found himself praying, praying that she was well, that she would listen to his pleas to marry him, for Marcus had learned that there could never be anyone else for him. She was, indeed, all the things he had called her: treacherous, deceitful and arrogant. But these flaws in her character no longer seemed so important.

From the very beginning she had lied. Not one word had been the truth. And this business with the Ainsleys. A trading post so close to Richmond. Her friendship with the very same savages who plundered, burned and killed. How did it happen? And so quickly. He shook his head in dismay. He did not know her at all. He only knew that he loved her and always would.

The more his mind dwelled on her, the clearer those flashing eyes became, and the more he remembered of the feel and smell of Victoria's skin. The smoothness of it. The spicy-sweet smell of the scented oil that left no trace of grease on her skin.

He pictured the scene he had witnessed so many times as she had emerged from the water and almost felt the coolness of her body. Once again he was aware of the heady aroma of warm grass and the sweet perfume of wild flowers.

Marcus could bear no more. He groaned and hunched down in his saddle, suffering in his own personal torment. Philippe winked at Spotted Wolf and the Indian nodded. He had seen lovesick men before.

When Marcus finally sighted the small village below them in a valley just coming green he knew that there was almost nothing he would not submit to to hold Victoria in his arms again. It was that *almost* that had proved to be the stumbling block, but he was determined to do whatever was necessary to have her.

"If I have to fight the whole damned Indian nation!" he thought somewhat overzealously.

The size and noisy energy of the welcoming committee that greeted the group with whom he was traveling unnerved Marcus as he realized how futile his last thoughts had been. He would do everything in his power to persuade Victoria to marry him. However, it was abundantly clear that he could not force himself on her. Not here. But sooner or later she would have to emerge from this cocoon of safety. Sooner or later she would have to return to civilization and to her business.

"And that will be the time to act if she refuses me again."

The thought was as bitter as bile, but he would do it. And he knew it.

Deciding to play his cards close to his chest, Marcus waited with outward calm for what seemed an unnecessarily long time while the others unloaded the horses and began to divide their possessions. He was about to explode with impatience when Philippe walked toward him.

"Ah, monsieur, it was so good of you to wait," he commented without the least trace of sarcasm. "Come, I take you to the mademoiselle now."

Ducking his head as he followed the Frenchman into a large, snug cabin, Marcus looked around the spacious main room of the structure. Then he saw her. She was sitting by the fire with a blanket wrapped around her. Her feet were clad in high moccasins and what little he could see of her deerskin skirt was edged with leather fringe. Her hair fell into two thick plaits over the front of the blanket.

Despite himself Marcus felt the long-controlled physical urge of his body begin to reassert itself, but it was a momentary reaction and one he did not welcome. As his eyes became more accustomed to the dim interior, he noticed that Victoria looked tired, that those eyes that always sparkled with one emotion or another were haggard—almost listless. His restraint, the restraint he swore to maintain, broke.

"Vickie!" His voice was soft, but the intensity of his emotions roughened the sound as Marcus closed the distance between him and the woman he loved. He raised her up to him.

"Vickie, Vickie," he murmured as his lips sought hers and lingered in the tenderest of kisses. "Are you all right?" he asked, then hushed his breathing in order to hear the barely audible whisper.

"You came," Victoria breathed, almost afraid to believe her senses. Yet Marcus was here. His hands were touching her. His lips had been soft against her own. He had come.

Marcus shook his head in dismay as he understood the doubt, the refusal to trust and to believe in him. ''Did you not know that I would come, that I would walk into the jaws of death if you needed me?''

And then he became aware of the difference in Victoria's body. He stepped back, and his eyes examined every inch of the woman who stood in front of him, still clutching the concealing blanket around her body. A slow, almost triumphant smile betrayed his understanding before he brought himself under the strictest control. This was no time to flaunt a victory that was not yet his.

''Remove the blanket,'' he ordered quietly, but everyone in the room, including Victoria, knew he would do it himself if she didn't.

So Victoria obeyed. She did not have the energy to fight. The blanket dropped to the floor and what Marcus had known was proved true.

Some warning sounded in his brain and he stared at Victoria through wary eyes. ''You left me knowing this? Why? Why did you run when you knew you were carrying my child? You must have known!''

She nodded. ''Yes, I knew, but I had to be free to make my own decision. I was not sure I would allow your child to live.''

The ease with which Victoria spoke the words belied the terrible struggle she had waged before making her decision, but she had no intention of letting Marcus know anything of that battle that had been fought with such intensity on her journey to Spotted Wolf's village.

Marcus took a step back under the force of the terrible truth, a truth he could not imagine. The look in his eyes was painful for Victoria to see. ''You would have killed my child? No, not even you could be so evil, so cruel. I don't believe you,'' he stated with certainty as the shock wore off and his mind began to function logically once again.

''No, my darling, you would have to hate me in order to do such a thing, and you have proved over and over again that you do not. No woman who comes to me so eagerly, who loves with such passion and such fury as you, could hate me. No woman who has touched and explored and claimed every part of me, as I have allowed only you to do, could hate me. No, my dearest, despite all the wrong I have done, you do not hate me. Neither would you ever have killed my child. This, I believe. I must believe it.''

His smile was wistful, almost sad. ''Somehow, I have not yet lost you completely. You do love me. Not as much as I love you, perhaps, but you do love me. I have known that since we crossed the ocean together on the *Maryann*, but it seems that we have a still wider and more turbulent ocean to cross, you and I.''

Marcus watched as a faint look of hope replaced the uncertainty on Victoria's face, but he understood that she was waiting for more. She was waiting for some commitment he did not as yet understand, so he continued to plead with her.

''You will, I hope, finally agree to marry me. You must, you know. That child you carry under your heart is as much mine as it is yours, and I will not give up my claim to it.''

His smile was soft, but there was a small twinkle of humor in his eyes as Marcus continued. ''So you see we must share our child and we can hardly do that if you continue to refuse my most honorable proposals of marriage.''

Marcus laughed as Victoria directed a scathing look his way. He knew that she thought him a great deal less than honorable, but at this moment he didn't care. Victory was so near that he could taste it, feel it. His smile was almost condescending. "Surely, my dear, you can see that the time for running away is past. You must think of the child now. You must marry me so that our baby will have a father and a rightful name. In turn, I will promise to love you and our child with all my heart. I will care for you and protect you. I will share with you all that I have. I can do no more."

Victoria shook her head in doubt. "I don't know, Marcus. It is not easy for me to even think of marrying you—or anyone else. But we will put that aside for the moment. The important thing, the reason I have asked you to come to this place is to discuss our child. If I should die in giving birth, which is always possible, you may, if you wish, take the child to raise. If you do not want him, then he is to be cared for by Henry Byrnes. And this, not marriage, is the reason I asked you to make a long and dangerous journey."

Marcus was confused. He was stunned. Victory had been so near and now he was uncertain of anything. What was his beloved tormentor up to now?

His skin prickled with suspicion. He was on guard, and he studied Victoria through narrowed eyes. He was absolutely certain that even at a time like this the little vixen was working him with all the skill of a weaver throwing the shuttle back and forth, patiently creating just the right pattern.

However, the prospect of a difficult birth seemed very real to Marcus in these primitive circumstances.

He remembered the agony that had racked the body of Ellen Ainsley and the certain death for both mother and child if Victoria had not been there to help. And who was here to help her?

Fear and anger struggled side by side in his mind. She wanted something and he didn't know what it was, something she refused to spell out. She was going to maneuver him into a corner just as she had done so many times in the past.

Despite his anger his voice was calm. "Not want my child?" he asked, allowing himself a slight reassuring smile. "There is nothing I want more, with the exception of his mother. At least admit that I have the right to give my son or daughter my name and the legal and social protection that that entails. Would you have the babe thrown out into the world a nameless bastard, my dear?"

The fires that danced in Victoria's eyes told Marcus that he had at last hit a vulnerable spot. He leaned back in the nearest chair and relaxed as he waited for the raging storm to crash over his head. Instead Victoria changed course once more. It was one of her most disconcerting traits.

She did not reach for the bait. Totally ignoring his line of thought, Victoria said nothing about the possibility or the undesirability of her child being born a bastard. Nor did she mention her own unfortunate claim to that title. Her voice oozed over him as a snake would surround the flesh of its helpless victim, and Marcus knew that he was at last going to learn what she really wanted.

"You talk of marriage, Marcus. What kind of marriage? A marriage between master and slave, with you the master, of course? A marriage where you would expect to control not only my body but my mind as well? A marriage where, by law and custom, you have every right to my entire fortune, to every shilling in my possession. And worse, the law allows you to treat me any way you choose. With the possible exception of beating me to death!''

She paused briefly to allow the venom of fear to work and then went on. ''You have always made your conditions quite clear to me, Captain. Now let me make mine clear to you!''

Marcus blinked back the surprise and the pain. Did she really believe what she had just said? Yet somehow he was almost relieved. She was going to spell out her conditions, but she was going to marry him. If he could accept the terms she was about to demand of him, she would marry him. Fearfully, uncertainly and with very little trust. She would step into a situation where she would no longer be in total control with great caution, and Marcus understood it all. He stared into Victoria's conniving eyes and waited.

''I will marry you if you still want me after you learn that I was born out of wedlock,'' Victoria began in the most casual of tones. ''It seems that I am one of those bastard children you were so careful to avoid until now.''

The bitterness of her last words lashed Marcus with her pain, but he would not allow her to emasculate him. He could not be the weak, spineless creature she seemed to want.

''Do you think I didn't know the circumstances of your birth, madam? That was one of the first things I learned about you after you ran from me in such fear. You ran instead of having the courage to tell me your

parents were not married. You ran and you hid like
some beaten child cowering in the corner! So you see,
my love, I do know. I knew before I came to Annapolis. You can no longer use that particular excuse for
avoiding doing what you know you must."

Victoria's eyes widened in surprise. Surprise that he
knew so much about her and surprise that he actually
thought her illegitimacy had been the reason she had
left him. "Do you really believe what you have just
said?" she asked incredulously. "Do you really think
for one minute that I would have hesitated to tell you
the truth about myself if I had thought there was any
chance for compromise between us? No, Marcus, we
never had a chance, for it was I who was expected to
do all the changing. It was I who was expected to bow
my head meekly to my husband's every demand, cater
to his every whim and overlook his every flaw. No! I
won't do it!"

Victoria's emotions had surpassed anger. She was
enraged, and she took a deep breath to calm herself.
"But this is getting us nowhere, and you're right
when you imply that I do not want my child to suffer
the same cruel slights and snubs I did for the
horrendous and unforgivable crime of being born a
bastard. But," she said more calmly, her voice taking
on a pensive, restless quality, "you are also right
when you say that I love you. You have good reason
to know my feelings, for if I did not love you, you
would be dead by my hand. I had many opportunities
that I ignored. Not because I have any compunction
against killing, but because it was you. I did not then
and I do not now want your death on my hands, but
neither do I want you to control my every thought,
my every action with an iron hand. I've had enough

of that!'' she snapped, surprising herself because she felt an anger that was not directed toward Marcus.

She paused and then pushed the fleeting thought from her mind. She had to protect herself and she had to protect her child. And at last Victoria made her conditions known.

''However, my love will not be an excuse for knowingly subjecting myself to an intolerable situation. Therefore, I have two conditions. The first is that you will in no way interfere with my life.''

Marcus looked at this fierce, determined woman and understood why she had been compared to a cat in two languages and by two cultures. The arrogance, the independence, the contempt seeped from every pore.

He sighed heavily. What she had said was quite true. At any time in his hunting lodge she could have put a knife deep into his back. Even before that, she had had the opportunity to seize the knife he had dropped to the floor of his cabin aboard ship. But she had done none of those things. Still Marcus did not understand the kind of love she offered him, a love where there was little trust. She was afraid. She was afraid of what he might do if she gave him legal power over herself and her possessions. Victoria was, in her own estimation, taking a monumental risk. He could hardly blame her if she tried to better the odds.

Still he would not lie. If her terms were unacceptable, he would tell her so. If she could not be won now, she could be forced later. He shook his head in denial of her first condition. ''My dear, you will be my wife in name and in fact. I have no intention of excusing you from those wifely duties it seems to me you enjoy as much as I. Are you really

serious? Do you actually believe I could keep such a
promise? You have good cause to know my nature.
Though I might make such a promise out of desperation to have you and my child, do you honestly
imagine I could keep it?"

Victoria was amazed when she realized that he had
misinterpreted her meaning entirely. It had seemed
so clear to her. Did he really not understand what she
must have from him?

She found herself stumbling in embarrassment over
her words. "That was not the kind of interference I
had in mind."

Marcus laughed out loud. Philippe and Raven's
Wing turned their faces to hide their smiles. Still
laughing, Marcus replied, "My pet, any other terms I
will gladly agree to as long as you are not foolish
enough to think that you will not share my bed."

Trying to reassemble some dignity out of a situation
that had gone awry, Victoria said lamely, "I have my
own way of living, Marcus. There will be times when
I will need to travel. I have a demanding business to
run. I will not be spending much time in Richmond."

Once again she clawed her way from the depth of
humiliation to the high protective perch of the cat
bird, and matching that small creature in pugnacious-
ness, Victoria made her first mistake. She threatened.
"You will not try to dominate me, Marcus. That will
simply result in my leaving you and taking our child
with me. My second condition," she continued
serenely, unconcerned with the obvious struggle
going on in Marcus, "is one I feel sure you will
consider an unnatural and unwarranted restraint.
However, it is one I insist on. You will not come from
another woman's bed to mine. You must make a

choice. Here and now.''

Philippe touched the knife at his belt lightly as he
saw the hands of the large and powerful man twitch
as dark blue eyes blazed with cold fire. ''*Sacre bleu*,''
he thought, ''the man is right. She needs a good
beating, but I cannot allow it.''

When he saw that Marcus had himself under
minimal control, at least, Philippe breathed a silent
prayer of relief. It would not be to his liking to kill this
man who had so meekly accepted the most personal
information being revealed in public, but he would if
it became necessary. He would do so in mercy, for
Spotted Wolf would see to it that it would take many
days and nights for the white man to die if he harmed
*Le Cougar*.

Then Philippe briskly rubbed his chin. Victoria was
not the only one who had revealed much of what had
transpired. Marcus Randall, too, had said a great deal.
Philippe thew up his hands in disgust. They both had
said too much. He folded his arms across his chest and
watched as the sparring continued.

Marcus breathed deeply. It was not the time for
anger. Nor was it the time to teach Victoria the lesson
she so sorely needed in manners and humility. He
would wait for a more opportune moment.

With the deceptive charm and sincerity he could
muster when it suited him, he put on a magnanimous
front. ''Although by law I shall be responsible for you
and your actions, my dear, you need not fear that I
shall try to curtail you. Neither will I interfere in your
business or your finances. I shall ask you to give up
nothing. I wish only to be a loving husband to you and
an attentive father to our child. Is that so wrong?'' he
asked, and did not wait for an answer.

Instead Marcus drove home his point. "You may carry on your business affairs to your heart's content. You may go where you wish, but if you expect me to live up to your second, rather impertinent condition, then I must have ready access to your bed wherever you are. Neither will I scratch and whine at your door like some mongrel cur. If you wish me to be faithful to you, then you must receive me when I need you," he finished coldly, not the least concerned that others were listening to the most private details of his life. As long as he won he didn't care who knew how the victory had been accomplished.

Victoria stared at Marcus for a long silent minute. She was uncertain about giving in. Yet Marcus had agreed to everything she wanted. Her child would have a father, and she would have a husband who promised not to interfere in her life, a husband who had also promised to be a faithful bed partner—under certain conditions. They were conditions she understood and approved of. Her smile was angelic. She had gotten exactly what she had wanted.

Hesitantly she began to confide a little of her true feelings to the man who would soon be her husband. "It was not easy for me to leave you in Williamsburg. It was even more difficult to run from you the second time, but we could not have continued under the rules you wished to impose upon me. Not even for you can I bring myself to agree to such servitude. Please try to understand that what I did was done because I was fighting for my life as I must live it."

This last thought reminded Victoria that she could not yet involve Marcus in her life—not until he knew what still lay ahead. Not all of it, of course, but enough so that he would know the dangers that might face him somewhere down the road. She would give him warning so that he might pull back now if he so chose.

"It's best I tell you now, before you commit yourself, that I have a half-brother who may or may not try to kill me."

Philippe's eyes narrowed, and the words seemed to explode like a musket shot inside Marcus's head. He had forgotten about Edward; he had forgotten that Mr. Jones's informant was all but certain Victoria's brother had made one attempt on her life and might very well try again.

"In that case, my love, the sooner we are married, the better. For several reasons," he added, smiling as he caressed the fullness of her womb with a gentle hand. "Can there be a binding marriage here?"

Deciding that it was wise to interfere before either of them had time to consider more carefully all the implications of what each had agreed to, Philippe interrupted. "*Capitain,* if you will allow it, I shall be happy to send for the priest who busies himself converting the Indians to the true faith. He has the power to marry you here with the full sanction of the church and with the sanction of the laws of France as well. And since you are in territory which France claims, such a marriage would also be honored by your own people, I think. Or so it would seem to me." He shrugged and considered the matter settled.

Marcus decided that legal or not it was the best option open to him under the circumstances. "I would like the marriage to take place as soon as possible, monsieur."

Philippe nodded his assent. "I shall send my son, Jacques, to fetch the good father. He should arrive in a few days.''

Studying Victoria's condition with a critical, but not too experienced eye, Marcus muttered doubtfully, ''I hope that's soon enough.''

''And I, monsieur! My woman assures me that the time is getting close, and she is an expert in these matters. But we will hurry,'' he promised, white teeth flashing in his dark face.

Spotted Wolf decided to accompany Jacques. He, also, would speak to the priest who could sometimes be difficult but who would agree to grant this favor if he wished to continue his work in this vast area. For Spotted Wolf could muster powerful allies who would join him in driving out all the foreign holy men if one of their number defied him.

Father Antoine, who was a practical man, listened carefully. He understood the vague threat that was so softly worded, and he smiled. The savages were not at all the childlike creatures he had been led to believe them to be so many years ago when he first set out for this land, aflame with the zeal of his mission. That flame burned not so brightly these days. The all-consuming zeal had diminished to something more comfortable to live with. The marriage of two heretics was a small price to pay in return for the privilege of continuing his work.

Two days later Philippe helped Marcus through the ritual of presenting two fine mares to Spotted Wolf. As the chief accepted the animals that were offered to him in exchange for Victoria's hand in marriage, he grunted his approval. The white man had done things properly. It was good.

Only then did Marcus and Victoria exchange vows. Marcus was filled with happiness that his two most cherished wishes were finally coming true. He would become a loving husband to the woman he needed and he was soon to become a father. If his good fortune held, a son would be born to him, a son who would continue the Randall line.

As she spoke the brief words, Victoria's mind was swirling with hopes and thoughts of her own. She had put her life into the hands of another. If she had miscalculated, if she had made an error in judgment, it would be the most costly of her life, for Marcus Randall now had absolute power over her and over the child who was yet to come. She prayed that she had not misplaced her trust, that Marcus would keep his promise to her.

The diamond and emerald ring Marcus had brought with him was slipped on Victoria's finger, and documents were signed and witnessed. Marcus sighed in relief. Whatever he did now was his right under the law.

Raven's Wing spread furs and blankets on the floor near the fireplace. "Now that you are married you sleep with your man. The sleeping bench will be too crowded for the three of you, I think." She laughed at her small joke, and Victoria smiled back.

Turning to Marcus, Raven's Wing struggled with the English tongue she considered so inadequate to express her thoughts. "*Le Cougar* is stubborn, but she loves her own and will fight to the death for them, *n'est-ce pas?*"

Realizing that the Indian was saying more than the words would indicate, Marcus answered, "Yes, madam, what you say is true, but there will be no need for her to fight alone. She has a family now."

"Ah, that is good, *mon capitain*. It is as it should be,"

Raven's Wing replied, satisfied at last that this man
would care for the woman who knew so little of love
and of the sacrifices it sometimes demanded.

When evening came and the family had retired,
leaving the two of them alone in the front room,
Marcus helped Victoria stretch out on the furs before
cradling her in his arms, not quite believing she
belonged to him, that he was about to become a
father. He smiled as he put his hand on Victoria's
belly and felt the strong movement of his baby, then
contented himself with holding her close.

The few remaining weeks passed and Victoria
became increasingly uncomfortable. The baby had
turned days ago and its birth was imminent. She kept
moving, doing what she could to help with the chores,
and Marcus managed to get himself underfoot as he
followed her everywhere, making sure she kept her
activities within reasonable bounds.

He walked with her to the creek and carried the
water bucket both ways. He insisted she sit and rest
frequently. He made a nuisance of himself, and
Victoria's temper was beginning to grow short.
Finally Raven's Wing pleaded with Philippe to keep
Marcus busy elsewhere.

The Frenchman laughed as he hugged his woman.
"It was the same with us, do you remember, *ma
cherie*? It is always the same until the man learns that
in some things his woman is stronger than he, eh?"

Raven's Wing smiled up at this man whom she had
married twenty-five years and fifteen children ago.
He was not perfect; no man was, but she loved him
and was content. "Yes, my husband," she replied
demurely, "but it is a wise wife who hides it."

The Frenchman's love shone in his eyes as he

smiled back at her. Then he all but pushed Marcus
out the door and kept him busy chopping wood,
making needed repairs to the cabin, helping care for
the horses and anything else he could think of. But
despite these heroic efforts, Marcus managed to make
frequent short visits to wherever Victoria happened
to be in order to assure himself that she was all right.

By the third day Philippe was at his wits' end and
was about to give up. He said as much at supper that
evening, but his wife motioned for him to be quiet as
she inclined her head in Victoria's direction.

Philippe nodded. He had seen it many times.
Victoria had her hands to the small of her back as she
arched to ease the pain. She paced the floor, refusing
food or drink. And finally, when the pain intensified,
when it came in ever more frequent waves, when she
could ignore it no longer, Victoria called for Raven's
Wing, who immediately sent Philippe to fetch the
women who had as much experience in helping at
times like this as she. Then the children who still
lived at home were shooed to their sleeping room.

Philippe guided the white-faced Marcus to an out-
of-the-way corner. The bodies of the women who
would help Victoria through her ordeal formed a
screen around her. From time to time Marcus caught
a brief glimpse of what was going on, and he could
not believe it. They had Victoria crouching like some
animal in the field. The front of her dress had been
pushed up to her thighs. The back hung down behind.
Two of the women held her outstretched arms.
Raven's Wing crouched in front.

Victoria struggled to give birth to her child. Her face
glistened with perspiration. Her breathing was sharp,
and Marcus wiped the sweat from his eyes. All he

could think of was Ellen and her dead son.

When she gave a sharp cry of anguish he started toward her, but Philippe put a restraining hand on his shoulder. "No, my friend, you can do nothing but distract her. She must concentrate on what she is doing. She must think of nothing else. It is her first child and a little difficult, I think. Then, too," he added uneasily, "she does not have the best of builds for an easy birth."

Finally Marcus understood. Raven's Wing was worried. And why not? Ellen, who was generously proportioned, who had a fine, full womanly figure had almost died. The wide girth of her hips had not helped. And Victoria! Her hips were as slender as a boy's.

Marcus slumped against the wall as he realized at last why Raven's Wing had sent for every midwife for miles around, why that mindless old fool chanted and beat incessantly on his drum just outside the cabin door and why Spotted Wolf had retired to his lodge to wait.

"My God!" he sobbed, and clamped his hands over his ears as another scream tore from Victoria's lips. But even as the sound of her ordeal faded Raven's Wing smiled broadly and received the child who finally slipped into her waiting hands.

Short, sharp breathing marked the end of Victoria's torment. She swayed with exhaustion against the restraining hands that still held her. Marcus hurried to her. Kneeling behind, he supported her weight against him until Raven's Wing indicated she could be moved, then he carried her to their bed of furs.

The round-faced squaw beamed into the new-born face of the manchild she held in strong hands.

Crooning softly, Raven's Wing turned him on his side and rubbed the tiny back until the child moved, made a thin mewing sound and contorted his face into what Marcus swore was a smile.

He tightened his arms around his wife as he stared in wonder at the stained bit of humanity that was his son. He watched until, in her own good time, Raven's Wing cut the cord and washed the infant in tepid water.

None of her husband's reactions to his son escaped Victoria's scrutiny. She was pleased, for only love shone from those dark blue eyes. She could taste her happiness, and the love that surged through her, for the life she had brought into this world was strong and fierce. Edward would never get to her son, not with two determined parents guarding him.

She smiled her contentment and turned to Raven's Wing. "Give the child to his father."

Tenderly, Marcus received the tiniest human creature he had ever held in his arms. The warmth from his son's body seemed to invade and swell in his own. His heart could not contain the love and joy that surged and grew with each beat. Softly, the tears fell, and he sat next to Victoria, who was propped up on their bed of furs. No one spoke. Every eye, including Victoria's, was moist.

"What shall we name him?" Marcus asked at last.

Victoria's face was gentle and unguarded. "It doesn't matter so long as his last name is Randall."

It took Marcus some time to control the ache in his throat. "Paul was my father's name. I would like to name my son for both grandfathers. Paul Andrew Chisholm Randall."

Victoria murmured sleepily. "Not much better than

Marcus Aurelius, but a little. It will do. We can call him Pac for short."

Marcus nodded absently. He didn't really care what his son was called. Like Victoria, he only cared about the last name, and that name proclaimed to the world that this was his legitimate son and heir.

Reluctantly, he placed the baby by Victoria's side, then leaned over to kiss his wife. Her face was tired and drawn. As he stood, Philippe commented, "A good job, I think, eh, *capitain*?" He put his hand on the taller man's shoulder. "The first one is always the most difficult. On the papa and the mama. Come, I get you a strong drink. In fact, I have one with you." He laughed, slapping the proud new father on the back.

When Victoria awoke, she found her husband sitting on the floor holding the baby in his arms once again. As the child began to fret, Marcus placed him in her arms, loosened the leather thongs that tied her dress in front and leaned her easily against him. His body shielded her from all eyes as she put the child to her breast. Marcus smiled as he watched his son fumble uncertainly to find his mother's nipple.

"I'm afraid he's as clumsy as his father." He laughed, fascinated, as the baby sucked hungrily, hardly stopping for breath.

He put his finger to the baby's hand and watched as the tiny fist clutched it. Victoria laughed softly as she watched the reenactment of the age-old scene. Her husband was going to be a good father, as good as her own had been, if such a thing were possible. How he would have loved his grandchild.

Marcus smiled at her. "Thank you, my love. Thank you for our son."

The day after Pac's birth Victoria was up, much to her husband's consternation, but Raven's Wing assured him that too much bed rest was no good. "Most of our women would not even have taken to their bed," she explained in halting English. "But I think your woman did well enough."

"Victoria does everything well," he replied, and Raven's Wing showed her teeth in humor at his pride in the woman who had bound him with threads he would be unable to break. She nodded and returned to her chores, thinking that men sometimes took a great deal of credit for something with which they had very little to do.

The days passed swiftly and the winds grew warm. Victoria was taught the art of keeping her child comfortable and dry by using moss when securing him to the cradle board. Raven's Wing helped her learn the easiest way to carry the baby on her back, thus freeing her hands for other things. And Victoria learned quickly, for she did not wish to be encumbered by this baby any more than necessary. Yet she wanted him near. She needed to know that he was safe.

When it was certain that the child would live Pac was presented to the clan and was named in the language of his uncle, Spotted Wolf. To them he would forever be known as One Who Smiles, for everyone assured Marcus that never had there been a baby with a better disposition or a happier countenance.

It was ridiculous, of course, for Pac ate and slept and did little else, but by now Victoria understood something of the excessive flattery in which Spotted

Wolf's people sometimes indulged, so she listened and made the appropriate remarks while the father all but burst with pride.

But deep in her heart she was troubled. It would not be easy to raise Pac to be the kind of man she wanted him to be. Not with his father spoiling him every step of the way. And she might have only a few short years, if that, to firmly plant her son's small feet on the path he must follow. Edward would not delay forever.

Marcus's mind was no less full of thoughts and plans for his son than was Victoria's. He was anxious to get his wife and child back to Annapolis and then to Richmond, for now that he was a husband and a father, there were certain legal matters that needed to be taken care of immediately.

And there were some changes he had to make in the running of his business. He had one good captain for the ship he had bought from Mr. Johnson but would need another for the new *Morning Star*. There would be little running off to foreign ports now. He intended to stay close to his family wherever they were, and he was determined not to allow Victoria to push him out of her life, for he fully intended her to be his wife and the mistress of Serenity—with all that her position implied.

So it was with open arms that he welcomed James Bryce, who escorted Tim and Robb to the village. Their animals were loaded down with the tents, supplies and gifts Victoria had instructed them to bring on their return trip. When her men had left her last year she had not been at all sure that she and her baby would not be returning to Annapolis as social outcasts. Now, Pac, at least, had a chance to escape the stain that never washed clean.

But there was one complication Victoria had not counted on. Tim and Robb were ready and more than willing to do battle with Marcus. In fact their fingers itched to get at the wicked knives each carried on his belt. They glowered frequently in his direction, daring him to take up the challenge.

It was a reaction Marcus tried to ignore, for in his mind they were justified. They just didn't understand the whole story. Apparently Victoria had said very little to them about her relationship with him. And why should she? They were, after all, only hired help. Still, he could not allow their open defiance to get out of hand. One way or the other, it must end.

The surly remarks rankled Marcus to the point where he would not be able to control his temper much longer. The tension increased to an explosive level. Finally Victoria stepped in. She took the two men by the arm and walked a short distance with them, just far enough to be out of hearing of the rest. Her voice did not carry any further than their ears.

"Marcus Randall is my husband," she began quietly. "I must ask that you put aside your bitterness. For my sake and for my son's."

She held each man's gaze by turn. "I must depend on you to guard Pac well, and there will be times when he will stay with his father in Richmond. You must do nothing that will make you unwelcome there; you must do nothing that will cause you and my child to be parted one from the other. This you must swear."

Tim and Robb straightened. Their chests swelled with determination. "Thought maybe that's the way it was. You and the cap'n. Married. Boy had to have a father," Robb grumbled, but Victoria knew it was settled. There would be no more open defiance. No more challenging of Marcus's authority. And they would stay close by Pac.

"Now," she said brightly, "shall we see to the distribution of the gifts?"

So the two seamen turned their attention from Marcus to the child called Pac, and the rough, coarse-mannered sailors became the butt of many jokes as they fussed over the child they would guard with their lives. Marcus settled for the undeclared truce. They didn't have to like him, but, by God, they would not defy him.

"I suppose those unlikely nursemaids are included in the bargain," he drawled with dry humor.

Victoria flashed a bright smile toward Tim and Robb, who had also heard the question and were waiting for the answer. "Marry me, marry my family," she quipped, and ignored the expression of smug satisfaction that settled haughtily on Robb's face. Instead she turned her back on the three of them and nodded to James, who began to unload the horses.

Marcus grunted in disgust. "Lord help us all," he muttered sourly, "when such as these are the best we can do for family," but he understood that the relationship between his wife and these two moth-eaten seamen ran deeper and stronger than he had suspected. There was still a great deal he had to learn about Victoria. Then, he, too, turned his attention to James and the unloading of the pack animals. He pursed his lips in appreciation as each item was spread on the skins of the rarest of creatures—the white tiger.

And now Victoria was anxious to return home. There were a great many things yet to be done. And all must be accomplished before another winter set in, for she could not drag Pac around the countryside in the bitter cold. Nor would she expose him to winter gales at sea or the bone-chilling dampness of life aboard ship. He must be kept warm and safe. And he must be surrounded by those who loved him and would protect him. Edward might manage to get to her, but he would never get to her son or to the man who would care for him in the event of her death.

# 15

The small party of travelers arrived at the farm on the last day of May. Entering through the back gate, which closed the wooded portion of the farm from the road, Victoria could hear the screeching, deafening noise coming from the saw mill that had obviously been completed during her absence. But once the tangle of trees and scrub had been cleared the mill would be converted for the grinding of grain.

Following the meandering path leading to the edge of a planted field, Victoria's heart lifted as she gazed across the expanse of sprouting wheat and oats. A little further along was Bess's pride and joy, the herb garden. And she smiled with pleasure as her eyes took in every detail of the house, which had been completed. The ugly structure had been transformed into a sparkling jewel. The orangerie completed the scene, adding its style and grace. Even the fountain was splashing water into the Italian-style pool.

It was then that the housekeeper spied them. She dropped the basket of wash she was carrying and ran to greet them.

"Oh Lord, have mercy!" she cried. "Miss Victoria! I've been so worried about you," the older woman babbled as she dashed the tears from her eyes.

Somewhat ashamed of her unseemly conduct, Bess took a sterner view of things. "Is that your baby you're hauling on your back like a heathen? Why, shame on you, miss! You give that child to me this instant."

It had been a long time since Tim or Robb had heard Miss Victoria laugh as though she meant it, and they watched through eyes that sparkled, trying to hide their smiles from Bess, whose short, plump body could swell with wrath if she thought someone was making fun of her.

Aiming a defensive kick at the raucous, threatening geese that had suddenly appeared from nowhere, Marcus dismounted and eased his wife from her horse. Then he removed the cradle board from her back and handed Pac over to Bess, who immediately lost interest in everyone else. However, she did manage to make one further comment, expressing her doubts as to what was going to become of the child with such a mother as an example.

This last snipe at Victoria's unwomanly habits proved too much for the rest of them, and they struggled with broad smiles, choking back laughter as they followed after the housekeeper.

Once inside nothing would suit until Bess had removed the baby from the carrying cradle. Victoria was about to take advantage of the lull in conversation by formally introducing Marcus when Josiah stomped into the house. In his agitated state, he had neglected to scrape the mud of the fields from his boots, and clumps of wet, red earth marred Bess's spotless floor.

Josiah's eyes were hostile as he glared from the baby his wife was holding to the man he had never seen before. Turning to Victoria, he muttered darkly, "Tim and Robb told us you'd likely be bringing a babe home with you." It was obvious what he thought of the situation, and it was just as obvious that his Puritan soul was grievously offended.

Anger flared in Marcus's eyes and James tensed, but before matters could get worse Victoria interrupted. "Yes, Josiah, I've brought my son home, and this is his father, my husband, Captain Randall. Marcus, this is my manager, Mr. Hubbard."

Josiah was stunned. Nothing had been said about a wedding. "You're married?" he asked incredulously, his face flushed with sudden embarrassment.

"Yes," Victoria assured him, smiling at this small triumph. "Would you care to inspect the documents?"

Josiah stiffened. The reprimand was well deserved. "That won't be necessary, miss. None of my business, anyway," he mumbled uncomfortably.

"But of course it is," Victoria replied matter-of-factly. "Particularly since I had intended to ask both you and Bess to do me the honor of being my son's godparents."

Marcus grinned broadly. Victoria was what she, herself, had termed an infidel, an unbeliever. Until this very moment the thought of having her son christened had probably never entered her head, but if it would serve her purpose, if it would ease her son's path, she'd do that and a lot more. This much Marcus already knew.

Josiah glanced at Bess, who was beaming, then turned back to his employer. "It's an honor for us, ma'am. We'd be delighted to stand for the boy."

"Good," she replied, smiling, for one obstacle had been successfully put behind her. "And now I believe it's time I showed my husband around Chisholm House."

"Aye," Josiah muttered darkly, "Chisholm House it is and Chisholm House it'll stay." It was not in his heart to forgive too quickly. Besides, he had made an accurate guess as to exactly what had happened even though Tim and Robb, for the most part, had been as close-mouthed as clams. He wasn't at all sure about the dark-haired scoundrel Miss Victoria had married.

Victoria gave a warning squeeze to her husband's hand. They had both heard the scandalous remark, and she couldn't blame him if he lost his temper completely. He had put up with a great deal from those who surrounded her. But she loved these people, and she wished to avoid hurting them, if possible. However, whether they liked it or not, Marcus was now master of Chisholm House, and they must accord him proper respect.

Looking into his scowling face, Victoria smiled as though nothing were wrong. "The north and south wings were finished in my absence. I can only hope my instructions have been followed since I was not here as I had planned to be to oversee the finishing touches." And Marcus understood that his wife was telling him in no uncertain terms that she did not appreciate the interruption to her life that he had caused.

His anger increased to the point where he was about to show Victoria that there were some things he didn't appreciate, either, but before he could act, she smiled and established his authority in this house.

"Now," she said brightly, "where would you like to begin your inspection of your new home, a home I hope will give you as much happiness as it has given me."

Josiah did not miss the words *your home*. Neither did anyone else.

Marcus smiled into his wife's upturned face and forgave her her impertinence. With just two words, she had settled the matter once and for all. He kissed her lightly, put his arm around her waist and replied, "Anywhere you choose, my dear, I'm anxious to see it all."

They walked from the room, and Marcus listened intently as Victoria pointed out one treasure after another, giving its history in a brief sentence or two, and he was uncomfortable.

Leroy Jones had spelled out Victoria's powerful friends and her great wealth to him long months ago, but Marcus was not prepared for what he saw. Only now did it begin to take on a reality of frightening proportions. Not he nor all his friends put together could match the value that was in this house alone. And this was only a small part of her fortune. Her real wealth lay in her ships and the commerce they carried on as well as in her holdings in various trading companies. There was no end to it.

He was relieved, therefore, when they reached the parlor in the main section of the house and Victoria looked not at the priceless collection of antiquities the room held but at a portrait hanging prominently over the mantle.

"I was three when that was painted. The other two

people in the picture are my parents. My mother died soon after the portrait had been completed.''

Marcus stared, fascinated, at the tall, slender man who held a laughing child in his arms. Their coloring was almost identical except for the eyes. Andrew Chisholm smiled out at the world through eyes of vivid, intense, cobalt blue. Even now a sense of power, of absolute assurance crackled from them.

Marcus frowned. Victoria's father had been ruthless, vicious and uncaring. He had destroyed those who stood in his way, and he had apparently raised his daughter to be just like him. Yet he seemed to have loved her, and the little girl in the portrait obviously adored him.

He continued to study the likenesses of this small family. Victoria had her father's coloring and his lean, slender build, but there the resemblance ended, for her face was almost a mirror image of the pale yet hauntingly beautiful woman who posed gracefully on her chair. Huge, sad, emerald-green eyes stared wistfully into his own. He shivered. It was as though she were pleading with him. But why? He tore his gaze away.

''They were very beautiful, my dear. They had to be to produce something like you,'' he commented softly.

But Marcus was filled with thoughts of his own as they toured the remainder of the central portion of the house. It was not until Victoria opened the door to her private suite in the new south wing that he began to pay attention once more.

His senses could not totally absorb the opulence of the sitting room. Dappled sunlight streamed through latticed windows. The distinctive open work of the

Moorish shutters broke up the intensity of the light, softening and diffusing it. Here and there it touched the surface of some reflective object. The effect was dazzling and almost overwhelming. The room seemed to dance with a life of its own.

Entering the inner chamber, he stopped just inside the wide double doors. His eyes were drawn to the soft folds of the diaphanous, pale-green silk, which, when released from its ties, would curtain off the large raised alcove that held a bed reminiscent of an Eastern harem.

The intricately carved legs were short and brought the luxuriantly covered mattress much closer to the floor than the high bed he was accustomed to. The headboard had been carved by a master craftsman and depicted a finely worked scene of Indian gods and goddesses. And it was wide, wider than any bed he had ever slept in.

The three walls that formed the recessed chamber were also covered in finest silk. Heavier silk, tassled in gold, formed a valance that gave a greater sense of richness to the alcove. Lacquered, highly decorated chests flanked the bed. Thick carpet gave way under foot. Golden statues in various states of undress stood guard. Each item was worth an immense fortune to a collector of antiquities.

As Marcus finished taking in the bedchamber itself, his eyes focused on the larger room, which seemed to be redundant. All the furniture was of another time and place. Brass knobs and pulls glistened; finely worked woods glowed with an inner sheen. Lounging chairs were covered in gleaming satins. Bright green pillows, embroidered and tassled with threads of pure gold, nestled in cream-colored chairs.

His mind could not catalogue it all, but Marcus realized the incalculable wealth that was housed in each and every room of this mansion. A large portion of Andrew Chisholm's fortune was at Victoria's fingertips. The man had seen to it that his daughter would be provided for in any circumstance.

Victoria had to repeat her question. "Do you want to see the rest?"

"This is not the end?" he questioned wearily, for he had already seen quite enough, more than enough. Compared to this bastion of wealth, Serenity was but a hovel. The house he had loved since childhood was suddenly diminished in his eyes.

"Of course it isn't," Victoria answered sharply, for she sensed his disapproval, and because she resented that disapproval she took him firmly by the hand and led him through a huge dressing room that was lined with mirrored cupboard doors and built-in drawers. It was a room whose innovative design and practicality Marcus had no time to appreciate, for Victoria opened another door, which revealed the room that had fascinated her from the very beginning, the room she was proudest of.

Marcus stared for some seconds before he realized what he was looking at. Once more his mind flashed to the harems of the East, for there, at one end, was a recessed pool of tile and marble. Spigots of gold had been fashioned into the shape of flying swans.

Obediently, he put his hand into the stream of water that flowed from the open mouth of one of the swans. His eyes reflected the fact that he was more than a little impressed. "It's warm. But how? Where does it come from?" he asked, looking around in vain to find the source of heat.

"It works on the same principle as any common garden fountain, except it's just a little more complicated and the water is heated. But wait!" she exclaimed eagerly as she walked to a pair of louvered doors and triumphantly flung them open. "Look at this!"

And Marcus did look. There was another, smaller room behind the doors Victoria had just opened, and in that room was a water closet. Sunlight streamed in the window and picked up the green and gold of the floor tile, which continued into this room from the larger one. Marcus whistled softly. Never had he seen anything like it. He had heard of them, of course, but this was the first he had ever seen.

"Does it work?" he asked suspiciously, and Victoria laughed in pride and happiness.

"Try it!" she crowed, and then laughed again as Marcus flashed her a look of sardonic humor.

"If you're not careful, I just might. But you're going to have to show me how this thing works," he added uncertainly as he studied the contraption more closely. He stepped back hastily as Victoria tugged on the chain and water came rushing and gurgling into the bowl. Then the valve closed as the tank above filled for the next time.

Victoria shrugged her shoulders. "That's all there is to it."

But Marcus shook his head in wonder as he fully appreciated all the technical skills that had been involved in completing Chisholm House. There was much more to be learned. The forces that made these marvels work were somewhere out of sight, but he would have to investigate later, for Victoria was urging him to look at the large oval mirror hung in the bathing room, a mirror whose gold-leafed frame swirled in graceful design over a portion of the glass.

He watched as she tilted the Chinese mirror slightly to one side. There was the click of a latch being released, and an invisible door popped open about an inch. Behind the door was a stairway.

"These steps can be reached from the library off the kitchen as well as from this room. There is also a third concealed door in the cellar. I'll show it to you later," Victoria explained, as though secret doors and passageways were a normal part of life.

Marcus released his breath slowly as he realized just how little he knew of Victoria's life. As they returned to the bedroom, his discontent showed through the words.

"How you must have laughed at my ridiculous hunting lodge, and how you must have missed all the luxuries to which you are obviously accustomed," he said softly.

Victoria's eyes clouded with an emotion Marcus could not read. "I have not always lived in luxury, Marcus. There have been times when I would have traded all of this for a drink of water or an extra blanket or even a portion of bread, but do not think yourself superior because you have suffered. I also know the meaning of the word."

Despite himself, Marcus smiled and put his hands to his wife's face. "I will try to remain humble, my dear," he murmured, the humor echoing from his voice. "Forgive me if I have become proud of my low estate."

But Victoria did not think he was the least bit funny. Too many people of lesser station puffed themselves up with the conviction that they were

somehow better, stronger and more worthy than the
man who possessed great wealth. They attributed his
material riches to luck or favoritism. They had absolutely no understanding of the discipline, the single-
mindedness and sometimes the great sacrifices that
were required to build a financial empire. But Victoria
knew. She knew what all of this had cost her father
and what it was to cost her still. She sighed and
opened several drawers in a beautifully fashioned
chest. "You can put your things in there. Now is there
anything else you need before I get my bath and
change into something Bess will approve of?"

"Yes, dammit," came the tight, urgent answer.
"There is very definitely something else I need, but it
will have to wait."

Victoria pretended not to understand the meaning
of his words. She ignored her husband's increasing
need for her and walked to the dressing room, closed
the connecting door and quietly turned the key while
Marcus removed the soiled clothing from his saddle
bags. He frowned in distaste. He had taken only a few
things with him to Indian territory and almost everything was in need of a good washing, including the
pants and shirt he had on now. But he could hardly
walk around naked. Not in this house. Perhaps
Victoria could find him something to wear.

Scratching the itchy stubble on his face, Marcus
headed for the door behind which Victoria had
recently disappeared. What he wanted most was a
pan of steaming hot water for a clean, close shave. He
reached for the ornate knob and turned. Nothing
happened.

"Damnation," he muttered beneath his breath, and
gave the door a few solid blows with his fist. "Open
this door, Victoria!"

Blithely ignoring the edge of irritation in his voice, Victoria slid lower in the water. "I'll be out in a minute."

Then her eyes opened wide and she sat straight up. The pounding had increased in fury. He meant to break the door in! The entire household would be in an uproar.

Thoroughly irritated by his childish behavior, Victoria climbed the two steps from the tub, stepped onto the tile floor and struggled to pull her robe over her wet skin. Blowing out a breath of exasperation, she stalked through the dressing room, dripping water over the expensive carpet. Turning the key and twisting the knob viciously, she jerked the door open. A few well-chosen words were about to escape her lips when she spotted Bess clutching Pac to her. The housekeeper's eyes were wide with shock and dismay. Victoria backed down. "What is it, Bess?" she asked in a reasonable, calm tone that belied the anger that still smoldered in her eyes.

"The child's frettin' a good bit, Miss Victoria. Won't quiet down for me. I think he's hungry."

Victoria directed a thoroughly nasty glare toward Marcus, who stood smirking, and while she saw to her son's needs he slipped into the room she had just vacated and enjoyed the comforts which, until now, had been totally outside his experience—and his purse.

After feeding Pac Victoria placed him in the center of the large, soft bed. She was almost dressed when Marcus came back to the bedroom cleanly shaven and washed with his hair still damp from the scrubbing. He dropped his boots on the floor as he rummaged for a last clean pair of hose.

"Never seen anything like it," he mumbled absently as he searched in vain for something else that might be worn one more time. "I've seen ruins of ancient baths complete with latrines, but never anything like those rooms. Not even the finest plantation in all of Virginia can offer anything close to it."

Victoria watched as Marcus picked up a shirt and discarded it. The pants were accorded similar treatment. She understood the problem. "I think my father's hose and boots might fit you, but I doubt that you could squeeze into anything else of his. However, I think Tim is about your size. Wait here," she suggested and then laughed, for where else would he go clad only in hose?

In a few minutes Victoria returned. She carried a pair of well-worn boots whose fine, soft leather had been stretched by frequent wearings. She also handed Marcus several pairs of expensive cotton hose. To this meager wardrobe she added a pair of Tim's breeches and a clean linen shirt. Marcus felt much better and his smile as he gazed at his son, who was sleeping in the middle of the large bed, reflected his contentment.

Once Victoria had assured herself that her son would be safe if left alone she and Marcus left this private suite to join the others in the kitchen. As they approached, the heady aroma of food cooking made them both realize just how hungry they were.

Bess, who had been shocked by her mistress's loss of weight, had decided that all meals from now on were going to be huge ones with an abundant choice of foods. At least until Miss Victoria had gained back the flesh she could ill afford to lose in the first place.

She had soundly berated the innocent and unsuspecting James, Tim and Robb for not taking better
care of their employer, totally ignoring the fact that
they had not been with her. She held that against
them too.

A hearty soup she had intended for supper was
served now. Thick slices of ham were warming.
Chicken was frying, and a variety of pickled and
dried vegetables and fruits were put in serving dishes.

Fresh bread was sliced; honey, preserves and butter
were placed on the table. The finest wine from the
cellar was ready for pouring. A large pitcher of cold
buttermilk was put within Victoria's reach.

Bess was beside herself as she shouted orders down
to Suellen, who was working feverishly in the
summer kitchen, preparing raisin-filled oat cookies,
one of the few sweets her mistress enjoyed. The
young girl raised imploring eyes to heaven, hoping
that her efforts pleased Bess or there would be no
tuppence for her this week.

The men stuffed themselves like gluttons, then sat
back sipping wine as Bess poured the steaming tea
and coffee while Suellen served several dozen cookies
for dessert.

Victoria, whose stomach would not yet accommodate a large meal, munched on one of the cookies
and sipped her tea. She smiled her approval as
Suellen stood by, waiting nervously for the verdict.

"Very good," Victoria lied gallantly and nodded her
head in dismissal.

The girl bobbed and let out her breath in relief.
"Thank you, ma'am. We're so pleased to have you
home, miss!" Suellen added with feeling, for Bess had
not been easy to satisfy in Miss Victoria's absence.

Putting down the half-eaten cookie, Victoria looked at Bess. "I would like to have a few friends in for dinner in a day or two. A small, rather intimate group, I think. Mr. Bordley, Governor Ogle . . ."

Bess interrupted. "Why, Governor Ogle's dead, miss. Didn't you know?"

Victoria frowned. It was distressing news. The governor had been most kind and helpful. He had been a friend. Now he, too, was gone. "No," she answered quietly. "I had no idea. When?"

"Early this month," Bess replied. "About the third of May, if I remember right."

"And who's governor now?" Victoria inquired.

"Mr. Tasker is filling in until a permanent appointment is made," Bess answered as she pushed the platter of chicken a little closer to Victoria's hand.

Victoria nodded in resignation. "Then we'll send the invitation to Mr. Tasker. The Dulaneys, of course, and perhaps another couple or two. And, Bess, I want everything to be done with elegance—*tres chic*." She laughed, putting the tips of her thumb and forefinger together, forming a circle as she clucked her tongue.

Everyone at the table laughed at her brazen admission that she was out to overwhelm her guests. Marcus was going to be introduced to a very distinguished few, but within days all Annapolis would be abuzz with news of the unbelievable additions to Chisholm House as well as the wealth it contained. The fact that Victoria had suddenly returned home with a husband and baby would become a topic of secondary interest.

The news, as Victoria intended, would be buried under the detailed descriptions of the food, the service, the furnishings, and anything else she could think of that would bedazzle her guests. Secretly, Victoria was flaunting the power that was hers, for she fully intended that her son be accepted in the finest houses, and the reason did not matter.

No one understood the secret smile as she continued. "I want an excuse to show the women to my apartment. For that purpose Captain Randall and I will drive to town tomorrow to purchase the most ornate bassinet money can buy. Someone will ask for whom it is intended, and I shall tell him. That will start tongues wagging. No one will refuse the invitation, and every woman will insist upon seeing Pac. In order to fulfill the request, I shall find it necessary to escort them through the house, up the stairs, along the gallery and into my rooms. That, I think, will give them all pause. Each woman who is to be invited has the intelligence to understand the power the wealth in this house represents. I don't believe they will wish to challenge it. Rather, it seems to me, they would wish to cultivate it. And us."

Marcus frowned. "But why, Victoria? Surely, from what I understand, you are already much respected in this town. And certainly I can earn respect on my own. I don't need to follow along in your wake."

"Ah," Victoria purred, "but Pac must. Our son must follow where we lead. And I intend to lead him to those people who can be of most use to him, here and in the rest of the world."

Marcus sucked in his breath audibly. There it was. His son was to fulfill the grandfather's dream. If Victoria had her way, Pac would be raised to be every bit as vicious and unscrupulous as Andrew Chisholm had been.

His mind rebelled. No! He would not allow his son

to fall heir to such a fate. There was so much more to life than the accumulation of wealth at any cost. It would be up to him to teach his wife that lesson, and he would begin tonight.

Pac was already six weeks old, and not since last August had Marcus relieved the tension that now threatened to burst the bonds of restraint. He needed Victoria. He needed his wife. He would take her tonight. Love for her husband and family must become stronger than loyalty to her father's demands.

Scheming eyes studied Victoria's profile as she outlined to Bess exactly what she wanted in the way of food and entertainment on the night she intended to introduce her husband and her son to the cream of Annapolis society. Marcus was satisfied. He would play along with her plans for a while, but gradually she would be weaned from this house of booty and plunder. She would be taught to love the simpler pleasures of Serenity.

Later that day Marcus turned his attention to more practical matters. He found a large wash basket that Bess lined and pillowed so that Pac might not be subjected to the dangers of sleeping in the same bed where his parents were making love. The basket would do for tonight. Tomorrow Marcus would see that his son was provided with furniture of his own. And he would be put in the dressing room, for Marcus was quite determined that his son would not become accustomed to sleeping with his parents. With any luck his first-born would have to give way to a new baby in another nine or ten months.

A year between children was long enough. His own brother had been six years his senior, but there had been several still-born and several miscarriages inbetween. And though he had adored his older brother, there had been no one to fill the void when he had died. No. Pac must have brothers and sisters to fill his life. His son must not be devastated as the father was when his only sibling had disappeared beneath a stormy sea.

Marcus frowned. He, himself, was not getting any younger. He had turned thirty-five only days after his son had been born. If he wanted a large family, there was not a lot of time left in which to accomplish it.Some men were done with siring before they turned fifty, and then, too, the length of one's life could not be guaranteed. But Victoria would not bear his next child squatting on the floor of a primitive cabin in Indian country. From now on his children would be born in the same bed in which he had been born, the bed that had belonged to his parents and then to his father alone, the bed Marcus, himself, had never used.

He frowned. He had not entered his parents' bedroom in many years. Now that he had a wife it would be put to use, for the room in which he slept was hardly suitable for the master and mistress of Serenity. At once Marcus penned a letter to Ruby, his housekeeper. Serenity must be made ready for its new mistress.

As Victoria tucked Pac away for the night, Marcus paid closer attention to the rooms in which he and his wife would spend their nights while in this house. He studied the scene on the ornately carved headboard. The intricate pattern faded away under his concentration and the cleverly interwoven figures came clear, depicting a story of lust and gratification.

Marcus arched his brow in disapproval even as his gaze drifted to the statuary he had not really noticed before. His eyes narrowed. If this was the way Andrew Chisholm had raised his daughter, it was a wonder she had not turned out worse than she had. Her father, it seemed, had exposed his daughter to the world's obscenities.

"My dear," he drawled in disgust, "this room is positively indecent."

Victoria smiled sweetly. "In that case, Marcus, you should feel right at home."

His laughter was soft and full of insinuation. "I hope to live up to that reputation, my dear, beginning now."

And Victoria did not resist as he began the ritual that would awaken her senses, the ritual that would bring the sweetest agony she had ever known until Marcus assuaged it.

It had been a long time since Victoria had thrilled to the deliberately tantalizing touch of her husband as he prepared to make love to her, a love that consumed them in its fires. And even before he touched her she was impatient to be in his arms, anxious to be fulfilled by the deep penetrating warmth of his body. She loved him all the more since he had made his promise to her. She had put her hand in his hand and wanted nothing more than to believe what he had told her—that he loved her, that he would force nothing on her, that he would not interfere in what she must do. He had promised all these things and she believed him.

Now, as she faced Marcus, Victoria put her hands to his face. She kissed him tenderly as her fingers moved to the buttons on his shirt. Then it was his turn to unhook the restraints that held her garment in place. And when the dress fell to the floor Marcus untied the shift that covered Victoria's nakedness.

Pushing the soft bit of cloth down the length of her body, his hand teasing all the way, Marcus returned the soft kiss, his lips caressing and possessing every inch of his wife's body. His tongue flicked and sent the sparks of desire streaking through Victoria. She sank to her knees with him, claiming his mouth then moving to his ear. It was more than Marcus could stand. He had waited so long for Victoria to come to him and now the dam burst.

Drawing his breath in sharply between clenched teeth, he removed the remainder of his clothing and led his wife to their bed. He had waited for this moment for almost a year, and he was determined to prolong the lovemaking despite the demands his body was making on him.

Once more they lay side by side, each ready to give and to receive the love of the other. Gently, Marcus touched his wife's face, tracing the line of her brow and then the curve of her lips. Victoria responded to him and ran her fingers lightly down his back as her body pressed against his. Then she gave a soft grunt as the air was forced from her body by a fierce, sudden embrace as she was closed tightly in her husband's arms.

Turning them on their sides, Marcus sought to penetrate his wife's body. Victoria shifted her leg to help him and then came to him with a sudden thrust of her body, straining to receive all of him.

A cry of unbearable desire escaped Marcus's lips as he plunged deep and held. He dared not move, but the throbbing of Victoria's body caused a quivering he could not control. "No," he sobbed almost inaudibly. "No. Not so soon."

Victoria held him tighter in her urgency. "Yes," she pleaded. "Now, Marcus. Now."

And as her body squirmed to enforce her words, Marcus could bear no more. Together they tensed, barely moving, waiting for the pinnacle of joy which would release them from this prison of desire. The pulsing increased in each of them. The rhythm became as one and the cry of released tension tore from Victoria's lips even as Marcus groaned and pushed ever deeper into the body that made him weak. And the passion flooded from him even as he sobbed his happiness and love.

And when the force of passion had played itself out, when the need had been satisfied and when they were exhausted from the efforts of their lovemaking, Marcus and Victoria lay in each other's arms quiet and still. Only the rapid beating of their hearts hinted at the demands of the passion that had filled them.

They lay content, knowing that their night was not yet done, and Victoria smiled as she remembered another such night aboard ship. Marcus, too, was remembering that night, and his smile was smug as he remembered with some pride his remarkable performance that fateful night. He had done well. He had made Victoria his own. Whether she had known it or not, he had made her his own during that long night of love.

His fingers caressed her breasts as they both relaxed, gathering the strength for their next strenuous effort, for neither of them was yet satisfied to let the other one alone. They needed to touch and to feel the joy of their love one more time before giving themselves up to sleep.

Marcus sighed softly. Somehow, despite their pride and despite their tempers, they would find a middle ground where they could keep their love safe, a love that was so strong it drove all else from their lives. He smiled into his wife's eyes as he leaned over her and began once more to stir the fires that never failed to consume them and leave them spent, their hearts beating with love.

Victoria returned his kiss and moved under him.

# 16

Stretching contentedly, Victoria breathed deeply, savoring the sweet, fresh air of this bright June morning. The heady smell of honeysuckle permeated her bedroom. She stretched again and smiled in smug satisfaction. The intimate dinner party had been a great success. Marcus, in his hastily but expertly tailored suit of heavy blue silk, had been absolutely splendid. The bootmaker, too, had put aside all his other orders so he might work straight through on the fashionable gold-buckled shoes that complemented the new, expensive suit. He had cut quite a dashing figure and Victoria remembered with pleasure how the usually ever-so-proper matrons had flirted coyly even as their husbands had tried to hide their envy of Marcus's masculine good looks.

Her own attire had been no less splendid. A pale-green gown of silk gauze had been taken in and adorned with leaves of gold that formed a graceful spray cascading diagonally across the bodice and down the side of the voluminous skirt. The magnificent emerald necklace had helped hide her protruding collar bone. In fact, only Stephen Bordley had seemed to notice her unbecoming loss of weight. Everyone else had been far too busy cataloguing every detail of her home. Even the extra servants she had hired for the occasion had done their jobs to perfection. And everyone had absolutely adored Pac, who had been at his smiling, cooing best.

Victoria laughed out loud. Her husband, too, had been at his best. It was quite obvious that he had been well schooled in the social graces, and he had played the part of the gracious Virginia planter to the hilt. Everyone had fallen under his spell. Several of the men had congratulated him on his great good fortune in siring such a fine son on the very first try, and Marcus had positively beamed with paternal pride.

All in all, it had been a fantastically successful evening. Her husband was now a member in good standing within the most powerful and influential circle of Annapolis society, and her son's position was assured.

Victoria enjoyed the luxury of lolling abed until her husband emerged from the bathing room freshly washed and combed. Grabbing her robe, she climbed from bed and went to take her turn while Marcus put on freshly laundered clothes that still smelled of strong soap and a hot iron.

He was extremely pleased with himself. He had carried off his role of loving husband and doting father to perfection. Victoria's pride in him had been obvious to everyone present. He had been accepted without reservation as the master of Chisholm House. Except, perhaps, for Stephen Bordley, who was obviously in love with Victoria himself.

"But no matter," he thought serenely. "My wife
and son will soon be safely ensconced behind the
fences of Serenity," for Marcus had no intention of
making Chisholm House his permanent residence,
nor did he intend for his son to grow up here.

After bathing and dressing Victoria returned to the
bedroom. Marcus was no longer there, so she made
her way to the new, sunny morning room where hot
tea and scones had already been set out on a small
round table. Settling herself comfortably in a gaily
cushioned wicker chair, Victoria picked up the latest
edition of the *Maryland Gazette* and began to look over
the list of ships that were presently in port and their
sailing dates. Some of the cargo that was enumerated
interested her.

As she glanced at the ads and various articles in the
local paper, Victoria sighed her contentment. Things
had gone well during her absence. The contraband
she had been so concerned about had been disbursed
by Mr. Coster, who had managed to take care of the
matter several days after she had been abducted. She
must remember to reward him for his dedication and
loyalty, for even though his head and leg had been
throbbing with pain, her agent had been carried to the
warehouse the moment he had learned of her dis-
appearance. Nothing had been left to chance.

Victoria's eyes danced with pleasure as she thought
of the perfect gift. Beatrice Coster, Howard's wife,
was a woman much impressed by the social graces of
the gentry. In particular she craved a fine tea set over
which she might preside as the lady of quality she
yearned to be. She would have it. One of the ads in
the paper had been for a finely made tea set newly
acquired from the estate of a wealthy gentleman late

of Philadelphia.

There were some fine silversmiths there. Victoria had seen examples of their work while she and Tim and Robb had been visiting that city. She would look into the matter today.

It was then that her thoughts were interrupted by Bess. "One of Captain Hensley's men here to see you, Miss Victoria."

A flicker of alarm showed briefly in Victoria's eyes. Richard would not have sent a seaman to this house unless there was trouble that he wanted to discuss in private. "Show him in, Bess."

Within seconds the seaman entered the room and stood awkwardly, shifting his weight from one foot to another. He was not accustomed to facing his employer alone and in such a grand house. "The cap'n says he'd be most grateful, miss, if'n you'd allow me to escort you to the *Trident.* Got urgent business, he says," the man managed in one breath.

Victoria recognized the sailor. "Jack, isn't it?" she asked casually.

The seaman smiled broadly. She had remembered his name. Out of hundreds of sailors who served under her flag, she had remembered his name. "Right as rain, miss. Been serving the cap'n and you for eight years come fall."

Victoria nodded. "And as I understand it, you're a fine seaman. Captain Hensley has spoken highly of you on several occasions."

The rough sailor blushed under the warm blandishment of his employer. She knew how to ensure a man's loyalty, right enough. Good food, good pay, and never a sign of the cat, the whip all seamen dreaded. She hired good men and treated them in such a manner that they stayed good men. As long as you did your job and gave faithful service, you pulled good duty. "Thank'ee, ma'am," he mumbled in uncomfortable pride. "And what answer shall I be takin' back to the cap'n?"

"Wait here while I change, and I'll accompany you back to the ship. Help yourself to breakfast if you like," she added casually, pointing to the tray of untouched scones.

As soon as his employer was out of sight, Jack stuffed one of Bess's still-warm raisin scones into his mouth. He grunted his approval, poured a little hot tea into a saucer and washed the sweet dough down.

Precisely at that inopportune moment Marcus strolled into the pleasant room, hoping to have breakfast with his wife. He stopped short and stared at the rough sailor who was downing tea from one of the best saucers. "You're here to see someone?" Marcus asked suspiciously.

The sailor choked on a bit of scone that stuck in his throat, struggled to regain his breath and finally managed to explain his presence. "Miss Victoria said I could help m'self, she did, guv'ner. Wasn't stealin' nothin', I swear. Cap'n Hensley sent me. Asked Miss Victoria to visit him aboard the *Trident* so's he can discuss some important business with 'er."

"I see," Marcus answered with more than a trace of curiosity in his voice. "And has my wife agreed to accompany you?"

Richard Hensley had learned of Victoria's marriage from Howard Coster. Consequently, he had given the sailor explicit instructions not to give his message to anyone other than Miss Victoria and not in the presence of anyone else—including her husband.

However, the hapless seaman had seen no way to avoid telling the master of this house what he was doing here. His agitation was obvious as he twisted his cap in large, rough hands. "Aye, sir," he mumbled.

Suspicion loomed large in Marcus's mind. "In that case I will accompany my wife as well. I've not yet had the opportunity of inspecting any of her vessels, something I'm most interested in doing. As you may know, I, too, am a man of the sea."

"Aye, sir," the sailor replied smartly. "You're name's known to me."

"I dare say to you and to a good many others," Marcus drawled with little humor. His unsavory reputation seemed to precede him to port towns he had not yet entered, and that situation must be corrected. No longer could his name be spoken in the same breath as brawling and wenching. He had a wife and son to protect.

His eyes flicked to his wife as she entered the room. He could tell nothing from her expression, which remained pleasant and serene, but he did not miss the look of utter consternation that flooded the sailor's face. Something was very definitely wrong. It was obvious that Victoria had hoped to slip unnoticed out the back door. She hadn't intended to tell him of her business in town. "Urgent business," the sailor had said.

He decided to force the issue. "I've decided to accompany you to your ship, my dear." His voice was matter-of-fact and showed no sign of his disappointment and distrust, but he had to admire Victoria's absolute control. Not a sign of emotion crossed that lovely, deceitful face. She smiled sweetly and nodded in agreement.

When the carriage pulled up to the docks Marcus helped Victoria down and followed her across the gangway and onto the ship. Captain Hensley stared at Marcus and then turned to Victoria. His eyes asked the silent question, which she answered.

"My husband has decided to accompany me into town, Richard. I don't believe you two have ever met. Marcus, one of my captains, Richard Hensley. Now, Richard, what's the problem?"

Richard knew from the clipped tones of Victoria's voice that she was not happy to have her husband here. However, since nothing could be done about it he was to get on with his report. Still, he proceeded with utmost caution.

"It's about the ships your father commissioned in southern waters," he said softly, hoping Victoria would turn the conversation into other channels, but she did not.

For a moment, Victoria did not reply. Obviously, there was trouble with the privateers who had shared their booty with her father. He never should have gotten mixed up in that nasty business, but he had been angry and had sought his revenge in a manner that could not be easily traced back to him. Then he had sat back and had watched the havoc as his enemies had been broken. His satisfaction had grown with each ship that had been sent to the bottom, with each grievous loss his enemies had suffered. And there had never been any survivors to tell what had happened. No trace of ship, crew or cargo had ever been found. But her father had received large amounts of money each time a heavily laden cargo ship had gone down.

''I see,'' Victoria replied just as quietly. ''And what is the problem?''

Richard shrugged and whipped a canvas covering off a small chest. ''Cordoba sends this,'' he said, and opened the lid.

Victoria's eyes narrowed. The chest was full of jewelry and coins. There was nothing unusual here, yet Richard was troubled. There was more to be told. ''Get on with it, Richard.''

There was no more Captain Hensley could do. If Victoria insisted that he tell her in front of a witness then he would do just that. ''Cordoba and the others say this is the last payment they intend to send. They feel that they had paid for their vessels many times over, and they want an end to it. They intend to do business as they choose. They learned of your father's death and feel they are released from their bargain with him. They do not recognize your rights in the matter.''

Victoria's face was calm, but Marcus watched her closely as she spoke. He, himself, was stunned by this newest revelation.

''Where are they?'' Victoria asked.

Captain Hensley met her steady gaze. He knew exactly what she was thinking. After working for Andrew Chisholm for seven years and then for Victoria for almost two years he had learned how very much alike father and daughter were.

Even though his employer had not yet reached her twenty-third birthday, she was every bit as cunning and as devious as Andrew Chisholm had ever been. ''They're now east of the isthmus, skulking just outside the sea lanes along the Spanish Main, waiting for anything they can find until this matter is settled.

But," he added meaningfully, "they won't stay together for long, not once you've released them from the agreement. They'll most likely break up the pack and each man will head out on his own."

"Making them that much more vulnerable to capture," Victoria added thoughtfully. "The fools have actually left the relative safety of the Pacific?"

Richard nodded. But it didn't make much difference. In any case her ties with the pirates must be severed, and there was only one way to do it. He hoped Victoria would give the right order, the only order she could under the circumstances.

Victoria let out a long sigh. "I can no longer risk being associated with them, Richard. I should have put an end to it immediately after Father's death, but I preferred not to deal with it. Now I must."

The older man nodded in solemn agreement and waited for the fateful words. His eyes flicked toward Marcus Randall. The pallor of the captain's face told the story. He understood which way the wind was blowing.

It was true. Marcus understood the problem, and his fear was overwhelming, but he was not afraid for himself. Even though he was legally responsible for his wife's actions, it was not his own fate that chilled his heart. It was Victoria's.

From everything that had been said or implied, she was engaged in piracy. It was a hanging offense. He clenched his fists in frustration. Everything would be lost, for he would not allow the admiralty to take her. There were places in the world where his small family could lose themselves and never be found. He would have to move quickly. He could not wait for the authorities to learn of her part in a crime that was despicable to every honest sailor who risked his life at sea.

But before Marcus could speak, Victoria announced her decision. "Find them, Richard. Hunt them down and raise the orange flag. Captain Rutherford should be in port within days. His ship is a sleek swift vessel and carries eight guns. But even more important is the fact that she can maneuver where the *Trident* cannot go. Yes," she mused, confirming her thoughts, "you will need the *Eye of Osiris* and probably the *Bayside* as well. Also, I will get word to Captain Crawford to meet you at the transfer point off the Carolinas. He is now captain of the *Blue Dragon*. She's a new ship—and fast. And she carries sixteen guns and mortar cannon. If you need more, say so now, for the first attack must succeed completely. Not a spar, not a single man is to be left in one piece. Everyone is to die."

It was the only order Victoria could give, and the four vessels Victoria proposed to put under his command would be enough for Richard Hensley to do the job thoroughly, for their captains were the finest who sailed the seas, the crews were rigidly disciplined and would not break in battle as the swifter, heavier-gunned ships outmaneuvered and destroyed every pirate vessel. Nothing would survive.

"They'll be enough," he confirmed quietly, and then asked the question that was uppermost in his mind. "What about Ramon? Is he to be treated any differently from the others?"

Marcus felt a twinge of jealousy as he saw the look of pain fill Victoria's eyes just before they closed. When they opened again the pain had been replaced by an expression that was as hard and as unyielding as any he had ever seen.

"No. He is to be treated exactly the same. This is the second time he has betrayed me."

Richard Hensley nodded. Ramon, the handsome young Spaniard Victoria had once loved, would be killed with the rest.

With fear still clutching at his heart, Marcus asked, "First, what is the orange flag? I can guess, but I want you to tell me. Second, who is Ramon?"

His voice had an ominous flatness of tone Victoria recognized, but she decided to tell him the truth anyway. She must do what must be done whether Marcus liked it or not. "The orange flag is a code. It simply means that everything is to be destroyed. No trace is to be left. And Ramon," she said, a bitter-sweet smile touching her lips, "is the man whom I loved with a passion that only a sixteen-year-old can feel. He was and still is a handsome man of Spanish blood—blood that betrayed him—and me. Unfortunately, he could not resist the charms of a married noblewoman, and even more unfortunately they were discovered together in bed by the woman's husband. Ramon shot first and had to flee Spain. He came to me and broke my heart with the truth. Marriage, of course, was out of the question, for if he betrayed me once, he would do so again. But to keep him from the hangman, father gave him a ship and he became a pirate preying on our enemies. He joined the two other captains who commanded my father's vessels, and together they sent a great many ships to the bottom, but not before they had looted them and had taken everything of value. But no prisoners, of course. No one who might identify them or their ships was allowed to live."

Stunned by the magnitude of what he had just heard, by the confessions of crimes his wife had so casually made, Marcus stared first at Victoria, then at Richard Hensley and back again to his wife. Finally his brain responded. "How many men have you killed? How many more will die at your hand?"

Instead of defending herself, instead of telling Marcus that she had opposed her father's actions, Victoria accepted the full blame for all of them. "As many as it takes to keep my neck out of a noose," she answered calmly, waiting for Marcus to make his decision. He could either keep her secret, thereby becoming an accomplice to her crime and thus being fully accountable to the law or he could abandon her to the mercies of the Admiralty Court. She waited for his decision.

With eyes as hard as flint, Marcus asked Richard Hensley the futile question. "There's no other way?"

Richard shook his head. "If even one of them survives, he'll talk. He'll tell who he works for. Your wife will hang."

"And if Victoria simply releases them from their agreement with her father, if she lets them have their ships?"

"You know better than that, Captain," Richard replied sadly. "If Victoria shows such weakness, if she lets them get away with this, not only they, but every other enemy she and her father have will attack. They'll see it as a sign of weakness and they'll turn on her like ravening wolves. It will be a blood-bath such as you and I will never again see in our lifetimes. She could lose, but she will fight. She will not go down without throwing in every weapon at her command. Would you do any less, Captain Randall?"

A forlorn smile touched Marcus's lips. "Under the circumstances—no, I suppose not. How many men will go to the bottom?"

Captain Hensley met his eyes and saw the decision that had already been made. "If we're lucky, about a hundred."

Victoria watched and waited. Her face showed no trace of the turmoil of emotion that was threatening the calm facade. Her eyes met her husband's.

"The quicker done, the better," Marcus answered grimly, but his eyes were hard and his jaw was set in a tight line as he took Victoria by the shoulders. His touch was not gentle. "After this there will be no more, or you will answer to me. You have a lot more than the admiralty to fear, my dear. Do I make myself quite clear?"

Despite the fingers that dug deeply and painfully into her arms, Victoria's smile was shining with love and joy. She put her arms around her husband and held him close. He had not abandoned her. He would not betray her. "I would do the same for you, my darling. I would gladly give my life for yours. One day, perhaps, I will have the chance to prove it."

Marcus let out a resigned sigh and rolled his eyes toward heaven. "I sincerely hope not," he responded sardonically, but a smile of pleasure touched the corners of his mouth. Neither had he missed the fact that his wife had not answered his question. She had made no promise that this would be the last of the killing and the last of risking her neck for money and for power.

With supreme confidence Victoria left the matter in Captain Hensley's capable hands as she walked arm-in-arm with her husband. They left the ship and

strolled to the warehouse, and while Marcus con-
versed with Mr. Coster, Victoria searched for the
bolts of silk that had entered the country entirely
legally. She smiled as she thought of Marcus wearing
the beautiful new clothes she intended to see that he
got. Nothing she could do would ever repay him for
the decision he had just made, but Victoria promised
herself that she would try to run her business in a
more acceptable manner. Marcus was risking his life
for her, just as she would do for him.

While Victoria was thus occupied Marcus gained an
even deeper insight into his wife's business, for Mr.
Coster revealed more than he should to the man who
now ruled the woman who ruled the commercial
empire. Or so Howard thought.

The wrenching experience Marcus had just been
through convinced him more than ever that his wife
must be removed far from Annapolis and far from the
circumstances of business that had already turned her
into a very casual killer. It seemed to mean very little
to Victoria that her own men would very likely suffer
heavy casualties, and Richard Hensley was no better
than a pirate, himself. It had taken him a long time,
but Marcus finally realized the depth of the violence
to which his wife would sink to insure her wealth and
her power. He grimaced in distaste and thought that
Victoria and Richard Hensley were two of a kind.

It was not until that evening, when the two of them
had retreated to the privacy of their rooms, that
Marcus began to apply the pressure that would
eventually force Victoria to live the life he intended
for her. His approach to the subject was casual. ''I
must return to Serenity very soon, my dear, and it

would please me if you came along for a brief visit. I
have trailed after you like an obedient hound while
you exhibited me and our son to your friends. Now
it's your turn to indulge me. I'm most anxious to have
one or two people learn of our marriage."

Victoria laughed. "Clay, for instance?"

"Yes, my dear. Particularly Clay, who never ceased
to remind me of my shortcomings all the while you
were gone."

Still smiling, Victoria shook her head regretfully.
"I'm afraid you will have to wait to savor your small
victory. I must travel on business now, for I cannot
drag Pac with me during the winter months. However, we'll come for a visit before Christmas. Perhaps
you can invite Clay and his family to spend some time
with us then."

Anger roiled to the surface. Marcus clenched his
fists to keep from striking his wife, who had just
hurled the greatest of insults. And she wasn't even
aware of it. Victoria had told him in so many words
that he paled in significance when compared to her
financial affairs, that he was worth a short visit for a
week or two of pleasure in his bed, but then she must
be off to do more important things than being his
wife.

His anger defeated his well-planned strategy as
Marcus reacted to his wife's indifference and
arrogance. "You will most definitely not drag Pac
halfway around the world on scurvy-ridden ships.
You will not expose him to a terrible death at sea.
Wasn't Ellen's baby enough for you? Must you
sacrifice our son as well? No, my dear," he continued
ominously, "you will not drag our son from one
pest hole to another as your father did with you. And

whether you accompany me to my home or not, Pac will go with me. Ruby raised me; she can raise him as well.''

Victoria's eyes narrowed dangerously, and the skin over her high cheekbones tightened. ''No one will raise my son but me,'' she muttered from between clenched teeth. ''Not as long as I have breath in my body.''

Marcus almost smiled. Defeat suddenly became a very likely victory, for although Victoria did not make a fuss over her child, she loved him with a quiet intensity that would compel her to any deed to keep him near, to keep him safe. Wherever he took the child she would follow. He had a new and powerful weapon to use in his particular war—their son.

He shrugged. ''That's up to you, my dear, but my son is going to Serenity. It's my home, and it's his as well. What you choose to do will not alter that fact.''

''You wouldn't dare!'' Victoria hissed, but she knew he would. He had boxed her in a corner. There wasn't a court in this land or in any other that would condone her actions. If it came to that, Marcus would win. Her child would be torn from her arms, and her marriage would be destroyed. ''Just like my father!'' she thought suddenly and slumped in defeat.

''Very well,'' she replied quietly, controlling the bitter resentment with difficulty, ''we'll go.'' She needed time and this was one way to get it, but Marcus was going to regret this action. He was going to regret it bitterly. Already Victoria had put aside her gratitude to the man whose silence would insure her very life.

The tension between them grew as the ship made its way up the James River. Victoria had refused all

intimate contact with her husband; she barely talked
to him, and Marcus chafed under the lash of his
wife's wrath. He had made a crucial error and knew
it. He had his child, but he certainly no longer had a
wife. Finally his irritation swelled to full-blown
anger, and by the time the ship tied up at his private
wharf he was ready to take a horse whip to Victoria.

But Victoria, too, was in a dangerous mood. This
was not what she had anticipated when she had set
down her conditions. It was unheard of! Of course she
had intended to include her child! It was understood
that where she went Pac would also go.

Marcus had twisted the covenant to suit himself.
He was obeying the letter but not the spirit of their
agreement. And the fact that he was perfectly willing
to let her go wherever she wanted as long as Pac
stayed with him enraged her even more.

Her self-absorption was such that she barely
noticed the comfortable home nestled securely in its
foundation of warm brown stone, nor did she act in a
civil manner toward the small, dignified black
woman who waited for them in the open doorway.
She acknowledged the introduction to the house slave
with no warmth or enthusiasm. The destructive
poison of self-pity had crept into her veins, and she
demanded haughtily to be shown immediately to her
room.

Marcus was beside himself. And when he had
escorted Victoria to his bedroom he turned on her.
''Don't think for one minute, my dear, that I shall put
up with your wretched behavior, and don't think that
I shall suffer for long months again without the
comfort of a woman's body.''

Pain seared through Victoria, but she instinctively

lashed back. "I don't give a damn what you do! You told me what seems a lifetime ago that you would release me when you tired of me. I shall expect you to keep that promise. Divorce is long and difficult, but if the right hands are crossed with enough silver, it can be arranged," she replied icily, driving the wedge deeper. But she had made up her mind. If Marcus sought out another woman, it was the end. Her life would continue, and she would keep her son.

Stunned by the mention of divorce, Marcus fought back the pain. In retaliation he wounded Victoria just as deeply. "There will never be a divorce, Victoria. My son will have both a mother and a father, and you will never obtain your freedom without my consent. No, my dear, there is a much simpler way to solve my problem, but do not concern yourself, for you shall be the first to know when I take a mistress to fulfill your duties. For the sake of our son, however, I shall be most discreet. I will do nothing to publicly shame or humiliate either of you and can only hope you will show me as much consideration."

"Consideration!" she said quickly, feeling as though she could stand no more. Her hand trembled as she put it to her eyes to block out a world that had suddenly become untenable. Without touching her physically, Marcus had delivered a mortal blow.

Victoria felt herself sway slightly, and her husband's arms were around her instantly. "Don't touch me!" she hissed, and Marcus recoiled as he would from a white-hot iron. Then he recovered, his pain and frustration stinging him to near madness.

"I will not put up with this, Victoria! As long as you are my wife, and that will be for as long as you live, I shall do what I damned well please with you," he snarled as he curled vicious fingers through her hair, pulling her face toward him.

Victoria struggled in silence, deeply humiliated by the thought that the servants would hear and know of this degrading treatment. She grimaced in pain as Marcus pinned her arms behind her, leaving ugly marks that would become bruises.

Her clothing was torn from her body with less thought than that given to skinning a rabbit. Hard, cruel fingers caught the tender flesh of the thigh in a viselike grip, forcing her to submit. Her strength was gone. She could fight no more, but neither did she respond. The searing pain that burned in her brain blocked out all feeling. She was numb, and she endured the despicable punishment in silence.

At last it was done, and Marcus covered his shame with a callous attitude. "And now, my dear, suppose you make yourself presentable. I would not have my slaves think I have married a common slut from the streets. You will put a good face on things, or, so help me God, I shall take a strap to you!"

Separating herself from the world around her, Victoria withdrew where no one could follow. As though in some waking dream, she washed and put on clean clothes. With great effort she lifted the brush and touched it to her hair.

Marcus watched and waited. His heart pounded in fear. He had broken her. He had forced her to take refuge from a world she could no longer tolerate, and he did not know how to make it right. He swallowed the ache in his throat. He would wait for her. No matter how long it took, he would wait.

Gradually, almost imperceptibly, Victoria's back straightened. Her head lifted. The practiced calm she had mastered through years of patience and self-denial began to spread its soothing ointment over her tortured soul. The total shame of cruel degradation eased its killing grip, but she was not yet ready to return completely to the pain Marcus had inflicted. She needed time. Time for the answer to come.

Marcus was appalled by the icy correctness of Victoria's bearing and speech, the aloofness of her mind. She was remote and unfeeling. He could not allow it to continue. If he did, he would lose her forever. Something had to be done to warm that cold skin, to put the fires of life back into her. He would try anything. But what? He didn't know.

Ruby, the slave who had run this house for almost three decades, hesitated. Something was very wrong between the man she had raised from childhood and this woman he had married. She shook her head in sorrow. The captain had waited almost thirty-five years before marrying, and from the looks of things he should have waited that much longer.

She had seen her share of cold, heartless ladies, but the one her Marcus had married was the worst of all. Not even the baby clothes she had so tenderly saved all these years made an impression. The new mistress hardly looked at them. She didn't even bother to pretend she was interested. Instead she turned her head, rudely ignoring Ruby and her kind efforts. "Don't care nuthin' 'bout the cap'n," she muttered sullenly as she banged one more pot onto the kitchen hearth and silently cursed the woman who had intruded into her life.

Marcus was aware of the depth of the rift between Ruby and Victoria. He, himself, was near the breaking point. It was his fault Victoria could feel no joy in the things Ruby held to be so precious. It was his fault the slave who would never knowingly hurt anyone had been deeply hurt herself.

He glanced over at his wife. Her stare was blank. There was no smile, no warmth to her features. He would have preferred tears, screaming, a tantrum—anything but this terrible reserve, this shutting herself away from him.

Not a single tear had been shed. She had defeated him completely, for he had wanted her to cry, to beg, to promise. But she had not. She had simply endured in stoic silence the vile treatment he had heaped on her. She had threatened to leave him, to divorce him, and she had denied him the rights that were his by law.

Having convinced himself that Victoria was equally responsible for what had happened, Marcus made a stiff, mocking bow in her direction. "Shall we go into the dining room for a glass of wine before dinner?"

Victoria lifted her eyes and looked at him, and Marcus dared hope. There was a spark of resentment struggling to survive in those green eyes.

Taking the chair he held for her, Victoria sat in silence, staring into the ruby wine. She made no move toward it, so Marcus held the goblet to her lips. "Please, my love, drink this. It will help warm you."

Again she raised her eyes to his, and Marcus winced. The anguish there was a mirror of his own. But she drank the wine. Again Marcus filled the goblet and held it to her lips. This time Victoria took hold of the heavy crystal and drank thirstily. She could not seem to get enough, and for a woman who rarely sipped a sociable glass it spelled disaster.

The second glass began to send a warm, comforting

glow through the numbing chill of her body. As she sipped the third, the deep-seated pain began to blur and soften. Her body relaxed, and she could feel her extremities begin to thaw. And suddenly she was aware.

"I'm getting drunk," she thought in surprise and didn't care as she drank the fourth glass. "Oh, well," she said aloud, "there's a first time for everything." And she put her fingers to her lips to stifle the giggle that she felt the terribly clever remark called for. Instead, she hiccuped.

"I hope so, my dear," Marcus replied dryly, filling the glass again.

The next morning Victoria could not remember what she had eaten or how she had gotten to bed, but she could remember feeling warm and safe in her husband's arms. And from somewhere out of the haze she remembered her husband's tears and his tenderness.

She sat up and her head throbbed. Moaning, she lay back down and eased it gently to the pillow. The drapes were drawn and the room was dark, but she was vaguely aware of movement. She closed her eyes against the pain as she felt Marcus sit on the edge of the bed.

"Not feeling too well this morning?" he teased, the amusement as well as the pleasure and satisfaction evident in his voice.

Victoria made a small, unhappy sound and rolled over on her side. She felt a cold, wet cloth being applied to her forehead as her body was turned gently. Her hand went gratefully to the coolness, and she opened her eyes to the diabolical smirk on her husband's face. She was too miserable to comment.

Instead she flashed him a nasty look and closed her eyes to shut out the widening grin.

"Our son has been howling for the last two hours, letting us know in no uncertain terms that he has been sorely neglected. And he stoutly refuses a pewter nipple. Prefers his mother's, and I can't say that I blame him."

Victoria's eyes flew open. What in the name of the holy mother, Isis, had she done last night? She didn't know, but there were vague shadows drifting across her mind, and they were terrible. She wouldn't have behaved like that.

Or would she? She was no longer sure, and that laughing hyena she was married to didn't help. How was she going to face anybody? She wished she could remember.

Marcus left the room and returned almost immediately, bringing a screaming Pac with him. Victoria held out her arms and took the child whose little face was wet with tears. It wasn't right. It wasn't right that this little creature she loved so much should be made to suffer because of two idiots who were old enough to know better. It must stop. Some compromise must be reached. She would have to sacrifice, but so would Marcus.

Her son sucked hungrily, and Victoria smiled into those wide emerald eyes that were so much like her mother's. As she bent her head to kiss one small hand, her hair tumbled around her, shielding her from her husband's fascinated gaze.

A renewed surge of guilt washed over Marcus. He had used his son to force Victoria into line. And he had threatened to take a mistress. He was not honoring the contract between them.

*Contract!* The word lay bitter on his tongue. He wanted more than a business agreement. He wanted a marriage.

Pac released his hold on his mother's breast and closed his eyes, worn out from crying. Marcus took his son from Victoria's arms and put him in the cradle that had been his so many years before. When he turned back toward the bed Victoria slid out quickly and picked up the robe she had last seen at the hunting lodge.

Marcus took it from her and held it up as she slipped into it. Then he turned her to him and fastened the tiny buttons. When he leaned down to touch his lips to hers Victoria turned her head, but Marcus did not press the matter.

"You seem to have made a remarkable recovery, my dear. Now if you are quite ready to come to breakfast, I should like to eat as well."

As the meal progressed, Victoria became increasingly uneasy, waiting nervously for Marcus to say something about her conduct last night. She was so uncertain of what she had done that she was sorely tempted to come right out and ask, but some instinct warned her to be quiet.

Not once through the entire meal did Marcus mention her immoderate drinking, and that made her even more suspicious. She glowered. Immoderate drinking, her foot. She had been riproaring drunk. She moaned and tried to sink lower in her chair. Neither was she comforted by the smirk on Marcus's face.

Finally she couldn't stand it. "I'm very sorry for my behavior. The drinking, I mean," she added defensively, for she had no intention of apologizing

for the actions that had driven her husband into a
rage. He was the one who had started it.

"But, my dear, you are perfectly charming when
you are drunk," Marcus replied easily. "If things
don't improve when you're sober, I might seriously
consider keeping you in your cups."

She blushed furiously. "Damn, I wish I could
remember!" she snapped, and was not at all
comforted by her husband's insinuating sneer, but his
next words soothed her troubled spirit.

"Pac will go with you," he said softly. "I had no
right to use our son as your jailor. You may leave
Serenity whenever you choose, and you may take him
with you. But not for too long, I hope. He's my child,
too, and it will break my heart to part with him for
even a day."

He took her hand in his before continuing. "You
forgave me last night when you were too drunk to
know what you were saying, so once again I beg your
forgiveness. I also promised to wait for you no matter
how long you stay away. It's a promise I'll keep."

Victoria's heart was full to bursting. For her sake he
was sacrificing his own needs and desires. He loved
his son every bit as much as she did, but because she
needed to go her own way Marcus was willing to
suffer the wrenching agony of separation. And he
would endure the celibacy she demanded from him
until she returned. It was enough.

A growing love shone through Victoria's smile.
"I'm glad I forgave you. Now, tell me, what did I do
last night?"

The rolling laughter surfaced from deep within.
When he could control himself Marcus wiped the
tears from his eyes. "My angel, you don't want to

know. But this I will admit. You fairly burst with a wanton abandon that even I cannot fully do justice to.''

Victoria drew in her breath and turned crimson. She knew she shouldn't have asked, and she didn't want to know any more.

Bruised hearts began to mend. Clay and his family put their own minds at rest. Whatever had happened that long-ago day in Williamsburg was past. They spent a pleasant three weeks with Marcus and his bride.

Clay chuckled indulgently. The bride and groom who had been married for less than four months had a fine strapping son who was already three months old. But Clay didn't give a damn. And if any man dared comment on that fact, if they should somehow stumble across it, there would be hell to pay, for never had Clay seen his brooding cousin happier or more content.

When the time came for Victoria to leave him Marcus did not complain. He kept his promise and stood watching as the ship that carried his wife and son so far away from him disappeared in the distance.

# 17

Marcus approached the imposing house that was guarded by a forbidding, spiked-iron fence. He pushed at the gate and it swung open. Before he had time to pull the bell cord a small peep door opened, revealing two reddish-brown eyes set in a band of freckles. "State yer business," the unfriendly voice growled.

"Captain Marcus Randall out of Richmond, Virginia, husband to Victoria Chisholm, father of Paul Andrew Chisholm Randall calling on Mr. Henry Byrnes," he rattled off confidently.

And he was right. Without another word the heavy door swung wide, and he stepped into the intimidating entry. He smiled as he recognized the tactics. He had heard his wife explain the strategy of exhibiting unmistakable signs of her great wealth where no one who entered her home could possibly miss them. Apparently she had learned that bit of devious behavior from Henry Byrnes himself.

"Wait here," Sean Rubley instructed. He didn't

sound any friendlier, and Marcus began to question the wisdom of this visit. But he had come all this way to talk to the man Victoria loved and trusted. He would not turn back now.

Within minutes a tall skeleton of a man, leaning heavily on his cane, appeared from behind one of the numerous closed doors. "I'm Henry Byrnes, Captain Randall."

"May I speak with you, sir? In private," Marcus added, glancing at the servant who continued to intrude with his presence.

"You can speak in front of Sean," Henry countered. "He'll just listen at the door, anyway. But come in, come in."

Following Henry into a cluttered, musty study, Marcus sat in the chair the older man indicated with a wave of his hand. Sean stood behind his employer's sagging chair and waited.

"Now, Captain," Henry began as he settled himself more comfortably into the dents and hollows that conformed exactly to his body, "what's on your mind?"

"It concerns my wife," Marcus answered and stopped, giving Henry Byrnes one more chance to dismiss the servant.

"I see." Henry sighed. "She's well, I hope. The few letters I've received indicate that she is in robust health."

Marcus laughed. "Indeed, sir, she's more than I can keep up with."

Henry chuckled in understanding. "If you have difficulty, Captain, you can well imagine what her father and I went through. Both of us were well in our dotage before Victoria came of age. But enough of the past. What is it you came here to say?''

Not sure just how to begin, Marcus hesitated. ''This is very difficult for me, but I had to talk to someone. You seemed the likely choice.''

Another moment passed. Henry did not break the silence. He waited patiently for this man to ask the questions he knew were coming. But he was not sure how he would answer. Everything depended on his judgment of Marcus Randall's intent and character.

''First, let me assure you that I am deeply in love with my wife. . . .''

''But!'' Henry interrupted cynically.

''Yes,'' Marcus admitted. ''There is a but.'' Again he hesitated, and he was tempted to forget this whole implausible quest when Henry stepped in, for he had seen the man's embarrassment and agitation.

''Sean, bring the captain and me a pitcher of wine and two mugs. We're going to be here awhile. And ask Tillie to send in a platter of cold meats and cheeses. A loaf of rye bread, too, I think.''

When the servant had gone Henry turned his full attention to the man Victoria had married. ''Now, Captain, out with it.''

Hesitantly, Marcus began to confide in the man Victoria seemed to respect and love. ''When we were married, sir, my wife demanded that certain conditions be met.''

''By you, I take it.''

Marcus smiled bitterly. ''Of course. The problem is simple. Those restrictions are becoming increasingly difficult to honor. As you probably know, Victoria refuses to live with me.''

Henry raised his brows. ''Does she really, now, Captain? Or is it that she refuses to live with you where you wish to reside? Are you not welcome in her home?''

Totally exasperated by this turn in the conversation, Marcus glared at Henry in disgust. ''Wives are expected to live in whatever homes their husbands can provide, I believe!''

''So,'' Henry translated, ''that's it. You are unable to force Victoria to conform to your demands. Never mind what she wants.''

''I see that further conversation is useless,'' he muttered and stood to leave.

''Sit down, sir!'' Henry commanded in a tone that indicated he would brook no defiance. ''May I suggest that you are acting like a pompous ass. You have no idea what you have gotten yourself into. It's about time someone enlightened you.

''For the sake of the young woman who is as dear to me as if she were my own flesh and blood, for the sake of the woman you profess to love so deeply, you will listen. And if you cannot live with the conditions Victoria demands of you, then get out of her life once and for all. It would be far the kinder thing to do. You cannot force her to bend her neck to your will. It simply will not work. She will not be bullied, sir. Not by you and not by me. And I might add that there were precious few times even her father could get away with it. That is not the way to handle her.''

''You're very good at flinging insults,'' Marcus snapped back, ''For you obviously have all the colossal arrogance so typical of your class. I can see now why my wife is such an obnoxious, headstrong, spoiled brat. She's been encouraged to ride roughshod over others without regard for their feelings or for the pain she causes. She is my wife, sir, and she will do as

I tell her. I had hoped you might be able to help me find a way to mend this terrible rift in our marriage, for I refuse to follow her from place to place like some blasted lap dog."

Henry smiled. The planter from Virginia had obviously suffered some rather devastating blows to his pride, and the wounds were still tender. "Sit down, Marcus. I may use your given name, may I not? If you please, sir," Henry insisted genially. Reluctantly, Marcus sat.

"What you say has some merit," Henry continued reasonably. "You are, indeed, in a most difficult position, but if you try to resolve this dilemma by force, you will lose her completely. Is that what you want?"

"God knows it isn't," Marcus answered, "but I've given her about as much rope as I can. I don't need a business partner, and I certainly don't need a whore for my occasional pleasure. Those things are easy enough to come by. What I want is a wife! She apparently has no intention of being one."

"You must give her time. I know, I know," Henry soothed, raising his hand to forestall the angry protestations, "you're growing impatient. But Victoria has much to do yet before she can even consider such a request, and I think she will never be content devoting all her energies to home and family. She wasn't raised to be wife or mother. She was raised to be exactly what she is—a cunning, conniving, somewhat ruthless ruler of a vast financial empire."

"Is there no hope at all?" Marcus pleaded. "Or am I condemned to live through this hell forever? I've tried forcibly bending her to my will, and you're right. It's no good. Somehow or other, she always wins."

Laughing heartily, Henry concurred. "I usually gave in as well, so you're not alone, but to answer your question, I was quite serious about giving her more time. Right now Victoria is fulfilling a promise to her father. It was his dying request. She will not dishonor it. Not for you. Not for me. We can only hope that she soon considers the promise kept, that there is to be some limit to her efforts.

"But she cannot be torn between two worlds. If you set yourself up as a rival to her father's interests, you will lose. At least at present. Wait. Be patient. She will choose the world that means the most to her, and when she does you must accept that choice."

It was a most unsatisfactory answer and not at all what Marcus had hoped for. He wasn't sure just what he had expected Henry Byrnes to do—accomplish some miracle, probably. But there were no miracles.

"I'll try." He sighed in bitter resignation. "If that's the best advice you can give me, I'll try."

"I'm truly sorry," Henry remarked with feelings of genuine sadness for the man who sat looking so disconsolate. "It really isn't Victoria's fault, you know. Before her mother died she was the happiest, the most loving of children. But from the beginning Andrew had marked her as his eventual heir. It was not until he lost Jeanine that that dream became an obsession.

"From the time she was three Andrew began to mold Victoria in his image. She was subjected to the most demanding physical and intellectual regimen. Her childhood was over. It was a dreadful existence for a child, and I shall not go into the details, but to his credit Andrew stayed by her side through it all. And to a man in his fifties that was no small feat.

"At any rate, Victoria thrived. She learned to out-
smart and outmaneuver the sharks of commerce who
even now circle, waiting for her to make a mistake.
She was trained well, and she is prepared. Her
domestic skills, however, are quite another story."

Henry smiled wistfully and closed his eyes.
"Nothing like her mother, more's the pity. If only
Jeanine had lived," he wished in vain. "But if Victoria
has just one drop of her mother's blood flowing in her
veins, she will be worth the wait—well worth the
wait."

His voice trailed off in remembrance, and Marcus
understood more clearly the unusually close relationship between Victoria and this shrewd old man. He
had loved the woman who had been her mother, and
so he loved the child as well. "I'm sorry, sir."

Henry opened his eyes and nodded. He did not try
to deny an obvious truth. "Victoria has never guessed
just how much I loved Jeanine Monet. Andrew, I
think, suspected, but he never mentioned it. As for
Jeanine, there was never any question. Andrew was
her life."

The early dark of late fall closed over the room, and
Henry lit the candles as the two men ate and drank
and talked half the night away. Each, in his own way,
loved Victoria deeply, and Marcus took what strength
he could from the old man's lifetime of love and
devotion.

For the first time in long, dreary months Victoria
awakened to the comforts of her own home. She was
more than pleased. Pac had adjusted to life aboard
ship with remarkable ease. While she had been

occupied with the tiring details of distributing her power, Tim and Robb had watched over her son like two mother hens. She smiled as she remembered, but then that smile disappeared.

She did not think it possible to miss anyone as much as she had missed Marcus. It was a constant longing that not even the profitable, clandestine trade agreements entered into in the West Indies, Portugal and South America could still. How many times had she turned to share a thought with him, and he was not there and would not be there? How many restless nights had passed so slowly while her mind wandered back to remember only the good times they had shared in his cabin?

But perhaps the worst was almost over. She had arranged her life in a way that would give her more time to spend with the man who had waited so patiently.

Buck Arnold, her Baltimore agent, who had shown a remarkable talent for business, would control her interests from that small tobacco port to the north and to the west. Howard Coster would oversee everything from Annapolis to her newly formed interests in Brazil. William and Ellen would continue to run the trading post that seemed to take in more and more furs each season. And Henry, of course, would take care of her European interests, as always. The legitimate ones, at least.

Still all her accomplishments were not making her any happier. The heady feeling that had always accompanied victory, the elation she had felt in the past when besting a clever enemy were gone. Her work seemed to have little purpose, for who was there to care if her father's influence had been

extended to yet another continent? Who was there to
care that gold and silver were piling up faster than she
could find suitable investments? And her answer was
bitterly truthful. No one. No one at all.

And still there was more to be done. The two
thousand acres her father had purchased from Lord
Baltimore was doing little more than providing
lumber for her trade in the Indies. Families must be
sent north to clear the land. Grain must be sown and
harvested. Cattle must be transported from England.
Animals that would form the beginnings of valuable
herds of breeding stock.

She had already informed Howard to be on the
lookout for workers whose services could be bought
from a ship's captain for the price of passage and a bit
more. But so far none of the ships that dropped
anchor at Annapolis had carried any indentured
workers not already contracted for. Even then, few
had any real skills to offer, and home-grown labor
was increasingly scarce as those with ability bought
up their own land or businesses. It was certainly not
like England, where one could pick and choose from
among the almost bottomless pool of labor at prices
that enabled manufacturers to sell their goods at a
pleasing profit.

Of course she could always purchase slaves, but as
far as Victoria was concerned, owning her own labor
force simply was not cost efficient. Neither did she
have any desire to play nursemaid to aging and sick
workers who cost more to keep than they were worth
to her in goods and services produced.

And there was something else bothering Victoria.
Clay had taken her aside before he and his parents
had ended their visit to Serenity. His warning had

been simple and direct. Marcus was a man not suited to a life of abstinence. His needs were very real and very strong, and she would be courting disaster if she refused to be a wife to him, if she refused to be there when he needed her.

His words still sent a shiver of fear through her just as they had when Clay first spoke them. "If you go through with your plans as you have outlined them to Marcus, you are thrusting temptation directly in his path. You cannot trip a man and then blame him for falling, my dearest, foolish Victoria.

"When you left him in Williamsburg he changed into someone none of us recognized. I've never seen him in so black and dangerous a mood. And he amazed us all. Not once during the time you were separated from him did he take another woman to his bed. He loved you then and he loves you now. If he betrays you, it will be because he thought he married a woman of flesh and blood, not some celestial vapor that floats periodically in and out of his life. My cousin needs you, my dear, not broken-hearted dreams of you, but you. He needs your strength, your warmth, and most of all your love. If you withhold yourself from him, if you allow your pride to come between you, then God help you both," Clay had said with great sadness.

But most of all Victoria heard over and over in her dreams the last words Clay had spoken on the subject. "If you loved Marcus enough to marry him, then you must love him enough to be a wife to him, for nothing else makes sense to my cousin. As far as he's concerned it all boils down to one simple question. Do you love him or don't you?"

She had not answered Clay, but tears had sprung to

her eyes even as they did now. Of course she loved him. She always had. And that was the problem. What did she owe him and what did she owe her father? There was no answer. There never had been.

Just as important, however, was what did she owe to herself? What did she want? She was no longer certain. There had been a time not so long ago when she thought she knew, when her path had lain shining before her, but all that had changed. It had changed when Marcus had intruded into her life, when he had upset all her neat, well-constructed plans.

And Pac. She smiled as she glanced over at her son, playing contentedly in his crib. Never had she known a love so deep and so strong as that which she felt for this joy that had come into her life. And except for her love for Marcus, she would have destroyed those faint beginnings of life within her. Had Pac been the seed of any other man, she would have killed him.

She laughed as her son went through his attention-seeking antics. Spotted Wolf's people had named him properly. They had given him a name that was prophetic. "One Who Smiles."

Then, once again, a frown darkened Victoria's face. What she was doing was cruel and inexcusable. Pac was growing up not knowing his father. And Marcus, who loved his son as much as she did, suffered anew each day he was parted from the boy. It wasn't right.

"*Damn, damn, damn,*" she cursed softly under her breath, and for the first time some faint twinge of sympathy for Lady Catherine tapped gently at the locked door in Victoria's heart.

Her father had been wrong. If Edward had been less than he desired, then he should have stayed at home to correct the boy. Money wasn't that important! She smiled in self-derision. Who was she to condemn? She was doing the same thing, the only difference being that she took Pac with her. And in so doing, she had excluded Marcus not only from her life but from his son's as well. It was the same thing her father had done to Lady Catherine.

Victoria slumped dejectedly onto the bench at the dressing table. Her hand twitched as she clenched the hairbrush and then was still. Clay was worried. So worried that he felt it necessary to intrude into her personal life, something Victoria knew was absolutely distasteful to him, something he would not have done except under severest provocation. And she had provided that provocation.

Then her eyes focused and she saw the pathetic, weak image that reflected back to her from the mirror. She laughed derisively at the indecision, the self-pity she saw there, and she made up her mind. Pac would definitely spend more time with his father. So would she, but she had no intention of plopping herself down at Serenity with nothing beter to do than oversee that poor excuse for an estate and raise a dozen or more children. For that's exactly what would happen if she gave in.

Her back straightened and her eyes snapped defiantly. She would work it out some other way.

At that precise moment one of life's not so uncommon coincidences occurred. Bess appeared at the door of the bedroom, waving a sheet of paper in her hand. "Howard says you're to come to town quick! There's some redemptioners aboard the *Flying Gull* that haven't been spoke for yet. But he says you must make the decision since the poor souls are in desperate shape. Some won't live out the week," Bess added accusingly.

Victoria raised her brows in a useless gesture of displeasure, but Bess paid not the slightest heed. Of course she had read the message from Mr. Coster. She had to decide whether or not it was important enough to disturb her mistress, who had precious little time to herself as it was.

For a moment Victoria hesitated. She was not anxious to descend into the stinking bowels of a ship whose captain had undoubtedly taken on more hapless souls than could ever be properly fed from the limited provisions aboard. And even food wouldn't help some of them survive as conditions deteriorated. The longer the voyage, the more who would die. Many never lived to see their destination. And if one member of a family died, the others were still responsible for his passage. Practically no children under the age of seven ever survived. She wondered how many of these desperate creatures still lived. Howard didn't say.

Reluctantly, she nodded to Bess. "Tell Bullen to get the carriage ready. I'll join him in a few minutes. And take Pac downstairs with you. He won't be going with me."

Bess swelled with righteous indignation. "I should hope not! You've already dragged the poor child halfway around the world as it is! The good Lord only knows what terrible things he's been exposed to."

"He'll survive," Victoria drawled sarcastically, and proceeded to pull on a pair of old boots that would be almost hidden under the skirt of a well-worn blue wool dress. She would wear nothing that couldn't be spared to the cleansing flames, for she did not know what she was going to find aboard the *Flying Gull*.

Howard met her at the warehouse and joined her in the small boat that would carry them the short distance to the spot where the *Flying Gull* rode at anchor. Even as they boarded, Victoria could smell the stench that was rising from the hatch like some bilious cloud.

As they descended, Victoria put her handkerchief to her nose. "Holy mother, Isis," she whispered as she saw what was left of the ship's human cargo. Quickly she bent to examine the refuse who moaned piteously at her touch.

With eyes that had been trained to detect the simpler illnesses she looked at each person carefully to make sure there were no signs of those diseases that could wipe out her entire farm and much of the town of Annapolis as well. If there was even the slightest indication of any of these terrible scourges, everyone would be left aboard to die.

But all she saw were those afflictions that could have been prevented. There were the familiar skin eruptions, the bleeding, spongy gums, the missing teeth and the clothes soiled from uncontrolled diarrhea. She could only guess at the number of ports in which these people had waited—first with hope and then in numb despair. She had thought her slaves had been in poor shape when she first saw them. Compared to these wretches, they had been the picture of health and plenty.

Without further comment she escaped to the open deck. Then she gave Howard instructions to bargain sharply for the eight she thought might survive. He was to offer nothing for the three who seemed close to death. If the captain were as desperate as he should be by now to rid himself of the whole lot, he would offer to throw in those three just to have them removed. In that event Howard was to accept them.

While her agent was letting the captain of the ship know what he thought of him, Victoria had herself rowed back to land. Quickly she walked to the small house she still rented, stripped and burned everything. Then she scrubbed down with the harsh soap that reeked of lye.

Hurrying up the stairs, she shivered in the cold house and rummaged impatiently through the few things she kept here. Finally she shrugged into a dress, silk hose and narrow-heeled shoes. The only outer garment to be found was a light, waist-length cape that would provide very little warmth.

She made a wry face. She had only herself to blame. There were quite a few things she had neglected in the months she had been away. But at least she was satisfied that she would be carrying no lice or other vermin back to the farm. As for the redemptioners, they would be scrubbed down with salt water and all their pitiful belongings would be burned. Howard knew what to do. They would be wrapped in blankets and transported to Chisholm House. Not one stitch they had worn would escape the fire.

Almost at a dead run, Victoria returned to the carriage she had not dared enter while still wearing the clothing that had come in contact with the new workers. Ordering Bullen to drive her to the nearby shop, which sold the cheap, coarse cloth she wanted, Victoria estimated the minimum amount that would be needed in order to cover their nakedness with simple, unadorned nightshirts. She sighed heavily. The women at the farm were going to have their hands full with the eight men and three women soon to be dumped on them. But that number would soon be reduced, for one of the men and two of the women looked as though they were beyond help.

Eleven blankets were sent back to the ship, then Victoria headed for home, the awkward bolt of cloth resting securely atop the carriage. Almost before the carriage came to a halt, Bess popped out the front door. She was plainly disappointed that her mistress had not brought the others home with her. Victoria simply muttered some dark and unintelligible comment and swept inside.

It was not until the cart rumbled to the back door and Bess got a good look at the pathetic cargo that she understood. "Lord bless us!" she cried in horror, then went to work.

One by one the new arrivals were put into the snug cabins of those who lived on the estate and had so much to share. Josiah prepared drinks made with lime juice imported from the West Indies. Nourishing soups simmered over kitchen fires. Additional butter and cheese were provided from the springhouse. Soon the tantalizing odor of baking bread wafted from the ovens of the bakehouse to hang in the cold winter air.

For a few days a desperate battle was fought for some of the lives, and in spite of their best efforts one of the women was lost, but all others survived. Everyone of them, however, would carry the marks of his ordeal to the grave, but they would live to work and to be of use to the woman who had saved their lives as surely as if she had pulled them from a raging sea.

At Josiah's request two of the younger men were kept at the farm. The remaining six men and the two surviving women were sent north with the necessary supplies. Daniel Hubbard went with them to help build a crude shelter, for winter was already upon them. Tents would be their only protection until a common house was built. Come spring, their work would begin in earnest.

Victoria laughed as she watched the motley group leave. They were going to a sparsely populated area, and the two ladies were going to find themselves the center of attraction despite some as yet unhealed skin lesions and a few missing teeth. She shook her head in good humor and turned back to the house.

This would be her first Christmas at home, and Bess was making the most of it. The marvelous smells of ginger and cinnamon filled the kitchen and drifted up from the cellar, where Suellen worked diligently. Trays of cookies graced the sideboard. Heavy, rich plum puddings cooled on the table, and fruited breads had been tucked safely away inside beautifully decorated tinware.

Wandering into the newly completed north wing, which housed the grand dining room, Victoria smiled as she dipped her fingers into the gleaming gold bowl and stuffed a few kernels of popped corn into her mouth, licking her fingers in appreciation afterward. Nobody made it like Bess.

And despite her frugal nature, Bess had lit every candle in the room. The bright flames threw their cheerful glow everywhere, highlighting each piece of silver, each item of crystal or gold. The effect was breathtaking, and Victoria reveled in it. At last the place was the way she wanted it.

It was not important that there was still not room for all the furniture her father had shipped from

London. It could stay in the warehouse until she found some diplomatic way to incorporate select items into the general changes she planned for Serenity. But she had to be careful. Marcus was very touchy about the difference in their financial situations, and her plans could only be accomplished through great delicacy and artful maneuvering.

At first she paid little attention to the raucous geese. Even seconds later, when she heard the soft pounding of hooves against the crushed oyster shell that made up the drive, she thought little of it. Then she knew!

Making a mad dash for the door, she raced down the front steps and ran directly into the path of the charging horse. In desperation, Marcus jerked and sawed at the reins, bringing the high-spirited stallion to a rearing, thrashing halt. Pawing the air and whinnying in terror, the horse struggled to retain its balance. Both man and beast were in grave danger if the animal went over backward.

Only when Marcus pressed his weight against his stallion's neck was equilibrium restored, and the horse landed heavily on all four hooves. Totally unconcerned by the havoc she had very nearly caused, Victoria's eyes danced with happiness as she held up her arms to her husband.

Throwing one leg over the saddle, Marcus slid to the ground and crushed his wife to him. He didn't try to speak; he just held her tight and waited for the trembling to cease. Then he wrapped her in his riding cape and hustled her into the house and out of the frigid air.

Tim and Robb materalized from out of nowhere. Bess came running from the kitchen, wiping her hands on her apron. The three of them talked at once, each smiling his welcome. Gradually Marcus was able to answer their questions.

Everyone, including Victoria, raised his brows in some astonishment when he told them that he had just returned from a trip to England where he had met with Henry Byrnes. "I must say the man received me most cordially once he was convinced I had not come to steal the family silver."

All of them smiled and chuckled at the small joke and waited for him to say more, but Marcus remained silent. Disappointed, Robb turned the conversation to generalities while Victoria sliced a large portion of mince pie that would quiet his hunger until the large meal of the day was ready.

But his hunger would have to wait. "Pac?" he asked anxiously. Victoria laughed and ran to the playroom to get their son. Handing the boy to his father, she watched through shining eyes as Marcus ignored everyone else and became reacquainted with his son.

The child laughed and squealed as he was bounced and rocked by a booted foot. His soft baby arms went around Marcus's neck, and the others turned away as tears ran down his roughened cheeks. Victoria blinked the moisture from her own eyes. She had no right to separate them. It would stop.

Regaining her composure, Bess poured hot coffee and sliced pie for everyone. Neither Tim nor Robb needed any urging to accept the silent invitation. Each man settled himself comfortably at the large kitchen table, ready to enjoy the latest gossip from England. Mr. Byrnes, it seemed, knew everything that was going on.

Victoria smiled at the comment. "He always has, for he has turned many a profit from another's misfortune, and there's no quicker place to learn of those misfortunes than the gossip mills of His Majesty's Court.''

Marcus looked at Victoria in an odd way, but he remained silent, and at that moment the entire group turned their attention to Ned, who was ushered through the kitchen door by a blast of wintery wind.

Doffing his stocking cap, the boy shuffled nervously. "Bullen says for me to deliver these 'ere saddlebags to the master, if ya please, Miss Bess."

Tim pushed back his chair and stood. "I'll take 'em, lad. And what about the captain's horse?"

"All rubbed down an' safe an' snug in 'is stall, 'e is. Munchin' on oats an' 'appy as a clam."

Marcus grinned broadly. He had forgotten how recently the indentured servants had arrived in this country. Little more than two years ago, actually. Not yet time enough for some of them to lose the speech and mannerisms of the streets of London.

"Sit down, lad," he invited cordially. "You look near frozen to death. Might you spare a cup of hot coffee for the boy, Bess?"

Bess smiled and rumpled the boy's hair. "And a piece of pie, too, eh, Neddy?"

The boy blushed to the lobes of his ears. "Aye, mum, if'n yer sure ya can spare it."

No one laughed. Not even Tim, who suddenly found it necessary to make some adjustment to the saddle bags he had just hung over the back of an empty chair. And Marcus found himself relaxing almost to a stupor in this warm room so full of various and wonderful odors, a room that spelled home. He sighed heavily as he shifted his son's weight to his left arm while he finished the large slice of pie with his right hand. Serenity could most definitely use some improving.

For a few minutes his contentment seemed to have spread to the others, for no one spoke a word as they leaned back in their chairs, each lost in his own thoughts. And Marcus fixed his longing gaze on Victoria. He wondered what Henry could have meant when he had warned him about the side of her nature he had apparently not yet seen.

It was not easy to believe that there could be any more violent side to her character than he had already suffered under. He had been soundly boxed about the ears, kicked, gouged and slashed. What more could she do?

It was the same question he had asked Henry, who had laughed at the recitation of violence perpetrated against the hapless captain until tears rolled down his face. But when he had brought himself under control and had gulped a soothing mug of wine, he had responded seriously.

"I hope you never find out, Captain. And I hope she never directs that bloodless, emotionless, almost detached violence in your direction."

But the thing that had nagged at him and would give him no rest was Henry's reference to Edward Chisholm. He stared into the fire and recalled almost every word of the old man's warning. "No," he had said sadly in answer to Marcus's question, "her natural instinct is to destroy her adversaries as was her father's, and I sincerely believe that she will never rest until this thing with Edward is settled. I have never known Victoria to forgive an enemy or to allow him to go unpunished, just as I have never known her to be disloyal to one she loves—no matter what the provocation."

He had smiled encouragingly at Marcus when he

had spoken the last words, but Marcus had blushed with embarrassment. He had tested that love and loyalty to the limit. His eyes twinkled and he grinned as he put his restless son on the floor. She had done quite a bit of testing herself.

Long before the rest of the household was ready to retire for the night, Marcus and Victoria retreated to their private apartment. Pac was dumped unceremoniously into his crib and the door to the dressing room as well as the door to the sitting room were locked. When Marcus returned to the bedroom he found his wife standing there with a simpering smile on her face.

She curtsied demurely. "And what may I do for his lordship?" she mimicked coyly.

The old, lopsided grin she had seen so little of this past year spread slowly across his face. "His lordship prefers to demonstrate his needs," Marcus drawled suggestively, and Victoria laughed as he approached menacingly. But it was more than a lover's game. It was as much a delaying action, giving each of them a chance to get over the awkwardness they felt after so many months apart.

Slowly Marcus began to make love to his wife. At first there was only the touch of his fingers, moving like gossamer wings over her face. Then the soft touch of his lips on hers as his arms drew her closer. Restraining hooks and buttons were loosened. Cumbersome skirts and boots were removed, but all was done with a fluid grace and a muted tension that finally burst into flame.

Still Marcus did not hurry. Once under the covers, he pressed his wife's body to his. He did not know nor did he care where the control, the discipline came from as he assured the frenzy of her need, until she wanted him as much as he wanted her.

When it was over they lay quietly, content in the warmth and secure in the certainty of the other's love. Victoria squeezed her husband's hand. Then she turned over on her side and smiled into his eyes. "You've been in this house less than nine hours, and already you've managed to get me into bed. You certainly don't waste any time," she remarked in wry humor.

"Five months is one *hell* of a long time," Marcus muttered sourly. Then they both laughed shyly at the unintended admission. He had waited, but it had been no easy victory.

With no warning whatsoever, Victoria flopped heavily on top of her unsuspecting husband and strangled him in a bear hug. The joy and love that surged through her could barely be contained in her slender frame.

Grunting as the breath was knocked out of him, and doubling up his knees under the shock of literally being bounced on, Marcus grabbed Victoria and rolled them both on their sides. Their lovemaking was fierce, intense and demanding. Nor was Victoria a silent, passive partner, and when Marcus lay back exhausted he felt a deep sense of contentment. It had been difficult, but he had waited. And he would continue to do so no matter how long the time.

# 18

The following day was Christmas. Marcus and Victoria were aware of the subdued excitement that ran through the household, and Victoria smiled smugly. This year she was ready to celebrate the holiday she and her father had never bothered with even though Henry had always remembered them on this day he considered to be very special.

Reluctantly, and only because Marcus absolutely insisted, Victoria agreed to attend an early service that was to be mercifully short. Pac, of course, would be dragged along and put on display. It was the whole reason for going.

Victoria sighed forlornly. There was little hope Pac would make a nuisance of himself and give her an excuse for making an early exit. "Perhaps," she thought wickedly, "a small pinch . . ."

Mildred Thompson and her family were of the Roman Catholic faith and had already set out for Mr. Carroll's nearby estate where they would be welcomed into the family chapel for the celebration of this joyous mass. Other members of the household would visit with friends once the necessary chores had been done. Bess insisted that she stay home to keep an eye on the huge goose slowly turning over the fireplace coals on a spit powered by a wound spring, but Victoria shooed her housekeeper and Josiah away for a few hours of well-earned relaxation.

When the house was empty Victoria's thoughts turned to the offering she would make to this Christian deity. Such hypocrisy annoyed her, for neither she nor her father put much stock in any of the numerous gods and religions they had encountered in their travels. They had always preferred to put their faith in themselves and in their own abilities.

Nevertheless, Victoria allowed herself to be stuffed into the carriage and jolted over frozen, snow-dusted ground. She smiled serenely as she acknowledged the heads that bobbed in polite greeting, and she sat on the hard, high-backed pew, her feet propped on a foot warmer, and suffered. She even managed to react graciously to the curious members of the congregation who delayed her at the conclusion of the service with their inconsequential small talk.

Marcus, of course, handled the whole situation with a disgusting display of charm and with perfect Virginia-born-and-bred manners—something that irritated his wife until she realized that the extraordinary show was being put on for Pac's benefit. If it killed them both, Marcus was determined that the sins of the parents would not be allowed to brand his son. No matter what he had to suffer through and no matter what Victoria must tolerate, their son was going to be accepted in the very best circles of society.

And that was something money could not buy.

Not at all happy with her role, Victoria played the part as skillfully as her husband until, finally, everyone's curiosity had been satisfied and she was allowed to escape to her carriage.

Christmas dinner was a magnificent affair, and the huge banquet table was resplendent with gold, silver and crystal. A succulent, full-breasted goose, crisp and browned to a turn, tantalized every palate, and Marcus hoped fervently that the meat that fairly oozed and melted in his mouth was all that was left of a particularly nasty beast who seemed to derive great pleasure from sneaking up behind him to deliver a devastating blow to his unprotected rear.

When the final drop of hard sauce had been sopped up by the last morsel of plum pudding and when the fourth bottle of wine had been emptied the contented group adjourned to the parlor. It was time to open the gifts, time to complete the Christmas Bess had looked forward to with such eagerness for many weeks.

Pac was first. With tantalizing slowness Marcus untied ribbons and removed crackling paper to reveal a doll Bess had crafted from old socks and various other odds and ends. The child was delighted and kept himself happily occupied while the adults continued to indulge Bess, who presented small gifts to the others. The men received knitted vests and Victoria promptly draped a white shawl over her shoulders.

Finally Tim and Robb could wait no longer. They unveiled a magnificent replica of the local schooners that glided so swiftly over the waters of the rivers and the bay. The amount of work that had gone into each detail of the fully rigged vessel was staggering to contemplate.

"It's beautiful," Victoria murmured appreciatively. "We shall treasure it always. In fact," she laughed, walking to the fireplace, "I think we shall display it on the mantel for everyone to admire." And pushing aside the fine French clock, Victoria centered the model in the place of honor, immediately below the portrait of her parents. Tim and Robb beamed, for they had not been certain whether their gift would be good enough for this grand house.

"I'm next!" Victoria laughed and began dismantling the small mountain of bundles and boxes she had piled in the corner of the room.

She had been wise enough to limit the extravagance of her gifts to the others, for she had no wish to flaunt her wealth, thereby making their small treasures appear insignificant by comparison. Bess received a length of fine linen and a few yards of lace. Josiah admired a serviceable shirt. Tim and Robb were delighted with the boots that had been specially crafted for them, and Marcus raised his brows in uncertainty as he examined the beautifully brocaded vest worked in threads of gold bearing the name of the finest house in France.

After a moment's pause he smiled and expressed his appreciation for so fine a garment. Victoria breathed a sigh of relief, and she was most thankful that she had put the two suits of heavy silk aside. She would find some other occasion to present them to her husband.

With eyes twinkling, Marcus reached into his pocket and handed Victoria a small package in return, and when she opened the box, Victoria gave a small, soft sound of joy as she sat spellbound. Removing the ring from its cushion, he slipped it on his wife's finger. "It does not compare to your other jewelry, my dear, but it is strong and enduring, as I hope our life together will be."

Silent tears ran down Bess's plump cheeks, for she had often fretted about the lack of a wedding band. Josiah blew his nose and finally decided to forgive the dark scoundrel who had forced his way into their family in such an unseemly manner. Only Tim and Robb managed to smile their approval.

Victoria gently closed the empty box and looked into her husband's eyes before replying softly, "I hope so, Marcus." Then she put the small, gaily wrapped boxes intended for the other families aside. Suellen would deliver the bright, shiny coins to Bullen and the others tomorrow.

Marcus was more than pleased by Victoria's reaction to the wedding ring, and he smiled his contentment as he lifted his son into his lap. She had not yet read the inscription, but she would find it and she would understand. "To the only mistress my heart shall know," was the promise engraved deep and firm inside the sturdy, wide band.

The days passed too swiftly, and soon it was January. Marcus had lingered longer than he had intended, but he found it almost impossible to leave.

The last few months had been difficult ones, and he had kept himself busy forging ahead in his own affairs. The trip he had just completed to England was to be his last one without his family. He had turned the new *Morning Star* over to Lyle Saunders, who was now captain of that vessel, and Marcus had been amazed to find how easy it was to relinquish a life he thought he could never abandon until now.

There was a break in the weather, and Marcus bundled Pac against the cold and put him on the saddle in front of him as he and Victoria made the obligatory tours of inspection from the house to the swift falls that powered the mill and the pumps, to each cottage and finally to the stable where Bullen was undisputed master.

As Victoria took Pac onto her horse and headed for the pasture fence so her son could watch the antics of the mares and the frolicking of the colts as they snorted and pawed at the snow, Marcus inspected the stallion she and Bullen had purchased for stud just before she had been so unexpectedly abducted by the man who was now her husband. Victoria could scarcely believe that a year and a half had passed since that night she would never forget.

As Ned entered the pasture to bring the mares and their offspring into the stable for the night, Victoria clucked Lady Fair toward the spot where Marcus and Bullen stood discussing the gleaming stallion, Black Knight.

"It's a magnificent animal, all right," Marcus commented as he inspected the sleek coat, the rippling muscles and the fine lines of the highly spirited animal. But as Black Knight reared and pawed the air, Marcus had second thoughts about the stallion. Those high spirits could very easily turn rebellious, and such a powerful beast could run away with a rider if he were not handled with great skill and strength.

Turning to Bullen, Marcus gave an order that caused the old man some concern. "My wife is not to ride that stallion under any circumstances. In fact, I'd prefer she not get anywhere near him.''

Bullen rubbed the stubble on his chin and turned perplexed eyes to the master of Chisholm House. ''Don't know as how I'd stop her, sir. Miss Victoria's got a mind of her own and she does pretty much what she pleases.''

No one needed to remind Marcus that Victoria did as she damned well pleased, and he was irked by the servant's refusal to carry out a direct order from the master of this estate. His eyes narrowed and his tone warned Bullen that he would be obeyed in this matter or there would be serious consequences to pay. ''If you cannot persuade your mistress, then come get me. I assure you, I can stop her!''

Victoria had overheard the conversation and would have taken offense at her husband's tone and at his presumption in telling her servants what she could and could not do, but that was before she had lived with Marcus, before she came to understand something of his moods and character. He tended to become most difficult on two separate and distinct occasions—when she rejected him and when he perceived her to be in danger. And she certainly had not rejected him lately.

Her handling of Marcus Randall had become a little more subtle, so with a suggestive smile touching her lips, Victoria slanted a provocative look his way. ''You need not worry, my dear. You are the only stallion I care to ride.''

For an instant Marcus was speechless, and then he grinned as he saw Bullen roll his eyes heavenward. Apparently the old retainer was quite used to Victoria's crude and vulgar sense of humor, and Marcus had to admit there were times when he thoroughly enjoyed that side of his wife.

"Then I shall not disappoint you tonight," he answered quietly, his eyes dancing with humor and mischief as he reached up to take Pac from Victoria's arms.

When Victoria had dismounted Bullen walked the two horses into the stable, where Ned would see to their care. Arm in arm, Marcus and Victoria trudged toward the house as dusk brought with it a penetrating chill.

At breakfast on his last day at the farm, Marcus asked his wife about the herb tea she always drank no matter where she was. "In fact, it seems to me you drag that tin of herbs around with you wherever you go."

An evasive expression flicked across Victoria's face and then was gone as she explained that the herb was the ground seed of the stoneweed, which was quite useful in soothing a woman's turmoils. It led to greater tranquility and peace of mind.

"Buy why just women?" Marcus asked in all innocence.

"It just seems to work that way. Apparently stoneseed has very little to offer the male constitution."

Marcus shrugged idly. He didn't think his wife needed a drug to calm her mind, for surely a woman who possessed the control he knew was hers did not need that sort of potion. But if it made her happy, there certainly seemed to be no harm in it.

Finally, and with great reluctance, Marcus bid his family farewell, but Victoria insisted on riding with him to the harbor, which was beginning to freeze over. Then she made her way to a point of land where she stood watching until the sails of the ship disappeared beyond the horizon.

January turned bitterly cold. Snow crusted over, wind howled through chimneys and rattled windows. Everyone was miserable until an unseasonable warm spell in February brought relief to the suffering people and animals. There were days when the sun reflected brilliantly from the white surface with a dazzling brightness that blinded the eyes. Dripping water could be heard as the encompassing blanket of white began to melt, and dark hollows under the branches of trees and the eaves of houses and outbuildings grew larger.

It was on such a morning that Victoria sat in the kitchen sipping a cup of hot tea while Bess busied herself kneading dough for the next day's bread. Her thoughts turned once more to her husband, and she wished she had sailed with him. Then she shrugged. Serenity would be no better in winter than this farm. And here, at least, she could direct her business by means of the carrier pigeons she had added to the Annapolis, Baltimore and Philadelphia offices. In this vast land, the ancient Persian messengers winged their way homeward in hours across terrain that would take her days, and the small feathered creatures gave her the advantage of time. She knew days ahead of her competitors what cargo would be arriving in which port. This information often allowed her to make purchase contracts that gave her a monopoly on certain products. She had already made thousands of pounds in just such a manner.

Her mind meandered from one thought to another, and Victoria sighed in total boredom. It was not just idleness. She was getting soft. The sharp, cutting edge of her mind was dulling. Things had come too easily. There was no challenge, no intrigue to keep her on her toes. She felt like some fat spider content in its gossamer orb.

Bess, who could never stand prolonged silence, broke through Victoria's mental wanderings. "Don't know what you see in that brew," she grumped uncharitably, fixing a distasteful look on the herb tea Victoria was sipping. "Tried it myself a few times. Didn't seem to settle my nerves any."

Victoria laughed out loud. "I think you're past the age of needing this particular herb."

Never one to admit she was not as young as she once was, Bess was miffed. "If it works for you, it should work for me."

"I believe, Bess, you're past the age of child-bearing. Of course, I could be wrong," Victoria added with an insinuating smile.

The housekeeper directed a sharp glance toward her mistress. Miss Victoria never spoke plain so folks could understand her meaning. "Child-bearing? Of course that's in the past. What does that have to do with anything?"

"It's something Raven's Wing told me about. The women of her tribe use stoneseed to limit the size of their families if they choose to do so. Apparently she didn't. But it must be used every day."

"Does it work?" the older woman asked suspiciously.

"Seems to. Heaven knows it's been tested severely enough," Victoria added with another smile that caused Bess to blush and jerk her head around to make sure Suellen was nowhere within hearing distance.

Narrowing her eyes in disapproval, Bess asked, "Does Captain Randall know?"

"That I'm using the herb? Yes, I told him."

Bess was exasperated. "Does he know what it's for!"

Victoria shrugged. "I doubt it."

"I hope he doesn't find out," the housekeeper muttered almost fearfully. "I've heard him say many times he hopes for a large family and you never said any different. It's a wicked thing you're doing, miss."

Victoria slanted the motherly woman a warning look. "I'll make my own decisions about that, thank you. And there's precious little Marcus can do about it anyway!"

But Bess wasn't so sure there was nothing Captain Randall could do. She had seen the love for his son shine from the man, and she knew he had his mind set on adding to his family, but she knew better than to say any more, for she had seen the hard light in Miss Victoria's eyes. There was no use arguing with her when she was being pig-headed.

Irritated by her housekeeper's sulking disapproval, Victoria turned her attention to Pac and smiled. He had pulled himself up and was holding tightly to the cloth of her skirt. His legs were flexing at the knees as he babbled in delight at this latest marvelous accomplishment. He was up off his knees and walking. And he was learning to fall a little easier. Again Victoria thought of Marcus and of how much of his son's life he was missing.

Suddenly her face went blank. Her mind turned inward, and she felt the icy grip of fear invade her body. She was not mistaken! She had heard Marcus call out for her. Something was terribly wrong.

"Bess!" she cried, as though awakening from a nightmare only to find it real, "get some clothes together for Pac while I throw a few of my things in a bag. Get Tim and Robb. I must leave for Richmond immediately!"

Bess opened her mouth to speak, but Victoria cut her off. "Now!" she snapped.

Tim and Robb came running as Victoria was cramming the minimum change of clothing into a small traveling bag. There was no time for neatness. An urgency tugged at her. She felt a desperate need to hurry. The journey would be much swifter by water if only the river had cleared enough to be navigated.

Victoria pulled on boots and breeches. Pac was wrapped securely against the weather, and Bullen brought horses around to the front of the house while Bess handed Tim a hastily filled basket of food, and Victoria silently blessed these friends who acted so quickly and calmly without asking questions.

The snow had all but disappeared from the countryside, but the narrow road had turned to mud, making it difficult going for the horses, so the small group cut across country, avoiding the dangerous ruts and the farm wagons that had gotten stuck in the wet thawing earth. The condition of the road gave Victoria hope. It was possible that the ice in the harbor was gone, that the warm weather for the past few weeks had broken up the solid mass of ice that had made navigation impossible.

As they trotted into town, she breathed a sigh of relief. A few chunks of ice were still visible, but the solid mass was gone. She could have her ship brought right to the dock. There was no necessity of endangering Pac's life by transporting him in a long boat through the rushing chunks of ice to the vessel that bobbed at anchor well outside the harbor.

Once water and a few more supplies were put on board Victoria gave orders to put her small coastal vessel under sail, and the tiny craft bobbed its way to open water.

When the small vessel nudged against the private wharf that served Serenity, Victoria jumped ashore and ran up the bank to the house. Ruby was dumbfounded to see the woman who had left so many months ago. It was too soon for the messenger she had sent to have gotten to Annapolis. He couldn't be more than halfway there.

"My husband!" Victoria said fearfully, hoping against hope that she had been wrong. "Is he all right?"

"The cap'n's mighty sick, ma'am." Ruby's face was contorted by the fear she felt. Then the old woman broke. "Lord Gawd, he's dyin'," she sobbed.

Terror slashed at Victoria's heart as she pushed past the older woman, heading for the stairs. Her heart was pounding so that she barely heard Ruby cry out.

"He's in his study! He's so bad, we can't even get him to his bed. Gonna die on that cot. That's what's gonna happen," the slave sobbed hysterically.

Bringing herself up sharply, Victoria clenched her fists. What Marcus didn't need was two incoherent, useless women on his hands. She turned back toward the small study off the kitchen and entered. An involuntary moan of despair caught in her throat. Marcus was so pale, so still lying there. She had to hold her own breath in order to make sure he was breathing. And the doctor was just sitting there, doing nothing, the red rags of bleeding scattered about the floor.

Ignoring the man who had probably done more harm than good, Victoria knelt by her husband's side. Feeling the thready, uncertain pulse, she bent close and whispered, "Marcus."

The glazed eyes that were too bright tried to focus. "Vickie, you came. I knew you would."

His voice was barely audible. She held his fevered hand in her almost frozen ones and bent close as he tried to speak from the haze of enclosing delirium. "Don't let them cut off my leg, Vickie. Don't let them do it," he pleaded in a voice that was hoarse with desperation and fear.

"Shh," she soothed. "I won't, I promise." Then, lifting the blanket, she saw the terrible wound high on the inside of the thigh. It was inflamed; the skin was stretched tight and had a waxy look. There was festering under the sutured surface. The telltale lines of red had already begun their race, and Victoria understood her husband's terror.

Amputation was called for. It was apparently what the doctor had been urging, the last desperate measure to save his life. But such an amputation would do as much to kill him as the wound itself.

Victoria's mind flashed back to the master who had taught her so much—enough to save Ellen's life and more. She would do it! She would take the risk.

Holding Marcus's hand tightly, Victoria asked, "Do you trust me?"

"With my life," came the fading response.

Victoria took charge. Her orders bordered on the belligerent. "There will be no more bleeding or purging." Then, turning to Ruby, she asked, "Do you have laudanum?"

Ruby nodded and Victoria continued. "I'll need moldy bread. Send riders to neighboring farms and to the slave quarters if you must, but get it!"

Ruby ran to the kitchen, where she gathered the laudanum and rummaged desperately through the slop pail for the loaf of partially eaten bread that was meant for the pigs. Ordinarily, in this well-run house, such waste would never had occurred, but this had been no ordinary week.

Gingerly, Ruby patted the bread dry where uneaten stew had been dumped on top of it, then took it to the woman whose orders she trusted even though she didn't understand what good they would do.

"Now," Victoria continued, "I'll need a large pan, clean rags and lots of honey. Then clean Marcus's razor in the strongest spirits you have and bring it to me."

Ruby paid no attention to Dr. Burke, who was protesting vehemently that the leg must be amputated in order to have any chance of saving Captain Randall's life. Victoria listened politely for a few minutes, then smiled serenely. "Your methods don't seem to have done much good so far, so suppose I try those I have seen work. And they are by no means new, Doctor. They were known to the ancient Greeks, among others, though one must search the old scrolls diligently to unlock their secrets. And now, sir," she said in the kindest of dismissals, "perhaps you would care to refresh yourself. I'm sure Ruby can find something for you to eat and drink. You must be very tired and hungry."

Jerome Burke glared fiercely at the arrogant interloper. He drew himself up and replied stiffly, "I'll bid you good night, Madam Randall, but I wash my hands of the matter. Captain Randall's death is on your hands!'' Then he flinched under the murderous glint in those pale eyes and beat a hasty retreat to the kitchen.

Before she had all she would need gathered around her Tim and Robb barged through the back door carrying Pac, the luggage and the few bits of leftover food. The two men handed Pac over to Ruby and prepared to help Victoria in the dangerous job ahead. They could see for themselves that she would be fighting for her husband's life, and the odds were not with her.

As Victoria prepared herself for the task ahead, she had made a firm decision. If her husband lived, it would be as a whole man. The choice was his and he had made it.

Taking the laudanum from Ruby's hand, Victoria began to measure. It was a large dose—dangerously close to fatal. But it would block the pain quickly. She lifted her husband's head and held the glass to his lips. "Drink, my darling," she encouraged quietly.

Obediently, Marcus swallowed the mouthful of strong narcotic, the mixture that contained the deadly distillate of the poppy. He sighed in relief, for now he could at last give up the battle to stay conscious. Victoria would ease his dying. If she could not save his life without mutilating him, she would let him go. She had promised. Confidently, almost with a feeling of euphoria, he fell asleep.

Victoria directed Tim and Robb to change the position of the cot. She had them line it up with the compass needle, his head facing north, and Victoria didn't care how much the learned men of science in this part of the world derided such practices, dismissing them as chicanery or worse. She would use every trick, every superstition and every piece of knowledge she could remember. She would not give in to what seemed inevitable, and she would not let Marcus give in, either. She had prepared herself to fight for his life with every ounce of strength and power within her.

Folding the blanket back, Victoria picked up the razor and carefully made a deep incision directly into the festering wound, cutting through stitches and flesh. Instantly the bloody flux spurted out, and the noxious odor from the poisonous fluid hung heavy in the room.

Not satisfied, Victoria pressed, squeezed and cleaned, cutting again and again until the bright, clear blood flowed. It was then she saw the problem. A deeply buried portion of the wound, high in the thigh, had been ignored. It had not been opened, nor had it been cleaned.

Holding her breath to steady her hand, Victoria exercised the utmost care as she cut deep. She was very near a portion of her husband's body where a careless move could render him impotent. She smiled in black humor as she thought that he would rather lose his leg.

When every vestige of pus had been excised Victoria turned her attention to the poultice. Mixing the scrapings of mold with a few drops of honey, she smeared the gaping wound with the sticky substance until there was no part of it that was not covered. Then she packed the tortured flesh with layers of cloth that had also been dipped in honey, ending with bandages loosely wrapped around the leg. Everything was coated again before Victoria covered her husband's naked body with a clean sheet and fresh blanket.

She smiled her gratitude to Tim and Robb, who were even now clearing away the vile reminders of the battle she had waged for the life of the person who was so very important to her.

Satisfied that she had done all she could for now, Victoria pulled up a chair and sat holding Marcus's hand, directing her energy into his body. Her concentration was fierce as she drove the unsettling memories of her father's death from her mind. No vibrations of fear must be passed to her husband.

Time had no meaning for Victoria. She did not know how many hours passed, but as Marcus began to stir, awakening from the drug-induced sleep, the sound of a rooster crowing at the rising sun rang out clear and strong, and Marcus heard it. He knew that he had returned to the woman he loved.

Even though the opiate still clouded his brain his eyes had lost the fevered glitter as they focused on the blanket, which clearly showed the outline of two legs and two feet. "Thank you," he whispered weakly.

Victoria looked him straight in the eye. "It's too soon for thanks," she said bluntly. "This contest is far from over."

A faint smile touched his lips. "I have never known you to lose any contest you wanted to win." Then he frowned. "Dammit, I'm hungry. What does a man have to do to get something to eat?"

Ruby laughed with relief and joy. She let go of the fear that had paralyzed her, and she let go of the last shred of resentment she had felt for the woman who just saved her captain's life.

Hunger was a good sign, and Victoria put her hand to Marcus's forehead. The fever was subsiding. "Very well, my love, we'll give you some nourishing gruel. If you keep that down, maybe we'll give you something more substantial. But first, drink the willow tea Ruby has made for you."

"You, madam, are getting a little bossy," Marcus teased.

"And you, sir, need a keeper to see that you stay out of trouble," Victoria replied good-naturedly.

He grinned. "Are you making an offer?"

"I'm giving it serious thought," she replied, surprised that she did, indeed, mean what she said.

Marcus tried to tighten his grip on her hand, but there was too little strength in his own. The effort tired him and Victoria had to lift his head so he could drink the tea that would ease the pain that would only increase in intensity.

After eating a few spoonfuls of the gruel Marcus slept fitfully for brief periods only to awaken and complain of still being hungry. Satisfied that he was going to keep his food down, Victoria fed him every several hours, commenting wryly, "You're more trouble than Pac. At least he sleeps through the night."

The following morning Victoria did not let her fear show as she unwrapped the wounded leg. The honey-smeared strips of cloth came out as one, pulling the poultice and what little festering there was cleanly from the wound. To Victoria the raw ugly injury looked beautiful. It was working! She smiled as she renewed the poultice and rewrapped the leg. The worst was over, and Ruby was given permission to indulge Marcus in whatever he wanted to eat, but the cups of willow-bark tea were to be continued.

By the time Marcus had consumed a thick stew, hot buttered biscuits and coffee he was a contented man. He lay back and slept more peacefully through most of the day. Only occasionally did he twitch as the painful process of healing began.

While he slept Victoria gave orders that Ruby rest as well, and despite their protests she insisted that Tim and Robb get some sleep. Before the two men retreated from the room to find a place to lay their weary bodies Victoria thanked them for their loyalty and their help. She made a silent oath. Never, so long as they lived, would either of them want for anything.

After everyone had retired Victoria settled herself in a large comfortable chair and prepared for the long vigil. She dozed fitfully, waking every few minutes to watch the even motion of her husband's breathing.

The next inspection of the leg showed no more infection, and the ominous streaks of red were gone. Silently, Victoria blessed the white-robed priests, all of whom were scholars and mystics, who had taught her the almost forgotten arts of healing, the arts a few enlightened men still guarded zealously. The ancient brotherhood of Karnak, site of the sacred temple, would receive an anonymous donation, and they would understand. Once more they had touched a life and had found gratitude.

Just after dusk Ruby roused herself from the much-needed sleep and prepared a small supper for Victoria and her men. She smiled at the new mistress of Serenity and was satisfied. She did not understand this strange woman, but Miss Victoria loved the captain and that was enough for the slave who had been a part of this family even before Marcus had been born.

Victoria asked the question there had not been time to ask before. "How was Captain Randall injured?"

"Wild pigs, damn 'em!" Ruby, who never cursed, did so now. "He was out huntin' 'em down 'cause they made a mess of his fields. One of 'em charged an' the cap'n shot it, but that ol' hog, he jes' kep' a'comin'. Got the cap'n with one of them tusks 'fore he died. Lord only knows how the cap'n got home. Bleedin' all over the place. Hardly enough strength to fall through the door.

"Doctor wanted to chop that leg off, but the cap'n said no. Said he'd rather die." The last vestige of disapproval died. "Mighty glad you got here, miss. Mighty glad," Ruby said quietly.

Ruby did not bother to ask how her mistress knew she was needed here. There were some things that couldn't be explained. But they existed, and she had seen such a bond between two people before. One got hurt and the other one hollered.

# 19

Two more days were all that was needed to assure Victoria that Marcus was out of danger. And she would not tempt fate. They had been extremely fortunate this time; they might not be so lucky again, so there would be no more suturing. The wound would be kept open to heal slowly from the inside. There would be an ugly scar, but that hardly mattered when compared to the possible consequences of tampering with that leg again. Enough muscle had been damaged, enough flesh severed. She would risk no more, and Marcus heartily concurred in that decision. He knew better than anyone else just how very close to death he had been. It was his second brush with the grim reaper in as many years, and there was a certainty fixed firmly in his mind that he would not survive the contest a third time.

His thoughts were abruptly jarred from their desolate path as Tim and Robb literally bounced into the room to share the companionship of another man. This farm was a lonesome place, and they said so.

Victoria took advantage of this mild complaint. "In that case you should be overjoyed to leave for a short while. Pac and I need a great many things from Chisholm House, and I'm afraid to let the captain out of my sight long enough to go get them myself. It would seem that he manages to get into all sorts of trouble the minute I turn my back."

Tim and Robb grinned sheepishly, but they were relieved, nonetheless, to be getting away from Serenity if only for a little while. However, they were totally unprepared for the captain's reaction to his wife's words.

A smile that could only be described as positively lewd slithered across Marcus's face. "There's only one kind of trouble I'm interested in, my dear, but that requires your earnest cooperation," he drawled in his most theatrically insinuating tone, but if he had meant to intimidate Victoria, he failed miserably.

Instead of blushing or lowering her gaze modestly she laughed companionably at his implied meaning. "All in good time," she purred, deliberately patting his injured leg.

Marcus winced in pain under her none-too-gentle reprimand, but his eyes were shining. "Planning to stay a little longer so you can take advantage of my weakened condition?" he asked hopefully.

Victoria and her two men lost their battle with the laughter that refused to be contained. Still chuckling softly and wiping her eyes, Victoria explained, "I'm planning to stay long enough to give that leg time to heal."

Thankful to be alive and in a playful mood, Marcus reached for her. His strength was returning, a fact he promptly tried to demonstrate, but Victoria smiled and slipped from his grasp. "If you're well enough for that, you're well enough to start exercising that leg."

"That, love, is precisely what I was trying to do," he drawled.

In mock despair, Victoria shook her head and frowned. "You, sir, are impossible!"

"And you, madam, are responsible!" Marcus shot back.

"I love you, too," she said quietly, then motioned for Tim and Robb to lift Marcus into a nearby chair. Carefully, tenderly, she cushioned and positioned the injured leg before draping the blanket over his lap. "I think we'll let you sit up for a while, especially since you seem to think a bed has only one purpose."

Marcus was about to reply when he gave a short grunt of pain and clenched his teeth as he leaned and tensed with the anguish of the sudden, sharp bolt that shot through him. It took his breath away, and he panted with the effort required to fight this newest agony. Perspiration suddenly appeared on his skin, and the dank, telltale odor of intense suffering seeped into the air.

Victoria waited for a moment or two, but when the pain persisted, when it was obvious that it would not pass quickly she instructed Tim and Robb to put her husband back on the cot while she measured a stingy dose of the opium tincture into a spoon and administered it to the man who was in such pain he could barely swallow.

It only took a few minutes for the opium mixed in an alcohol base to do its work. Gradually the pain flowed from Marcus's body and he relaxed into his pillows, sighing in blessed relief.

"Ah, well," he said, smiling ruefully, "it seems I

shall have to wait a while longer. Blasted nuisance!"

"You're very fortunate to be alive," Victoria replied seriously. "Don't begrudge your body time to heal itself. The pain is its way of telling us we're moving too swiftly. Be patient, my darling."

He touched her face with his hand. "Thank you, Vickie, for saving my life, but mostly I thank you for not allowing them to butcher me. I would have preferred to die. My only regret would have been leaving you and our son."

Tears came into Victoria's eyes, and she covered his hand with her own. "I'm glad you did not leave me," she whispered. "And Marcus," she continued almost shyly, "I read the inscription."

After Tim and Robb had gone the days passed slowly. The two sailors had been right. Serenity was a lonely, somber place. There was no Suellen, who fairly danced and skipped through her chores, frequently singing at the top of her lungs. And there was no Bess, quick with a kind word or the latest bit of gossip. And there were no companionable evenings of music as Josiah coaxed indescribably beautiful notes from his old violin and she plunked a soft accompaniment on the guitar. Neither were there any chestnuts or popcorn crackling over an open fire. But worst of all, Pac was growing up surrounded by much older people just as she had done.

Deciding that there were some things that could be changed, Victoria began. Whether she wanted a helper or not, Ruby got one—a young girl of about eleven who was totally untrained in service, but a child who had a warm, bright disposition. Ruby took to her at once. Her husband, Zeb, was saddled with

two young boys who were to be trained by him to do
the heavier chores around the house. And once again
Victoria began to parcel out a few farthings here and a
penny there, depending upon the skill and diligence
of the workers, and once again a few coins clutched
tightly in hands that seldom held them worked
wonders. Even Ruby decided that she approved of the
changes, particularly since there was an old cracked
cream pitcher that now held enough silver coins so
she did not have to run to Marcus every time she
needed to buy something she could not get by
bartering for it.

But there was nothing that gave Ruby more
pleasure than watching the children of field hands,
who had never possessed so much as a penny, walk
proudly to the first peddler to brave the remnants of
winter. She smiled as she watched them buy their
first little treasures.

Just as Victoria was getting a firm grip on Serenity
Marcus lost all patience. He was tired of this little
room, and he would no longer be held prisoner, left
alone while everyone else was busy—too busy to pay
proper attention to him. Besides, he wanted to sleep
in his own bed.

Victoria scowled in mocking imitation. "Feeling
that well, are we?"

Marcus was in no mood for sarcasm. His leg was
healing. He had even taken a step or two with a bit of
help from the two boys Victoria had assigned to the
house. He was sick and tired of being an invalid. "I
intend to show you tonight just how well I am, my
dear," he bragged foolishly.

But Victoria could not resist. "Oh, and are you one
of those men who only make love at night under the

blankets?'' she threw back at him as she passed
hastily through the doorway and into the kitchen.

As she proceeded out the back door the last sound
she heard was the soft chuckling coming from the
sickroom. Marcus was still smiling to himself as he
heard the back door close behind his wife. Apparently
Victoria did not forget a thing, for he remembered
speaking words very much like those a long time ago,
that first night aboard his ship, the first night he had
made love to her.

Cataloguing even the minor details as she walked
around the outside of her husband's home, Victoria
decided that some improvements were called for. The
comfortable but modest house could be enlarged with
very little trouble. At least two rooms downstairs and
two or more rooms upstairs could be added without
disturbing the general style and line of the house to
any great degree.

A new master suite was something she would insist
on. There must also be a new dining room, for some
of the things she had sent for would be out of place in
the large room that was used for almost any desired
purpose, including the setting up of trestle tables for
large dinner parties.

No, Serenity would have a proper dining room with
all the wealth and grace Marcus would allow in his
house, but it would be touchy for he had a stubborn
pride that would rebel if she tried to force too many of
her father's treasures on him. Victoria smiled. The
changes would take place gradually, item by item. He
would barely notice.

As she continued to inspect the grounds, Victoria
wandered beyond the few slave cabins and beyond

the dormitory-style building where many of the male
slaves were housed to the stream that cut across her
husband's property. She followed it through a
heavily wooded area for perhaps a hundred yards,
where the ground began to mount at a sharp angle
and she began to climb over protruding boulders.

It was a wild place that delighted her heart. The
sound of water swirling and cascading over rocks
brought the joy of living back to a young woman who
had been too long immersed in a world of cunning
and violence. For a few minutes that world faded as
Victoria stood at the top of the rugged terrain with the
wind blowing through the trees, bringing with it the
sweet fragrance of a new and warmer season to the
rolling hills of Serenity.

# 20

Before the week was out Tim and Robb returned to Serenity, bringing all manner of goods with them. Additional clothing for Victoria and Pac was put away. The two suits she had had tailored for Marcus were added to his wardrobe.

Heavy silk was to be transformed into drapes for the large room that would soon become an extravagant drawing room. Ancient bronze shields were burnished and hung on stairwell walls. Bright spermaceti candles burned in silver candlesticks. Delicate crystal and decanters were arranged on the sideboard, and a huge silver tureen graced the highly polished table in the private family dining room.

It was then that Marcus rebelled. He had no intention of living off his wife's charity and said so. "I'm perfectly capable of providing for my family, Victoria, and I want no more of your father's possessions brought into this house. Is that understood?"

Admitting to temporary defeat, Victoria agreed.

Secretly, however, she was pleased that she had
managed to do as much as she had, and she was more
than satisfied that Marcus was taking such an interest
in the pigeons that had been transported from
Annapolis. Serenity was to become yet another stop
along the "pigeon mail" route she was still establish-
ing.

During one of those restless times when Marcus
had hobbled outdoors accompanied by Tim and
Robb, Victoria sat at the oversized kitchen table,
sipping her herb tea. "What was Captain Randall's
family like, Ruby?" she asked as the black woman
was demonstrating the art of kneading dough to her
young helper.

Ruby's hands paused in midair. Marcus never
talked about his family, and she was not sure she
should discuss them, either. Finally she shrugged.
Miss Victoria was the mistress of this house. When
she asked a question she deserved an answer.

"Mr. Paul—he was the cap'n's daddy," she began.
"And his mother, Miss Eugenie, was an angel if one
ever lived. Had hair lighter than yours and eyes as
blue as a summer sky. Never a cross word," Ruby
said gently, her gaze seeing the ghosts of some other
time.

"Mr. Marcus, he loved that lady. Worshipped the
ground she walked on. Loved his daddy, too, but in a
different way. And his older brother, Alexander. He
idolized that boy."

Pausing as she remembered the long ago, Ruby
nodded to a silent thought. "Miss Eugenie, she's Miss
Josephine's sister, but then you know that. But Miss
Jo, she could tell you all 'bout Miss Eugenie."

"Afraid she never said a word," Victoria remarked

ruefully, realizing that she should have shown some interest. She should have asked.

"Mr. Marcus, he don't talk 'bout his family. It still hurts too much and I guess Miss Jo, she don't want to open old wounds."

"Tell me about them, Ruby."

The slave sighed heavily and wiped her hands on her apron before settling into the wooden rocker. The chair squeaked as she rocked gently back and forth. "Mr. Paul, he come to this place almost ten years to the day before Mr. Marcus was born. Not a whole lot a' money, but a powerful lot a' pride. He worked hard an' he worked the few slaves he had hard. Then he met Miss Eugenie and from then on he was a changed man. Married 'er in lessen two weeks.

"Well, then, Mr. Alexander, he come first. Then all kinds a' trouble. Miscarriages, still-born babies, crop failures. Everythin' seem to go wrong all at once, but they got through.

"And when Marcus was born, why that made everythin' jes' fine, but he was the last live chile Miss Eugenie ever had."

The slave wiped a silent tear from her cheek as she remembered the suffering. "Then it happen. Miss Eugenie, she went to visit her cousin in Charleston. Mr. Alexander, he went with his momma 'cause Mr. Paul couldn't get away. We heard weeks later that their ship was caught in a terrible storm off the Carolinas. Everybody dead. Everybody gone," Ruby sobbed.

"Mr. Paul went crazy. Plum outta his mind. And Mr. Marcus grieved like a dog who jes' lost his master. It was awful and Zeb and me couldn't do nothin'.

"Sixteen he was. Mr. Alexander. And Marcus was ten. Mr. Paul—he tried to do right, but he jes' grieved himself into his grave. Four years an' he was gone. The cap'n was never the same. Kinda went wild. Not mean or hurtful, jes' not-carin'-'bout-nothin' wild."

Ruby gazed at her mistress in silence and then said what needed saying. "Till you came along. Now he's got somebody to love and to care about again. An' that boy a' his. Jes' like Mr. Alexander all over again. 'Ceptin' for the eyes. Mr. Alexander's eyes was blue."

A bittersweet smile touched Ruby's face. "When he was no bigger'n a yearlin' Mr. Marcus used to say when he grow up he gonna have a big family so's he wouldn't never have to be alone again."

It was a painful moment of understanding. Marcus had lost everyone he had loved, and when she had threatened to leave him or when she rejected him all the old fears came rushing back. He fought to keep her the only way he knew how. The violence he had so frequently unleashed on her was his desperate attempt to hold onto her. Losing his family once again was more than he would be able to bear, and his need to be surrounded by his own was as much a necessity for Marcus as food.

"Thank you, Ruby," Victoria said softly, and knew that she had a great deal to think about.


With the arrival of warm weather the tempo at Serenity picked up. For the first time since the death of his father Marcus began to build up his farm. Fallow fields were turned. Grain was planted. Stock was increased, and Marcus thought Victoria's suggestion of a slaughterhouse and a pickling plant was a good one. He was gone from the house for longer and longer periods of time.

The only thing that bothered Victoria during this busy season was a letter sent by Henry. It seemed Edward was making plans for a lengthy journey. It could be to America, but Henry was not sure. He would write as soon as he had definite news.

However, the news she had already received was enough for Victoria. Edward was covering his tracks. He was being extremely cautious.

Tim and Robb were sent to the farm owned by James Bryce's brother-in-law. They were to leave word that James and his men must come to Serenity at once. A letter was dispatched to Leroy Jones in Williamsburg with explicit instructions. When Edward came she would be ready for him, and Pac would be well guarded.

Busy overseeing the work of the plantation, Marcus had little time for his wife or son, so Victoria would pack a picnic lunch and join her husband for a leisurely meal wherever Marcus happened to be occupied at that moment. Pac always managed to delay his father a few extra minutes. This time together was precious to Victoria, for she did not know how much longer she had before either her life or Edward's was done.

James and his men arrived two weeks after Victoria had sent for them. They made themselves at home and settled into a routine of helping around the farm and guarding Pac wherever he went.

The softness of spring was burned away by the summer sun. July brought with it an oppressive heat that was only made worse by the rains that seemed to leave the air hotter and stickier than ever. However, it was perfect weather for swimming, and Victoria decided that it was time for Pac to learn.

Slipping a robe over a sleeveless short shift, Victoria

took Pac to a secluded cove where they would be shielded from the curious eyes of river travelers. James kept watch from a discreet distance.

The water in the wide cove was much cleaner than the basin in Annapolis, which was often filled with effluent. Even dead bodies bumping against the bulkhead were not unknown occurrences, but here the air and the water seemed fresher and purer.

Victoria waded in, carrying Pac. The water was warm, and only an occasional cold current spoiled the feeling of perfect relaxation.

Gradually Victoria eased her son into the water, supporting him with her hands, teaching him to trust. In a few days he was confident enough so she could gently and slowly remove her hands from under the child's floating body.

When he found out that he was not going to sink Pac took to the water like a little fish. He splashed and paddled until he suddenly found himself swimming, and he struck out further each time, but Victoria was never far from her son. When she thought he had gone far enough, she herded him back toward shore. There was no fear and no panic, but she firmly taught respect for the water and for Pac's limitations.

After weeks of practice Victoria decided to share her son's accomplishments with his father, and she invited Marcus to accompany them to the cove the following afternoon. When they arrived at the narrow beach she stripped Pac of his clothing. The boy's brown body gave mute testimony to the fact that he had frequently been naked under the hot sun.

Pac made for the water like a destruction-bent lemming, and Marcus stiffened, feeling the cold sweat of fear trickle down his back as he watched his only child paddle out into deeper water. He wanted

desperately to interfere. That tiny head bobbing in the
water looked so helpless, so vulnerable.

Marcus sat down and removed his boots and shirt,
ready to go after his son, who was by now a good
twenty yards from shore. It was only when he saw
Pac turn back and paddle unerringly toward him that
he dared have hope. He would make it. He was safe.

The bronzed boy clambered out of the water and
ran to his father, throwing himself on Marcus, eager
for the praise he had always gotten from his mother.
And despite his very real doubts about his son's
newest accomplishments Marcus did not disappoint
him. He swung his child into the air and nuzzled and
nibbled at his neck, growling playfully, until Pac was
reduced to the helpless high-pitched laughter typical
of an overexcited child.

Marcus put the boy on his shoulders for a
triumphant ride home. Victoria picked up the forgotten clothing and trailed behind. She was careful
not to catch up to father and son, who were happily
chattering away even if most of what Pac said was
incomprehensible to other ears.

Victoria was satisfied. Marcus and Pac were very
close. If anything should happen to her, her son
would be all right, and he, in turn, would sustain her
husband.

When they reached the house Pac ran inside to tell
Ruby of the day's adventure while Marcus relieved
Victoria of his boots and shirt. Sitting on the steps, he
pulled her down beside him. "He's still only a baby,
Vickie. Don't push him too hard."

Victoria smiled into her husband's eyes. "Don't
coddle him, Marcus. Teach him everything there is to
learn. Concern him only with dangers that are real or
he will accomplish nothing for fear of terrors that

exist only in his mind. And teach him to love, my dear.'' Her smile was wistful. ''It is something you can do better than I.''

Marcus studied Victoria's face for a long minute. He was not sure just what she was telling him, but it was more than the words she spoke. Finally he stood and escorted her inside.

While Victoria returned to her room to dress, Marcus sat in the kitchen listening to his son recite every detail to Ruby, who was trying to put clothes on the excited happy child.

When Pac ran outdoors to play Marcus turned the subject to the thing that worried him constantly. ''Have there been any more messages concerning Victoria's brother?''

Ruby shook her head. ''Nothin', Cap'n.''

''Perhaps Edward has changed his mind,'' he mused more to himself than to Ruby. ''Surely the man has enough money to keep him happily occupied for a lifetime. Yet Victoria seems certain that he's getting ready to play out his hand.

''I can't understand it. How can a brother think of killing his sister? For that matter, I don't understand Victoria, either. She never speaks of Edward, but I know she plans to kill him if it becomes necessary. I can only hope that things between them improve.''

There was little for Ruby to say. Miss Victoria would do what she had to do and nobody would be able to stop her. That much, at least, Ruby had learned about the new mistress of Serenity.

Changing the subject, Marcus confided in the woman who had looked after him for so many years. ''There's something I've been meaning to discuss with you, Ruby. I don't want it mentioned to Victoria until I'm sure of my own feelings, but it looks very likely that my injury has made me incapable of siring any more children. What would you think of my adopting another child or two? How do you think Victoria would react?"

"Hmph!" Ruby snorted. "Nothin' wrong with you. Can't get a chile long as Miss Victoria's takin' the stoneseed. Don't need to adopt no chile lessen you want to."

Marcus sat motionless as the full meaning of Ruby's words sank in. "No," he said in disbelief. "Victoria wouldn't do that. Not without telling me."

"Woman's gotta have a rest 'tween birthin's," Ruby defended. "Can't expect Miss Victoria to have one chile right after the other."

The anguish in Marcus's voice made Victoria stop even as her foot was about to touch the bottom step. "No, Ruby, you're wrong. My wife would not do such a thing. She would not take some damned herb to prevent her from conceiving. She loves me. The very fact that she gave birth to Pac proves it. And she agreed to a large family. She would not go back on her word. Adoption might be the only answer."

Quietly, Victoria retraced her steps and returned to her room. Some decisions had to be made—and quickly.

That evening Victoria did not bother with a nightgown. She slipped under the sheet and pressed close to Marcus. He took her in his arms and searched those deceitful eyes. "Would you care to tell me what stoneseed is really for?"

"To prevent an unwanted pregnancy," she answered truthfully. "I thought I had more important things to do."

"And now?" Marcus questioned.

"And now I know I was wrong." Her smile eased

the pain in Marcus's heart. She had used the
stoneseed only for a little while. She still loved him.
She would give him the one thing only she
could—another child.

He held her in a tight embrace. She had come back
to him. "Are you sure?"

Victoria understood the question. "I'm sure," she
answered.

With infinite tenderness Marcus kindled the flame
that would bring his wife to him with as much need as
his own. Once more he prepared his wife's body to
accept his seed, and Victoria responded to her
husband's touch. She drew in her breath sharply as
the familiar shock tingled and pulsed its way through
her. The need for him grew, and when Marcus came
to her she was ready.

This night of love was special. It was somehow even
more intense than at any other time since Marcus's
injury. Once more he felt invincible, and once more
he carried his wife to the top of the mountain.

A sharp cry and quick short breaths traced the
easing of flooding passion. Victoria held Marcus
tightly, straining against him until the need slowly
subsided. Then she lay quiet and content in his arms.

"Do you have any idea how much I love you?" he
asked.

"Probably as much as I love you," she answered
with certainty.

In late September, just a week after Victoria's
birthday, the news she had been waiting to hear
came. Edward and several friends had arrived in
Williamsburg. Leroy Jones had seen to it that the dock
workers who were questioned gave all the right

answers. Edward would be heading for Annapolis as soon as he could hire passage for his party.

First Victoria told Marcus, then Tim and Robb. Finally James Bryce and his men were alerted, but Victoria was calm and confident. Edward was doing exactly what she wanted him to do.

She waited patiently, and when hay had been piled safely in the barn, when apples had been plucked from the few trees in the small orchard Victoria decided it was time to go home. Marcus objected strenuously and tried to insist that she stay at Serenity until Edward wearied of waiting and returned to England, but Victoria had no intention of allowing her brother to live through another winter if she could prevent it. He would be getting impatient by now and would be anxious to seize the advantage she would apparently offer him.

She faced her husband. "I am going home, Marcus. With or without you."

Seriously considering carting his wife off to the hunting lodge and keeping her there by force, Marcus stood and looked into that quiet set face. There was no sign of compromise. Victoria was quite determined that the encounter with her brother should take place, and no delaying tactics of his would change the outcome.

If she must go, it would be easier to bear if he were there to judge the situation for himself and protect her, if necessary, so he gave in. James and his men would be there to help watch over her, and Tim and Robb would stick like glue. They were a formidable group and no man in his right mind would risk an attack, no matter how cleverly planned or how deviously carried out.

# 21

The morning of departure was a bright beautiful day with none of October's chill in the air. The small ship slipped quietly downriver past the beautiful crimsons and yellows beginning to tinge the leaves of the trees along the bank. It was the first autumn Pac could appreciate, and he stayed at the rail with his father, who would net a colorful leaf from the water and watch as his son examined the orderly tracery of it in wonder.

While her husband and son were occupied Victoria took advantage of the opportunity to engage James Bryce in quiet conversation. The woodsman argued with his employer but finally agreed to her plan should it become necessary. As soon as they landed, he and one of his men would head for the Ohio country. If they moved quickly, they could contact Spotted Wolf and get back to the place of rendezvous she had planned on.

James reluctantly promised to say nothing to Captain Randall, a man he had come to respect in the past months, but he was so agitated with this stubborn woman that he forgot himself and spat in the wind with disastrous results. Victoria put her hand to her face to hide the smile and decided it might be wise to retire to the small crowded general quarters below deck.

There had been no privacy aboard the small coastal vessel, so when Bess welcomed her mistress home and started to follow her upstairs to help unpack Marcus firmly refused the offer. He closed and locked the door of their bedroom behind them, stood with hands on hips and watched as his wife obeyed his unspoken command.

Victoria began to undress slowly and deliberately. The devil's own gleam was in her eyes as she took an extraordinary amount of time with each shoe, each stocking and each button. Marcus lost patience with the whole tantalizing process and finished disrobing her at a less leisurely pace.

She had teased him and now it was his turn to play. His fingers barely brushed her flesh, his lips seared and tormented. His warm breath kindled the fire within her. The slight penetration was agonizing in its unfilled promise. He felt the pressure of his wife's hands on his back urging and finally demanding. He smiled as he deepened the penetration and felt the tense lifting of her hips to meet the slow downward motion she wanted.

All the desire was there. All the passion flared, and when it was done they lay side by side, physically and emotionally spent. Marcus roused himself before he dozed off and went to the other room to bathe. Victoria stretched luxuriously, waiting for him to finish so she could take her turn.

Dressed in a plain light wool, she put her arm around her husband's waist as they descended the wide stairs of the sunlit south wing of her home and joined the others. No one commented on their late appearance for the unusually grand eleven o'clock snack.

Everything was going well. James was at the table for the special gathering. Marcus suspected nothing, not even the fact that she was now carrying his child. "Just a little longer," she thought, and felt not the slightest guilt for what she was doing.

James, however, was not happy. He stared in disapproval as Victoria and Marcus escorted Pac outside. It was now that he must ask Bess for the corn and sugar mixture that would be his only sustenance for the next week. But if Bess were curious, he was to tell her the same trumped-up story Victoria intended telling her husband. He was going to Miss Victoria's property north of Baltimore to see how the indentured servants were making out.

Packing the supplies they would need for man and beast quickly, James and Luke headed for the mounting hills in the distance. They rode two of Victoria's finest horses, who would keep the steady pace needed to get them to Spotted Wolf on schedule, for if they weren't at the right place at the proper time, Victoria's plan would fall, and it would be she, not her brother, who would be in danger. Timing was crucial.

Delaying her husband in the front yard until she was certain that James and Luke were well away, Victoria made a great show of inspecting each and every fruit tree that had been planted along the drive. Then, when she was sure James had gone, she led the way to the log cabins of the indentured servants, where Pac found several young children to play with, and she found women eager to gossip about all that had taken place since she had left Chisholm House.

The idle chatter began to bore Marcus so he left Victoria under the watchful eye of Clint Porter, one of James Bryce's men, and wandered off in search of Josiah and Daniel to discuss a few things more to his interest.

Young Daniel had been mightily impressed at the amount of goods making their way to the warehouse in Baltimore. The land to the north was producing a quality and quantity of grain that exceeded their expectations, and the farmers who were buying their land from Victoria shipped all manner of farm goods for her vessels to transport.

"Yes sir, Captain Randall, we've got a prosperous business going. Why, Miss Victoria is the envy of merchants up and down the coast," he boasted, proud to be a part of it all.

Marcus tried not to smile at the young man who was just realizing what others had seen long ago. Victoria had already forged a small empire in this land, one that might soon rival the one she still commanded on other continents. Her wealth and power were formidable, and he suddenly wondered what kind of fool Edward Chisholm was.

If the man intended any mischief, he and his friends would face a solid wall of resistance from people whose interests lay in keeping their fates closely tied to Victoria's. Those who were indebted to her would not soon find another creditor who wanted them to succeed and who did everything in her power to insure their success, for idle land and idle wagons were little more than an albatross around his wife's neck. But land that produced and wagons that rolled over every back road fed the insatiable appetites of her ships, which were the real source of her enormous wealth.

Marcus had taken a few lessons from his wife and the growth of his own business was beginning to impress those who had known him in the days when he had paid little attention to money because he had been more interested in the adventure of sailing and the challenge of outwitting the Admiralty.

All of that had changed now that he had a family to provide for if only Victoria would let him, for she was still much too independent to suit Marcus. When she decided something needed doing she did it. Not yet had she learned that marriage must be a partnership, that no serious moves can be made without the agreement of the other person.

Despite their physical love, Victoria's mind was not open to him, and Marcus doubted if she even realized just how often she shut him out of her life completely. Their bed was the only place where they truly belonged to each other and, as grateful as he was for that, he wanted more.

At precisely one o'clock the dinner bell rang, interrupting his thoughts. He and Josiah walked leisurely back to the main house. The farm was being made ready for the coming winter season and there were only a few things left to do. Butchering would be done at the end of this month or next month, depending on the weather. Not until then would the tempo of work pick up for a little while and then settle down to a more leisurely pace.

After Marcus had seated his wife at the table he

looked around for the two men who were missing.
"James and Luke aren't eating with us?" he asked
Bess, and before Bess could reply Victoria told her
husband the agreed-upon story that her men had gone
to her property north of Baltimore to make certain
everything was running smoothly.

It was a story Josiah did not believe for one minute.
He read the doubt on Captain Randall's face as well,
but because he knew Victoria did nothing without a
well-thought-out purpose, he turned the conversation
to the new governor who had arrived in Annapolis
during the month of August.

Victoria listened with interest as Josiah described
the celebration that had taken place welcoming the
new governor to the colony, but she was concerned
about her business now that Horatio Sharpe would be
overseeing the colony. Like his brother, John, Horatio
was shrewd and discerning. To make matters worse,
he was a man of integrity who would try to enforce
the laws that protected England's interests, for
England understood little of these colonies just as she
had, and the new governor's efforts would not be
popular with many who disregarded those laws.

It was one of those not unusual coincidences that as
Victoria was thinking about Governor Sharpe, one of
his servants arrived with an invitation to a costume
ball to be held in two weeks. It was to be a gala affair
to welcome several gentlemen recently arrived from
England.

Victoria could not believe her luck. The timing
would be perfect and would fit her plans exactly, for
she had no doubt who the gentlemen from England
were. Among them would be Edward Chisholm. The
others being honored were undoubtedly his friends,

who had come to help him carry out his plans.

The calmness of certainty and the acceptance of her fate settled over Victoria as she showed the invitation to Marcus and asked if they might attend. The ball was to be held in the Assembly Room in Annapolis, and the entire governor's set would be there.

Marcus was not too thrilled by the idea of a costume ball; neither did he want his wife in Annapolis while Edward Chisholm was there, but it was one way to find out if the man was here to cause trouble. Yes, they would go. He would meet Victoria's brother face to face. Only then would he know what action he must take, but they would go well guarded and he would go as a frontiersman. That, at least, would give him an excuse for carrying a pistol.

Her husband's plans fit in with Victoria's own. The deerskin dress she had worn in the Ohio country was brought out and properly fitted. Additional fringe and beads were sewn on to enhance the rather plain garment. A set of buckskins was put together for Marcus.

On the evening of the ball Marcus and Victoria were accompanied by heavily armed bodyguards. Bullen and Ned carried pistols. Aaron and Clint preceded the coach, and Tim and Robb protected the rear as they traveled the road that led past deserted fields and heavily wooded land.

Marcus did not relax until their carriage pulled up to the entrance of the Assembly Room. Even then, he did not relax completely. He kept a watchful eye on Victoria as Governor Sharpe greeted them and personally offered to introduce them to his guests of honor.

While the governor looked over the assemblage in

the crowded room, trying to locate the newly arrived Englishmen, Victoria spotted her brother with no difficulty. He was standing near the table that held the potent liquid refreshments, and he was in the company of three other men who, except for the color of their fashionable attire, resembled one another in manner of dress, indolent posture and look of total boredom on their faces.

Victoria's eyes never left her brother's back, and he seemed to feel her presence for he turned slowly and smiled as he recognized the woman dressed as a squaw. Brilliant blue eyes, the most frightening eyes Marcus had ever seen, flicked briefly to Victoria's husband and then immediately dismissed the Virginian as being of little consequence. Edward Chisholm had room in his mind for only one person.

"La, if it isn't my elusive sister," he said with a slight bow as he approached Victoria and Marcus. "What a charming sight you are, my dear, in your braids and moccasins. Your costume is complete even down to the knife you are wearing at your waist, and I see that your husband is also quite convincingly armed." He laughed inanely, a high-pitched laugh that caused Marcus's blood to chill in his veins.

Edward was dressed as a pirate, a choice of costume Victoria thought suited her brother perfectly, but her husband was assessing the strength of this man before him. Edward Chisholm was undoubtedly the most beautiful specimen of manhood he had ever seen. His mane of wavy blond hair curled over the collar of the thin cotton shirt that was open at the throat. Chest and arm muscles flexed easily with his every motion. He wore provocatively close-fitting breeches, and his long legs were encased in soft leather boots that

accentuated their strength and power. He, too, was
wearing a pistol in the broad belt that encircled his
trim, firm waist. There was a field of power that
emanated from the man, drawing everyone within
range to him. Marcus was deathly afraid for his wife,
and he moved closer to her.

Once again the laugh of madness echoed softly
around them as Edward correctly interpreted the unconsciously protective motion. He turned those eyes
of blue fire back to his sister, who was standing
calmly with no emotion visible on the face he was
going to smash and mutilate.

"You do not seem surprised to see me, Victoria.
And I had so hoped that you would be. I have traveled
all the way from England just to see you once again,"
he mocked.

"No, I'm not surprised, Edward. Your movements
are known to me, and I think it would have been wise
had you remained in England," she replied in a voice
that did not carry beyond the small group.

Marcus cringed. She was challenging her brother, a
man who was powerful enough to crush her in his
hands. This brief encounter between brother and
sister had dispelled all hopes he had harbored of a
peaceful settlement of their differences, for there was
no possibility of misunderstanding the intent of either
of them. There was only one solution Edward would
accept, and that was Victoria's death.

Henry had been right. Edward Chisholm was not
sane, and at this moment Marcus wondered about his
wife's state of mind as well. She could not possibly
attack this man and survive.

Marcus was deeply concerned. The aura of danger
and destruction surrounding Edward was strong, yet

his wife had not once turned to him for help or protection. It was as though he had ceased to exist for her. Like her brother, she had room for only one person in her thoughts, and he was not that person.

Sir Charles Northington, one of Edward's friends, felt extremely uncomfortable. Edward was giving away the whole purpose of their miserable trip to this miserable country. He moved forward and introduced himself, trying to put Victoria at her ease. A warned enemy was a dangerous enemy, and Edward had warned her. That much was obvious. Now he must try to undo the damage.

"I fear your brother has had a little too much to drink, Madame Randall. Please forgive him. He is not at his best when in his cups. Indeed, this trip was for the purpose of checking on some investments I have here and to visit for a brief time with Governor Sharpe, who was a good friend of my dear brother before his untimely death. Edward and these two other gentlemen graciously consented to accompany me on my dreary journey."

Sir Charles felt that his efforts were rewarded when Victoria smiled up at him, and he thought it a pity that such a lovely creature had to die so young. His answering smile was just as charming as he wondered exactly what Edward had in store for this woman he hated with such single-minded purpose.

He and Edward had killed before, and his friend had proved himself to be a master at causing such exquisite pain that the victim begged for death. The thought showed on Charles's face and his mouth, still smiling, curled upward at one corner as he envisioned this woman at their mercy.

The soft voice was the same one Victoria had heard

on that foggy March night in London, the night Ben
Ives had been killed, the night she might also have
died. Charles Northington had been the other man
there to help her brother. The soft words of re-
assurance did not hide the cruel twist to his lips.
Charles was once again ready to help Edward.

"Ah, Sir Charles, I am so relieved to hear that
Edward did not come to carry on the silly feud that
has marred our relationship for so many years. You
don't know how often I've wished that my brother
and I might be friends," she pouted prettily.

Turning to Edward, she spoke contritely. "I am so
sorry if I have misjudged you, brother. I hope that
your stay in Maryland will be a pleasant one. Unfortunately, it will be some weeks before I can
entertain you as befits my father's only son, but I
must travel to a rather desolate area to check on my
properties. I fear that I shall have to get an early start
tomorrow, but perhaps when I return you will do us
the honor of staying at Chisholm House." Her eyes
took in all four men, and the other three understood
that they, too, were included in the invitation.

"It will indeed be a pleasure for us to accept your
kind invitation, madame," Charles interposed before
Edward could say any more to ruin what he had so
cleverly accomplished, but he found it difficult to
believe that this beautiful, totally feminine woman
was the infamous Victoria Chisholm, who directed
one of the most powerful mercantile companies in
England. She appeared to be nothing more than a
lovely, rather stupid little twit who posed very little
danger to them.

"You must tell me more about your journey,
madame," Charles said congenially. "I have heard a

great deal about the dangers of the frontier and must confess that I have a morbid interest in them."

Marcus was perplexed as he listened to his wife outline every detail of some imaginary journey. He could not for the life of him understand why she was involving herself in such lies unless it was to discourage her brother from staying any longer. Perhaps she hoped that he would tire of this nonsense and go back home, leaving them all in peace, but he doubted it. She had insisted on returning to Maryland to meet her brother. She had been ready to face Edward, to meet any action of his with a fiercer action of her own, and it was unthinkable that Victoria had been taken in by Sir Charles, with whom she was now chatting so amiably, especially when Edward was not even trying to hide the expression of contemptuous amusement on his handsome face.

"La, sir," Edward said, turning to Marcus now that his little cat-and-mouse game had been interrupted. "It seems that I am suddenly a man with a family once again. I understand that you and my dear sister have a handsome son. You are to be congratulated, Captain, and I am quite pleased to learn that I am an uncle. The courts would consider it a direct line of inheritance, I believe. Victoria and I, after all, do have the blood of our father flowing in our veins. That same blood connects your son with me. Yes," he remarked casually, "the same blood unites us and our fortunes. So you see, I really must become acquainted with my nephew. He should not be a stranger to me."

And suddenly Marcus understood the depth of evil in this tall, handsome, utterly mad human being who stood with such languid unconcern in front of him. Not only Victoria's life was in danger but his own and

Pac's as well, for Edward Chisholm wanted more than their deaths. He wanted the fortune that he might inherit if Pac were the last to die. Edward would be the last surviving blood relative who had a strong enough claim to win in the courts, no matter what his or Victoria's will might contain. Edward had powerful friends who wielded great influence; they would assure his victory. Edward had only to make certain of the order of death.

Victoria was to be first. Marcus understood that now. He would be next, and finally Pac, Pac, whose line was direct, whose blood was the same as Edward's. A chill of fear shivered through Marcus.

Edward saw and understood the thoughts racing across his adversary's face. It was a marvelous game, one he would enjoy to the utmost. It was too bad that Victoria could not be spared long enough to see the culmination of his plans, but, no, she must go first. It was too bad, but it was unavoidable.

Since he had first set foot in this small provincial town, he had made discreet inquiries about his half-sister, and he had learned enough to enable him to make his plans. The long weeks Victoria had kept him waiting were not wasted, for he had learned all he needed to know about Marcus Randall and his lack of family. Edward smiled serenely into the dark blue eyes that had turned hard and cold. His sister had made a mistake. She had given him time to plan what he must do.

It was at this moment that Sir Charles turned to Marcus. "I say, Captain Randall, your wife has been telling me the most fascinating stories about the frontier. Will you be accompanying her on what can only be a frightfully dangerous trip?"

Marcus answered abruptly. "Where my wife goes, I go!" Edward's smile was genuine. He was delighted. He would rid himself of Victoria and her husband at the same time. That would leave only Pac, and as the boy's uncle, he would easily win guardianship. In that case he might even allow the boy to live just long enough to turn his life into a living hell. What sweeter revenge could he ask for? Then when he tired of the game, the son of his despised sister would meet with a fatal "accident."

It was all very clear in Edward's mind. Already he could feel the power of his triumph surge within him. Turning to Victoria, he bowed slightly and murmured, "Ah dear sister, I do so look forward to our next meeting."

"No more than I, dear brother," she replied in a tone that caused Marcus to study his wife's face closely, but he could read nothing there except openness and friendliness.

Sir Charles was satisfied. His friend's plans to do away with his sister would begin sooner than expected, and since he wanted no more said he excused himself and propelled Edward toward the governor, who had been surrounded by a group of people who probably wanted one thing or another from Horatio Sharpe.

Marcus took advantage of the opportunity, grasped Victoria's arm and guided her forcibly to the door, where they accepted their outer garments from the handsomely liveried slave. Hurrying Victoria down the steps, he waited impatiently until Bullen eased their carriage around from the back of the hall. Instantly the four bodyguards took up their protective formation and Bullen, under Marcus's explicit orders, drove straight through to Chisholm House.

"He means to kill all of us," Marcus said through tight lips.

"I know," she replied, and then drew closer to him, feeling the comfort of his presence.

Even as Marcus held her close Victoria's mind was on the plan that would not change. She had not fooled her brother, but he was willing to take the risk, to accept her challenge, to meet her on her own terms. He was that confident. The fool!

But Edward must be lured far from her son and her husband. He must not get to them. They must be kept safe no matter what price she had to pay. This she had understood from the beginning. And, if possible, Edward must be killed in such a way that suspicion would fall elsewhere. This was the critical part of the plan.

As the carriage came to a halt in front of Chisholm House, Bess heard the clatter and got out of bed. Josiah hastily pulled on his pants over his nightshirt and took his loaded rifle from the wall. It was much too early for Miss Victoria and the captain to be returning from the ball, and he could take no chances with night riders under the present circumstances.

A gust of cold air swept the returning party into the house, where they headed immediately for the kitchen. Marcus was busy explaining the situation to the others as Bess renewed the fire, put water on for tea and brewed the coffee. Keeping her hands busy in a time of trouble always seemed to help.

Victoria walked to the cupboard and took out several cups. Reaching to the back of the shelf, she removed a small vial of white powder, which she sprinkled into one of the cups. When the coffee was ready she poured the dark liquid over the powder, which disappeared without a trace. Handing the cup to Marcus, she began to blow on the scalding tea Bess had put in front of her.

Agitation and deep concern were etched on Marcus's drawn face. He was making plans to get Victoria and Pac to Clay, where they would be protected until he could take care of Edward.

In the middle of his orders to Tim and Robb a sudden and debilitating dizziness overcame him. Haunted eyes tried desperately to focus. "No, Vickie," he began, and did not finish. His head slumped forward as he collapsed to the table, knocking over the cup of coffee from which he had taken only one sip.

Victoria moved her hand gently over the thick dark hair. Her heart was sad as she contemplated the profile of the face she loved. Marcus might never forgive her for this. Once again she was shutting him out, but he and Pac must be kept safe, no matter what the consequences for herself. She sighed heavily as she leaned down and kissed the bronzed cheek and then buried her face in the sweet-smelling hair. "I love you," she whispered into the unhearing ear.

Victoria had Marcus carried to their room and placed on the bed while she dressed in the male attire she had worn most of her life, the attire that would not encumber her movements. Tim and Robb put up a futile fight when they learned that they were to stay behind to guard Marcus and Pac while Victoria lured her brother deep into the wilderness, but she cut them off sharply. The two seamen barely recognized the mistress they had come to love. She paid no further attention to them or their concern as she

moved with icy calm and shut them from her mind
completely.

Josiah was to go into town just before first light and
rouse the small crew who ordinarily manned her
coastal vessel. Howard was to see to fresh water and
supplies. She and the two frontiersmen would be in by
nine o'clock, when everything must be ready for
immediate departure. Her destination was to be kept
no secret. If anyone should inquire, he was to be told
that she was sailing as far as Baltimore and would
then cut cross country to a place a few miles beyond
Frederick Town.

Just before dawn Josiah left on his errand. Everyone
understood what was expected of him. Marcus would
sleep for at least forty-eight hours and after that they
were to make no effort to restrain him, but Pac was to
be kept indoors under close guard until they had
news of her.

Tim instinctively knew, but he asked anyway.
"What news, Miss Victoria?"

"You'll know if and when it comes, Tim," she
answered gently.

When she arrived at the wharf Victoria made no
attempt to disguise her purpose. Quite openly and
calmly she chatted with the three sailors who would
see her to Baltimore. She looked around casually and
spotted another small ship riding at anchor just outside the harbor. It was a vessel she recognized as one
that was frequently hired out to those in need of
getting from one place to another without waiting for
the uncertain transportation on a larger ship.

To make absolutely certain that Edward was
aboard, Victoria had one of her crew make inquiries
around the dock. He reported that four gentlemen

had hired and boarded the vessel several hours before. From their descriptions it was obvious that Edward and his three companions were onboard, staying out of sight. If it had been otherwise, Victoria would have returned to the farm regardless of the risk of being cut down before she got there.

Just before her coastal vessel passed the other small ship making ready to sail, Victoria went below. She was quite certain that she had been carefully watched from the moment she had arrived at the wharf. She could feel Edward's hatred reaching out to her. Watching to make sure the rented ship followed her own, Victoria smiled to herself as it stayed a good distance behind. It promised to be an exhilarating game.

# 22

There was a strong favoring wind that carried Victoria's ship toward Baltimore. If the fates were kind she would have another day before Marcus roused from his drugged sleep. She had not dared make the dose any stronger or he would not have awakened at all.

The ship that had been following Victoria's pulled into the opposite shore when her own vessel headed toward her dock on the west side of the basin. Chatting pleasantly with Buck Arnold in his warehouse office, Victoria waited patiently until the rental of horses was arranged.

Buck, however, was not pleased when he heard his employer's plans, and he provided her and her two companions with a word of warning. Trouble was building up near the area she was heading for. He expected there would be a showdown before long between the English colonists and the French, for both were trying to enforce their claims to the territory west of the Alleghenies.

As they began their journey, there was no haste and no sense of urgency. Clint thought that Victoria's patience and control were worthy of James Bryce himself. And that was no mean compliment.

The deceptively leisurely pace soon put some distance between Victoria and her pursuers, but she kept close watch on the ship that had followed them as it edged to the Calvert Street wharf. Edward's tall form and his golden hair shining in the slanting rays of the sun were unmistakable as he stepped ashore.

Victoria's first stop was at the farm of a German family who had moved from Pennsylvania. They had bought a small parcel of land from her and were now prospering raising pigs, pork being the staple meat on everyone's table. And although Victoria delayed long enough to accept a cup of cider and to chat for a few minutes, she was alert; this seemingly unhurried pause in her journey was intended to confuse her brother. He would expect her to know she was being followed and act accordingly. She must cause him to doubt that knowledge. Edward must feel safe, and it was the doubt she must plant in his mind that would make him vulnerable.

Darkness had closed in by the time Victoria's group reached the next farm on her inspection schedule. She refused an offer by the wife of the family to sleep indoors, saying that she did not wish to disturb the household when she departed before dawn the next morning.

Therefore she had her tent pitched well away from the house with a small fire built in front of it so that anyone who watched would have difficulty seeing past the fire to the tent. However, Victoria had no intention of trapping herself inside a tent. Instead she and her men retired a short distance from camp to wait and to watch.

No one came. She imagined that the night, the strange terrain as well as fear of ambush kept Edward at bay. He had not yet begun to doubt.

Victoria was wrong. Edward saw the fire and did not understand. Always before, his sister had been elusive. She had slipped from his grasp and had covered her tracks. Never had she so boldly advertised her presence as she was doing now. It was not like her. It was contrary to her rules. She should be setting her trap, trying to keep her exact position unknown.

Perhaps Charles was right. Perhaps his bastard sister had not expected him to follow her into dangerous territory. Could she possibly have changed so much that she did not know? He had been certain that she was ready to face him; now he was not sure. But one thing had not changed, he did not trust her. He would watch a little longer before he made his move, but he was not happy that her husband was not with her, and he kept watching the trail behind him. He would leave Captain Randall to others, but Victoria he wanted himself.

Another long day passed as the two groups worked their way closer to the final destination. The three riders in the lead party seemed to be in no hurry as they stopped briefly, first at one farm and then another, but the steady pace of their horses rapidly closed the distance between them and Frederick Town.

Again a fire was built as the deepening shadows closed in on them, and still Edward did not come. Finally Victoria knew. She had won. Her brother was uncertain. He was beginning to doubt. She smiled grimly as she and her men spent another sleepless night, but she was not worried. The sense of danger had all but disappeared. By noon tomorrow or a little later it would be over.

The increasingly rugged terrain rose before them, leading from the valley of the Monocacy River, when the frontiersmen grunted as they heard the unlikely sound of a night owl hooting in broad daylight. They had made it.

"I didn't think it was possible, ma'am," Clint said quietly, without turning his head as he continued moving ahead of her on the narrow trail.

"This is where I leave you, gentlemen," Victoria responded as she saw the three innocent-looking stones piled one on top of the other.

Clint and Aaron stopped their horses and made a show of saying good-bye. They thought that any damned fool would understand the slightly exaggerated gestures as they left Victoria and continued as far as the next bend while she nudged her horse off the trail and melted into the surrounding forest.

Sir Charles Northington was jubilant. He made the fatal error of believing what only one of his senses told him. "I was right, Edward," he crowed. "She hasn't spotted us. She doesn't suspect a thing. Her men have left her."

Edward shifted uneasily in his saddle. He had not slept for several nights. He was irritable and on edge. It was possible, of course, that Charles was right, but he couldn't take any chances now. He had followed that green-eyed bastard into the most God-forsaken wilderness he had ever seen. This was not the time to be careless, not when he all but had her staked out awaiting his pleasure.

There must be a farm nearby, although he couldn't see it, for surely his sister would not have left her guides in the middle of nowhere. If that was the case, he must hurry before she reached safety or before her employees returned to her.

He ordered two of his men to track Victoria's companions just far enough to make sure they had actually gone on while he and Charles cautiously followed his sister into the woods. They were to hurry back to him at the first sound of trouble. Victoria was treacherous, but she certainly was not stupid enough to face the four of them by herself. Charles had to be right. She suspected nothing.

Dismounting a short distance from the path, Victoria slapped her horse's rump, and the animal trotted deeper into the woods before slowing to follow the sparse tufts of grass.

Spotted Wolf emerged from a dry creek bed that was well screened by brush and signaled to *le cougar*. She made her way noiselessly to his side and waited until she heard the cautious approach of mounted riders.

Edward stopped and listened. He could hear nothing. He inched forward cautiously, signaling to Charles to be quiet. For some anxious minutes he wondered if Victoria had gone in another direction. Then he heard the sound of the horse ahead.

Barely nudging his own animal, Edward eased forward when he heard the rider just a short distance away head off in another direction. He turned to direct his friend to circle in order to cut Victoria off while he followed them behind.

Charles was not there. Edward's skin began to crawl and perspiration broke out on his upper lip. He backtracked and saw Charles Northington lying on the ground with a knife wound in his back. The man was obviously quite dead. His hired horse was grazing not ten feet from the body.

Edward Chisholm understood at once. His sister had gotten behind them. She had divided his force and he had been the one to fall into the trap. His high-pitched laughter startled the birds, and they flew to the safety of the open sky with a roaring of wings. Edward did not hear the knife that pushed the air softly and stopped his laughter abruptly, turning it, instead, into a soft gurgling sound as the life slipped from him.

Spotted Wolf sauntered over and matter-of-factly scalped both men. Victoria removed her knife from her brother's back, wiped it clean in the earth and leaves and walked quickly toward the sound of her horse.

As she led the animal back to the spot of ambush, James hurried to a better vantage point where he could see the road without being seen himself. The sound of a horse that had obviously been ridden too hard and too long had caught his attention. He stepped out onto the trail and waved down Marcus Randall.

"Afternoon, Cap'n," he drawled pleasantly as the exhausted man threw one leg over the saddle and leaped to the ground.

"Victoria," he gasped hoarsely. "Have you seen her, James? Edward and his men are following her. We must get to her!"

"They ain't followin' her anymore, Cap'n. Miss Victoria's just fine." He grinned. "Just managed as nice a piece of knife throwin' as I've seen in a while."

Marcus didn't understand, but his questions were forestalled by Clint and Aaron, who approached through the trees leading two horses, each with a dead body draped over the saddle. James had no more time for Marcus. There was still work to be done.

Signaling the two men to follow him, he led them deeper into the forest, where the others waited. The full meaning of James's words and the significance of the two dead men being transported with arms and legs flopping grotesquely suddenly became clear to Marcus. No one would know that the party had been separated and killed by different people in different places.

The scene of carnage was spread out before him. Edward and Charles lay where they had fallen. The other two men were dumped nearby, and before Marcus had a chance to protest, two silent Indians took their scalps with one swift motion of their knives. Clothing, pistols and jewelry were stripped from the bodies.

Marcus looked around. James and Luke were here, not at the two thousand acres Victoria owned north of Baltimore. Philippe was here as well as his constant companion, Spotted Wolf. Clint and Aaron, of course, he knew about.

It had all been planned weeks ago. Victoria had known from the beginning what she was going to do. Once more she had kept the truth from him. She had played him for a fool.

Victoria paused in her eager rush toward her husband. She saw the fierce anger that clouded his eyes. She stood for just a moment, not knowing how to proceed. She had hoped he would understand and forgive her, but he had not. Still, she must do something to close the rift she had created once again between them.

Continuing toward her husband at a more dignified pace, Victoria prepared herself for any reaction, and she didn't care what it was so long as the coldness left Marcus's eyes. If he would just understand!

To her total consternation, Marcus just stood there, staring down at her with not one spark of forgiveness showing in his eyes. His expression had not changed, and he seemed to be waiting for Victoria to make the first move.

And because she loved him Victoria humbled herself in front of her friends. It mattered very little to her that they might think her weak and unfit to command. At this moment nothing mattered except her husband.

"Do you remember, Marcus, that I told you I would gladly give my life for you? It was not something I said lightly. I meant it. And this was the time. There is nothing I wouldn't have done to protect you and Pac from Edward's madness. If only one of us could survive, then I wanted it to be you, for if Pac is to have only one parent, it must be you. I want you to live to raise our son and this was important enough to me to risk losing you. Please tell me I haven't done that. Please tell me that the child I'm carrying will have both a mother and a father."

The shock registered in Marcus's eyes as he realized the depth of Victoria's desperation. Not only had she risked her own life but that of her unborn child as well. And she had done it so that he might keep his son.

Marcus drew in a deep breath and nodded. He drew Victoria into the circle of his arms and rested his cheek on the top of her head. "But no more, my dear.

I can tolerate no more. Do you understand what I'm saying to you?''

"Yes,'' Victoria answered, and tightened her arms around his waist.

Spotted Wolf was growing impatient. "We must go,'' he reminded Victoria. "It is not yet finished.''

Marcus frowned. He didn't understand, and Victoria explained. "It must look as though we had nothing to do with Edward's death. We will go to a farm a little way down the road. Only after we are there will Spotted Wolf, Philippe and the others raise an unholy racket to make it sound as though Edward and his men were killed while we were at the farm. We will have an alibi. Our hands will be clean.''

"Far from clean, my dear, but I suspect Edward's death was an absolute necessity. That being the case, I would just as soon have no suspicion come our way.''

Victoria smiled at Marcus, and her eyes were bright with happiness. He would support her story. He literally held her life in his hands, but he would support and help her.

Swinging up onto her horse, she heeled the animal into a swift trot. Marcus followed close behind. Clint and Aaron pulled up in the rear. It took only a few minutes to reach the small farm where they were welcomed by Rebecca McIntyre, who was extremely pleased to see visitors. She informed Victoria that her husband was at the edge of the field clearing a little more ground but would be in for dinner in a matter of minutes.

Insisting that her guests be seated, Rebecca served buttermilk and cold biscuits, chatting amiably all the while. It was such a treat to have someone to talk to, and she was anxious to hear all the gossip from the Tidewater area.

Suddenly the conversation stopped and the occupants of the isolated cabin froze, straining to hear the unmistakable sounds of the high-pitched shrieks of attacking savages. Then came the sounds of rifle and pistol fire. Becky's eyes were wide with fear as her hand gripped the back of a chair. Her husband was alone in the woods. She raced for the door, but before she could escape through it Clint stopped her.

"Me and Aaron'll see to your husband, ma'am," he offered genially, for he understood exactly what Becky had planned to do. He understood the futile gesture.

Becky looked at the men gratefully and stepped back. Aaron, Clint and Marcus slipped out the door and made for the far end of the field. At the same moment Bruce McIntyre bolted for the cabin under the safety of the three guns that were poised to protect him.

The small house was made tight, and Bruce McIntyre waited anxiously to see what the next few minutes would bring, for he had no way of knowing how large the raiding party was. He might soon be fighting for his life and for the life of his wife if the Indians decided to attack his home, and he was extremely grateful that his creditor had chosen to make an inspection tour at this particular time. The three armed men were a Godsend. He and his wife by themselves would not have stood much of a chance.

The shouting subsided briefly and then, like a sudden and terrible wind, the Indians and a white man rode past his home screaming and waving their muskets, from which streamed four bloody scalps.

Each man in the raiding party led a saddle horse, and several of the Indians were wearing odd bits of clothing taken from their victims.

Bruce McIntyre shuddered. There was very little protection for the lonesome farmer in these parts. Even a small band of Indians such as this one could strike fear into a man's heart.

When he was certain the raiding party had gone its way Bruce edged cautiously toward the barn, where he retrieved several shovels. He had some burying to do, and it wasn't going to be pleasant.

Finally convinced that there were no savages lurking in ambush, Bruce relaxed and breathed a sigh of relief. He was grateful that the three armed men who had come with Miss Victoria seemed willing to go with him. He didn't trust the savages and never would.

Marcus insisted that Victoria stay with Mrs. McIntyre while the men did what had to be done. Victoria offered no objection as her husband and the others headed in the general direction from which the noise of ambush had first come. Clint and Aaron led the way and smiled as they saw the obvious trail of bloody pieces of clothing that led to the bodies of the four Englishmen.

The gruesome evidence lay before them. There would be no question in anyone's mind that these men had been surprised and butchered by savages who had been led by a dreaded French *coureur de bois*.

The charade was played out to the end as Marcus feigned surprise and shock at the identity of the men. One of the victims was Miss Victoria's half-brother, but it was a mystery what he was doing so far from Annapolis, where they had last seen him.

As Marcus unflinchingly told the lies he knew were necessary to protect his wife, he wondered if this might be the side of Victoria Henry had warned him against, for she had coldly and calmly calculated the deaths of these four men, just as she had ordered Captain Hensley to send a hundred seamen to their deaths. But that matter had yet to be resolved. It was entirely possible that one of the pirate crew would escape. If that happened, Victoria's life would once again be in danger.

Marcus blew out a long breath. If that happened, he would have to flee with his family. He roused himself from the useless conjecture and turned his attention to the task at hand.

After erecting crude markers over the graves the men returned to the farm, where Becky was waiting anxiously for the news of what they had found. Bruce explained briefly and left the identifying of the dead men to Captain Randall.

Marcus acted the role skillfully as he broke the news to Victoria that her brother had been killed, and he watched in grudging admiration as her face mirrored disbelief that then gave way to shock. Becky rushed to her side to offer whatever comfort she could, but Marcus had seen the lights of triumph dance brilliantly in his wife's eyes.

Accepting the well-intentioned but misguided sympathies of the farmwoman, Victoria lifted a distraught face and requested that the McIntyres write an account of what had happened so that the document might be sent to England for the families of the poor dead men.

At that moment there was nothing the McIntyres would not have done for Victoria. Obligingly, they wrote what they believed had transpired and gave the letter to Captain Randall, who folded it carefully and put it in the pocket of his vest.

The moment Victoria had what she wanted, she was ready to leave. She thanked Becky and Bruce for all they had done and promised that she would have her agent, Buck Arnold, find another family for the small parcel of land she still owned just north of the McIntyres. She acknowledged that it was, indeed, too dangerous for them alone, especially since the only two rangers in the area were miles away.

Once outside, Marcus whispered urgently, "Where are James and Luke? What happened to them?"

Victoria smiled sweetly. "Why, my dear, they are at my farm north of Baltimore just as I said. Or at least they will be very soon. And they will make very sure that they are seen by several people who will, if necessary, swear to that fact."

Marcus shook his head in resignation. "I might have known," he answered.

When Victoria and her companions arrived in Baltimore she decided to stay at the Indian Queen Inn for a day or two while Clint and Aaron returned to Annapolis carrying the account written by the McIntyres to Governor Sharpe. After he had read the deposition and had questioned the well-rehearsed men Victoria would return to face him.

Within three days Victoria huddled below deck as the small vessel that carried her homeward was buffeted by rising winds and waves. She would be thankful when they finally reached the warmth and comfort of Chisholm House. She was tired of hunkering over smoky fires eating indigestible foods

as she shivered from the damp and the cold that
seemed to seep right through her.

Edward was dead and soon those who could
identify her as the owner of pirate vessels would also
be dead. She would be safe at last, and her father's
reputation, such as it was, would not be made any
worse.

It had gone well. Now, if Captain Hensley could
carry out his assignment, the most pressing of her
problems would be out of the way, and she could turn
over even more of the responsibility of running her
complicated business to the agents and managers who
were proving themselves so capable.

As Marcus helped his wife out of the carriage, the
front door of Chisholm House opened to receive
them, but before Bess had a chance to say a word she
was almost knocked off her feet as Pac surged past
her. The boy ran to his mother, hurling himself down
the front steps, sure that she would catch him, but his
father intercepted him before the force of his charge
could hit Victoria.

Marcus swung his son high in the air, hugged him
tightly and then put him into his mother's outstretched arms. Victoria nuzzled and laughed with
him as she trooped up the steps and managed to get
inside the doorway that was a mass of confused
humanity.

Tim and Robb and Bess all tried to speak at once
while grabbing hold of Victoria's arm or slapping her
on the back, and Pac simply would not release his
stranglehold from around his mother's neck. Finally,
like a congealing blob of gelatin, they flowed to the
kitchen, where Victoria sat down and slid her son to

the floor.

"I knew it!" Robb crowed. "I knew you'd come back. Told ya not to worry, didn't I, Cap'n?" The boasting in Robb's voice gave way to a choking sob as he grabbed a towel and pressed it to his face to hide the unmanly tears.

"Yes, Robb, you told me," Marcus replied gently, and put his hand on the seaman's shoulder.

When the emotional storm had passed, when Victoria had told them only part of the truth, she retired to her room, where she disrobed and stood studying herself in the mirror. She was still slim and her muscles were firm. Soon, though, her waist would begin to thicken with the growth of her second child. She smiled serenely. She was still happy about the choice she had made. She wanted nothing more at this moment than to give her husband another child.

The soft laughter startled her and she turned her head to see Marcus standing there, grinning broadly at her display of vanity. "If it helps, I find you absolutely ravishing."

"Ravaged is more like it." She laughed companionably, not minding in the least that her husband had misunderstood her rather ruthless and totally honest self-appraisal.

Marcus laughed with her and held her briefly in his arms. "Go get your bath before you catch your death of cold. I'll be in to help you in a few minutes."

Victoria entered into the spirit of the game and muttered something about his having helped quite enough and disappeared into the next room, where she gathered her robe and slippers before proceeding to the bathing room.

The warmth of the water soothed and relaxed

Victoria. Not even her husband's intrusion nor his insistence that he help her bathe disturbed her equanimity, but when Marcus started to go too far with his help Victoria slapped his hand. Marcus took the unsubtle hint, backed off and, still grinning, began to stroke his razor over the strap.

Governor Sharpe, accompanied by several of his council members, called upon Captain and Mrs. Randall the next day. The men listened to Victoria's calm recounting of the trip to Baltimore and to several of her farms along the way to Frederick Town. Her husband had felt ill when she had left and had not joined her until she had almost reached the McIntyre farm, which lay several miles beyond the town. It had been while they were at the farm that they had heard the terrible screams of the attack.

It was at this point in her narration that Victoria told a small part of the truth. "As you might know, Governor, my brother has hated me for years. I left England because of him. He made one attempt on my life and, had I stayed, would surely have tried again. As far as I'm concerned, Edward got exactly what he deserved."

Horatio Sharpe smiled knowingly. Victoria Chisholm was not going to hide behind tears and fainting spells, something he most certainly would not have believed. There was not the slightest doubt in his mind that Madame Randall had arranged for her brother's death, but he could not prove it. There was no point in pursuing the matter. Besides, he fully agreed with her. Edward Chisholm was most deserving of his death. No one had been more surprised than he when the man had suddenly appeared in this colony.

Now that it was all over it was clear to the governor that Edward had come to Maryland to kill his sister. Instead he had died at the hands of a group of marauding savages. This was the story that had been sworn to by those who had been there at the time, and he would have to accept the story as fact.

But before the governor could speak Marcus stepped in. "If you will excuse my wife, your excellency, I insist that she rest for a while. This has been a very difficult experience for her and I fear it has already done much to endanger the child she is carrying. I can allow no more. I am sure you understand."

Then, without waiting for an answer, Marcus put his arm around Victoria's shoulders and turned her over to Tim and Robb, who had never been far away. The two faithful seamen would see their mistress to her room.

Returning to his guests, Marcus made it clear that any further inquiry into Edward's death must be directed to him. "I must assure you, gentlemen, that what you have heard from my wife will agree in every detail with the deposition we sent you from the McIntyres. I assure you that my wife was unaware of her brother's latest murderous intent until he had been killed by Indians. Only then did she realize that she had been followed, and only then did she put the pieces together. That should end the matter."

Horatio Sharpe smiled in admiration for the man and his wife. "I assure you, Captain, your wife's story agrees in every detail with what I have been able to learn from the other witnesses. There will be no more questions. I believe I understand the situation fully and offer my deepest apologies for finding it necessary to inquire into this matter.''

Satisfied that the worst was over, Marcus offered his visitors some of Victoria's finest brandy, an offer the men accepted gratefully, for this had been a nasty business and all were relieved that it had ended so well.

Then, just as Marcus had finished pouring a generous portion of the amber liquid into each man's glass, Bess appeared at the door. ''A gentleman to see you, Captain. Says it's urgent.''

Marcus frowned in annoyance, but Bess would not have interrupted unless the matter was, indeed, urgent. Nor would she have neglected to have announced the visitor by name unless she did not want his guests to know who was calling. Something was wrong.

Turning to Governor Sharpe, Marcus spread his hands in a gesture of exasperation. ''Will you excuse me briefly, gentlemen? I'll return as quickly as possible. Meanwhile, help yourselves to more of what I assure you is an excellent brandy.''

Following Bess to the kitchen, Marcus froze momentarily until he looked squarely into the eyes of Richard Hensley. He smiled as he saw that those eyes were dancing with a light of accomplishment the man of the sea could barely repress.

''It went well?'' Marcus already knew the answer.

''Yes, Captain. It went well, indeed. It's over.''

With shoulders slumping as the heavy burden was lifted, Marcus nodded. ''Thank God,'' he said softly. ''I think this is news my wife would welcome hearing immediately. Bess will show you the way to our room. I would come myself, but I have an informal board of inquiry to deal with at the moment."

Richard chuckled knowingly. "I heard all about that particular incident. So Edward is dead. It's about time!" he added, not in the least perturbed by all the violence that seemed to swirl around Victoria.

After Bess had escorted Captain Hensley to the back stairs Marcus returned to the drawing room with a new feeling of confidence. Nothing could be proved against Victoria. Everyone, including the McIntyres, had sworn that the attack had occurred exactly as Victoria had stated. It was time the governor returned to his home.

By the time Marcus was able to join his wife Richard Hensley had given his report and was gone. He entered the sitting room of their suite and saw Victoria resting in an oversized leather chair, where the rays of the diminishing sun of autumn touched and warmed her. And, as always, the golden glow of her hair and skin seemed to absorb those rays.

Her eyes were closed. Her features were relaxed, but Marcus felt a stab of pain in his heart, for Victoria looked so very thin, so very fragile and so very lost in the large chair that had been made to accommodate her father's frame.

Marcus walked toward her, his footsteps silenced by the soft thick carpet underfoot. He leaned over and kissed his wife tenderly, and Victoria opened her eyes.

A strange expression, one which Marcus could not define, shadowed those expressive eyes, and for the first time he felt a twinge of pity for this woman who had been asked to endure so much, this woman who had suffered through conditions he could only imagine. And she had done it all for love. She had adored her father and had gladly suffered any pain, any anguish for his sake.

Marcus pulled up a straight-backed chair. He lifted Victoria's thin hand to his lips. His thumb touched the wide gold band she had never removed and he smiled into those weary eyes.

"Richard said it went well."

"Yes," she replied, and her voice was unsteady. "If you call sending almost a hundred men to their deaths going well, if you call sending a man I once loved to the bottom going well, then it went well. At least we didn't lose any of our own men."

Without warning, Victoria's eyes filled with tears and she turned her head away, but Marcus turned her face toward him with gentle hands. "It's over, Victoria. All of it. As for the men who died—you had no choice. Neither did I when I agreed to such a plan, for your life was in my hands, and I would protect it at any cost. But the blame is as much mine as yours. Although," Marcus added in his practical way, "the men were cutthroat pirates. We did the honest men of the sea a favor by getting rid of them. They would have been captured and hanged eventually. But they would have talked. We both know that. They would have taken you down with them. I could not allow such a thing to happen any more than you could.

"And as for Ramon," he continued softly, "I am deeply sorry. I know that you do not love easily and to earn your trust is even more difficult, but Ramon betrayed you long before this final action became necessary. He was indeed a fool."

Victoria nodded. She had done what she must, but the cost had been high—very high, indeed. "And Governor Sharpe?"

Marcus smiled. "Governor Sharpe will ask no more questions. He will report exactly what we told him. Whether he believes it or not is one thing, but he cannot prove otherwise. No, my dear, it's done. You're free and you need never look back."

She took a long tremulous breath. "Yes," she sighed. "I'm free and we are safe, you and Pac and I. It's over. It's done at last."

And suddenly Marcus understood. It was just as Henry had said. Victoria had been bound by her father's wishes. She had carried them out, not allowing herself a life of her own choosing. But now her task was done.

"And now?" he asked, still holding her hand in his.

A wistfulness touched Victoria's face. "And now, dear husband, I shall go with you to Serenity. There is much to be done if our home is to accommodate a growing family." She smiled impishly and all the cares of the past years seemed to melt from her shoulders. "You did say you wanted a large family, didn't you?"

Marcus laughed out loud and scooped his wife from the chair. Victoria had made her choice. The ghost of her father would no longer rule their lives. She was coming home—to him!